FORBIDDEN FIRES

"You must not tempt me, Miranda," Blazing Star said sadly, passion burning in his eyes. "You cannot be my woman."

"Why do you speak of what cannot be? Why can't you admit to what there is between us. I need you, Blazing Star," she said boldly. "Can't we share our love for just a short while? I swear I will let you go when the time comes."

"Do not ask for the forbidden," he said hoarsely.

Miranda's dark brown eyes filled with tears. "You say I should not love you, but I do. You say I cannot have you, yet I want you more than life itself." Sobbing, she turned and walked to the bed and flung herself face down upon it.

Blazing Star went to sit beside her. "Do not weep, my love. It is like a sharp lance in my body to see you suffer this way."

Miranda rolled onto her back and looked up at him. There was no need for words; her eyes said it all. He lowered his head to seal his lips to hers, to fuse their destinies into one.

Never had Miranda known such excitement and happiness as here in this handsome warrior's arms. His warm breath caused tremors to sweep over her tingly flesh. His hands were skillful as they roamed her silken skin. Soon there was no spot upon her that did not cry out for him to conquer it and claim it for his own. And as she murmured his name, caressed his muscular, bronzed chest, she knew there was no turning back . . .

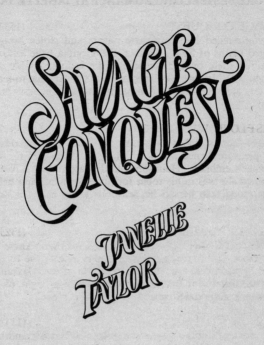

SAVAGE CONQUEST

JANELLE TAYLOR

ZEBRA BOOKS
KENSINGTON PUBLISHING CORP.

ZEBRA BOOKS

are published by

Kensington Publishing Corp.
475 Park Avenue South
New York, NY 10016

First printing: February 1985

Printed in the United States of America

For Michael, Angela, and Melanie, whose help and support prevent "warring winds" from destroying my deadlines and creative flow.

And for my good friend Elaine Raco Chase, whose letters, calls, and wit help me retain my sanity.

And lastly for my good friend and helper, Hiram C. Owen.

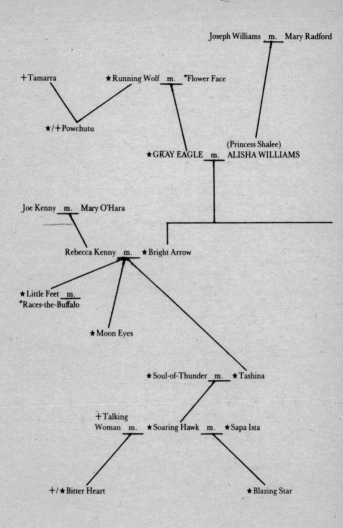

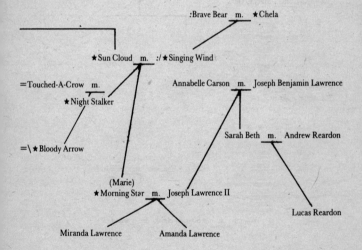

Tribes:
★ Oglala Sioux
= Brule Sioux
" Sisseton Sioux
: Blackfoot
+ Cheyenne

:Brave Bear   m.   ★Chela

★Sun Cloud   m.   :/★Singing Wind

=Touched-A-Crow   m.

★Night Stalker

Annabelle Carson   m.   Joseph Benjamin Lawrence

=\ ★Bloody Arrow

Sarah Beth   m.   Andrew Reardon

(Marie)
★Morning Star   m.   Joseph Lawrence II

Lucas Reardon

Miranda Lawrence   Amanda Lawrence

Chapter One

Alexandria, Virginia
May, 1873

The past nine weeks had been difficult for the two young women sitting on the floral sofa in their brightly decorated parlor. Their mother had loved bold color schemes, but the lively shades didn't match the girls' solemn moods. Both were trapped in painful silence as they struggled to come to grips with a horrible truth—Lawyer McVane had just told them that their parents must be assumed dead, at least legally. Joe and Marie Lawrence had gone sailing in early March; only debris of their shattered craft had returned. Even if the girls did not want to accept this agonizing fact, they knew it was time to make some decisions about their current situation. They couldn't spend their lives feeding on grief and false hopes.

Amanda Lawrence shifted to glance at her fraternal twin sister, Miranda. Amanda's light blue eyes were filled with uncommon doubt and sadness as she met Miranda's somber brown gaze. Amanda felt as though she were looking in a mirror. Despite their different coloring—Amanda's flowing curls were light and dark blond, her complexion fair, and her eyes bright blue, while Miranda bore sleek chestnut locks, an olive complexion, and tawny eyes—they could have passed for identical twins. But the two eighteen-year-olds were completely unlike in personality.

They had always been very close. Amanda knew her sister was more beautiful, but it had never been a source of jealousy or trouble between them. Most men viewed Miranda as a sensual, enticing creature with an aura of mystery and a provocative innocence. Miranda was more than exquisite; she was warm, gentle, and unselfish. She was direct and honest but always tactful, carrying out her social obligations with grace and charm, but preferring close friends and simple events to crowds and soirées. Miranda seemed to be waiting, planning, dreaming of something vital to her existence, her destiny, her happiness.

A well-bred young lady from a wealthy and prominent family, Miranda concealed her "unfeminine" yearnings for adventure. In truth, she and Amanda could ride and shoot better than most men. Miranda could even fight better than most men, having been taught the "ancient arts" of self-defense by Ling, their Chinese cook's son. The last thing Miranda Lawrence wanted to be was a refined lady condemned to household chores and a "proper marriage," or so she had proclaimed at every available chance.

Miranda had never loved the parties, dances, theaters, dashing suitors, elegant clothes, and jewels as the outgoing Amanda did. Amanda would be the first to admit she enjoyed being coy and flirtatious. Why not? After all, Amanda Lawrence was wealthy, a Southern "blue blood," a valuable "catch." And men didn't have to tell Amanda that she was ravishing; the mirror did that. Even so, Amanda Lawrence accepted her beauty and acquired charms as blessings, gifts from Fate to be treasured and used to her best advantage.

Amanda knew what she wanted from life and was determined to have it. But how she wished the war hadn't destroyed that enviable Old South life style of belles and balls, of romantic duels, of grace and beauty, before she could taste and enjoy them. Dreams of such days had filled her youthful head until the nightmare of war with kin against kin had awakened her to their passing. Amanda felt she had been denied something essential—some loss of history, of ancestry, of heritage. She would never know such times, such daring and romantic men, such elegant evenings, for the Old South was gone forever.

Perhaps, Amanda mused, it was time for her to mature. She was no longer a child but a woman responsible for her own fate. In these past weeks, Amanda had come to realize life was more than looking and behaving the irresistible lady, more than having fun. Her parents had tried to teach her to be independent and brave, to be basically honest and caring. Suddenly her carefree search for the perfect storybook marriage had lost its magic.

Amanda had never known real fear before this dire period, and the taste of it was sour. Her parents had always been there as a defense between her and the cruel world. She didn't like feeling vulnerable and, in a brief moment of fear and panic, she had almost surrendered to a protective marriage. But now the initial shock had passed; the intense agony had dulled. Amanda's thinking was clearer and braver; she was ready and willing to challenge her future. She had spent a great deal of time with her father at his shipping firm, and she recognized that the first step toward her new life was obviously there . . .

"I don't care what Lawyer McVane says, Randy. I'm not going to sell Papa's business," Amanda stated calmly. "I'm going to run it myself," she announced.

"But, Mandy, you're a woman," Miranda argued. Her beloved sister had always believed she could do whatever she wanted, and she did understand and love the business, but what smug businessman would deal with a female owner? Their only source of livelihood could be crushed.

Amanda looked down at her shapely body clad in a lovely gown of sapphire, grinned, and playfully jested, "From my point of view, Randy, I do believe you're right. However, our competitors and customers will soon learn that brains can also be encased in a nicely rounded package." They laughed musically, feeling happy for the first time since they had heard about their parents' accident. Yes, it felt good to laugh and smile again.

Miranda gazed at the renewed life in her sister's eyes, thankful it had returned. She asked, "Mandy, are you going to marry Web?"

Disturbed by the nearly inaudible question, Amanda hesitated before candidly replying, "I don't know, Randy."

"It isn't like you to be so indecisive. You're not seeing anyone except Weber Richardson. Do you love him?"

"Do you remember what Mama told us on our eighteenth birthday? She said we would know the right man for us when we met him. She said she knew Papa was to be in her life-circle the moment she looked into his eyes. They loved each other so deeply. Do you really think it happens that way?" Amanda inquired seriously, for no suitor had made her feel and think the way her beloved mother had described.

"Yes," Miranda responded quickly. "That's why they wouldn't arrange any marriages for us. We must choose for ourselves. What do you think about when you look at Web? Does he make you feel warm and tingly inside?"

"I've sampled lots of stolen kisses, Randy, but none as good as Web's. He can be so romantic and dashing. Every single girl in town is after him, including many widows and even a few married tarts. It's exciting to know he's chosen me. I'll soon be nineteen, and if I wish to marry well, who's better than Web? Yet . . ."

Miranda's heart had been racing with panic until her sister wavered. "If you have any doubts, wait until after our birthday," she coaxed.

"First, I must learn if Web loves and wants me more than he wants Papa's firm. That should come to light when I take over."

A knock sounded loudly on the Lawrences' door. Their housekeeper/cook had been given the day off to allow them total privacy for the meeting with Lawyer McVane, so Amanda rose to answer the summons. She was both pleased and annoyed to find their first cousin, Lucas Reardon, lazing against the portal. As much as she adored this kinsman standing before her, she was eager to continue her conversation with her sister.

A broad grin claimed Lucas's mouth, creating little wrinkles near the corners of his dark green eyes and full lips. "A bad time to call, Mandy?" he astutely surmised, his grin widening and eyes sparkling.

"No, and yes," Amanda replied, stepping aside to allow him to enter. "Lawyer McVane just left. Randy and I were discussing the implications of his advice. A glass of sherry, Luke?" she offered.

Lucas sat in a plush chair, watching both girls with intense interest. Sometimes he wished he weren't related to the radiant beauties but, between the war and the recent accident, they were the only family he had left.

At one time, Lucas's father had been in business with Joseph Lawrence. But when Joe sided with the North and his father with the South, all bonds had been severed. Joe had always claimed that he remained neutral, not having the heart to battle either side. But there had been times when Joe's decisions had greatly affected one side or the other. The North hadn't fully trusted him because he was Southern, but Southerners despised any kinsman who didn't aid their cause. Now, Joe was dead and the twins were all alone, except for their cousin.

Lucas understood how his cousins must be feeling at this moment. It had been only nine years ago when his parents, Sarah Beth Lawrence and Andrew Reardon, had been slain during a battle near their home. Time would dull the anguish, but it would never completely vanish.

Amanda passed the sherry to Lucas then sat near her sister. "What brings you here today, Luke?" she asked, observing a curious strain in his expression and voice.

Lucas's smile faded, a worried scowl replacing it. "It's been weeks, my loves. What are you two planning to do with the business? Any offers?" he inquired, sinking back into the cushiony chair, crossing one booted foot over his sturdy thigh.

"Plenty of offers, but we'll accept none," Amanda announced. "We're keeping Papa's business, and I'm going to manage it. Right, Randy?"

Lucas's mouth fell open and his leafy eyes became large circles. "You can't be serious, Mandy! A woman in shipping? You'll lose every account within a month. They'll laugh you off the docks."

Amanda puffed up with pride, jutting out her dainty chin. "I know that business inside and out, Luke," she declared smugly.

"From the books and your father's mouth, Mandy-love. What about the warehouses, the workmen, the ships? You planning to do the rounds on them? The first sailor or loader who caught you alone would toss you on your fanny and take liberties. It isn't safe or smart. I can't allow you to take such foolish chances," he stated firmly.

"Don't be such a pessimist, Luke. You should know I can take care of myself. According to McVane, Randy and I own the business now. What I don't know, I'll learn, or I'll find someone who does know. Perhaps I'll hire a strong man who can do the rounds for me," she teased, eyes twinkling with merriment.

"Make sure he's an honest one, or he'll steal you blind while your nose is in those books," he warned seriously.

"If you're referring to Web, drop it, Luke. He's only taking care of things until Randy and I get matters settled. He made us an excellent offer, but we're not selling. For now, I can use Web's assistance. One day you'll have to tell me why you two dislike each other," she insisted, probing for a response which he refused to give.

Lucas and Amanda discussed and debated this topic for a long time as Miranda quietly listened and watched. She was amused by the verbal battle, for she already knew what the outcome would be.

Miranda studied Lucas as he conversed with her sister. Miranda and Lucas were very close; he was a friend, a teacher, a companion, a confidant, a partner in daring adventures. At twenty-seven, her handsome cousin still possessed a boyish mien and boundless energy. His dark green eyes glowed with a vitality she envied; they almost seemed to burn brightly from some inner fire. Lucas was strong and agile, which discouraged other men from provoking him. But her cousin rarely fought, for he was intelligent and perceptive. He could talk himself out of most troubles.

Lucas had a combination of traits which made him very attractive to women. He had a most enchanting and winning grin—when Lucas Reardon smiled, it was with his entire face, his entire being. His sable hair fell into a natural part down the middle then winged backward as the feathers near a hawk's throat. Just above his collar, his thick hair curled upward, almost impishly. Yes, Miranda decided to herself, Lucas Reardon was a man to stir a woman's heart, body, and soul—if she weren't his blood kin. Next to Amanda, Lucas was the most special person in her world; there wasn't anyone she admired or trusted more than Lucas.

In a humorous display of defeat, Lucas threw up his hands and shrieked, "I yield, love. Just remember

I'm around if you need me."

All three joined in shared laughter. Miranda asked, "Luke, what are you writing now? I haven't noticed any articles in the paper recently."

Lucas sighed heavily. "I quit the paper, Randy. I wasn't doing any good there. It'll be years before the North listens to our side of the war. With that damn cartoonist, Nast, and his other jaundice-eyed cohorts, still portraying us as barbarians in *Harper's Weekly*, the South might never be vindicated or understood. You'd think he did enough damage to us during the war. Did you know that even their school books now carry the Northern bias against the South? Sometimes I think those journalists and newspapers did more to continue the war and hostilities than the soldier. How do they sleep at night after writing and publishing such injurious trash? What about truth and honor?"

"What can you do about it, Lucas?" Amanda questioned, knowing how much it meant to Lucas to set the records straight.

"I just wish there were some way to get reports or books to the Northern people. All they hear and read is how bad it still is down here. They're led to believe we're savages ready for another uprising. They take minor events and exploit them. The only path to lasting peace is for both sides to learn the truth about each other. And I want to be the pathlighter," he eagerly announced.

"But how?" Miranda asked, listening intently.

"I've worked and waited a long time to get into a

position to be of use to the South. As Richelieu said, 'The pen is mightier than the sword.' I have a plan to strike a heavy blow at our Yankee conquerors. When it's in motion, I'll tell you two all about it," he revealed conspiratorially then winked at Miranda.

Miranda witnessed the mischievous look on Lucas's face, one she had come to know well. "Give, Luke; what's so funny?"

Cuffing her chin, he would only whisper, "You'll be the first to know, Randy. I just might have a vital role for you."

Following a light dinner, the three carried their desserts into the parlor to sit before a warm fire. The weather had turned slightly chilly, and the three sat on the floor near the fireplace as they chatted and enjoyed the treats prepared earlier by the housekeeper. Amanda still insisted on formal evening meals in the dining room, including proper clothing, silver, crystal, china, and candles, but tonight they also enjoyed the serene atmosphere of the sitting room.

"I'm glad to see you two smiling again. I've been plenty worried," Lucas confessed. "I wish there were something I could do."

"Just standing by us is enough, Luke," Amanda remarked softly. "We'll take care of everything until . . ." She went silent.

Lucas's head jerked upward. He stared at the golden-haired girl, and then at Miranda. Both their expressions shouted "trouble." His heart thudded heavily. "Until what?"

"Randy and I won't believe they're dead until we view the bodies. Maybe a passing ship found them. They might be alive somewhere. Papa was a skilled sailor; the *Merry Wind* was in excellent shape. And the weather wasn't bad. It doesn't make sense, Luke."

"The *Merry Wind* was found shattered on the coast, Mandy. You're dreaming, loves. If they survived, we would know by now. Don't build up for a crushing fall. They're dead," he stated with finality.

Miranda looked at him and shook her chestnut head of hair. "Hope is a free commodity, Luke. It isn't impossible."

"Don't do this," he pleaded, distressed by this unexpected defiance of reality, wishing he could alter it. Their gazes battled for a time. Lucas argued reluctantly, "You're denying the evidence."

"Evidence of a broken ship but not our parents' certain deaths," Miranda retorted.

Lucas looked from one girl to the other. "What if the bodies are never found? What if they're never recovered?"

"Then Randy and I have each other. At least Mama and Papa had a happy life together, and they have us to carry on for them. But as long as we can retain a glimmer of hope, it will see us through this dreadful period. When the time comes to accept the 'evidence,' we'll be strong enough to do so. But not yet, Luke, not yet. You must admit, we've survived the roughest part and we're getting on with our lives. Don't fret. We're going to be just fine."

Another knock sounded on their door. This time, Lucas went to answer it. "What do you want, Richardson?" he asked, not bothering to mask his dislike for this man who was hotly pursuing his cousin.

"I came to speak with Amanda, if you don't object, Reardon. Isn't it time for you to get over Marissa's loss?" Web hinted tauntingly.

"You never cared about her, so why did you ruin her?" he flared angrily. With luck, his investigative work on Web would pay off soon. With proof, Amanda would be compelled to see it was more than male pride and rivalry between them.

"If you care so much, why not take her back?" Web scoffed.

Before Lucas could reply, Amanda joined them. She was puzzled by the endless hostility between these two vital men. As they stood facing each other in the entrance hall, the currents of antagonism were so strong they were almost a tangible force. Amanda was piqued by their childish behavior. She was weary of trying not to take sides and of trying to settle their mysterious dispute.

"May I come in, Amanda?" Weber asked in a thick southern accent. If his secret plans worked out, Weber thought to himself, Lucas would soon be long gone, putting a halt to his nosing around. Luke always provoked him into acting badly before Amanda, and those reporter's instincts could soon get them both into trouble.

"Of course," Amanda responded, hoping they

would conduct themselves like gentlemen tonight. She almost stomped her foot in irritation when they exchanged surly grins. It was evident they were going to be as nasty as the rainy weather outside.

Lucas stalked into the sitting room, leaving them in the hallway. He sat beside Miranda this time, flashing her a frown. Amanda and Weber joined them, each taking a chair before the sofa. Amanda served Weber coffee and listened to his business report.

Although Weber was courting Amanda, Lucas never missed that flicker of desire for Miranda in Weber's dark eyes. Positively, this ex-Rebel craved both the Lawrence Shipping Firm and one of the Lawrence girls. Weber had leveled his sights on Amanda, but Lucas felt Web would just as soon have either sister if the firm was included in her dowry. Lucas was alarmed by Amanda's blind spot where Web was concerned, but as much as he hated to admit it, he knew Web could be a real charmer. If only Amanda knew the real Web . . .

Weber Richardson was a die-hard Southerner to the soul. During and after the war, there had been rumors of his cruelties to Yankee prisoners, even female ones. Web despised the North and what she had done to the South, to his family, to him. The Richardsons had lost everything: power, riches, property, and family. And Lucas was very eager to learn how Web had come back into money and property so quickly. Web owned a smaller shipping business near Joe's. Unknown to the girls, Web had once approached Joe about merging the two firms and marrying Amanda. But Joe had refused both requests. Undoubtedly Joe had recognized those same bad traits which dismayed Lucas: Web was conniving, greedy, vindictive, and cold-blooded. Now that Joe was gone, Lucas felt he must protect the girls from Web. But to attack the man verbally without proof would place Mandy on Web's side. Too, Web was dangerous and wily. If only some suitor would come along to distract Mandy and save her from Web, Lucas wished silently.

Lucas wondered what women saw in a man like Weber. Sure, he was nice looking, wealthy, and influential. At thirty-four, Weber was what the Northerners called a "typical Southern aristocrat." His features were prominent, strong, and arrogant, but Lucas knew all that to be a facade.

Miranda's thoughts were similar to Lucas's. There was something about Web Richardson that unsettled her. How she wished Amanda would never see him again.

Miranda admitted that Weber Richardson was imposing. He was educated and well traveled, and he could be witty and romantic. It was obvious women found him immensely attractive, but she wondered if Amanda had any real affection for Weber. So far, Miranda had carefully concealed her reservations about Weber. For now, she would allow Amanda to make her own decisions about him. But Miranda had glimpsed flickers in Web's eyes which chilled her heart. Just thinking of him sent shivers of dread through her body.

"Cold, love?" Lucas inquired, pulling her from

her dark thoughts.

"Let's get some brandy to warm me," she replied, sending Lucas a look which said it had been her thoughts and not the weather which had inspired her tremors. Lucas smiled and nodded.

When Miranda and Lucas left the room, Weber quickly arose and went to Amanda, pulling her to her feet. Before Amanda knew what he had in mind, his arms were holding her tightly and his mouth was settling over hers. He murmured huskily, "I've been waiting all day for that. You're driving me wild, Amanda. Why must you resist me? No man is more suited to you than me," he whispered confidently.

"Behave yourself, Weber Richardson," she scolded playfully. "It's too soon to think of such matters."

"If you won't agree to marry me or become affianced, at least don't see anyone besides me," he entreated.

"I've seen no man but you in over three months. Still, only by comparing you to other men can I judge if you are truly the right one for me," she jested coyly, grinning at him.

"But you've dated every man within fifty miles," he argued. "I have to be away on business for a few days. When I return, we need to be alone and talk. I have something important to ask you."

His tone revealed what he had in mind—sex and marriage, in any order. Uncertainty washed over her. Web's kisses were nice, but they didn't stir her desires. And she didn't know if she was ready for a permanent relationship. Right now, Amanda didn't want any complications in her life, including marriage. Maybe

Weber was the ideal choice for a husband, or at least a business partner. Each day he was becoming more amorous and persistent even though Amanda had not encouraged him. What would he do, she wondered, if she refused him?

"Please, Web, not here. Randy and Luke will return any moment. We'll have dinner and talk when you come back."

"At my home?" he suggested, eyes glowing with interest.

"At the Duke House," she refused laughingly, wondering what was missing between her and Web—or, perhaps, only in her.

He shrugged. "One day soon I hope you'll tire of leading me a merry chase, Amanda. Be mine. I promise you won't be sorry."

Amanda pulled away as she heard voices nearing the room. She realized that if she kept refusing to make any commitment to Web, he would demand one or leave her and her business. But did she care? When he discovered she was taking over the firm, his reaction would tell her a great deal. She decided not to tell him her news until his return. Since her parents' deaths, she had acted both spineless and brainless, but that was going to change. Web could take it or leave it!

As Miranda was pouring four brandies, another knock sounded at the door. "This is certainly our day for company," Amanda declared, her voice unnaturally high with tension. To escape Web's mocking gaze and to recover her wits and poise, she went to answer the summons. It was raining hard, and the night air was nippy and brisk.

"Yes?" she asked shakily of the man whose back was to the open door. Even though he was wearing a rain slicker, Amanda could tell he was several inches over six feet and powerfully built. She thought it odd he was wearing a western hat over his coal black hair.

He spoke in a stirring tone as he turned to face her. "Would you please tell Joseph Lawrence that Reis Harrison is here to see him?" he stated politely, sweeping off his hat and running strong fingers through his hat-ruffled hair.

In the darkness, neither could make out the features of the other. As the damp breeze teased at her clothes and hair, Amanda invited the stranger inside to deliver her depressing news. There was nothing menacing in his stance or voice, and there were two strong men inside the house who could offer their protection. She closed the door and leaned her forehead against it, summoning the strength to utter words which ripped at her heart. She inhaled then slowly released her breath.

Reis sensed something was terribly wrong. He waited patiently for the young woman to speak. As he removed his rain slicker and tossed it over his right arm, his eyes slipped from her silky head of blond curls down her slender body, to return to where her eyes would be once she faced him. When she did, her words, "Joseph Lawrence is dead," temporarily went unnoticed as his entranced senses hastily absorbed every detail about her.

Reis had heard the silly phrases "breath-taking" and "heart-stopping," but in his thirty-two years no woman had ever made his breath catch or his heart race. Now, without warning or preparation, he was assailed by both sensations. The instant her pale blue eyes fused with his rich blue ones, all wits and words were lost to him. Like some foolish lad, he gaped at her.

Once Amanda's gaze met his, she was unaware of anything except this vital man. Amanda had been wooed by countless suitors, and she knew instinctively this man was special. What could be more pleasurable, she imagined, than losing herself in his arms?

Amanda had not closed the door securely, and a sudden gust of wind flung it against her back. She jumped and gasped. Reis's hand shot over her shoulder to press the door shut, bringing their bodies into close contact, making each aware of the nearness of the other. Reis's palm flattened against the door and his arm rested lightly on her shoulder.

Amanda could feel the warmth of his breath upon her forehead. Never had she seen such handsome features. He had startlingly blue, mesmeric eyes, which flaunted a softness and sparkle that tugged at her thudding heart. His lips were full and inviting; his jawline was wide and his chin squared. If a man's nose could be beautiful, his was. Such strength of character was stamped upon his tanned face, and when he smiled, his whole face lit up like a candle in the darkness. His eyes and mouth had tiny creases near their corners—the kinds of lines which implied he was a man who loved life and was pleased with his role in it.

Without realizing she was inspecting him from head to foot, she noted his clothes. Surely his garments were specially tailored for that well-developed and well-toned physique. But why was he wearing western attire? His snug shirt, black leather vest, dark blue Levi jeans and black knee boots were not the usual dress for men in this area.

When Amanda realized she was leaning sideways and examining him from ebony head to black boot, she blushed in embarrassment, an uncommon reaction for her. What was wrong with her? To cover her lapse, she asked, "Who are you, sir?"

Reis straightened, placing his wayward hand on his hip. "Reis Harrison, Miss . . . ," he replied entreatingly. Reis was bemused by his novel loss of self-control. Surely she was an angel sent to Earth to warm his heart and soul. Her hair coloring was a mixture of lemonade and aged brandy. Her eyes were as striking as a peaceful summer sky.

"I caught your name, sir. What business do you have with Joseph Lawrence? As I said, he—he was killed in a recent accident," she told him hoarsely, eyes dewy.

Reis could tell she was upset by her words and her previous behavior. Then again, he was also unnerved by this vision of beauty. He quickly detected her spark of courage and pride. Reis Harrison, an ex-Yankee officer presently employed by President Grant as a special agent, was accustomed to getting his wishes, one way or another. Right now, Reis found this female more intriguing than his case . . .

Killed? Reis mentally echoed. "May I extend my

condolences, Miss..." He tried to obtain her identity once more.

"Amanda Lawrence, Mister Harrison." She took his cue.

"Wife or sister or daughter?" he inquired anxiously, praying her answer wouldn't be his first query.

"Joseph Lawrence was my father, Mister Harrison. I'm the new owner and manager of Lawrence Shipping. So if your business concerns the firm, you'll have to deal with me now," she informed him crisply, anticipating a mocking attitude.

Reis read her emotions accurately and smiled. "I have no qualms about dealing with a woman, even if she is extremely beautiful. I do hope you don't use your distracting charms to take advantage of a client. Shall we get acquainted and discuss our business over lunch tomorrow? I just arrived and wanted to introduce myself. Shall we say noon at the Windsor?"

At his bold flattery, surprise registered on Amanda's face. When she read no trace of guile in him, she smiled. "If all male customers and clients take my news as well as you did, Mister Harrison, I shall consider myself a believer in miracles. Thank you. I would prefer to discuss these matters tomorrow, as I have guests tonight."

"At your convenience, Miss Lawrence. It is Miss?" he pressed.

Amanda laughed softly and parried, "It is Mister, isn't it?"

"If there's anything better than a breath of fresh air, it's a charming and witty lady," he teased. He boldly reached for her left hand and held it up to view the third finger. "Why that finger's naked I'll never understand, but I am most grateful," he murmured.

Not to be outdone, Amanda audaciously repeated the action on his hand. "Since many men don't wear gold bands, is there a Mrs. Harrison?" she brazenly inquired, refusing to break their locked gaze.

"Not yet. Would you care to apply for that position?" he asked mirthfully, eyes glittering with appreciation. His cheery mood was contagious and his easy smile was infectious.

"Shouldn't we get acquainted first?" Amanda fenced deftly, warming and tingling all over.

Reis's glowing eyes eased over Amanda, then he chuckled. "Is there some dark secret about you which might change my mind? A nasty temper? Some hideous scar? Perhaps you're a witch?"

The smoldering fire in his gaze ignited her very soul. Amanda laughed at his comical look. The conversation was ridiculous, but so much fun. "The truth is out, sir; alas, a witch."

As Reis trailed a finger over her lips, he murmured, "What but truth could pass such sweet lips. A bewitcher indeed." Neither had kissed a total stranger before, but both were sorely tempted.

"Is there some problem, Amanda?" a frigid voice asked from down the hallway as Weber noisily approached them, having missed Reis's words but not his interest in Amanda.

Amanda quickly stepped aside, as if guilty of some offense. Weber joined them and Amanda eased her inexplicable tension by introducing the two men. "Weber Richardson, meet Reis Harrison. Reis and my father were friends, Web. He came to pay his respects and to discuss some family business. As I said, we'll chat tomorrow," she stated to an astute Reis. "Web is also a friend of the family," she added nonsensically.

"Haven't we met before, Harrison?" Weber asked suspiciously. His eyes chilled and narrowed as he scanned the vaguely familiar taut frame and handsome face near Amanda.

"Where?" Reis cautiously speculated, implying no recollection. He wondered why Amanda had insinuated that they had met before, but he went along with her deception. Apparently she didn't want Richardson to know he was here on business. Answers could come later.

Weber stepped closer, slipping his arm around Amanda's waist and smiling down into her baffled expression. As Amanda watched and listened, there it was again, that brief flash of intimidating coldness which warned her to keep Weber at arm's length. "Why don't you invite Harrison inside for a brandy? Since I'm handling your affairs, he can discuss his business with me," he stated boldly, wanting to study this man who caused ripples of warning and fury in him.

As if Reis wanted to do the same, he didn't decline or speak. As both men waited for Amanda's reaction, she grasped intangible sensations which didn't sit well with her. With unsuccessfully disguised annoyance, she chided, "You don't handle family or personal matters, Web, only business ones," trying to sound playfully casual. She looked up at Reis and said, "I'm sorry, Reis. I hope you don't think me rude, but it is late. Web and my cousin Luke were just about to leave." Somehow she wanted Reis to know she and Weber weren't alone. How dare Web act as if she were his property! "My sister and I have family matters to discuss in private." To Weber, she said, "I'll see you later. It's been a long and tiring day for me and Miranda."

Weber knew he had angered her and was being dismissed. Before he could contrive an excuse to stay, Miranda and Lucas joined them. Lucas asked, "Is there some problem, Mandy?"

"Web was just leaving," Amanda answered. Turning to Reis, she said, "This is my cousin, Lucas Reardon, and my sister, Miranda. Luke, Randy, this is Reis Harrison, one of Papa's friends. Goodnight, Web," she added to make her dismissal and vexation clear.

Miranda accepted Reis's handshake and smiled warmly. "It's a pleasure to meet you, sir. Shall I take your coat?"

Reis's eyes went from one beauty to the next. "You're almost twins," he muttered in surprise. "With different coloring."

The girls looked at each other and smiled. Miranda hugged Lucas and said good night, her eyes motioning for him to usher the despicable Weber out with him. Lucas grinned, only too delighted to comply. Weber couldn't refuse without acting a fool, so he left.

When the door closed behind the two men—one frowning and one smiling—Amanda invited Reis to have a brandy. She smiled sheepishly as she told him, "I'm sorry about that little lie, Mister Harrison. Sometimes Web is a bit presumptuous. He has a bad habit of trying to be too helpful," she jested.

Knowing Weber Richardson was probably lurking outside to see how long he remained, Reis was sorely tempted to accept the invitation. He would have, if Amanda had been alone. But he politely refused the offer, giving the late hour as his excuse. He slipped on his rain slicker and said good night, sending Amanda a smoldering smile which could have melted an entire snowdrift.

As he walked away from the house with a fluid and confident stride, Amanda stood in the open doorway, oblivious to the cool, damp air, watching him until the shadows devoured him. She closed the door and leaned against it, sighing peacefully.

Miranda giggled and commented, "He's quite a man."

Amanda sighed again, eyes dreamy. "Yes, he is, Randy. We're meeting for lunch tomorrow," she divulged happily, then revealed who Reis was and why he had appeared at their door tonight.

"Aren't you spoken for, Mandy? What about Web?" Miranda asked softly, observing her sister's

33

interest in Reis.

"Who?" Amanda teased playfully, winking at Miranda. "Besides, Reis is only business, my first client."

Their gazes fused; they burst into mirthful laughter.

Reis stood before his hotel window watching the gentle rainfall and sipping a tepid brandy. He hadn't expected to find Joseph Lawrence dead under mysterious circumstances. Reis flung himself across his bed without bothering to undress. This case was suddenly very complex and perilous. He hadn't imagined he would meet a dream like Amanda Lawrence and positively not on this crucial trip. More so, he hadn't envisioned confronting Lieutenant Weber Richardson here! Perhaps that sadistic ex-Rebel officer had forgotten the awesome day when they had met, but Major Reis Harrison never would.

Reis had tried to accept his losses during a vicious war. He had tried to repair his torn life, to master his bitterness, to govern the urge to track that one foe and justifiably slay him. After all, if every person gave in to vengeful impulses, the conflict between the two sides would never end.

Somehow all these facts and people were intertwined, and he dreaded untangling them. Only President Grant knew why Reis had been sent here. With so much greed and corruption surrounding him, Grant didn't know who to trust. It was up to

Reis to find some answers for him, answers to halt some explosive problems, answers to who was involved and why.

He cursed the heavens for putting Amanda in the center of this new crisis, for there could be no middle ground . . .

Chapter Two

When Miranda entered the sitting room the following morning, she found her sister pacing the floor, a look of annoyance wrinkling her forehead. Miranda watched from the doorway for a few moments before asking, "What's wrong, Mandy?"

Amanda halted her movements and glanced at her discerning sister. Waving a paper in her tight grasp, she replied, "See this? It says Mister Reis Harrison doesn't want to meet with me today. He could have sent his refusal before I was dressed and ready to leave," she declared angrily, unaccustomed to being put off by a man.

Miranda was quick to notice how lovely her sister looked this gloomy morning. Clearly Amanda had taken extra pains with her clothes and hair. She had been so excited about this appointment. Now, she looked distressed. Obviously, Amanda was suffering more from disappointment at not seeing Reis than from singed pride. "What does the letter say? Why did he cancel the meeting?" Miranda probed curiously.

Amanda stated skeptically, "He claims the weather is too bad for me to leave home. He wants to postpone our talk for a few days. He says he has other business he can settle first. Damn him!" she muttered, jerking the ribbons loose from her stylish hat and tossing it on the sofa with her cape. This action revealed the extent of her edginess, as Amanda was always careful with her clothes and belongings.

"Amanda Lawrence! You shouldn't speak so crudely. You recall how often Papa had to change plans at the last minute. The weather's awful. I think he's most considerate."

"You believe this excuse about the weather and other business? He probably thinks I don't have the brains to run Lawrence Shipping!" she declared, wanting her sister to convince her otherwise.

"Mandy, you stop this! You shouldn't judge him guilty of deception until you have proof. He didn't strike me as a dishonest or calculating man. If you hadn't found Mister Harrison so handsome and charming, you wouldn't be so vexed by this note. I saw the way you two looked at each other," she teased knowingly. "Mandy, don't spoil things before giving him a chance to explain," she entreated, praying this vital man could pull Amanda's attention from Weber.

"Spoil things?" Amanda echoed. "There's nothing to spoil. We only met last night, and we've nothing in common but business."

Miranda gayly challenged, "That isn't the way it looked to me, nor to Weber. Did you see the look on his face when you dismissed him like an errant child? I'd bet he wanted to choke you and Mister Harrison." Miranda's voice waxed serious as she asked, "Mandy, isn't Weber getting awfully possessive of you? You two aren't betrothed. Why did Weber act so rude and hostile last night?"

"Probably jealousy. You met Reis; can you blame Web? Reis was being flirtatious when Web joined us. Actually, I was rude to Web first, but he made me so mad!" she confessed.

"Web was definitely trying to show Mister Harrison he has a prior claim on you. From the way you two acted, maybe Mister Harrison thought he had interrupted a lover's spat. Maybe that's why he canceled; perhaps he's waiting to see if you're available," Miranda hinted slyly.

"Don't be silly, Randy. Reis was just playing a game with me. He probably thinks he can enchant every female he meets. I bet he had no intention of doing business with us. I could flog myself for acting like a fool! That damn Yankee probably thinks Southern girls don't know how to do anything but look pretty! Just wait until I see Mister Reis Harrison again; I'll straighten out his thinking," she threatened. She would not be an amusing game for any man.

"Don't do anything you'll be sorry for, Mandy. Mister Harrison doesn't appear the designing type, like some of your other suitors. He probably knows you're flooded with offers, and he's afraid of the competition. After all, he is a stranger and a Yankee."

"Reis Harrison didn't strike me as a man afraid of anything. But if he thinks to entice me by seeming disinterested, he's wrong!" Suddenly Amanda's expression grew thoughtful.

"What is it?" Miranda inquired, coming to stand by her sister.

"Before you and Luke joined us, something odd happened. Web asked Reis if they had met before. Reis didn't say yes or no. But the way they looked and acted . . . It was like—"

"Like what?" Miranda asked anxiously.

"Fierce enemies meeting again. Worse than the situation between Web and Luke. I wonder why," Amanda murmured worriedly.

"Are you forgetting Web was a Confederate officer and Reis was a Yankee less than eight years ago? Some men can't forgive or forget those times. From what I've seen, Web hates all Yankees. And if Reis thinks you and Web are close, that might cause resentment toward you. You did tell white lies to both men. If you'll remember, the trouble started last night when Web confronted you two in the hallway and acted as if he owned you," Miranda speculated.

Amanda wondered if Weber was the real reason for Reis's change of plans. Or was Reis merely used to having his way where women were concerned? She wanted to learn more about both men, especially that magnetic stranger who was affecting her emotionally. "I think I'll go down to the office," Amanda announced.

"But the weather is too bad to go out," Miranda debated. "If you run into that dashing Reis, he might think you're chasing him. I wonder what Weber will have to say about Reis dropping your meeting?"

The cunning hints struck home. Amanda didn't want either man to speculate wildly on her actions. Web would be gone by midafternoon, and Reis was out there somewhere. She was being childish and impulsive. Postponing a business meeting with her was not a crime, an insult, or a rejection.

"You're right as usual, Randy. I'll go to the office tomorrow. I want a good look at our books while Web is away. If Reis's business is near our firm, it wouldn't be wise to run into him *accidentally*."

Miranda stared at her mercurial sister. "If he merely put off your talk until the weather clears, why are you acting this way?"

"Because he could have delivered the message himself. It was storming last night when he came here. So why does he suddenly use the weather as an excuse to avoid me? If he truly thinks it's too bad to go meet him, he could come here," she rationalized.

"What privacy could you have if Web called again? He could have learned Weber is handling the firm for you. Since Reis doesn't know how often you see each other, it might be Web he wants to avoid."

Amanda met her sister's mischievous smile. "You think so?"

"You know more than I about men and romance.

He's different, Mandy. I've never seen you act like this about a man. I think something happened between you two the moment you met, just like Mama said. Reis Harrison is a rare find, and I think you're a fool if you mess it up before you see that fact too," her sister blurted out.

Before Amanda could tell her how silly or absurd that was, Miranda danced toward the door, humming to herself. Just before closing it, Miranda warned devilishly, "Watch out, Mandy; you might be falling in love with Reis." Amanda stared at the closed door, allowing those startling seeds to take root in her fertile mind.

That's ridiculous! she mentally rationalized. *How could I fall in love with a perfect stranger? Perfect. Perhaps you're too perfect, Reis Harrison. Of all the men I've ever known or seen, none have compared to you. Can Randy be right? Did you cast some magical spell over me last night? If not, why can I think of nothing but you? Why did I go to sleep thinking of you? Awake thinking of you? Why am I so afraid you won't come around again? Why does the thought we've met for the first and last time cause me such sadness and anguish? Is this a cruel joke by Fate? Have you done to me what I've done to so many men? I must see you again, Reis. I must understand these crazy feelings.*

Around eight that evening, the housekeeper answered the door and delivered a note to Amanda. Her anger returned twofold when she read it. "How dare he!" she shrieked aloud. "Listen to this, Randy:

'Miss Amanda Lawrence, I have reserved a private table at the Windsor for our lunch and to discuss a possible business deal. I shall expect you at noon.' It's signed by Reis Harrison. Not, 'will you meet me'; or, 'is it convenient'; just an order!''

Miranda wanted to tell her sister she was over-reacting, but she knew Amanda wouldn't listen. A masterful man was a new thing to Amanda. Men had always pursued her, falling over themselves and each other to gain her eye or to carry out her wishes. Suddenly, here was a man whom she couldn't control or bewitch, one who made her the huntress and not the prey for a delightful change. Obviously this Reis wasn't overly impressed with her beauty, wealth, and station. Miranda wondered how her sister would deal with this unspoken challenge, a challenge poor Reis might not realize he had issued. Apparently her sister had much to learn about a real man.

"I'm not going," Amanda stated defiantly. "If Mister Harrison wants to see me, he can ask, not summon! He should pick me up in a carriage. Him and his stupid notes! When I don't appear, that should teach him a thing or two about ladies and manners!"

"You're being spiteful, Amanda Lawrence. He's arranged a business meeting, not a date," Miranda reminded her stubborn sister.

"Then perhaps I should think twice about doing business with an ill-mannered rake. How does he know I'm not busy tomorrow? He could have asked," she reasoned petulantly.

"First, you're angry because he cancels; now, you're angry when he sets a new appointment. What's wrong with you, Mandy? Do you or do you not wish to see him? You could lose his business by behaving like a spurned woman or a spoiled brat. Go and meet with him," Miranda encouraged.

"I can't," she vowed willfully. "If I rush to meet him, he'll think he can treat me in this despicable and rude manner. Mister Reis Harrison needs to learn a valuable lesson about women. If I had been a man, he wouldn't have canceled the first meeting; and he surely wouldn't set up a new one in such an offensive way. If we're to do business, he must treat me equally and respectfully."

"Be honest with yourself, Mandy," her sister advised gravely. "You're really upset because he's ignoring you as a woman. If he's stung your pride, don't let it show. You can't bedazzle every male. Are you afraid of him?" she conjectured seriously.

"Afraid of him? He didn't appear to be dangerous," she replied.

"That's not what I meant. He frightens you in some way."

Amanda flushed guiltily. "There is something about him which confuses me. He made a fool of me last night. He flirted outrageously with me, and I responded likewise. Now, he feels he can treat me as he pleases. I won't chase any man, and certainly not a total stranger. I don't like losing control of such a situation," she admitted.

"What's so terrible about giving the reins to such a

44

stimulating man? How many times have you complained about suitors who lack courage and brains? You don't want someone you can lead around by a ring through his nose. If he intrigues you, Mandy, discover why."

"For one who claims to know little about men and romance, you offer a great deal of advice," Amanda teased her sister. "What about you, Randy? Have you ever met anyone intriguing?"

"Not yet, but I will one day," Miranda replied confidently.

"How so, when you stay home all the time? You think some irresistible stranger is going to appear at your door one stormy night to sweep you off your feet?" she continued merrily.

"Why not? It happened with you," she ventured boldly.

"Miranda Lawrence, you never give up, do you?" she wailed.

"Not when I see that same look in your eyes as I saw in Mama's. Have you ever met a man like Reis? No," she answered her own question.

Still, Miranda couldn't persuade her sister to accept the appointment with Reis the next day. Instead, Amanda went to visit friends, just to be unavailable if Reis called. Actually, Amanda was disturbed by the way she had behaved with Reis. She had never met a commanding and imposing man, and she didn't know how to deal with one or the sensations which he aroused. She had acted like an infatuated and foolish young girl, and knew she had to be wary of his powerful effect. She refused even to send a note of regret or refusal.

When Reis came by in midafternoon to see why Amanda hadn't arrived for their meeting, Miranda was too embarrassed to speak with him. Knowing she couldn't lie with a clear conscience or straight face, she ordered their housekeeper to tell Reis that Amanda was out for the day. She was bemused by the message Reis left for Amanda: "If Miss Lawrence decides to meet with me, tell her to contact me at the hotel before I leave Friday."

Amanda was given the cool message upon her arrival home. "First, a command appearance; now, an ultimatum. Just who does he think he is, Randy? Mrs. Reed said he looked terribly angry."

"He should be. You insult his manners then behave just as rudely. The least you could have done was send a note to say you weren't coming," Miranda scolded her. "Is this any way to handle business? If you don't want to be treated like a spoiled woman, then don't behave like one. If you want him to pursue you, Mandy, then you'd best give him the opportunity before he leaves Friday."

"Why are you speaking so hatefully, Randy?" she quizzed.

"Because I'm mad. You rant about how all males are alike; then when someone different comes along, you're furious because he doesn't behave like all the rest. I don't understand you, Mandy. You haven't chosen a sweetheart because not one man you've dated has stood out from the others. Suddenly a strong and virile male magically appears on your doorstep, and you're chasing him away because you can't wrap him around your finger like all the rest who aren't worth having."

"That isn't true, Randy. I'm just . . ." She fell silent, turning her back to her sister. How could she explain her feelings?

"Just what?" the dark-haired girl demanded.

"You asked me if I was afraid of Reis. Maybe I am. Oh, Randy, he makes me feel and think such puzzling things. I'm at such a loss when he's near. I'd probably act like an idiot at our meeting. Can I risk falling for the only man who doesn't seem interested in me?" Tears glimmered on her lashes.

"From what I observed, Reis is most impressed by you."

"But in what way, Randy? I won't argue that he found me charming or desirable. What if that's all he sees and wants from me? He's dangerous, Randy, for he has the power to hurt me." With that fear spoken aloud, she knew she must deal with it, with the source of it.

"You're serious, aren't you?" When Amanda nodded, Miranda smiled and suggested, "Why don't you find out how you affect him? It isn't like you to be a coward or to be so insecure."

"That's the problem," Amanda sighed. "I haven't been me since I met Reis."

Reis sat at the table in his room, making notes and

planning. He had done some checking on Richardson, Amanda Lawrence, and both shipping firms. He didn't like what his search had revealed or the implications. He couldn't figure out why Amanda didn't want Weber to know he was here on business, not after discovering that Weber was in control of her firm. More confusing and plaguing was the fact that Weber and Amanda were rumored to be heading for the altar. Very strange . . .

He pondered Amanda's reasons for deceiving her sweetheart and temporary partner. But if Amanda was in love with Weber, why had she flirted with him? Who had killed Joseph Lawrence, and why? Reis couldn't believe his convenient death was an accident. Had Joseph found out too much? Amanda had wanted their meeting kept a secret from Weber, but why conceal it and why refuse to set up another one? What was Richardson's involvement in this mystery? Reis cautioned himself to forget vengeful justice against Weber until this mission was completed. The situation was getting more complicated and suspicious every minute. Amanda couldn't know who and what he was, so why was she avoiding him? Or was it merely a feminine ploy to entice and to baffle him?

The answers he needed were concealed in the Lawrence firm. Like it or not, Reis would have to use Amanda to get them. She was a proud and stubborn beauty. He couldn't wait around and hope for her to make the next move. Doubtlessly she was used to getting her way with men. If he had the time, he would spark her interest by showing a resistance to her charms and beauty, giving her a much-needed lesson. Then again, maybe he had been overly confident in his approach to her, for he was also accustomed to getting his way with the opposite sex. Frankly, her rebuffs were a shock to him. If Amanda Lawrence expected and needed romantic wooing, then she would receive it, and receive it from a master . . .

The following day was clear and warm. Miranda lifted the basket of fresh flowers and turned to enter the house. She was surprised to find Reis leaning negligently against the gatepost behind her. "Mister Harrison, I didn't hear you arrive. Have you been standing there long?"

"Only a few moments. I didn't want to startle you, Miss Miranda. You looked so deep in thought. It's a lovely day, isn't it?"

Miranda glanced skyward and smiled. "Yes, it is. Spring is one of my favorite seasons. But I fear the recent rains nearly destroyed the flowers." She waited for him to reveal his reason for being there.

As if reading her thought, he said, "I came by to see if Miss Amanda could join me for lunch or dinner, if she isn't occupied today. I would like to get our business settled as quickly as possible."

"My sister isn't home, Mister Harrison. And I don't know when she'll be returning. Would you care to leave her a message?"

"Please call me Reis. If I've offended your sister in some way, Miss Miranda, I would appreciate your passing along my apology." When Miranda lowered her lashes and didn't immediately respond, Reis had his answer. "Is there some reason why she doesn't wish to meet with me?"

Miranda looked up at him. "I don't discuss my sister with strangers, sir. You'll have to speak with her yourself," she told him politely. "However, it would be wise to invite rather than to summon her," she added slyly.

A broad grin captured Reis's mouth and eyes. "Thank you, Miss Miranda. I thought that might be the crux of the matter. I fear I've had little dealings with ladies. I'll call again later, if that's agreeable?"

"You may call me Miranda or Randy," she offered. Her hesitation was noticeable before she added, "Mandy went to Papa's office to work on the books. Perhaps you could drop by and see her there."

"I was under the impression Weber Richardson handled the business for her," he probed.

Miranda didn't realize her distaste for Weber was revealed in her eyes and voice when she replied, "After the accident, Weber was to take care of matters only until Mandy could do so. Weber is away for a few days," she informed him, hoping he would catch her hint.

"May I ask a rather personal question, Miranda?"

"Such as?" she inquired curiously.

"Rumor has it that Amanda and Weber are to be married. Is that true?" he asked.

Miranda knew she shouldn't answer such a loaded question, but she couldn't stop herself. To remain silent would imply a positive answer and discourage a possible pursuit by Reis. Even if nothing happened between Amanda and Reis, perhaps he could destroy any relationship between Mandy and Weber. She knew it was wrong to interfere, but she felt compelled by Reis's intent gaze. "Only if Weber has his way, which he hasn't to date."

"You don't like him, do you?" he inquired.

"I don't think he's right for my sister," she parried.

"Neither do I, Miranda," he readily concurred. "I hope this doesn't sound too forward, but I hope to sever that relationship."

Miranda gasped in astonishment at the confession, then smiled. "I hope it doesn't sound too forward to wish you luck, Reis."

Reis was in high spirits as he left Miranda. If Amanda was anything like her twin sister, he was in for a delightful adventure. He whistled as he strolled down the street, plotting the surrender of a golden-haired minx. He halted by the hotel to set his plans in motion.

Amanda had been reading for hours. She had gone over all reports and books available. But there was one book missing, and she wondered why. The only explanation was that Weber had taken it to work on while he was away. Weary from her labor and recent loss of sleep, she dozed lightly. She didn't hear the key as it turned in the lock, sealing her in this private world with a determined Reis Harrison.

51

He came forward to halt at her side, eyes passing over her from head to lap. He bent forward, his lips pressing against hers ever so lightly, then firmly and passionately as hers parted and responded.

He held her face gently between his hands, as his lips refused to end the long-awaited kiss which was more intoxicating than he had expected. Amanda's arms eased around Reis's body as she arched upward. When Reis's lips pressed light kisses to her eyes, she murmured dreamily, "Why did you wait so long to come, Reis?"

Reis realized she was half-asleep, but her words exposed her hidden thoughts and thrilled his heart. She had called his name, not Weber's.

Reis sat on the edge of the desk, Amanda's chair between his spread thighs. He placed his hands on either side of her shoulders, knowing she would bolt the moment her senses cleared.

Amanda opened her eyes then froze briefly in confusion. "What are you doing here? How did you get in?" she exclaimed.

"You shouldn't leave the door unlocked when you're alone, Amanda. Sorry, but I couldn't resist kissing you," he declared huskily.

Her cheeks flushed a deep crimson. "How dare you take such liberties when I'm senseless," she chided him. "What do you want?" she asked nervously, warming to his quick and easy smile.

"To talk, after we have lunch," he calmly announced to the befuddled Amanda, pointing to the picnic basket on her desk.

"Lunch?" she repeated as she stalled to clear her wits, which was nearly impossible while gazing into those expressive sapphire eyes.

"At your service, ma'am." As Amanda watched, Reis withdrew fried chicken, baked bread, and wine from the basket. As he spread a cloth over the desk and arranged the items, he remarked, "It isn't much or fancy, but it'll fill our stomachs while we talk."

Struck speechless, Amanda remained silent. Reis poured two glasses of wine and handed one to her. Amanda accepted it with a shaky hand. He set a plate and utensils before her, then lay a rose across her plate. "That's to say I'm sorry."

Bewilderment filled her blue eyes. "For what?" she questioned.

"I'm not quite sure, but I seem to have offended you into avoiding me. Could we make a fresh start?" he beseeched her.

"Just what are you trying to pull, Mister Harrison?" she asked suspiciously, touched by his romantic gestures.

"The wool over those entrancing eyes so I can think clearly," he murmured roguishly, grinning at her.

Amanda couldn't suppress her laughter. "I will say one thing for you, Mister Harrison, you are a most persistent and surprising man."

"I hope that's a compliment," he retorted hastily. "Shall we eat, then discuss future business?"

53

"Why not? I am ravenous, and this looks delicious."

To her further delight, Reis prepared her plate. As he worked, she eyed him intently as she sniffed the fragrant rose.

They ate in silence, but for his offer of more food and wine. When they finished, he promptly cleared the desk. He pulled a chair up before it, then sat down and met her amused gaze. "Well?"

"Well what, Mister Harrison?" she replied.

"Do we do business together?" he ventured.

"What did you have in mind?" she asked, leaning back in her chair as she teased her nose with the flower.

Their eyes met and danced with desire. "Business this afternoon and dinner tonight?" he suggested warmly.

Temporarily ignoring his last invitation, she asked, "What kind of business? Have you dealt with my father before?"

"I haven't, but the men I represent have. They've been doing business with another firm for months, but they've decided to deal with yours again, if you'll agree. They asked me to handle it for them."

"Why did they change to another firm?" she asked astutely.

"Businessmen always look for faster and cheaper service. They've decided it's to their advantage to return to Lawrence Shipping," he explained without actually lying to her. When this matter was settled, he would reveal the truth, that he and Grant had coaxed the clients to aid in this investigation. Reis had already uncovered certain facts in this case. A theft or switch in products was being done by this firm and on a ship employed by this firm. It was Reis's job to find out how the switch was carried out, by whom, and for what purpose. There was more to this intricate plot than ruining Northern-owned companies or destroying "traitorous" Southern sympathizers and carpetbaggers. He suspected that Joseph Lawrence had been innocent in this illegal and cunning deception. Perhaps he had been killed after discovering his firm was being used. Reis needed to find out the connection between Amanda and Weber, which didn't seem romantic on her part. But many aristocratic marriages had nothing to do with love.

Reis and Grant had discovered some of these evil profits were being used to finance the activities of the despicable Ku-Klux-Klan and to purchase black votes to put certain Southern whites in influential positions in national, state, and local governments. When money failed to produce the desired results, the Klan used other means to get their wishes. During a preliminary investigation, Reis had uncovered several interrelated plots which dismayed him and the President.

Reis had unmasked Northerners who were still victimizing Southern planters or exploiting them. He had found traces of dangerous hostilities still lingering in certain areas. He had discovered diehard ex-Rebs who were causing trouble disguised as antagonistic ex-Yankees. He had learned of unfair tariffs which were favorable to the North but devastating the South. There were Northern interests which were preventing progress in the Southern railroads and mills, which would lessen the proceeds in the North. There were Southerners seeking any means to recover power and property confiscated during and after the war. Most discouraging and perilous were the hints at an attempt to one day revive the Confederacy—gold, weapons, and supplies were being purchased and shipped to the South and concealed. It troubled Reis that most of his clues pointed to involvement by this firm.

Damn! he swore mentally. Hadn't this war done enough damage to the North and South? Why couldn't it be over once and for all? Sometimes Reis didn't know who to blame. If the damn newspapers and embittered writers would stop stirring up trouble with those poisonous pens, matters might settle down. Reis warned himself not to be vindictively blind where Weber was concerned. It bothered him to realize that he hoped that bastard was responsible so he could arrest him. No matter how much he despised Weber, he couldn't let the guilty parties escape while trying to pin something on his enemy. He had never allowed personal feelings to color his duty, but it was difficult where Amanda and Weber were concerned.

He sighed heavily then noticed that Amanda was

staring at him. He reprimanded himself when she commented, "If you're tired or bored, Mister Harrison, we can discuss this tomorrow."

"I'm sorry, Amanda; it's hard to concentrate with you before me. How about we take a walk and get some fresh air to clear my head?"

Chapter Three

As he requested, Amanda gave Reis a tour of her office, docking area, warehouses, and a ship which was in port. At first, she had been subdued. But Reis watched the suspense and excitement which flashed over her eyes as she took in the sights. He could tell she was just as curious about these areas as he was, just as pleased to inspect them. He observed her as she laughed and chatted with workers whom she had known for years, or accepted words of sympathy and encouragement about her parents. As if he inspired feelings of confidence and safety, if he lagged behind she would glance around to locate him. An almost timid smile would brighten her face when her blue eyes touched upon him; a smile which he always returned.

Once as they discussed the differences in local and foreign markets, their gazes had locked and they had fallen silent for a time. A noisy loader had broken the magical spell. As they continued their tour, Reis knew she had spoken truthfully; she knew all about this business, but not from experience. Even though she took this business seriously, she was like a child with a new toy.

As the sun moved closer to the horizon, Amanda obviously began finding things to discuss or examine. Reis wondered if she were reluctant to leave him or the docks. No matter, for it was getting late and cool.

As they watched a flatboat pull anchor and glide down the river, Reis inquired, "Is this your first visit here?"

"I've been here many times with my father, but never alone. I mostly helped with the books. I hope that doesn't change your opinion, Reis. I'm sure I can learn anything I don't know." She was eager to prove herself, and she needed Reis's three accounts to begin.

To her relief, he smiled and agreed. "Is safety the reason why you hired Weber Richardson? The docks aren't any place for a lady, even a brave one. In fact, we're inviting trouble to remain after dark."

"Believe it or not, Reis, I can take care of myself. But I'm not stupid, so I wouldn't come down here alone. I didn't exactly hire Web; he was kind enough to take control and run things after . . . the accident. I'm grateful to him, but I'm ready to take over now. This business has been part of my life for as long as I can remember; I've even gone on trips with Papa to make deliveries, to entice new accounts, or to check out problems, so I can handle those matters when they come up. To sell it seems like cutting all ties with my past. If I didn't have the business, I wouldn't have anything to do. A woman can't read and sew all the time. It's important to me, Reis. This isn't some childish whim. I promise you I won't disappoint your friends."

As they returned to her office to lock up for the day, Reis offered, "I'll make you a deal, Amanda. If I can hang around for protection and advice while you adjust to your new position as owner, you can have these three accounts. That way, everyone's interest will be safeguarded. I'll even work for free." He winked at her.

Amanda looked up into his handsome face. "You want to help me get started? But I thought you were leaving Friday," she hinted.

"That was just a sneaky trick to make you see me sooner," he told her. "For the next few months, my job is to see to my friends' business. That appears to include assisting their shipper, if she agrees."

Her heart fluttered at the idea of working side-by-side with this intoxicating man. How would she keep her mind on business! Suddenly she remembered Weber and, before she could stop herself, she blurted out her worry. "Web won't like this at all."

"Does that matter to you? You are the owner," he teased.

Amanda tried to cover her mistake and to keep Reis off balance. "It just seems kind of traitorous to fire him and to hire you. The firm might be out of business right now if he hadn't taken care of it. I was planning to take over completely when he returns, but I don't want him to think it's because of you," she rationalized aloud.

"Are you in love with him? Going to marry him?" He caught her off guard with those blunt and jarring questions.

"That's none of your business, Reis," she informed him curtly.

"But it is, Amanda," he refuted, backing her against the wall and pinning her to it with his steely body. "If you're another man's woman, I can't do this," he whispered, nibbling at her right ear. "Or this," he added, closing her lids with kisses. "Or this," he murmured again, sealing their lips. When she didn't resist him, he pulled her into his embrace, fusing his mouth to hers.

Amanda's arms were caught between them and her lips were helpless to do anything but yield to his masterful assault. She moaned softly as she pressed closer to him. Sensing a thrilling innocence in her response, Reis knew he must halt this madness or risk seducing her on the wooden floor. He had just enough presence of mind to realize the damage that could do to their budding relationship. If he didn't cease this tempting game, all would be lost. He ached from the flames which were licking painfully at his loins, flames which didn't want to be doused by words or self-control. He stared into her passion-glazed eyes. At least he knew she desired him as much as he desired her.

He stepped backward and inhaled raggedly. Amanda sank weakly against the wall, staring at him. "My God, Amanda, do you know what you do to a man? How you tempt him beyond control? If I thought for one moment you knew what you were doing . . . ."

Amanda's hand came up to touch her lips, lips which throbbed with hunger for his. She had never been kissed like this or had any man cause such bittersweet sensations to attack her mind and body. "Why did you do that?" she asked hoarsely. She had been so mesmerized that he could have taken anything he desired from her. Why had Reis halted? Web wouldn't have!

"I've been wanting to since the first moment I met you, but I was trying to control myself until we got to know each other better. I'm sorry if I offended you." He stepped to the desk and sat on its edge.

"Do you go around stealing kisses from any female who catches your eye?" she inquired, moistening her dry lips. She wanted to ask why he hadn't seduced her, but she dared not. Still, she found it odd that she felt no shame or embarrassment at her unbridled response.

"No, but you're not just any female. Will you have dinner with me tonight?" Reis changed the subject but kept his distance.

"If you promise to control such wild impulses," she jested, regaining a measure of poise. She must keep his power over her a secret. Maybe it was her imagination or wishful thinking, but Reis also appeared unnerved and puzzled by her effect on him.

"Ouch," he winced playfully. "You wouldn't want me to lie, would you?" he tested her as the passion faded in her blue eyes.

"Of course not," she stated too quickly.

"Then I can't make such a promise. But I will try to behave." He tensed as he awaited her response. Damn, but he wanted her!

"You, sir, are a rake," she declared, then laughed.

"It's one of my dark secrets. I hope it doesn't change your mind. However, I don't have a nasty temper or any hideous scars."

Both recalled their first conversation on which he was playing at that moment. "Do you have other dark secrets, Mister Harrison?"

Hearty laughter filled the quiet room. "Why don't we let you decide?" he murmured in a stirring tone.

"All right, Mister Rake. Do I meet you somewhere, or will you pick me up at home?" She accepted his stimulating challenge. She had to learn why this man was so unique, so irresistible, so unsettling.

Reis noted the softened eyes which watched him. He should warn her not to look at him like that, but he couldn't deny himself. "I'll pick you up at seven, if that's agreeable. First, I'll see you home safely." He lifted the borrowed basket and turned to face her. "Ready?" he asked, his tone sensually provocative.

Amanda grinned but didn't make the naughty comment which was teasing her tongue. He certainly had a way of making her feel like freshly churned butter beneath a blazing sun. She couldn't decide why she felt so carefree and daring around Reis, so happy and alive. She nodded and followed him out, locking the door.

As they approached a busy street, Reis took her hand and guided her across. At the other side he didn't release it, and Amanda couldn't break this pleasing contact. Even if she had thought about someone seeing them, it wouldn't have worried her today. His hand was so warm and strong but his grip so gentle. Nothing felt more natural than strolling with Reis, or more serene than being in his company, or more enticing than his touch. Amanda was glad she wasn't wearing gloves, for his flesh was delightful.

Reis left her at her front door, saying he would return later. The moment he was out of sight, she raced inside and up the stairs to decide which gown to wear. Miranda had been watching from her window. She sighed happily and smiled, heading for Amanda's room.

When she knocked, Amanda sang out for her to enter. "Did you get much work done?" she asked innocently.

Amanda whirled and laughed. "I saw Reis this afternoon. He's taking me to dinner tonight. That should please you, dear sister."

"It obviously pleases you, dear sister," she teased, witnessing Amanda's exuberance and starry eyes. Amanda had never pursued a man; but from the way she was acting, it appeared she intended to start with this one. Miranda was happy for her, as Reis seemed a perfect match.

"Yes, it does," Amanda stated honestly. She told Miranda about their deal and visit. "Need I say you were right?"

"It's just like Mama said, isn't it, Mandy?" she asked hopefully as she observed her ecstatic sister.

Amanda giggled as she vowed, "Even better."

When Reis came for her that night, he couldn't believe his senses. She was even more beautiful, if possible. "The way you look, you're not planning to help me keep my word, are you?" he chided her, remembering that she hadn't pulled her hand from his or spurned his touch at her office. Did she think he was made of iron? Did she think he could govern the situation between them without her help? Where was the arrogant ice maiden she was alleged to be? Doubtlessly, spurned males considered her such because she had refused their advances. He realized that only a rare and lucky man could win Amanda's love and stir her passions. Fortunately, he thrived on challenge.

She laughed merrily. "If that was a veiled compliment, Reis, thank you. You look quite handsome yourself."

"A woman who isn't afraid to speak her mind. Excellent."

As they dined in a candle-lit corner of the restaurant in the Windsor Hotel, she asked, "Where are you from, Reis?"

"Texas, but I live in Washington," he replied casually.

"That explains your western attire, but I thought you were a Yankee," she remarked, her mind spinning at his nearness.

"You say that as if it's a nasty word, Amanda. If it makes a difference to you, I was in the Union army," he informed her, knowing Weber would tell her, if he hadn't already.

"Why?" she probed inquisitively, lowering her fork and focusing her full attention on him. Something different about him tugged at her mind, but she was too enchanted to comprehend it.

"Do you really want to discuss my past politics? Do you hold some grudge against the Union?" he inquired anxiously, dismayed that she had broached this particular subject tonight. After dropping his pretense, he should have expected it, as Amanda was smart and alert.

"Of course not. Papa remained neutral because he didn't feel either side was totally right. We never had slaves on our plantation, but we are Southerners. When Virginia sided with the Confederacy, we were included in the hostilities whether we wanted to be or not."

"But your father held on to his plantation and shipping firm," he asserted genially, hoping she would explain how and why. He had to make certain he could trust this winsome beauty.

"Yes, but it was difficult. We made enemies on both sides," she answered sadly as she recalled unpleasant memories.

Comprehending this point, he stated, "But the war

has been over for years, Amanda. Are you having problems with someone?"

"I know it's over, but many don't accept it. There are Northerners and Southerners who still won't do business with us. Sometimes I think the conflicts will never end. Is it over for you, Reis?"

"Any man who battles his brother gets scars from it, Amanda, wounds which heal slowly or not at all," he answered candidly. "Each man must find his own cure or method of treating such injuries."

"Do you have any family?" she asked abruptly.

"No," he stated sullenly. "Would you like some dessert?"

"What happened to them?" She persisted despite his chilling mood.

He met her gaze and replied evenly, "Rebs killed them while I was off fighting other Rebs. Afterward, they burned our ranch to the ground. I still own the property, but I've never gone back."

"I'm sorry," she murmured, wishing she hadn't pressed him.

"Dessert?" he asked again, seeming to look right through her. He was suddenly tense and distant. Could he trust this woman who had ties to a snake like Richardson? If he was wrong about Amanda, she could destroy him and crush this vital mission. Until he was sure of her, he dared not get too close.

"No thanks," she replied, witnessing a withdrawal in him.

As if anxious to end their evening, the moment they finished he remarked, "It's late. I'd best get you home. I'll see you tomorrow.''

Reis paid for their meal then escorted her home, all in moody silence. At the steps, he bid her good night and turned to leave.

"Reis," she called to him in panic. He halted and turned, his expression concealed by shadows. He seemed so remote. "Nothing," she murmured, scolding herself for spoiling a lovely evening, pondering how she had done so.

In the moonlight playing upon her face, Reis saw the effects of his rash behavior. Tears glittered on her lashes; her expression exposed hurt and confusion. From what he had learned about her, this was unusual behavior for haughty and coy Amanda Lawrence. Reis knew he had upset her and he didn't want to push her away, but he couldn't explain matters to her for a long time. This case was forcing him to relive some painful times, times he hadn't allowed himself to think of in years. He surged forward, caught her in his arms, kissed her soundly, then hurried away before she could respond or speak. Whatever her part in this messy and hazardous affair—innocent or intentional—Reis felt he must find a way to protect her, to save her from danger.

Amanda stood there, utterly bewildered. If any other man had treated her this way, she would have berated him furiously and refused to see him again. Oddly, she wanted to comfort Reis, to go after him. She concluded Reis must have some hidden scars, if not on that firm and virile body, then surely on his soul. She must never mention the war or his family again, if he returned. That had to have been the source of his abrupt change.

Change, she mused to herself. She slipped her arms around the porch pillar and rested her cheek against it, concentrating on this mysterious and arresting man. All at once, she knew what had been bothering her all evening. Until he had kissed her this afternoon, Reis had spoken with a northern accent; since then, his voice had altered to a stirring blend of western and southern drawls!

Amanda was puzzled. That's why she had assumed he was a Northerner. The change had registered in her mind; that's why thoughts of Yankees and Rebs had come forth. But why would a man use a phony northern accent then switch to a southern one? Was it intentional or accidental? Did he think her so dense she wouldn't notice?

But he had confessed to being from Texas, to being a Southerner! Was this some kind of game she didn't understand? She couldn't help but feel duped, and she needed to know why he had deceived her. What was he doing to her? What did he want here? She tried to recall every word he had spoken and every expression since their meeting. No explanation came to mind. Amanda was very adept at playing wily games with people, and she felt that Reis was up to some mischief. Before he gained too much influence over her, she vowed to uncover his sport and its rules.

Amanda left the house early the next morning, anxious to get to the office and complete her study of the books before Weber's return. After opening the safe, she was astonished to find the missing book behind the others. Her eyes widened in confusion. Weber had not returned to Alexandria, so how had this book found its way back into a locked safe and office? How could she have overlooked an item of its size and importance? She sighed in frustration and scolded herself for her carelessness.

Clearly the book must have been there yesterday. She ordered herself to clear her wits. This book contained the most recent business dealings of her father's firm, with some personal entries at the rear. Perhaps the names of Reis's clients would offer her a clue to his sudden appearance and curious conduct.

Reis had told her that his friends had changed firms months ago. Perhaps her father had made helpful notations about those dissatisfied customers. Sure enough, Amanda located the three names which had halted business with Lawrence Shipping, all at the same time—their three largest accounts! She was shocked to learn that all three had switched to Richardson's Shipping.

She carefully went over those three records. There were old notes about shipments and cargoes, coded messages which only her father could understand. Was it possible those clients had created phony complaints just to cancel with him?

Amanda wondered how Weber's firm was handling that much business. If Weber had pulled some trick to gain those accounts, he would have destroyed this enlightening evidence, knowing she would eventually see it. After all, Weber had been in control of her firm and its books for two months. Was it true that Reis's friends weren't receiving the cheaper and faster service they had sought from Richardson's? Did Web know he was losing these accounts back to her? Had he gone to see these men, to try to hold them? She knew Weber wanted to expand his business, needed to do so. Was Weber afraid of losing everything a second time? Reis or no Reis, if these men were trouble, she didn't want to have them back.

Amanda returned her attention to the critical book at hand. She went over every fact and figure listed there. When she doubted her conclusions, she went over them again, and again.

When she couldn't deny the implications of those pages, she lay the book aside and closed her eyes to rest them. Amanda was alarmed by the shocking discovery that the firm was in terrible financial condition, the plantation had been sold, and the townhouse was mortgaged. How was that possible? Her father had said nothing to them. If business didn't pick up, the company wouldn't survive through June. What would happen to her and Miranda? Even if they sold their possessions and jewels, the money wouldn't last long.

Was this why Weber was pressing her about marriage? Not to gain a lucrative company and a wealthy business, but to spare her from humiliating bankruptcy? Was this why he didn't want her to take over, to keep her from learning the grim truth? She recalled him saying something about choosing him for himself and not for his position. She had taken the remark as a joke. Weber was so proud; he didn't want anyone to think she was marrying him for his money. He wanted them affianced before this news could be revealed. Did he hope to save her company by absorbing it into his? One thing appeared certain. Weber wasn't after her for the business; he couldn't be, for he knew its condition.

Amanda felt awful that she had had such wicked thoughts about Weber. One particular item plagued her; Weber had loaned her company a large amount of money to pay the bills for the past month . . .

What a selfish fool she was! While dear Weber was trying to help her, she was romancing another man. How could she take over and run a business that was losing money every day? How blind she had been. So much for Luke's suspicions and contempt. If not for Weber, she and Miranda would have lost everything.

How could she accept the accounts Reis was offering to her? From her father's past notations, they had switched to Web's company. They had to be his three largest accounts, and to take them away might ruin him, alienate him. Could she do such a cruel thing after all Weber had done for her and her sister? Far worse, how deeply would it hurt Weber if she put Reis Harrison in his place, in the firm and in her life? Did Web truly love her and want her for herself?

Why hadn't Weber told her how things really stood? He must think her ungrateful and insensitive. From the way it looked, Weber had supported her and Miranda for the past two months and never claimed any credit or repayment. Now that she was indebted to Web, what would he expect or demand in return? Did Web want her totally dependent upon him before telling her about the sorry state of her business and personal finances? Were his actions selfish or lovingly generous? This situation was painful and complex.

Amanda realized that Weber would know she had discovered the truth when he returned to find her in the office with her nose in the books. She should get out of here quickly and not return until she decided what to do with this dreadful information. She quickly put things as they had been left before his departure. She could only pray that he wouldn't discover her probing actions and force a talk before she was ready.

But what about Reis? her heart screamed. She told herself she couldn't think about the mysterious Reis at present. Her way of life was on the verge of collapse; her future survival and happiness were at stake. Until she searched her heart and conscience about both men, she shouldn't see Reis again.

Amanda didn't like what she was thinking and feeling. Only a few months ago, her conscience wouldn't have troubled her at all, but today it did. If she had known Reis longer, or knew him better . . . Reis was a cunning stranger, and she couldn't expect anything from him. There were strong hints of genteel breeding and wealth exuding from Reis. If she confided in him or if he learned the truth, he might think her interest in him was selfish and greedy. Could she marry Weber when she wanted

Reis? Could she refuse to accept Web's proposal if her and Miranda's livelihood depended upon her submission to Web? Her decision would have been simple and quick if Reis Harrison hadn't entered her life one stormy night.

Weber would return in a few days; he would insist upon that talk he had mentioned. Could she risk losing Web by seeing Reis? Yet, if she didn't see Reis, how could she uncover his true feelings? Even if she accepted Reis and his clients, her firm couldn't be saved. If Reis left as mysteriously as he had appeared, where would she be then?

Such thoughts and plots made her feel cheap and heartless. Yet, what choice did a woman have but a profitable marriage? So many times she had toyed with men, tempted them with a treasure they could never have. Now vengeful Fate was dangling a tempting treat before her hungry eyes and bound hands, teasing and tormenting her. Reis was a dream; Weber was reality. Fury and frustration overwhelmed Amanda.

"Hell's bells!" she shrieked, flinging a book at the wall to reduce her tension and anger. "It's too late," she murmured.

"Are you all right, Amanda?" Reis's compelling voice asked from the doorway. "You shouldn't leave that door unlocked," he chided for the second time, wondering at the meaning of her last words.

Startled, Amanda whirled, drilling her fiery blue eyes into his tanned face and worried expression. "What do you want, Mister Harrison, besides the opportunity to scold me like a child?" she panted coldly, her ire directed at the forbidden object of her desire.

"I know I was rude last night, Amanda, but aren't you overreacting?" he reasoned tenderly. "I'm sorry," he stated simply.

She had to get rid of him, to halt this temptation, to cease this punishment! Her pride demanded she make him think his deception was behind her rejection of him and his accounts. "You traitor, I wonder what I find different about you," she scoffed, daring to stroll around the towering man as he remained stiff and alert. She halted before him, placing her hands on her hips and glaring up into his inquisitive gaze, her eyes exposing more anguish than anger.

Reis's hands snaked out and seized her gently but firmly. "What's gotten into you, woman?" he demanded. If he didn't know any better, he might think her hysterical. What did she mean by "too late" and "traitor"? Was she pledged to Weber? Was she in trouble?

"What happened to your Yankee accent, Reis?" she blurted out. "It took a while to comprehend the change, but I did. Get out!"

"That was a naughty trick, but I had my reasons," he began.

"I'll just bet you did," she injected acidly before he could finish.

"Since two of my friends are Yankees and the other is what you called a 'sympathizer,' I wanted to know how you felt about Northerners. To pass as one usually extracts such vital information. I should have explained when I realized the test wasn't necessary with you."

Amanda continued to glare at him. "What other games are you playing with me, Mister Harrison?" she sneered accusingly. "Is romancing your female partner a new approach to crafty business?"

"I've never mixed business and pleasure before. Do you want the accounts, Amanda?" He evaded an answer which could have been damaging. "Are you in the mood to settle it now, or shall we wait until later?"

Amanda swallowed the lump in her throat. She knew what had to be done and did it bravely. "Since Weber Richardson handles such matters for me, I suggest you discuss it with him when he returns," she bluntly informed him.

Reis couldn't help but show disbelief and anger at those words. "I was given the authority to assign them to you, not him. Are you refusing them because I go along with the deal? Or you're afraid to annoy dear Weber? Have you suddenly lost your courage and confidence?"

Amanda couldn't say anything more without giving away her motives for this behavior. "If you don't mind, Mister Harrison, I would prefer that you forget our previous talk and meeting. Any business you have for Lawrence Shipping must be approved by Web. I'm really tired, so I'm going home. Goodbye."

Reis was alarmed by the way she spoke her last word. He was confused by this change of heart, this loss of spirit. Richardson hadn't returned, so he couldn't have threatened or misled her. "Would you have dinner with me?" he coaxed, smiling at her.

"I can't," she declined unhappily. She retrieved the book and completed her task. She knew he was watching her intently, disturbingly.

"Mandy, what did I do to earn this frosty treatment?" he asked from behind her as he slipped his arms around her waist.

Amanda stiffened and tried to pull free, but he wouldn't allow it. There was only one way to make Reis leave her alone, to stop tormenting her and tempting her. "I shouldn't be seeing you alone; it's wrong. Web has asked me to marry him, and I've . . ."

When she faltered, Reis's heart skipped a beat as he feared the rest of her statement. His embrace tightened, as if he could halt the words from coming forth. He could feel her tremors, sense her turmoil, and detect her withdrawal from him. Despite their closeness, Weber was between them. How? Why? "Don't say it, Mandy, please," he beseeched her. "If you loved him, you wouldn't be suffering. Damnit, you can't marry him! You want me!" he stormed at her.

If only having was as simple as wanting, she thought. "I didn't say I had agreed to his proposal yet. But I can't think seriously about it while I'm seeing another man," she deliberated aloud. "It isn't fair to Weber, or me, or to you. I owe Weber so much," she murmured.

"No matter what he's done for you, Mandy, you aren't obligated to marry him to repay a debt," he argued frantically. "Hell woman, you can't buy or trade love!"

Amanda remained silent, praying he would say the words which could change her mind, which could halt her necessary decision. But Reis kept quiet about his personal feelings and wishes. She debated sadly, "Why not? Women have done so for centuries, either by choice or compulsion. There are things about me and Weber which you don't know."

Reis turned her to face him, but she lowered her head. He gripped her chin and lifted it. "Then explain them to me," he coaxed.

"I can't. Please don't try to see me again," she told him. She waited to see if he would force answers from her. He didn't.

Reis's brain was working fast and hard on this mystery. She was frightened by something. She might become defensive if he pressed her. She couldn't love Weber Richardson, but she felt compelled to marry him. What hold did that devil have over her? Whatever it was, she had discovered it this morning. Before he made demands on her, he needed to investigate this problem. He would never allow her to marry Weber. Not when she wanted him instead.

"Are you afraid of me, Mandy?" he asked softly. At her baffled look, he clarified, "Afraid I'll change your mind about Weber?"

"What could you possibly say or do to influence my decisions?" she inquired, eager for his explanation.

Since he had no proof that Weber was part of the crimes he was investigating, he would have to keep his opinions secret for now. Also, he wasn't in a position at present to force a battle over Amanda. His only course of action seemed to be in showing Amanda her own feelings.

"You said it was wrong to see me. But isn't it worse to marry one man when you have such strong feelings of desire for another?" The moment he made his rash statement, he regretted it.

"And who might I desire more than Weber, my conceited rake?" she questioned.

He chuckled. "I see you know whom I was referring to, but not from conceit, Mandy." As his thumb gently rubbed over her quivering lips, he vowed tenderly, "No woman has ever kissed me as you did."

"If I misled you, Reis, I'm sorry. You do have a cunning way of clouding a woman's senses. I've been under a great strain lately, and I wasn't myself. If you'll excuse me, I'll be leaving."

"You're misleading yourself, Mandy, not me. As to clouding senses, you're the expert there. Before you make your decision, just realize that marriage is forever," he warned gravely.

"Forever," she echoed the word as if it were a death sentence which she couldn't avoid.

"Look at me, Mandy, and tell me you love him," he insisted.

"Why else would I marry a man?" she eluded his trap.

"I damn well intend to discover that answer," he stated boldly. Reis caught her face between his hands and lowered his head to fuse their lips. When she tried to prevent this stirring assault on her warring senses, he skillfully parted her lips, probing the sweetness of her mouth. His arms entrapped her as he invaded her heart and mind.

Amanda didn't know how many times Reis kissed her, but she knew she didn't want him to stop. Her arms encircled his body as she feverishly responded to his rapturous invitation. Reis's hands wandered up and down her back, causing tingles to sweep over her entire body. An age-old craving grew at her core, spreading its need over her quivering and fiery flesh.

Amanda snuggled up to Reis as he nestled his face into her fragrant hair. Such yearning filled her, a yearning to explore this fierce aching which plagued her very soul. A soft groan escaped her parted lips as Reis's hand drifted over a firm breast, his palm stroking the taut point through her dress. When his tongue danced merrily around her ear, she shuddered with intense need. Soon, his mouth fastened onto hers, taking her beyond the limits of reality.

She swayed in his embrace as his hands and lips worked magical wonders over her face and body. The tension built within her until she ardently meshed her mouth with his and unknowingly dug her nails

81

into his back as she tried to pull him even closer to her. She desperately wanted him; nothing and no one else mattered now. She instinctively knew the only way to appease such an awesome hunger, and she was willing to feed it then and there. Whatever might happen after this blissful moment of wild passion, she knew she must have Reis Harrison this one time.

Reis was snared by his own trap, too enflamed to think or care about anything but making love to Amanda. He trembled with the urgency which raced through his smoldering frame. He wanted her, needed her completely.

"Yield to me, love," he urged hoarsely. "You're driving me wild. I hurt all over with wanting you. You can't marry Web, Mandy; he's no good for you. He can't make you feel the way I do. If you loved him, you wouldn't be in my arms. Forget that heartless Reb," he pleaded earnestly, unaware of his rash error which struck Amanda forcefully.

It took Reis a while to realize Amanda was pushing him away from her, that she was suddenly resisting him with all her might. "Let go of me, Reis. Stop or I'll scream," she threatened wildly.

Reis leaned away from her. "Mandy?" he whispered huskily.

"I'm not some harlot to be rolled on the floor," she panted at him. "Stop doing this to me. You don't want me; you only want to hurt Weber. I don't know why, but I won't let you use me like this! Get out of my life and stay out," she demanded weakly, hardly aware of what she was saying but aware of how she was hurting without really knowing why or how to stop the knifing pains in her heart.

"Doing this to you!" he thundered in return. "You can't tease a man with surrender, then go cold on him! I need you, Mandy. If you don't need me, then why entice me? You're a witch, Amanda Lawrence. You enchant a fellow then punish him for his weakness. If it's only games with you, then stay clear of me, woman. I don't respect the rules. The next time you get me this hot, you'd best plan to cool me down," he warned, anger flashing in his deep blue eyes. "A man does crazy things when he's pushed beyond control or reason. If you want me to steer clear, I will. But first you'll have to convince me that's what you want."

Amanda was afraid she couldn't convince him with desperate lies, so she didn't try. Instead, she snatched her cape and raced out before he could stop her panicky flight. The office keys were lying on her desk; the safe was still open. Reis locked up hurriedly, then followed her to make sure she reached home safely.

He forcefully cooled his anger and his passion. He secretively returned to her office to search for the motive behind her vexing mood. He scanned the contents of her desk and the safe, then went through her files. He put everything back in its place, then locked the safe. He made sure all lights were out and the door was secured. He stuffed her drawstring purse into his pocket and headed for her house.

He would leave her purse with Miranda, hopefully

without an explanation. Then he would head to the privacy of his hotel room. He had some thinking and planning to do. It all made perfect sense to him, even if Amanda was mistaken and impulsive . . .

A mischievous grin tugged at the corners of his mouth. Devilish lights twinkled in his eyes. If he planned this scheme just right, he could obtain all his wishes. He would take Weber's rope and tie up that menacing Rebel and that fetching tart, one victim on each end with a cunning and victorious Reis in the middle!

"When I finish with you, you'll never forget the first and last time we clashed, Weber Richardson, you bloody son of a bitch. As for you, my exquisite butterfly, you'll never escape me. You were mine from the moment we met. You just try to fly away before paying me what you owe me. That Reb's debt is nothing compared to mine!"

Chapter Four

Again, Amanda refused to come downstairs for dinner, this time pleading a headache which Miranda knew came from some emotional upheaval. Each time she approached Amanda's door, she could hear muffled sobs which rent her tender heart. She and her sister had always been close, sharing even their innermost feelings. What was so terrible that Amanda felt she couldn't share it? Miranda knew her sister would confide in her when she was ready. Until then, Miranda silently suffered with her.

Since Reis was the only person Amanda had spent time with today, it evidently had something to do with him. What had he said or done to cause Amanda such anguish? It had to be something important because Amanda was always so calm and controlled. It pained Miranda to think she might be to blame for assisting Reis's torment of her sister. Miranda couldn't understand her sister's drastic swings in mood and behavior. But somewhere behind them was a charmingly handsome rogue.

The night was long for both girls. When Reis had delivered Amanda's purse last night, that told Miranda her sister had raced from Reis's company. This morning, lovely flowers and an invitation to dinner and the theater arrived, but Amanda declined both. She told Miranda and the housekeeper to refuse all gifts and messages from Reis Harrison. She made it bluntly clear she didn't wish to see or hear from him, that he was not to be allowed in her home.

It was midafternoon before Amanda ventured downstairs to sip hot chocolate and to nibble some cake. She looked so pale and weary, as if she hadn't slept all night. Before the housekeeper left to do shopping, Amanda convinced her she simply wasn't feeling well. She sat on the floral sofa and gazed off into empty space.

"Randy," she spoke faintly, "I know you're concerned about me, but I'm not ready to discuss this yet. I just need a little time to sort out some feelings and make a decision." Amanda couldn't bring herself to tell Miranda how critical their situation was, not until she decided how to resolve it. Amanda wasn't blind, so she was aware of Miranda's feelings for Weber. She knew Miranda would battle an enforced marriage to Weber as fiercely as the South had battled the North. But would marriage to Weber be so terrible in light of her scant options? Until she fully comprehended this dire episode herself, she could neither defend Weber nor praise him. She berated herself for suspecting some ulterior motive in Weber. But her dear sister had suffered enough lately, and she couldn't add this additional burden to Miranda's slender back. Until settled, it would be her problem.

"Did you and Reis quarrel?" Miranda asked helplessly.

To prevent any further mention of Reis, Amanda edged into lying when she replied, "I won't be seeing him again, Randy. He's even worse than the others; he's tried to seduce me twice in two days. Every time he's near me, he can't keep his hands off me. I'm not some cheap slut to be pawed or ravished. The accounts he was dangling before me as bait are nothing more than troublemakers. Papa got rid of them months ago; now Reis thinks I'm too stupid to refuse them. He even claimed he goes along with the deal. I don't trust him, Randy. He acts like the only thing he wants is to get into my bloomers! He's a smooth charmer, and I should have known better."

Miranda gaped at her, eyes and mouth wide open with shock. "But he seemed so nice, Mandy. I don't understand." Had she misjudged Reis? Or was her beloved sister fibbing to her for the first time? Miranda knew that change was often for the better, but Amanda was being forced to change too much too rapidly. Miranda was alarmed by the pain in her sister's ice-blue eyes. Perhaps the key word in Amanda's tale was "seduce," not ravish.

"You have a lot to learn about wily males, dear Randy. All men are nice while they're trying to get you under the sheets with them. I've never been fooled like this before, and it angers me. And yes, it hurts, too. I thought Reis was so special, so different. You asked if we quarreled. I suppose we did have a one-sided dispute. When he kept pressing me, I thought the best way to cool his passion was to tell him Weber had proposed, which he has many times. Instead of cooling his ardor, I inflamed his temper. He was furious; can you imagine that? Then he proceeded to prove I don't love or want to marry Weber by assailing me with embraces and kisses! And he excused his lewd actions by claiming that I am besotted by him!''

Miranda had a gut feeling that Amanda was defensively exaggerating. Reis didn't seem like a man who would force his attentions on a woman. Surely Amanda hadn't tried to play coy games with the masterful Mister Harrison. Didn't Amanda realize that her looks and actions toward Reis were sensually provocative? Besides, if Reis was enchanted by Amanda, that would explain why he was so bold and persistent. Perhaps he was trying to prove something to Amanda. "Is that why you ran out on him so quickly that you forgot your purse?''

"Please, drop it for now. I'm too upset to discuss it further.''

"Did you tell him just that Weber had asked, or did you also tell him you had accepted?'' Miranda boldly continued the conversation with a point which worried her. To Miranda, it seemed the quarrel had been over Reis's passion and jealousy—two emotions which hinted at affection.

"I told him the truth, that I was seriously considering Web's proposal," Amanda announced incredibly. Before her sister could speak, Amanda added, "I know you don't like Web, Randy, but you won't be the one marrying him; I will. There's a lot you don't know about Weber, but I'll tell you everything one day soon. I must decide how important Reis is to me before I mess it up between us. Please, Randy, trust me to make the right decision."

"By 'mess it up,' you mean with Reis?" Miranda inquired softly, fearing to silence Amanda if she wasn't careful with her words and mood. Miranda's heart thudded heavily, for it sounded as if Amanda had already made her decision in favor of Weber. Had she been this assured with Reis? It didn't make any sense; why was Amanda viewing Web in a new light? There had to be much more to this turn of events!

"I'll admit I was infatuated by Reis's good looks and charm." She inhaled loudly, then used her previous thought as her last argument. "Reis is a playful dream, but Weber is reality. A fantasy fades with time, Randy; reality is always there."

That comparison revealed much about Amanda's feelings and fears. Miranda entreated, "Just make certain Reis is only a dream before you say yes to Weber."

"I did, Randy, last night," Amanda confessed sadly.

When Miranda held out a note for her sister the

next morning, Amanda sullenly reminded her, "I told you, no more messages."

"It's from Weber," Miranda stated crisply.

"From Weber?" she inquired suspiciously. "He's back?"

"Evidently," came the reluctant response as she handed the missive to her wary sister.

Amanda read it and frowned. "He wants me to come down to the office to meet him for lunch," she stated in visible dread.

"Are you going to yield to this summons, this command performance?" Miranda inquired almost belligerently.

"Please don't treat me this way, Randy," her sister pleaded.

"What way?" Miranda innocently asked. "You're going to marry him, aren't you? Out of spite to Reis over a disagreement?"

"Don't be silly. I haven't decided yet, but I am leaning toward yes. Randy . . . Never mind," Amanda responded, dropping the topic.

"You'd better dress quickly; it's eleven now." Miranda was dismayed by the resignation she was detecting in her sister. But why were those normally bright eyes so somber?

"I'm not going," Amanda stated surprisingly.

"You're not?" Miranda asked in gleeful disbelief.

"I don't feel like rushing. I'll send Weber a note of regret. He can come over tonight if he wishes," she told her sister casually. "Randy, don't mention anything to Weber before I do."

The note never reached Weber as he hurried around checking out matters. When he called later that day, nettled with Amanda for ignoring his message, Miranda hoped her sister would refuse to see him. But, to Miranda's distress, Amanda appeared eager to see him. She had donned one of her loveliest gowns, matching slippers, and most appealing perfume as if she were setting the stage for a drama.

When Amanda realized the reason for Web's black mood, she apologized sweetly, then explained the mix-up. "I've had so much on my mind since McVane's visit. And the weather's turned so damp and chilly again. I thought spring was in full bloom." She pouted prettily to distract him. It might be wrong, but she needed to hang on to Web until she made her final decision. As she had done so often in the past, Amanda used all her charms. Yet, this time she didn't enjoy the coyness.

"I saw your new friend today," Web stated caustically.

"My new friend?" she echoed in confusion.

"Reis Harrison," he replied tersely, as if that told all. "You've been seeing him while I was gone. Why, Mandy? He's not a family friend. Why did you two go down to the docks and warehouse?"

"We had dinner one night at the Windsor, and I gave him a tour of my property. He wanted to meet the new owner of Lawrence Shipping. He represents three clients who want to sign with my company. Did I commit some crime?" she asked playfully to reduce his anger. She wondered just how much Weber had discovered.

"Since I'm handling the firm, why didn't you refer him to me?" he questioned, his gaze and voice accusing as he stared at the exquisite beauty who was sitting so gracefully before him.

Amanda knew this was the perfect time to clarify some points, while keeping other facts a secret. She didn't want Web to discover what she had learned. She had to mislead him carefully. She smiled and responded cheerfully, "Because I wanted to surprise you with the new accounts. Don't be so cross with me, Web. While you were gone, I wanted to see if I was capable of handling the business, to see if a customer would actually deal with a female owner. I only talked and listened, Web; I didn't make any deals. When he pressed me for an answer, I told him the matter would have to be settled with you."

"You did?" he asked in astonishment. "Then why meet with him?"

"Ego. And because he sent a message he was leaving by Friday if I didn't meet with him. We talked over dinner, then he asked to see how we run things. He seemed pleased and agreed to assign the accounts to me." She refilled his coffee cup with a steady hand.

"If everything worked out, then why didn't you complete the deal? Did he say why he was so anxious to sign and leave so quickly?" he asked, trying to appear and sound as poised as she was.

"He didn't say, and I wouldn't ask. I wanted to hand you the contracts when you returned, but that seemed rash. I was afraid of making mistakes. He asked questions which I couldn't answer. I realized there was much I didn't know. I thought I could run Papa's business, but now I'm not so sure. It's more complicated and risky than I realized," she confessed cunningly beginning to drop her desperate hints.

"What kinds of questions did he ask, Mandy?" he quizzed, feeling a mixture of elation and wariness. Was she truly backing out?

Amanda didn't ask about Web's emphasis on "questions" or his strange expression, but she noticed them. She hastily contrived a logical reply. "About laws, and tariffs, and schedules, and such. I couldn't even give him prices for shipments. He must have thought I was awfully dumb."

"If that were true, why would he offer you the accounts?" He needed to know what Reis had told Amanda without arousing her suspicion. Just what was this Yankee trying to pull?

A reason escaped her keen mind. "I don't know."

"He's been deceiving you, Mandy. Perhaps his interest is in you, not the accounts. He claimed he was here to do business with the Lawrence firm, and you said he verbally agreed to a deal. So why is he visiting all the others and asking so many questions about your company, you, and your father?"

"Is it uncommon to check out a firm and its owner?" she asked.

"Not before a deal is made. But it seems suspicious to do it afterward. From what I've been told, Harrison was nosing around yesterday and today.

Don't trust him, Mandy," he stated firmly.

Amanda quickly concealed her surprise and pain—she wouldn't think about Reis right now. She laughed saucily. "You can hardly blame him for checking out my firm's stability. He certainly didn't expect to deal with a female. As I told you, I didn't agree to a contract. Wouldn't that explain his checking around? Why are you so mistrustful? Do you know him, Web?" she inquired.

"Yep, I know who he is," he informed her, hatred flaming in his eyes. "It took a while to recall when and where we met. I guess I was trying to forget the bloody bastard. Fact is, I thought he was dead; I wish he were. I'm warning you, Mandy; stay away from him. He's sly and dangerous. He's a vengeful Yank."

Amanda was startled by the vehemence in Weber. She hadn't been mistaken; they had met before. "He didn't mention knowing you. Why did you think he was dead?" she questioned curiously.

"Because I shot him during the war," he stated casually. "Evidently my aim was bad."

"You what?" she exclaimed incredulously. Weber was clearly furious to find Reis still alive. Had Reis also recognized Weber that first night? If so . . .

"If you see him again, Mandy, ask him about his friend Sherman and their grisly escapades through the South. Make sure you don't carry a gun to your meeting with him. If he tells you the truth about his war ventures, you might finish where I left off. I can see from your shock that he didn't tell you about our meeting years ago."

Amanda paled and trembled. Web must be lying! Reis wasn't like that. But Web knew her well enough to realize she would check out such a grim accusation if Reis mattered to her. Web stood up and looked down at her. "The next time you see him, Mandy, it will be the last time you see me. I love you and I want to marry you; I want to protect you and take care of you. The firm's yours and you can do as you please, but not with my help and not with our enemy."

Suddenly Amanda realized that for the first time since their meeting, Weber was calling her by her nickname and she wondered if that meant something special. In an effort to comprehend Web's feelings, she answered softly, "The war has been over for years, Web. Both sides did wicked things to the other. The hatred and bitterness must end. Let them go, Web. Evidently Mister Harrison doesn't hold a grudge against ex-Rebs; he came to do business with my father. Perhaps he doesn't know you shot him. After he learned you handled matters for me, he was still willing to sign with me. To stay in business, I need all the clients I can find. If I decide to work in the firm, I'll have to prove myself, Web."

"Forgive and forget?" he sneered sarcastically, as if those words were evil, those emotions impossible. "You're too naïve and trusting. You don't know what the war was like, Mandy, but you know what Sherman's outfit did in the South. Every man who rode with him is just as guilty. Picture the blood of friends and family spattered all over you. Imagine showing up after a battle to see arms, legs, entrails, and brains all over the ground. You've never had someone die in your arms, Mandy, die with his blood soaking into your clothes, and then have to wear them for weeks or months. Do you know what it's like to have enemies chasing you day and night? No rest. No sleep. No food. Freezing your ass off while you hide like a coward to stay alive one more day to do it all again. Damnit, Mandy! They stole everything from me, from us! You say let it go? How? At least twice a week I wake up seeing and hearing those gory sights and sounds again, sweating and squirming like a beaten animal.''

When Weber felt his vividly crafted words had had the desired effect, he became silent. He sighed dramatically, as if fatigued by a tale which had been cut from his very soul. That should give Amanda some sympathy for him and some contempt for Reis! That should keep her away from Harrison and his damaging secrets! "Marry me, Mandy. We can merge the two firms. If you want to work there, no man will refuse to deal with my wife," he coaxed. "This Harrison is trouble, Mandy. He's deadly and cunning. I have a bad feeling he didn't come here for the reason he told you. Watch out for him, or you'll live to regret it. I told you I shot him during the war. If he didn't know I was connected to the Lawrences before his arrival, he knows now. My feelings for you are no secret. Don't let my foe use my love against me. He could be after revenge, Mandy.''

"Revenge?'' she echoed the wicked word.

"What better vengeance than stealing my woman

and destroying my business? Did he tell you the three accounts he offered you belong to me? Did he tell you it could ruin me to lose them? There are many ways to kill a man. What could be worse for a man than losing everything precious to him, all of his reasons for living? It's me he's after, Mandy. Don't be a pawn in his vindictive game."

Amanda was horrified by Weber's speculations. She wished they didn't sound so diabolically logical. "Surely both of you shot many men during the war. Why would he single you out for revenge?" she questioned sadly.

"Because he thinks my outfit was the one which burned his home and killed his family. He started tracking us, killing off my men one at a time. The only reason I survived was because I ambushed him before he could murder me too," he informed her, his gaze never leaving hers.

Amanda was afraid to ask if Reis was correct, but her eyes exposed her alarm and turmoil. He shook his head and asked, "Do I seem like a Sherman to you, a devil who could slay innocent people?"

Amanda couldn't imagine any man being so evil, so she was compelled to shake her head. Weber grinned and hugged her tightly. Just before leaving, he asked, "Will you consider my proposal, Mandy?"

"That's exactly what I've been doing for days, Web. I promise to give you an answer very soon," she told him, then smiled.

After Weber left, Amanda was trapped by deep and grave thoughts. After all this time, had she been given a glimpse into what had made Web the way he was now? Had the war taken a cruel toll on him?

Web had been born to and trained for a genteel life. After all was lost, he had changed. Web glorified the Old South, the Confederacy, the Rebel soldiers. Web had been compelled to find a new role in life, even as he yearned for the one lost forever. He believed that wealth and power would make things right again. It saddened Amanda to see the wasted energy and emotions that churned inside Weber Richardson. Should she try to help him, to change him? And at what cost to herself?

Amanda sought the privacy of her room for some necessary soul-searching. There was so much she didn't understand, didn't know, didn't want to accept. She pondered how she could investigate Reis Harrison and Weber's story. Weber was so full of hatred and bitterness; could she trust him to be honest with her? If only she didn't know what was inside that book!

When she closed her lids, Reis's image appeared before her mind's eye. Could a man with such gentle eyes and sensitivity have done such evil things? Was there any man worse than Sherman, or the men who had ridden with him without halting his devastation? If Reis had trailed and slain Weber's men, had it been a mistake brought on by grief? She recalled what Reis had told her about men doing crazy things when pushed beyond control and reason. Did these facts explain why he didn't want to discuss the war, why he had reacted so strangely and coldly? Had he been pressing her because he knew Weber would expose his secrets? She remembereed the way he had looked at her, the way he had kissed her. It couldn't be true. It couldn't . . .

Amanda realized her time was running out. Considering everything she knew, there was only one answer to her mingled dilemmas. But when she thought of what would follow her surrender to Weber's proposal, she shuddered. Could she be a wife to him? Could she forget Reis?

Miranda was in her room reading in bed. She knew the hour was late and her sister was still pacing her floor. Amanda had been extremely quiet and melancholy after Weber's visit this afternoon. She had even refused dinner and sought privacy. This abnormal behavior panicked Miranda. It was time to unravel the mystery.

When she heard Amanda go downstairs, she tossed the covers aside and followed. She found her sister sitting on the rug before a cheery blaze, knees propped up and feet crossed at the ankles. Amanda's chin was resting on one knee as she tightly hugged her legs. The flickering flames seemed to perform a wild dance upon Amanda's pale face and in her blank eyes. What pained Miranda the most were the sparkles off the teardrops which were silently flowing down Amanda's cheeks and dropping to her gown. What was causing Amanda such anguish?

"Mandy?" she called softly. "Can I help? You need to talk?"

Amanda fused her solemn gaze to Miranda's

entreating one. Amanda burst into uncontrollable sobs. Only once before had Miranda seen her sister weep this way, the night the news came about their parents. Distraught, Amanda blurted out Web's charges against Reis. She told Miranda everything, except the reason why she was going to marry Weber Richardson.

"But, Mandy, you can't marry Weber because Reis hurt you," she argued. "Even if what Web said about Reis were true, it happened years ago, during the war. Reis didn't strike me as a vengeful and cruel man. You just can't marry Web to hide from Reis. You're in love with Reis, aren't you?"

"If that were true, it still wouldn't make any difference," she replied tearfully. "Web is the man I must marry."

"Must? Why must you marry a man you don't love? See Reis, Mandy, and let him explain," she begged her irrational sister.

"I can't. There's nothing he can say or do to change matters. Oh, Randy, there's so much you don't understand," she wailed.

"Then make me understand," she pleaded fiercely. How could level-headed, proud Amanda Lawrence do such a reckless thing?

"If you ever get trapped between two men, you'll learn that love can't always be the deciding factor in choosing between them. I must do what is right for me, Randy. In time, I'll forget about Reis. Weber loves me and needs me," she vowed, as if that were a curse.

There were no words to ease such agony. All Miranda could do was listen, listen and be there for solace. For the first time, Amanda had met a man who touched her deeply. How tragic that she believed Reis wasn't what he appeared. Yet, Miranda sensed some unspoken motive for her sister's drastic decision, one she must discover. Amanda had never been a coward or a quitter, so why had she become both at this late date? Just above a whisper, Miranda asked, "But whom do you love and need, Mandy? What if Reis didn't come here for revenge on Weber? What if you discover the truth after you're wed to the wrong man? It's wrong to marry Weber when you're in love with Reis."

When Amanda gained control of her emotions, she murmured sadly, "Web did kill him, Randy, at least for me. How can I possibly have anything to do with a devil like that? Why did Reis come here? Why? I despise the things men do in the name of honor! I hate revenge! The war's been over for years; when will a Southern daughter no longer have to ask her love the color of his uniform?"

Chapter Five

For a week Amanda refused all visits and messages
from Reis Harrison, but it was one of the hardest
things she had done in her life. When Reis appeared
to halt his siege upon her, Amanda didn't know
which emotion was greater, relief or disappointment. Once she had admitted to being in love with
him, she realized it was too risky to see him even
briefly or to read his urgent requests for an
explanation. She feared Reis would mesmerize her
again, deceitfully convince her she was mistaken
about him. She couldn't allow it, if she were going to
marry Weber; and that seemed her only path to
survival. She was exhausted from battling her
warring emotions.

Wasn't love supposed to be simple and serene? she
wondered. Wasn't it supposed to bring happiness,
not sadness and pain? Shouldn't it be the most
natural thing in the world to marry the man you

love? How could such dark clouds hover over the flames of love and cruelly douse them before they could burst into a roaring blaze of passion and commitment?

Amanda knew she had to regain a measure of joy and confidence or pretend she had, or else many people would become curious about her mood. She couldn't go on suffering and wavering. She would find the courage to carry out her decision before anyone discovered her motive. Yet, she knew she was stalling, stalling Weber and the inevitable. Soon Weber would force the issue. It was only a matter of time before he exposed his actions and her obligation. She kept waiting for Weber to reveal her dire straits, to learn how he was going to use them as a persuasive tactic.

Amanda hadn't mentioned her father's books to Weber or shown any desire to take over from him. She wondered if he found that suspicious, considering how anxious she had been not long ago. She had used lingering grief and self-doubts as excuses, but they were wearing thin and tasting foul upon her lips.

Knowing the reason for Amanda's behavior, Reis avoided any embarrassing contact when she was with Weber. Although he watched them furtively, he was assailed by doubts and fears himself. Somehow he had to uncover Weber's game. He had to prevent her marriage, to win her for himself. But she needed time, time to relax and time to become wary of her close friend. He needed to come up with a ploy of his own, one to get her alone with him . . .

But Reis's subtle strategy had one drawback, one he didn't recognize: as he stayed away, it became easier for Amanda to convince herself that he should remain out of her life . . .

Weber continued to give Amanda business reports, reports she felt were false, designed only to keep her happy and naïve. Feeling she must begin to show some interest in the firm, she began asking simple questions. Weber was evasive about certain information, as if reluctant to give up this hold over Amanda until he was ready to use her dependence on him to his advantage. Not a day had passed since his vilification of Reis that he had not tried to convince Amanda to marry him. Unfortunately, Reis had shown Amanda what was missing in other men, in Weber, and in her emotions.

Amanda threw herself into chores at home, trying to shut out the emotional demands of both Reis and Weber. She told herself Reis was just another man, a past enemy, a treacherous beguiler. But Reis wasn't just a man. He was unique. Amanda was torn between wanting him and rejecting him. Why did Reis have to be the one to bring her emotions to life? Why did thoughts of him torment her day and night? How could she punish him for her misery? Had Reis lied to her or misled her? If she questioned him, would he? Amanda finally realized she was being a coward. She was too frightened to seek the truth, fearing the revelation could hurt her more than she was hurting now.

Miranda witnessed the rising turmoil in her

sister—the desire to see Reis and to hear his side was fiercely battling the fear of how to handle what he would tell her. She wondered how her sister could agree to marry Weber when her thoughts were filled with Reis.

Needing a distraction, Miranda met Lucas Reardon for lunch and a stimulating conversation. As she was strolling home, she bumped into Reis Harrison as she rounded a corner. Miranda wondered if Reis had arranged the meeting. They smiled genially at each other and exchanged greetings. As Miranda brushed past him, Reis gently caught her arm.

"Miss Lawrence, could you tell me why your sister is avoiding me? Did I say or do something to offend her?" he inquired, setting his plan into motion, a plan which could use an understanding partner.

"It seems we've had this conversation before, Mister Harrison. Why don't you ask Amanda, not me?" she suggested softly.

Reis sighed in frustration. "I've tried countless times. Amanda is a very special lady. I thought we were getting close. Then something happened which I need to understand. Is it because of Weber or me? How can I solve a problem which she refuses to clarify?"

Miranda looked up at him. Unless she was mistaken, he was distressed by Amanda's behavior. Did she have the right to interfere? "May I ask you a question first, sir?" she countered.

"Of course," Reis responded curiously.

"Why did you really come to Alexandria, Mister

Harrison?'' she questioned candidly, her eyes clear and her tone direct.

"I'm here on business, Miss Lawrence. But I sense that isn't the meaning behind your question,'' he astutely remarked.

"What kind of business, sir?'' she pressed boldly.

"Private,'' he replied, watching for any clue to her scheme.

"When is revenge a private business, sir?'' Miranda asked softly, stunning him and confusing him.

It wasn't what Reis had expected to hear. "Revenge? I don't follow your meaning. I came here to clear up some shipping problems with your father. That first night at your home, Amanda said she had taken control, and I would deal with her. I must confess I was wary about dealing with a woman, but Amanda is a most unusual one,'' he remarked mischievously, then grinned at some pleasant thought.

His voice waxed grave as he continued. "Everything was going fine, then she backed away from our deal the morning after we'd had dinner together. She seemed nervous, almost frightened of something. I'll be honest with you, Miranda; I did steal a few kisses, but it's not just a romantic rebuff I'm getting. She's rejecting me on all levels. She told me to discuss my deal with Richardson. That's a little tricky since he's the one who holds those accounts at present. We spent a lot of time together while Richardson was away; we toured the docks and discussed business. I'm positive she's capable of running that firm herself, so why hand it over to him? Why refuse to take back accounts which he enticed from your father months ago?"

He looked into Miranda's troubled gaze as he inquired, "Is it a matter of loyalty to him? I found her crying in the office one afternoon. When I tried to comfort and question her, she raced out as if terrified of me, or something else. Suddenly she won't have anything to do with me. Why is she refusing to see me? I must know, Miranda; she means a lot to me. Maybe I was dreaming, but I thought she was feeling the same about me."

Seeking her own clues to this riddle, Miranda bravely asked, "What happened that last morning in the office before she raced home? Why doesn't she want Weber to know you two met and talked there?"

Reis made no attempt to hide his astonishment at those words. To see how much, if anything, Miranda knew about their situation, he told her that Amanda had been going over the books, when he arrived. He disclosed her behavior, her refusal of his contracts, and her odd request to keep their talks and visits a secret from Weber. "She didn't want him to know she'd been in the office or seen the books. Since both are hers, I thought her request strange, but I honored it."

Miranda became pensively silent. What was going on with Amanda? She had been enchanted by Reis Harrison; she had been ready to take control of their firm; she had seemed prepared to drop Weber from her life. Then suddenly it all changed. She was rejecting Reis and the firm, and accepting Weber. Why? What had she seen in those books? Positively, Amanda was keeping something alarming and critical from her . . .

"Miranda, is something wrong? Do you know what the problem is?" he inquired gently, although Reis was positive Miranda didn't know the dismaying situation which Weber and McVane had cleverly arranged with their false entries.

"No, but I intend to learn what's troubling my sister. You're right about one thing; it started that morning. It's gotten worse during the last week since Weber's return. Did you ride with Sherman during the war? Did Weber really shoot you?" she asked bluntly.

Reis stiffened. "So that's it," he murmured coldly. "Just what did Richardson tell your sister about me?"

Instead of answering, Miranda asked more questions. "Did he tell Mandy the truth about you? Do you think he burned your ranch and killed your family? Did you track his troops and kill all except him? Did you come here to take revenge on him? Is Mandy a cruel part of it?" she probed, barely stopping to take a breath.

"I must know everything he said about me. Is Amanda going to marry this Richardson to punish me, to spite me?" He clenched his fists in frustration.

Before Miranda could help herself, she blurted out, "I hope not!"

"So do I, Miranda, so do I," he quickly agreed.

Miranda's piercing gaze traveled over Reis's face. "You didn't answer my questions, Mister Harrison. Tell me how you know Weber."

"If you don't mind, I'd rather explain all of this to your sister and let her explain it to you. It's a long, painful story. I will tell you this much, Miranda; it wasn't like he said. About the only truth he told was that he shot me. Weber Richardson is a sly and dangerous man. It might help if you remind Amanda that he has been in full control of her books for months; whatever's recorded there, he entered it. Perhaps she shouldn't trust everything she reads in them. And she certainly shouldn't feel obligated to marry him because of what she thinks he's doing for her," he stated mysteriously.

Miranda gazed inquisitively at him. "You know what's in those books, don't you? You know why she feels she must marry him."

"If I told Amanda what I suspect, she wouldn't believe me. Besides, I can't explain to either of you how I know such things. Weber has set a cunning trap for Amanda, but she's so confused she doesn't see it. Try to inspire some suspicion about those books and Weber's claims. You might also let her know that Lawyer McVane is a close friend of Weber's. If I were you two, I wouldn't trust him so completely. Weber has Amanda convinced I'm the enemy, but I'm not, Miranda. I'm going to save her from that devil, even if I have to kidnap her!"

Miranda smiled warmly. "I don't know why, sir, but I believe you. If it matters what my sister thinks and feels about you, I would explain things to her as quickly as possible," she suggested.

"How? I can't get near her," he stated in exasperation.

Miranda grinned as she offered a solution. Reis chuckled. "What happens when Amanda discovers you've helped me?"

"If I haven't misjudged you, sir, she'll be delighted —after she flogs us all for pulling such a trick! If I'm wrong about you, you'd best fear me and Luke more than Weber." They joined in mirthful laughter, then shook hands before going their separate ways to dress and prepare for their impending charade.

It was nearing midnight when Miranda returned home from dinner with Lucas and Reis. She was apprehensive but excited about putting her daring scheme into motion. She was grateful Lucas had agreed to play a role in this delightful drama. Reis had met them at a small and quiet restaurant near the edge of town. After talking for hours, Miranda and Lucas were both eager to assist the bold Mister Harrison.

Lucas was willing to help just to get even with Weber for stealing his sweetheart, then casting the unfortunate and tarnished girl into the street to work as a cheap prostitute. What made the sore fester rather than heal was Weber's constant reminders of his foul deed, his tauntings about Luke's taking Marissa back into his arms. For all of Lucas's previous affection, he couldn't bring himself to love or touch Marissa again, not after Web's use and abuse.

111

But since Marissa's betrayal, Lucas hadn't fully trusted another female, except for his twin cousins. Both girls hoped Lucas would find someone very special one day.

"You're late, Randy. I was beginning to worry," Amanda chided her sister. "Where have you been? It's midnight. No lady should be out this late, even with her cousin. Why didn't Luke come in?"

Miranda prayed she could carry off this act, as she was always so honest. "I'm sorry, Mandy; time took wings tonight. But I don't think you want to know where I was or with whom. Luke isn't the one who brought me home. It's late and I'm tired. Good night."

When she headed past Amanda for the steps, Amanda seized her arm and shrieked, "Just a minute, Miranda Lawrence! Don't you dare leave this room until you explain yourself."

Miranda looked indecisive and tense. "You won't like it," she warned before adding, "I had dinner with Luke and . . . Reis Harrison. Luke was busy making notes, so Reis saw me home. You said you didn't want to hear his name mentioned, so I wasn't going to tell you."

Amanda's mouth fell open and she gaped at her sister in disbelief. "Why on earth would you do such a thing?" she demanded.

Miranda gazed at her innocently. "Have dinner with Luke? Or stay out so late?"

Her eyes filling with outrage, Amanda shouted, "How dare you be seen with that damn Yankee! And to allow him to escort you home? I told you what Weber said about him."

"I know what Weber said, and how he feels about Yankees. Frankly, I don't care. As you put it the other day, you'll be marrying Web, not me. I can see whom I please," she stated sullenly to stun Amanda into a confession of some kind. "The war is over for me. I like Reis. So I'll see him again if I wish," she announced saucily. She anxiously waited to see how that news would affect her sister.

"You can't be serious!" Amanda stormed in dismay. "What about me and my feelings?" she panted.

"What about your feelings?" Miranda probed nonchalantly, perceiving the fury and tension building within her distraught sister.

"You know I was seeing Reis! How could you do this?" Amanda inquired sadly. Had Miranda been impressed with Reis from the beginning? Did she think he was free for the taking now? How could her own sister be so traitorous? If Randy and Reis became close, that would put Reis in her life once more! How could she bear to see him with another woman, especially her sister? If Randy knew what Web had done for them, she wouldn't despise him so much.

"I believe you've told me many times this week that you're going to marry Weber. Surely you can't have serious feelings about Reis, then marry Weber?"

"I told you how I felt about Reis, and why I had to stop seeing him! You can't bring him into my life again. Please, Randy," she beseeched her sister. "It's just a mean trick to get back at me."

"For what? Besides, once you marry Weber, you won't be living with me any more. So I won't be forcing Reis's company on you. If you told me the truth about loving Reis, you would never marry Web. I can't believe my own sister would be so conniving and cruel. Even if you can't marry Reis, there's no reason to marry just anyone! I'm shocked by your behavior, Amanda Lawrence, and hurt."

"But you'll be living with me and Web," Amanda informed her.

Before Miranda could stop herself, she shouted, "Never!"

Amanda stared at her twin. Should she reveal their financial situation? Should she expose Weber's rescue from humiliation and poverty? Without money and with their property lost, Miranda would be forced to live with them. "You're thinking only of yourself, Randy. What about me? Must you be so hateful to Web?"

"No, Mandy, you're the one being selfish and dishonest. If I didn't love you above everyone else, I wouldn't try to prevent this terrible mistake. I can't pretend I like Weber; I don't. What about Reis, Mandy? How can you hurt him this way? And how will Web act if he learns the truth about your feelings? It's wrong to play with other's lives and emotions."

"Hurt Reis? If he cared about me, he wouldn't be chasing after my sister! Don't you see, Randy? He's after revenge on Weber."

Miranda scoffed sarcastically, "According to Weber, you mean. You're hurting Reis by acting this way. I've seen the look in his eyes when he asks about you; it isn't spite or treachery. Why did you lead him on, Mandy? He seems bewildered by your stinging rejection. If revenge is a part of things, it's Weber's revenge on Reis. Web's keeping you and the business from Reis. You spent time with Reis; do you honestly believe he's so evil and cruel? I just can't accept Web's allegations. I can't understand why you won't give Reis a chance to explain. It's absurd to refuse a simple talk which could settle everything. What makes you so positive you can trust Weber implicitly?" she challenged coldly. "You're a fool if you discard Reis Harrison!"

"How do you know so much about me and Reis?" Amanda asked.

"You always said I was uncannily intuitive," she retorted slyly.

Amanda knew her sister would try to talk her out of her self-sacrifice if she revealed the truth. She couldn't make such a risky confession. Miranda was too taken with Reis; she might disclose the truth to him. This situation was becoming more and more complex. If only her sacrifice didn't include Reis.

Amanda quietly asked, "Are you going after Reis?"

Miranda came back with a question of her own, "Are you really going to marry Web?" Each girl studied the expression of the other.

"Is this some game to make me jealous?" Amanda

inquired warily.

Miranda realized her sister wasn't going to tell her anything vital. To prevent trouble between them, Miranda ceased the ruse. "To put your mind at ease, dear sister, it's nothing more than friendship. If I'm not mistaken, Reis was falling in love with you until you messed it up between you two. Reis is giving Luke some information for a book about the war. You'd be surprised how Reis's version of it differs from Weber's," she hinted casually. "It's a shame you're tied to Weber. Reis is quite a catch. The more I see him, the more I'm convinced you two are perfect for each other. No, Mandy, I'm not romantically interested in Reis," she sighed. "Goodnight, Mrs. Richardson; you should get used to that name. As you wish, I won't mention Reis again. But it pains me to realize how much you've changed lately; you don't even trust me enough to tell me why you're forcing yourself in a despicable marriage. What hold does Web have over you?"

Appalled, Amanda questioned, "What do you mean, Randy?"

"I'm not blind or dim-witted, Mandy. I just wish you could talk to me like before. If you haven't given Web your answer yet, please search your heart again. If I were you, I would ask both men lots of questions and very soon. If you can't turn to Reis or Luke for help, then confide in me. We can work out whatever's bothering you."

"Why do you insist something's wrong? Why would I need help? With what?" She tested to see if

Miranda knew about their circumstances.

"I'll make a pact with you, Mandy. I promise not to say another word and I'll stop worrying about you, if you can look me in the eye and swear things are fine with you. Swear you love and want Weber."

Amanda paled slightly. "How can things be fine when you badger me all the time? You constantly insult Web, even knowing how close we are. You go out with Reis, then expect me not to be upset." She tried to distract her sister with defensive questions.

Tears formed in Miranda's tawny eyes and her lips quivered. "I never thought the day would come when you would build a wall between us. I want to help, but I don't know how to reach you, Mandy. I wish Mama were here," she murmured dejectedly, then burst into racking sobs and fled to her room.

Amanda seemed glued to the floor. Anguish and guilt attacked her viciously. She wanted to go after Miranda and explain, but she was too emotional to carry on a conversation. She needed to think and relax. Tomorrow, she would find a way to confide in Miranda, to make her understand.

Neither girl slept well that night. Miranda made a desperate decision to visit the plantation, leaving Amanda alone to think. When Amanda awakened, Miranda was already packed and gone. Before taking the train to Richmond and hiring a buggy to Morning Star Plantation, Miranda stopped off to see Reis. She told him of her failure to reach Amanda and of her travel plans and asked him to send word to Lucas. When Reis asked about the servants with

117

Amanda, Miranda told him there was only their housekeeper and cook, Alice Reed; tomorrow was her day off, so Amanda would be alone for two nights and a day.

After putting Miranda on the train, Reis hurried to make preparations for a brazen move . . . He had decided it was past time for Amanda to learn some facts about herself, Reis Harrison, and Weber Richardson!

After Amanda arose and dressed, she headed for Miranda's room, finding it empty. She went downstairs, but Miranda couldn't be found there either. Odd, she thought, since it was only ten o'clock. Amanda worried over her sister's absence until four that afternoon, then panicked when Lucas dropped by to explain Miranda's departure.

"I would have come by sooner, but I was busy with an interview. Miranda said she didn't leave you a note, but she had to go away for a while. She seemed upset, Mandy. What's going on between you two?" Lucas questioned, as if he didn't know about Miranda's plans.

Amanda was frantic. *Morning Star isn't ours any more. When she arrives, she'll be confused and distressed. She'll wonder why I didn't tell her. If she starts getting suspicious, she might learn everything.* "Luke, can you go after her?" she entreated anxiously.

"Go after her? Why? It isn't strange for her to visit there, but it's awfully strange that she wouldn't leave you a note or tell you herself. Did you two quarrel?'' he asked, watching Amanda's reaction closely.

"She's angry because of me and Web," Amanda told him.

"Then it's true, you're actually going to marry him?"

"I know you don't like Web, but Randy has no reason to be so spiteful. Are you planning to desert me too?" she asked sarcastically.

"If you marry Web, I won't come around again, if that's what you mean. But I have a strong feeling that Randy didn't leave because of you and Web. Why are you sitting home instead of working? And why are you being so nasty to Reis Harrison?" he asked sternly.

"Since when do you have the right to interfere in my private life, Lucas Reardon?" she snapped at him.

"Since you seem to have lost your senses and appear determined to ruin it! Since you choose Web over Randy, me, and Reis! I don't know what you're trying to pull, but you'll regret it. I'm not going after Randy; she said she'd be home in three days. You don't have to worry about me intruding again. I'll be moving west soon."

"Moving west? But what about me and Randy? You're the only family we have left," she shrieked, dreading his loss.

"Soon, dear cuz, you'll have a whole new family. Weber and all the tiny Webers," he said coldly.

"If you don't care about me, then what about Randy? You know she'll never come to live with us."

"As soon as she returns, I plan to ask her to go west with me. You know how she feels about your mother's people, and I need her help."

Amanda was staggered by that news. "You can't take Randy on such a dangerous journey! I won't allow it!"

Lucas's voice became soft and compelling as he protested, "If she wants to go with me, you can't stop her, Mandy. Once you marry Web, there's nothing to keep her here. She wants to meet her grandfather and uncle. She wants to see what Indian life is all about, how your mother and her people lived. I'll protect her; you needn't worry. Besides, the Indian hostilities are under control. Nearly all the tribes are on reservations now; they can't even own guns. They've got soldiers and forts everywhere for protection. It's easy to get there—there are trains, riverboats, stages. It's been a dream of hers for years. Your parents were planning a visit this summer, remember?"

"But why are you going out there?" Amanda asked.

"It concerns that book I'm writing. Would you believe three of the most notorious Yankee leaders—Custer, Sherman, and Sheridan—are assigned to the Missouri Division which includes the Dakota Territory? How's that for research luck? They'll be more willing to talk out there, little suspecting I'm an ex-Reb out to extract the truth about them. This is a chance of a lifetime, Mandy. I'm not sure how I was selected for this assignment, but I'll be damned if I refuse it! Randy could use the diversion. Don't try to stop her," he coaxed gently. "Who knows, she might find her own true love out there, hopefully a Reis Harrison."

"Why are you two shoving Reis down my throat! I have to marry Web!" she rashly screamed at him.

"Why?" Lucas snarled.

Cornered, she declared heatedly, "Because I love him!"

"Like hell you do," Lucas debated, then stalked out of the house.

Weber came by to visit briefly around six, just before the housekeeper was to leave. Amanda tried to act cheerful, but she was exhausted from chores. When Weber chided her for not leaving such menial labor to the servant, she smiled and told him it was good exercise and a distraction from her sadness. Then Weber asked about Miranda. Amanda claimed she was visiting friends in Boston. If Weber suspected she was lying, he didn't let on to her. He told her to get some rest and he would see her in two days.

She looked surprised, so he explained he would be away on business. "If you have any problems while I'm away, contact McVane. I've hired him to manage both our firms while I'm gone. He'll be working out of your father's office. You rest, my dear; you're looking pale. See you in a few days." He stood up to leave. "Oh, yes." He turned back to add, "You don't

121

have to worry about Harrison bothering you again. He checked out of the hotel and left town."

"Did you two settle any business?" she asked, trying to sound calm. No wonder Weber felt it was safe for him to go away for days. *Gone,* her heart sighed painfully. And with McVane in her father's office, there was no way she could sneak in to go over the books again.

"I guess he decided to leave the accounts with my firm, for now. Since his vindictive plot failed, he's probably gone off somewhere to sulk or to make new plans. I'm glad you didn't see him again, Mandy. The men on the docks and in the warehouse have been teasing me about seeing you there with him. Give Randy my regards."

Amanda suffered through a lingering kiss, then waved farewell from the front porch. Had Weber been trying to tell her he knew about her times with Reis? Did Web truly think Reis would show up here again? Sometimes Weber could be so damn cocky! Suddenly Amanda wiped her lips. How could she ever make love to Web when a simple kiss turned her stomach?

Her heart ached. Her parents were lost to her forever. Reis was gone. Luke was leaving soon, perhaps taking Randy with him. By now, Randy was learning of their loss of Morning Star, the plantation that bore their mother's Indian name. When Randy returned, she would demand more answers. Was it too late to tell the truth? Reis was gone, and she didn't know where to locate him. And even if she found him, would he care or listen?

If they lost the townhouse and business too, could she find some way to survive without selling her soul to Weber? If she sold her jewels and anything not mortgaged, would there be enough money to live on after she repaid Weber? Besides Luke, there was no family or home to run to for help. Pride would demand they seek another place for a new beginning. What kind of decent work could she and Randy do? What would happen to them? She had read and heard so many wicked things about working women, about their vulnerability and abuse . . .

Amanda paced the carpet in her bedroom until she could have screamed from tension. As if to drive herself into mindless slumber, she downed two glasses of Irish whiskey taken from her father's private stock. Clad in a silky nightgown of azure blue, she threw herself upon the bed to ease her spinning head. She hazily scolded herself for drinking on an empty stomach.

As her mind drifted like a cloud, she had the strangest sensation that hands were binding her arms and legs. She felt as if she were being wrapped in a blanket then carried from her room. From a distance, she heard the clicking of boots as they descended the steps. Cool air wafted across her cheeks, then warmth covered them. She tried to force her lids open, but she was too tired to expend the energy. She was clasped against some firm object, and strong arms were protectively encircling her body. Comfortable and limp, she snuggled against the warmth of the object, then inhaled his manly odor and murmured peacefully, "Reis . . ."

The man looked down into her sleeping face, asking himself why she had called that name as he gagged her tempting lips. Soon her little game would be over!

Chapter Six

Miranda sat in the swing which hung from a towering tree, swaying back and forth as she sank into deep thought. The trip to Morning Star had been uneventful, but her visit was anything but dull and tranquilizing. Now that she was here and making odd discoveries, she didn't regret coming. But without her parents and Amanda, it was lonely and cold. The longtime servants couldn't seem to relieve the melancholy mood of their deceased employer's child. They had tried to clear up her somber mood and calm her anxiety, but instead they unknowingly increased them. They told her how much the plantation had prospered, which pleased her immensely. They asked what would happen now that her parents were gone, but Miranda couldn't tell them. She revealed that her sister was considering marriage; if it took place, Miranda would come to live here.

Tomorrow, the overseer had promised to take her on a tour of the entire plantation. He wanted her to inspect the replanked barns, to meet the new workers and speak with old ones, and to see how he was rotating the crops. Miranda didn't know anything about crops, but she could meet the workers and view what she and her sister owned. Clearly, this plantation was beautiful and valuable. Her father had always made certain the majestic ante-bellum mansion was in excellent repair. Without her family, the house seemed enormous and formal. Perhaps she could persuade Amanda to sell the shipping firm, refuse Weber, and move here to begin a new life.

Earlier in the day, Miranda had made several disturbing discoveries. The overseer had told her he had been instructed by Daniel McVane to send the monthly reports to Weber Richardson, and Weber had made two visits out here. Worse, Weber had been hinting to him about a probable sale of Morning Star.

Miranda tried to recall the overseer's words. Weber had Mister Farley making full reports on each area of the profitable plantation. The money was being transferred to Daniel McVane, their lawyer. Why had McVane failed to mention these enormous profits during their recent conference? He had made it sound as if the plantation had been steadily losing money since her family's last visit a year ago! Had McVane been misinformed or had he deceived them?

Since Weber had made two visits, why hadn't he corrected McVane's errors? Something funny was going on, and she was determined to discover what it was. It was a wild idea, but what if Amanda had uncovered some crime against them when she checked the books? And what if she was being threatened into marrying Weber? No, Amanda wouldn't agree to such evil even to save her life! But what if Weber and his unknown cohorts had threatened those Amanda loved: herself, Luke, and Reis! Amanda would do anything to protect them, even sacrifice herself to a demon like Weber.

Luke and Reis kept hinting that Weber was sly and dangerous. Blackmail would explain Amanda's irrational moods and her reluctance to confide in her sister. That would clarify why she was refusing to talk to Reis. And her sudden surrender to Weber's proposal! Why else would she take Weber, a man who couldn't even walk in the shadow of Reis Harrison! A bright and daring female like Amanda wouldn't lose the man of her dreams over a silly dispute; she would fight for him and demand an explanation for his behavior. She must have found something in those books to terrify her, to entrap her!

Miranda decided to send Lucas a telegram the next day, using the code which they had worked out long ago as a childhood game. Reis and Luke could do some snooping on their end while she remained here a few more days to see what worms she could unearth.

Amanda dozed for two hours in the warm embrace of her abductor until a violent storm began to pelt her face with raindrops and to saturate the blanket and her gown. She shivered and stirred, confused by her surroundings and predicament. She was bound and gagged! Held securely by powerful arms, she was being taken away on horseback by a black-clad villain! She assumed she was having a nightmare and struggled to awaken. Finally, she was forced to comprehend she was being kidnapped, wrapped in a sopping blanket and a flimsy nightgown!

She squirmed to sit up in the man's arms, but he wouldn't allow it. The wet blanket clung to her body. She moaned and thrashed her head, unable to speak. She was helpless and nearly naked! Wet curls clung to her cheeks and forehead. Who was doing this to her? Why? Terror filled her and she shuddered.

Aware she was coming around, the man slowed the horse to a walk. He pushed back the hood to his rain-slicker and his black hair was soaked instantly. Beads of water dripped off his chin and nose. When lightning flashed across the heavens, her eyes became large circles as she viewed his face and the implication of this scene. Her breath caught in her throat, and her heart started thudding heavily.

White teeth gleamed in the next flash of lightning as he grinned down at her. Reis roguishly vowed, "I said you can't marry him, love."

Amanda simply stared at him. She wondered what he was planning to do with her. Web said that Reis had left. Obviously, he had been lurking in the shadows until he was given a chance to abduct her. If Reis wanted revenge on Weber, would he kill her before letting Weber marry her? His cunning seduction had failed; now what?

When she ceased her futile struggles, Reis grasped her around the waist and set her up straight across his lap. He tenderly brushed the wet curls from her face then smiled and caressed her cheek. When she tried to turn away from his piercing gaze, he held her chin firmly.

As Reis observed her ever-changing emotions, he told her softly, "There's no reason for you to be afraid, Mandy love. I only want to talk with you. Since you refused to see me and hear me out, you left me no choice but to force you. If it takes all day and night, we're going to settle this matter. If you refuse to explain yourself by then, I'll hold you here until you relent. No tricks, no lies, and no silence, woman. Right now, I don't care about Weber's war crimes, only about you. I can promise you won't be harmed by me, and I'll take you home as soon as you tell me why you suddenly rejected me and agreed to marry him. Hellfire, I won't lose you without knowing why."

As her eyes narrowed and her teeth clenched beneath the gag, defiance and fury glittered brightly in her lovely blue eyes. Reis knew this wasn't going to be easy, but he did have some tricks up his sleeve. "We'll be at the cabin before dawn; then I'll untie you and remove that gag. But if you try anything, I'm not adverse to giving you a good spanking. In fact, you need one," he warned playfully.

The look in her glittering blue eyes shouted, you

wouldn't dare! He chuckled and replied, "Oh, yes, I would, love. You are the most exasperating and infuriating female alive. It's about time you started using those brains and wits again. If it takes a good spanking to bring you back to life, then I'll be most willing to provide it," he declared arrogantly.

Amanda's chest vibrated in heavy respiration. She glared at the smug devil, wanting to claw his handsome face. She wiggled frantically in his arms until he warned, "Be still, or I'll drop you in the mud."

That threat called an immediate halt to her thrashing. "That's more like it. It's nearly morning; get some sleep. You'll soon have the privacy and opportunity to severely tongue-lash me." He laughed mirthfully as they rode away into the stormy streaks of predawn.

Within an hour, he reined in the animal at a grove of trees. He slid her bound feet to the mushy ground, then agilely dismounted. He tied the reins to a tree, then scooped her up in his arms. Amanda kicked wildly, wanting to walk. Clutching her tightly, Reis laughed again, heading for a cabin in a small clearing. Although it was raining noisily, she could hear the rush of a nearby stream. She didn't know where they were, but it was secluded, and intimidating.

Reis placed her bare feet on the wet dirt while he unlocked the door. He carried her inside, kicking the door closed behind them, and deposited her at the entrance. After lighting a lantern, he turned and eyed her intently. She almost appeared comical, entrapped in the blanket with silvery blond curls dripping water. If this situation weren't so serious, he knew he could easily burst into hearty chuckles.

Unable to move, Amanda stood there, shaking from cold and suspense. Removing his rain gear and tossing it over a chair, Reis pulled a knife from a sheath at his waist. He came toward her. Amanda wanted to back away in fear but couldn't.

When he witnessed her reaction, he sighed in frustration. "I'm just going to cut the ropes, Mandy. Be still. We need to get you dry and warm before you take a chill."

It wasn't the knife which alarmed her; it was the beguiling grin on his face. When he removed the confining blanket, she felt naked in the wet gown which clung revealingly to her curves. He squatted to cut the rope around her ankles, then stood to sever those on her wrists behind her back. The moment her feet and hands were mobile she struck at him with both, wishing she knew how to fight like Miranda and those skilled Chinese. How dare he bring her here alone, bound and barely covered! What if someone saw them? Not having removed her gag yet, she berated him with muffled curses.

Reis captured her hands, then flung her to the bunk and pinned her beneath him. "I do believe you're aching for some discipline, love. Behave, or I might forget you're a lady and I'm—" He didn't finish that statement. It was too soon to say, I'm the man who loves you. "Settle down, and I'll build a fire and fix coffee. Deal?"

When she didn't nod, he slipped the gag down to her neck and insisted upon her answer. "Is it a deal, love? A truce?" His rain gear had been of little service; he was just as soaked as Amanda. His wet garments molded to his hard frame; that view and their contact made her too conscious of his virility and appeal.

Distressed by her attraction to him and her helpless position, Amanda screamed at him, "You sorry son of a—"

Reis's hand clamped over her mouth, denying the crude word to come forth. "Instead of a spanking, I might wash that mouth out with strong soap. Better still, I might do both! As soon as you get warm and dry, you're going to do plenty of talking. You owe me, love."

When he removed his hand, she shouted, "Owe you! I owe you nothing, Yankee! Get off of me! Take me home this instant! Are you too dense to know kidnapping is a crime? Or too wicked and arrogant to care?"

"You're a bright girl, Mandy. That means you should hear all the evidence before taking sides on a vital issue. Stop acting like a spoiled brat and listen to me!"

"Listen to your lies again? You claimed to be here on business; that isn't true. Why are you trying to hurt me?" she inquired angrily. She struggled once more, causing their bodies to mesh provocatively. When her strap slipped precariously from one shoulder and the tail of the ice blue gown wadded between her exposed thighs, she wisely halted.

"The business offer was true, Mandy. Tonight, the only thing which concerns me is your dark image of me. Hell, we're not strangers! How could you believe Web, Mandy?" he asked accusingly, acutely aware of every inch of her rain-kissed body.

Unlike her tanned sister, Amanda was as white and smooth as fresh cream. When she was calm or happy, she looked like a siren who should be perched on a rock in the ocean, luring sailors to blissful enslavement. Lord, how he wanted to lean over and spread kisses over that slender throat and those satiny shoulders. He wanted to capture that mouth with his. He yearned to turn that defiant sparkle in those blue eyes into a blaze of smoldering desire for him. He craved to have those arms and legs hungrily entwined about him. There wasn't an inch of her he didn't long to taste or explore!

"Look who's talking about washing out my mouth! You curse and lie worse than I do," she scoffed cynically, as his flaming gaze sent warm tremors down her spine. She feared the power of his hypnotic gaze and enchanting facade. If only he didn't have that roguish smile, those remarkably blue eyes, that sun-kissed flesh, that ebony hair, that . . . that everything disarming!

"Ah, so you have been lying," he baited her, attempting to keep his mind off her body. The light color, clingy material, and nearly translucent condition of her gown left little to his imagination. Despite his efforts at self-control, his traitorous body had reacted to those taut points which had appeared when her body had thrashed against his. His eyes darkened with passion at the memory.

"I didn't mean it like that!" she protested quickly as inexplicable sensations washed over her body and clouded her reason. "I'm cold and wet! My feet are freezing!" she panted, changing the subject. Truthfully, she didn't care if she was soaked, and the heat of his body was tormenting bliss. Her breathing became labored.

"Then behave while I make a fire and coffee." He stood up and smiled down at her, his gaze leisurely traveling from her straggly hair to her bare feet. Her gown had slid upward, offering him a pleasing view of shapely legs.

Amanda seized the wayward material and covered herself. "Did you think to bring along my clothes?" she sneered uneasily.

"Nope," he mischievously quipped. "But you'd better get out of that wet gown. Wrap a dry blanket around you," he suggested, chuckling at her embarrassment and outrage.

"You're insane if you think I'll wear nothing but a blanket around you, you lecherous fiend!" she shouted, sticking out her tongue at him.

"That wet gown's gonna get awfully uncomfortable. It doesn't hide your many charms anyway," he announced devilishly, grinning.

"You!" she cried in rising distress. "You'll be sorry for this!"

"If you explain and I explain, then neither of us

will be sorry or miserable. That is, if you're the woman I think and pray you are. If not, I'll be signing my life away," he vowed mysteriously, his expression suddenly grave.

He stripped off his shirt and boots, then warned her to turn her head while he exchanged his saturated pants for a blanket. "You can't be serious, Reis Harrison! No gentleman would subject a lady to such indignities! Surely you don't expect us to talk while undressed?"

"I didn't plan on the storm, Mandy. If we don't get dry and warm, we'll be too sick to settle matters. I should have brought us both some clothes; I honestly didn't think about it. You needn't worry; I've never raped a woman, and I won't start with you."

Amanda's cheeks flamed a bright red as she presented her back to him. He eased out of his pants and wrapped the blanket around his slim hips, tucking the edges in at his narrow waist. He hung his pants and shirt on rickety chairs, then set his boots near the hearth. He told her she could change while he made a fire.

As he knelt before the fireplace, Amanda turned and stared at his muscled back. There was nothing between them but a thin blanket and a scanty nightgown; soon, just two blankets. Except for the noise of building a fire and a gentle rain falling outside, they were sealed in a perilously sensual world of provocative solitude. Her heart began to pound so forcefully that she imagined it could be heard in the stillness.

Her eyes scanned the room which was dimly lit by one lantern and the approaching dawn. She noticed a gun and the knife, but both were near him. She feared this was some cunning trap, to show Weber that Reis could have her if he so desired. Damn, how she wanted him! But what would happen afterward? Was a beguiling seduction part of his vengeful scheme? Could she trust him? He claimed he only wanted to talk, but this romantic setting made her doubt his intentions. Could she trust herself alone with him, alone without clothes before a cozy fire?

Panic flooded her. Before Reis realized her intention, she raced to the door, flung it open, and fled outside into the light rain. She ran as if demons were pursuing her. She didn't get far before Reis was close behind. He shouted for her to halt, but she rashly fled toward a boggy area. The squashy surface tugged at her feet, impeding her progress. She dodged low-hanging tree limbs and moisture-laden bushes, then tripped on a fallen branch, plunging full force into a mushy area of yielding earth.

When Reis made the clearing, he grabbed her arm and tried to pull her from the muddy quagmire. She fought him wildly, causing him to stumble and fall into the shallow and slushy pit. As they struggled and argued in the morass, both were covered with sticky and clingy mud. Even so, Amanda continued desperately to struggle for freedom.

Reis shouted for her to stop fighting him and get back inside the cabin, but Amanda was terrified of being alone with him. At last he had her pinned to the ground, sinking into oozing mud. The dark mixture clung to her body, matted her hair, and stained her gown. She could feel it squeezing between her fingers and thighs. Realizing at last that she could not escape him, she ceased her movements and reluctantly went limp.

"Why the hell did you run like that?" he thundered at her, sounding angered and baffled. "I told you you're safe with me!"

"I don't want to hear any more lies!" she scoffed cynically.

"Just where can you go dressed like this?" he reminded her. "Sometimes I don't think you have a brain in that beautiful head!"

"Let me up, you brute! My gown is ruined. Look at my hair! My God, I'm covered in mud! You'll pay for this, Reis Harrison! You just wait until Web comes after me!" she threatened.

"I wish to hell he would! Then I'd force him to tell you the truth! I think you're in for a big shock when Randy comes home; you'll learn you still own Morning Star and it's very prosperous. And your townhouse isn't mortgaged, and your firm is making more money than you could count in weeks! It's all a ruse, Mandy love," he snarled at her.

"What are you talking about?" she asked in puzzlement, halting all struggles and staring up into his scowling face. How did he know such things? What was he trying to pull?

"That ledger is pure fantasy—lies recorded by Weber and McVane. Every month you grow richer,

Mandy. It's a cunning plot to get you to marry him. If I didn't know how sly and convincing he was, I'd think you were the dumbest female alive," he declared sullenly.

"How do you know so much about my affairs? And how can you make such ridiculous charges?" she demanded.

He replied with shocking words. "I'm an agent for President Grant. I know plenty of things. I took extra care to investigate you, Miss Amanda Lawrence. It seems I studied you too closely. I'm not here for revenge; I was sent by Grant on a secret mission. I never expected to find Richardson here. And I sure as hell didn't expect to meet someone like you. There couldn't be a worse time for romance, but I'll be damned if I allow that bastard to entrap you with lies!"

"You're the one who's lying! I've known Web for years. You're a total stranger. Why should I trust you?" she sneered. *A presidential spy? Investigate her? What in heaven's name was going on!*

"Because you'll make the biggest mistake of your life if you don't hear me out," he replied. His voice softened as he continued, "Listen to me, Mandy. You won't face poverty if you reject Weber. You're a very wealthy lady, despite what that phony book claims. Would I lie about such an easy matter to check out? Don't ask Weber or McVane; go ask the bankers and check with your accounts," he challenged. "Since I'm investigating Lawrence Shipping, I know how much business you've been doing. So why aren't those clients and shipments listed in your books? Why are only bills listed and no profits, profits which I know your firm's earned recently?''

"You keep talking about my books; how do you know what's in them? And how do you know where Randy is?" she inquired skeptically.

"That night you ran out on me, you left the safe open. I checked to see why you had panicked and turned on me. Knowing the state of your firm, I knew you were being tricked. I didn't have to guess by whom. He's taking money from your firm, Mandy, not making loans to it. And he isn't supporting you and Miranda, as you've been led to believe. I couldn't steal evidence to prove my claims to you without exposing my investigation to Weber and McVane; and without proof, I feared you wouldn't believe me. I saw Miranda before she left. I wonder how Weber planned to explain your ownership of Morning Star after your wedding. And why the townhouse is still yours.''

She wondered if he was daft, or staggeringly accurate. "But Web said you were after revenge," she protested.

"I swear he deceived you, Mandy. I didn't ride with Sherman. I was in his camp briefly while on a mission for President Lincoln. Weber was a captive then; that's where he saw me first. Later I learned he was the one in charge of the troop which burned my home and killed my family. As soon as Luke completes his work, he'll show you the facts; Weber and his troop were infamous killers and destroyers.

Weber would make Sherman look like an angel. I did track his men, trying to capture them. I underestimated Weber. He betrayed two of his own men in order to ambush me. I hate him, Mandy, but not enough to use you or any innocent person to gain justice. He knows how much time we spent together while he was gone. He told those war lies to keep us apart. He might even suspect who I am and why I came to Alexandria. I've been trying to find a way to protect you and my mission. But if I don't take you into my confidence, you'll marry this snake and ruin both our lives."

"How would my marriage ruin your life?" she asked sarcastically.

"It won't, if it's to me," he nonchalantly informed her.

"To you?" she murmured incredulously.

"That's right, my love. When this is over, I want you to marry me. Will you?"

"But we're strangers!"

"Does that alter your feelings, or mine?" he speculated. "Marry me, Mandy. Give us a chance to be happy and safe. Besides, we were never strangers. From the moment we met, we knew it was fated between us. You also sensed it that first night, didn't you?"

Amanda was speechless with surprise and confusion. Reis took advantage of her silence and questioned, "You spurned me because of what you saw in that book, didn't you? You felt obligated to marry him, to trust him, obligated to reject me. You don't love him, Mandy."

"Who are you, Reis? What's this about a secret mission for the President?" she probed.

Reis outlined his mission for her and his assumptions, then finished by saying, "I think your father was innocent. I told those clients if they would resign with Lawrence, I would follow the next few shipments to see how and where the changes were made and by whom. I realized there was more to this mission when I met you and Richardson. I think Richardson's behind this deception. He needs Lawrence Shipping and your plantation to carry on his covert activities, and he needs you as a respectable cover."

"Do you realize what you're saying, Reis? You're implying he's a traitor, a criminal, and a scoundrel. I know Web has his bad traits, but to think he's . . ." Amanda sighed heavily, forgetting she was lying in a mud hole beneath the man she loved but feared to trust.

Yet Amanda had a terrible sensation that Reis might be right. Crazy thoughts flashed through her mind. She recalled curious questions Weber had asked right after her father's death about these same three accounts. Could she totally trust either man? Was she the pawn in some monstrous game? Amanda tried to push aside her wild imagination. Coincidence? A deadly game?

Her quizzical gaze fused with his entreating one. "Why should I believe you, Reis? How do I know this isn't some trick to get me on your side, to use me against him? How can I accept such treachery on the word of a stranger? I'm so confused," she confessed.

"All I ask is that you go and talk with your banker. See if you're really on the verge of bankruptcy and see if you've lost the plantation. When Miranda returns, you'll know that isn't true. Don't tell Weber where she is, or she might not get back alive. You haven't told him, have you?" he asked, alarm racing through him.

"No," she replied, sensing his fear for her sister. "But Web wouldn't hurt Randy," she argued.

"She wouldn't be the first female he's injured or killed," he told her. "He has a lot at stake here. I know you find that impossible to accept, but you must. Luke's been investigating him a long time. He hopes to get proof of Weber's crimes then split you two with it."

Amanda didn't know why she was listening to such tales. "If what you say has even a grain of truth, then why would Web do such things? How can I accept this monstrous charge without proof?"

"Greed, Mandy love. He wants all and more than he lost during the war. He wants money, power, and fame. He can't risk involving his company, so he was using your father's. When I first arrived, I didn't know if you could be trusted since you and Weber were so close."

"But you just said my father was innocent," she shrieked.

"That might explain his accident, Mandy. Perhaps he discovered what was taking place and tried to stop it," he speculated softly.

Amanda went white and shuddered. "Are you saying you think my parents were murdered? You think Weber . . ." That was too much evil to accept, and she resisted that horrible accusation.

"I don't know yet, Mandy. But I suspect it wasn't an accident. You've got to realize how dangerous and desperate Weber and his men are." As soon as Reis made those statements, he grimaced. "Listen to me, Mandy. You and Miranda have to be careful until I solve this mystery. If they think you two are suspicious of them, they could harm you. Damnit! I should never have involved you! I must be a fool! What the hell could I be thinking!" he berated himself.

"You forget everything I said, Mandy. Don't you dare see those bankers! And keep this pretty nose out of your office and books. If Weber or his men think you are on to them, they could get rid of you and Miranda just like your parents. Besides money and power, their lives are in peril; they've committed treason, a hanging offense. Luke's in danger too if Weber learns of his investigation. Just remember: you aren't indebted to Weber, and I love you. Just keep quiet and safe at home until I arrest them. Don't give them any reason to harm you and your sister. Will you do that for me?" he pleaded earnestly.

"This is another trick, isn't it?" she asked painfully. Was he afraid if she did some snooping she would discover his lies? Could she be so mistaken about Weber, so blind and gullible?

Reis captured her face between his hands and shouted at her, "Tarnation, woman! All I need is a little time to prove it. Just don't marry him before Luke and I can save you. If you think you need money, I'll give you any amount. If you think I'm lying, then marry me. I have everything you want or need," he vowed.

"Marry you?" she repeated, eying him strangely. "Why?"

"Secretly, Mandy," he added a curious stipulation, then explained his reason. "If Weber thinks you're siding with me, that means you're against him. I won't put your life in danger, love. If you marry me, we'll have to keep it a secret from everyone but Randy and Luke. You'll have to pretend to remain friends with Weber. Otherwise, you'll have to go to my home and wait for me there." Reis didn't have a home anywhere, but he would buy one if she would live in it! This was a dangerous ploy, but one he couldn't resist.

"But why marry me secretly?" she probed, still doubtful.

"Marriage is legal and binding. Would I go so far just to hurt another man? Surely you would trust me then?" he tested.

"If what you say is true, then Web had me fooled completely. Who's to say you don't have similar motives?" she fenced nervously.

"Right now, you have only my word," he stated candidly.

Reis slowly bent forward, his lips coming into

contact with hers when she didn't move aside. He kissed her tenderly and leisurely, then leaned away. "I swear I've spoken the truth, love, all of it."

Amanda gazed into his eyes and felt she could trust him. Suddenly she realized she was finally free of the pain of the last few weeks. She didn't have to marry Web! Reis loved her and wanted to marry her! She had nothing to fear! In spite of the gloomy weather, her heart was full of sunshine and joy. Despite her slushy surroundings, she had never been more comfortable.

She smiled at him and teased, "You're a mess, Reis. So am I." She took handfuls of mud and smeared them over his bare chest, shoulders, and back. "You forgot to tell me you like to play in mud."

"It seems I'm not the only one," he responded, covering her arms and chest with it. "Now, you'll really have to remove that gown; it's ruined, love. But we have a problem; there's only one blanket left."

"Surely your clothes will be dry soon," she retorted playfully.

"Not if I can help it," he jested merrily, kissing the tip of her nose. "Can you believe this, us playing in the rain and mud?"

"And dressed like this?" she added laughingly.

"Or undressed like this?" he parried devilishly.

"I might be sorry, Reis, but I believe you," she murmured.

Reis's mouth came down on hers, this time passionately. He parted her lips and invaded her mouth. His arms went around her neck and shoulders, lifting her head out of the mire. Almost simultaneously, her arms encircled his steely body. Suddenly the mucky hole seemed sensual and cozy.

His desire mounting, he unwillingly pulled away. "Are you brave enough to wash this off in a chilly stream?" he inquired roguishly.

She laughed and retorted, "Do we have any choice? Any chance there's some soap in that cabin?"

He chuckled and said, "I doubt it. We'll have to make do with just water. At least we can wash each other's back," he teased.

Amanda grinned. This was as wild and wonderful as their first meeting. He had a way of relaxing and enchanting her. She was no longer afraid of him, of herself, or events surrounding them. Reis said he was hers, and that was all that mattered now.

As if reading her thoughts, he chuckled and noted, "We do have a crazy way of bewitching each other, don't we? You make me feel so alive, so carefree, Mandy. It's like being a kid again, having fun and doing silly things. You realize we're perfectly suited to each other?" Reis helped her to sit up near him, yet he didn't extract them from the mud.

Amanda glanced down at her condition, then giggled as she curled her legs behind her and looked up into his amused expression. "Evidently, Reis Richardson. Maybe I'm just exhausted from fleeing your persistent chase," she jested, wiping off clumps of mud from his chest and arms. She nestled into his embrace, murmuring, "Since you're so handsome and strong, I suppose my defeat isn't that bad. I yield to your superior strength, my dashing Yankee conqueror. How could I possibly reject a suitor who captures me in such an . . . unusual manner?''

Reis hugged her tightly, then scooped her up in his arms and struggled to free his feet from the engulfing mire. She laughed as they swayed precariously. She taunted playfully, "You did threaten to drop me in the mud, but I didn't think you were serious. From now on, Mister Harrison, I shall have to respect your words.''

Chuckles came from deep within that muscular chest. "Let's get you bathed, dried, and warmed. We still have some matters to discuss, Miss Lawrence.''

"Such as?'' she hinted curiously.

"Such as what will happen with us,'' he replied, tightening his grip on her as he stepped from the delightful quagmire. He headed for the stream, carrying her effortlessly. He gingerly waded into the rain-swollen stream to an area just above his knees. Suddenly he halted and stiffened, but not from the biting liquid nipping at his bare legs and feet.

"I think we have a problem,'' he stated nervously, comically, as his soggy blanket, heavy with mud and water, pulled from his lithe body, leaving him stark naked with Amanda clutched in his arms while the capricious covering was swept away by the strong and impish currents.

Chapter Seven

Amanda burst into uncontrollable giggles.

"It isn't funny, Miss Lawrence. How do you propose I protect our modesty now?"

She thought but a moment before merrily suggesting, "Of course, it serves you right for being so improper in the first place, but I could close my eyes while you sit down or chase your naughty garment."

"Then what?" he pressed in rising humor, relieved that she didn't seem overly concerned or embarrassed by their predicament.

"We can wash off this mud. Then I'll return to the cabin and hide in my blanket," she offered a seemingly simple solution.

"There's only one dry blanket left. What about me?" he wailed.

"Since you're responsible for this episode, you can either use my wet blanket or your slicker. Once you build a fire, you'll be warm enough," she blithely mocked his helpless position.

"How about you use my shirt and I use the blanket?" he hinted.

"But your shirt is wet; I'll freeze," she shrieked. "Surely a man who vows love for a distressed lady can be unselfish and gallant?"

"You wouldn't be cold in my arms," he debated, grinning down at her. "I'll tell you what; let's bathe and then decide how to handle this new business."

Amanda closed her eyes tightly as she suppressed more giggles. He lowered her to the ground and nudged her into the murky water as he sank beneath its protective surface.

Amanda instantly bolted to her feet and squealed as the biting water nipped at her bare flesh. She whirled and stared down at him. "You lied, Harrison; this water is like ice!" Her teeth chattered and she wrapped her hands around her arms and rubbed them frantically, unintentionally shoving her breasts together and causing them to bulge from her low neckline. "Surely you don't expect me to sit down?"

Reis laughed heartily. "It's not so bad once you get used to it. You certainly can't remain a little piglet. That mud will eventually dry and become most scratchy," he argued, beginning to wash the mud off his body with gentle movements. "You know something? With your hair dark with mud, you almost look like Randy."

Amanda stood there indecisively. Reis caught her hand and pulled upon it, encouraging, "Get it over with, love. The water won't get any warmer."

She gritted her teeth and stiffened as she sank into the stream before him, grimacing in discomfort. Before she could begin her own cleansing, Reis tenderly captured an arm and scrubbed it, then the other one. He told her to turn around and he would wash her back, which she did. With a rakish grin, he remarked, "You'd best wash the front, or I might become excited and break my promise."

Amanda shrieked again as she splashed water on her chest time after time until the mud was gone and then did the same with her face. "This water is almost as dirty as us," she complained, trembling. "What about my hair; it's filthy and full of tangles," she fretted.

"Duck under the water and swish it around," he replied.

"That's easy for you to say; this water isn't that cold to you. Let's see if I can make you just as miserable," she threatened, splashing water on his chest and in his face.

"Two can play at that game, love," he taunted.

"Not if I escape first. Are you forgetting you can't get up?" She wickedly reminded him of his state of nudity.

He grinned sensually and huskily murmured, "I can chase you, love; and if you turn around, you've only yourself to scold. Lay your head across my arm and I'll scrub that hair for you," he offered sweetly.

She eyed him suspiciously. "Another trick, my daring rogue?"

"Since I'm to blame for getting you dirty,

shouldn't I repair the damage?" he deliberated aloud, winking at her. "Surely you don't expect me to get inflamed while sitting in freezing water?"

"Reis Harrison! You crude brute," she chided his bold remark.

"If you want help with that golden mane, you'd best hurry; I'm getting numb—everywhere," he added wantonly.

Amanda gasped in astonishment, then scolded, "You're awful! But if what you say is true, then I should be perfectly safe."

She moved to sit at his left leg as directed, since he was left-handed. She slowly leaned back over his right arm which was propped on a slightly raised knee to prevent any intimate contact between them. He quickly worked with the cascade of hair which was dangling in the water until it was as mud-free as possible. "That's better. But what about that muck under your gown?" he asked mirthfully.

Their gazes met in amusement, then became serious as they fused. Unable to stop himself, he pulled her to him and kissed her intensely. One kiss led to another until the chilly water swirling around their locked bodies couldn't cool the heat of fiery passion.

"Amanda, love, I want you," he whispered against her lips, his hands moving up and down her arms as if to rub away the chill of her flesh. It was a brief, simple statement, but it said everything.

"I want you too, Reis," she responded feverishly, twisting her lips against his as she pressed closer to his taut frame. "Make love to me," she entreated him, enslaved by unbridled desire. This was the third time he had tempted her to mindless frenzy; this time she yielded.

He lifted her and carried her to the bank where they sank entwined in the wet grass, unable to wait until they reached the cabin to sate their mutual hungers. He removed her gown without removing his mouth from hers, then trailed a damp hand over the curves and planes he had dreamed about since meeting her. Reis tried to caution himself to teach her about love gently and slowly, but she was too eager and inflamed to be mastered, too impassioned to be restrained.

Amanda had wanted him for so long that she couldn't wait a moment longer. Her body was like an ember near a blazing fire, one which would die slowly if it didn't become a part of that potent blaze. As his lips teased her breasts to firm suspense, their taut peaks burned from the warmth of his mouth. Her hands moved over tanned skin which she hadn't dared to touch until now. When she was aquiver and breathless, he tenderly moved over her and gently joined his eager flesh to hers. She arched toward him in wild abandon, lost in the ecstasy of their union. There was no pain—only joy.

His deft hands and lips worked as skillfully and ardently as his throbbing manhood, until he brought her to the pinnacle of exquisite pleasure. Together, they passed through rapture's gates. Blissful serenity engulfed them, their lips still touching as they descended from the heights.

Here in this private hideaway with her body stained with obstinate mud, lying on the saturated earth beside a rain-swollen stream, Amanda had given herself freely to the man who owned her heart.

Reis propped himself on an elbow and gazed down at her, such tenderness emblazoned upon his handsome features, such love shining softly in his eyes. "You all right, love?" he inquired apprehensively.

She smiled, her entire face brightening. "Never better," she vowed, caressing his pleasing jawline. "You?"

"Never better," he happily concurred. "I love you, Amanda Lawrence, more than I could imagine possible. You cast your spell over me one stormy night, and I can never again be whole without you."

She laughed and teased, "Then I suppose it's only natural to prove it on a stormy morning. I love you, Reis Harrison. I've been so lonely and miserable without you," she confessed, her mood a curious blend of shyness and boldness.

"I've never been so afraid in my life as when I nearly lost you. I know it was crazy to kidnap you, but I had to do it. The state you were in—I didn't know what you would do next. I don't want you to be angry with Luke and Randy, but—" He hesitated briefly before confessing their daring ploy. "I don't want any more secrets between us, love. I must finish this mission, my beloved angel. We have a decision to make: do we marry later, or do we marry now in secret?"

She smiled. "I'm greedy and selfish, Reis; I want you as quickly as I can have you. But I'll comply with your orders from Grant."

"I think it would be best for both of us if we find a way to marry soon. I want to make sure you're mine, and it will be easier to spend time together. You'll be happier as my wife, not a mistress."

His meaning was clear. She had surrendered to passion today, but marriage would prevent her from feeling guilty over a pre-planned affair. "You know me too well, Mister Harrison," she teased mirthfully.

"I plan to know you even better. Say, inch by inch?" he murmured, a finger intoxicatingly encircling each nipple in turn. "Your greed is nothing compared to mine, woman," he declared, leaning forward to torment each faint, brown point with his tongue.

"I must need a lesson or two—I thought you said you were numb?"

"A fire such as you ignite could thaw any frozen object," he told her, taking her hand and clasping it around the proof of his claim.

"Then why not share your flames, my dashing Yankee; I'm chilled to the bone," she coaxed, stroking him boldly.

"All I have and am belongs to you, my love. You have but to ask or take what you will," he stated softly and truthfully.

"For now, all I need or want is for us to be one again," she told him shamelessly, her eyes never leaving his penetrating gaze.

His lips covered hers before making torturously slow and sweet love to her. Afterward, they lay together for a time until it began to mist once more. He splashed off in the stream and coaxed her to do the same, then tossed her the gown which he had rinsed for her. Ignoring its iciness, she wiggled into it. Hand in hand, they returned to the cabin.

Soon Reis had a cheery fire going and coffee warming. The aroma filled the small cabin and teased their noses. Amanda sat on a cured cowhide before the fire, clad in Reis's shirt which was nearly dry. Wrapped in the last blanket, Reis poured two cups of coffee and joined her. They didn't talk for a time, simply enjoying each other's nearness and company.

Amanda's voice broke the peaceful silence. "Reis, how do you plan to get me home dressed like this?"

"Like I stole you, in the middle of the night," he teased. When she asked if he had known her housekeeper would be off, he grinned and nodded. "If someone asks why you didn't answer the door, say you were bathing or sleeping, which you were—just somewhere else," he playfully rambled on.

"You mean Weber, don't you?" she asked gravely. "How do you plan to unmask him?" She wondered how she could pretend with Web.

"Just leave that to me. No playing the detective to end this matter sooner. Just be patient and cautious. He's dangerous, Mandy. Just carry on as usual," he instructed for her safety.

"Are you sure? You don't mind if he takes me out, and hugs me or kisses me?" she inquired behind giggles.

"If he lays a finger on you, I'll break it off," he vowed possessively. "Just as soon as I locate a minister out of town, I'll arrange our wedding. You and I can sneak off, get married, then sneak back. You'll be safe as long as Weber doesn't know you're in cahoots with me. That is, if I can't convince you to leave town for a while?"

"It sounds so exciting," she murmured dreamily.

"There's one other thing, Mandy; confide in Miranda. At times, we might need her help to . . . get together secretly. She's worried about you," he added at her coy grin.

"You like Randy, don't you?" she inquired happily.

"Yep. She's a lot like you; and yet she's very different. I think I've discovered a wonderful family for myself," he sighed contentedly.

As they consumed the food which Reis had wisely brought along, he expounded on his mission and Weber's treacherous deceptions. They passed the day talking about their lives and families or discussing their future. Once more they made love, this time on the narrow bank in the warm cabin. Around eleven that night, Reis couldn't stall the inevitable any longer; it was time to take Amanda home before Friday's dawn exposed their rendezvous.

Snuggled in a blanket in his arms, Amanda was quiet on the return trip. Once inside her home, Reis kissed her good night and cautioned her again about Weber before leaving. To keep Weber from getting suspicious about them, Reis promised to contact her through Lucas, and she was to do the same with him. She was surprised to learn he was staying with her calculating cousin. Under such precarious circumstances, she realized it would make things easier for herself and Reis.

During the day, Amanda managed to avoid Weber by visiting friends. Later, Lucas came over for dinner and a leisurely conversation. When Weber came by around eight, he was vividly displeased to find Lucas there and more displeased when Lucas wouldn't leave them alone. Weber and Lucas exchanged surly jibes, which Amanda pretended not to notice. Soon Weber announced that he had to leave and rose to do so. Lucas smiled and remained seated.

Amanda felt she must see Weber to the door. When he tried to kiss her good night, she turned away, informing him she had the sniffles and he might catch them. In preparation for such an awkward moment, she had been sneezing and sniffling during his visit. Giving Amanda one final, searing glare, Weber left sullenly.

She rejoined Lucas in the sitting room. He grinned and stated, "That was quick thinking, Mandy, pretending to have a cold. Reis will be delighted when I tell him," he teased fondly. "Did you see the funny look on Web's face when you mentioned a possible visit to Morning Star? Where did you tell him Randy is?" It was apparent that Lucas was thoroughly enjoying this charade.

They both laughed. "Web thinks Randy is visiting friends in Boston. Once she returns and we tell her everything, we can all relax. I did find it odd that Web didn't say anything when I mentioned the plantation. I wonder when he's planning to use that little ruse."

"When I'm not around to make trouble," Lucas declared.

"How could he keep it a secret from you? Surely he knows I would mention such a shocking matter to you during one of our vists," she reasoned. "Why alter the books, then not use them?"

"I'm leaving soon, remember?" he responded, not venturing a speculation on her last question. Who could understand Web Richardson!

"But Reis is staying with you," she replied in bewilderment.

"I've told him he can use my place as long as he wishes. I have to leave within two weeks. Until then, I can be your messenger."

"Are you really going to invite Randy to go along?" she fretted.

"Why not? That would give you and Reis lots of privacy," he hinted roguishly. "He told me you two are getting married soon. Just be careful, Mandy. He's right; Weber is a devil. You leave the investigation to Reis, you hear me?"

Amanda grinned and jested, "Yes, cuz; I'll be good."

"I know you, Amanda Lawrence. Don't go

sneaking around just to help Reis. You could stumble onto something which might endanger his life as well as your own. I hope he works fast and hard; you can't tell Web you have a cold for very long," he stated between chuckles.

"I would ask you to come over every night, but that would look suspicious. Besides, he would only start visiting during the day. Oh, Luke, how will I ever carry this off?" she worried aloud. Just the thought of Weber touching or kissing her was repulsive.

He mockingly lessened her tension. "Do these ears deceive me? Is Amanda Lawrence doubting her feminine wiles? You'll be great. You have Reis, so now I can stop worrying about leaving. I'll be back before winter." With comical animation, he suggested, "There is one thing you can do to roughen the waters with Weber; pick an argument with him. Then while you're pouting and reconsidering his proposal, that will give you and Reis extra time."

Amanda brightened in elation. "Over what?"

"How about over Randy?" he proposed astonishingly, then explained himself.

"You really think he has a fever for her?" she questioned, alarmed and surprised that she hadn't noticed such undercurrents.

When Lucas expounded on his observations and opinions, Amanda concurred. "Damn, I must be blind! He hasn't bothered her, has he? That explains why she's always so tense and remote when he's around. Why didn't she tell me, Luke?"

"Because you're always so defensive of him. Like me, she was probably afraid you would think she was only trying to separate you two. Don't forget, she doesn't know why you felt you must marry him. Nothing against you, my lovely cousin, but he merely wants a Lawrence. You fit his plans better than Randy, but he would settle for her. I bet Randy will be delighted to unmask that scum. And after your violent quarrel, it will seem natural for Randy to go away with me. Ah, yes, it's ingenious," he bragged, not realizing the repercussions of such a reckless charade.

"I must confess, I agree, Luke," she complimented him. "Then by the time you and Randy return, Reis and I will be settled down. You will take good care of her?"

"If she tags along. I haven't asked her yet. In fact, she doesn't know anything about this trip. I was saving the news as a surprise. I'm not sure how I landed this enviable assignment, but I'm taking it before they change their minds. Fact is, now that I've heard their proposal, I think I would even go at my own expense." Lucas didn't tell Amanda that taking her sister along with him would solve another problem: it would keep Weber from getting rid of Amanda and pursuing Miranda, now that Reis was in the picture.

"I know her, Luke; she would give anything to go to the Dakota Territory. Why shouldn't she have her dream? I am getting mine," she announced gleefully, dancing around the room.

"I'll drop around tomorrow afternoon with a note from Reis," he tempted her. "Would you like to send him a message tonight? Your housekeeper won't be off again until Sunday. Can you wait another day?"

Amanda hastily wrote three words on a page: "I love you." When Lucas accepted the missive and departed, she sighed restlessly as she headed for bed. Last night she had been with Reis; tonight, she must be content to dream of him. Two days ago, she had been utterly miserable; today, her heart sang with ecstasy.

Fortunately, Weber didn't come by to see her Saturday. Unbeknown to her, he was biding his time until the interfering Lucas Reardon left town, just as he had arranged. It was late in the day before Weber learned that Reis Harrison was not only still around but was living with that sly cousin of Amanda's. He would do some checking around before confronting her on Sunday afternoon . . .

Amanda wanted to send a telegram to her sister, encouraging her to hurry home but she dared not for fear of revealing Miranda's location. If Weber was as crafty and deadly as Lucas and Reis believed—which she no longer doubted—surely Weber was watching each of them. She desperately wanted to help solve this mystery but obeyed the wishes of Reis and her cousin. Now that she was acquainted with the facts of the situation, she didn't want to hinder her love's work.

Amanda remained in the house, continuing her illness ruse. She couldn't help but be disappointed, even slightly miffed, when Reis neither sent her a message nor made a stealthy visit on either day. This solitary game was becoming boring.

The sun came out bright and warm on Sunday morning. Amanda wanted to go outside, to go riding or picnicking with Reis. She warned herself to be patient and careful until Miranda's presence supplied a good reason to quarrel with Weber.

Oddly, Lucas didn't visit on Saturday or Sunday; Amanda worried over his absence. She fretted over Reis's behavior when he had made no contact with her since his daring escapade of Thursday. If he were as lonely and anxious as she was, he would have found a way to see her, or at least send word by Lucas! After their intimacy, did he think he could take her for granted? Did he think he owed her no explanation?

By late afternoon, she was tense and moody. She had spent the night listening for Reis's footsteps. Her hair was mussed, her face pale, and her cheeks flushed when Weber called. Thankfully, her appearance and mood added credence to her charade.

When she opened the door, Weber verbally assailed her before she could speak. "What in hell's name is going on, Amanda?" he snarled.

She looked at him in bewilderment. Lines of fury etched his forehead, and his teeth were clenched tightly. His dark eyes were cold, their gaze intimidating and accusatory. "I beg your pardon?" she murmured curiously.

"Why is that Yankee staying with your bloody cousin?" he snapped, his body stiff with rage.

"What Yankee, Web? Luke lives alone," she argued innocently.

"Reis Harrison!" he thundered, refusing to calm down and speak politely.

"Reis Harrison?" she echoed. "But you told me he had left town. Why would he be at Luke's? Did you decide to do business with him?" she asked, hoping her questions sounded logical.

"You haven't seen Harrison in the last few days?" he demanded.

"Certainly not!" she threw at him as if insulted by his tone. Actually, she was angry that it was the truth. "As for Luke, he was here the same night you were. I haven't seen him since then. Why are you attacking me like this? You know I haven't been well," she scolded him petulantly.

"When is Lucas leaving for Dakota?" Web inquired coldly.

"How did you know he was? He only told me Friday night; that's why he came over. He said it was a secret," she stated beguilingly.

"Is that Yankee going with him?" Weber went on, ignoring her question.

Puzzlement filled her eyes. "Why would they travel together? And how would I know such things? Your hateful questions are confusing," she informed him brusquely. "Luke isn't in the habit of explaining himself to me or anyone. If you don't mind, I need to go lie down again; I'm weak and shaky," she stated peevishly.

"Have you seen a doctor?" He suddenly became solicitous, actually smiling at her. Right before her eyes, he reversed his mood.

"If I'm not feeling better by tomorrow, I plan to see Doctor Ramsey. What I need is rest and quiet," she stated pointedly.

He grinned in false remorse. "I'm sorry, my dear. I shouldn't take my anger out on you."

"No, you shouldn't," she frostily concurred. "You know something? I see new facets to you each week. Sometimes I don't think I know you at all, Weber, and that troubles me. You are far too bossy at times. If you behave in this hateful way with a woman you're wooing, I wonder how you would treat a wife."

Weber tensed, then forced himself to relax. He chuckled and wheedled, "That's not true, my sweet. Besides, you'll have plenty of time to know me better once we're married. Have you made a decision yet?"

"How can I make any decisions when I feel terrible and you act so mean?" she replied, leaning against the door.

"You've had lots of time and privacy," he insisted.

"Do you realize how much has happened to me these past few months? I need time to adjust, Weber. If that seems selfish to you, then I'm sorry," she purred sarcastically.

"When is Miranda coming home? You need someone to take care of you," he remarked, tempering his vexation with feigned worry.

"She planned to be away for a week, but she could stay longer. I've been so irritable lately that I'm awful to be around. And you make it worse with your meanness. Once I feel better and get things settled with the business, I'll be fine."

"What about the business?" he pressed curiously.

"You don't mind handling it a while longer, do you? I'm just not ready to deal with it. I can't decide whether to sell it or run it." She sighed dramatically as if utterly fatigued.

"Don't worry your pretty head, my sweet. I'll take care of everything for you. Just concentrate on getting well, and on me," he added, cuffing her chin, then bid her farewell.

That night Amanda couldn't get to sleep. It was after midnight when she stood before her bedroom window looking out over the garden. Moonlight filtered through the gauzy drapes and outlined her body against them. But for stirrings and singing of nocturnal insects and birds, all was quiet and serene.

Suddenly a mellow voice teased from behind her, "How can you daydream at night, my love? A sick lady should be in bed."

She whirled, his name escaping her lips as she rushed into his beckoning arms and hugged him tightly. "It's about time you remembered I'm alive," she scolded Reis playfully. "Besides, I dream of you all the time. Where have you been? What's happening out there?"

"One question at a time, love. We've got to be more careful than I imagined. Richardson's having your house watched and he's having me and Luke followed. I had a time losing my shadow and sneaking in here. I found a minister not far away who can marry us, but getting to him in secret will be difficult. I sent Miranda a telegram; she should be coming home tomorrow. One thing that'll help distract Weber is a trip I need to take."

"A trip?" she wailed apprehensively. "Where? Why?"

"I have to follow the shipment that's leaving at dawn Wednesday. I'm staying hidden until then. Hopefully Weber will think I'm gone for good and lower his guard. When I get back, we'll see that minister first thing. You haven't changed your mind?" he asked.

"Never," she happily responded. "Do you have to leave?"

"It will speed up solving this case, and we both want that."

"But I'll be alone here, Reis. Luke is taking Randy with him," she said frantically.

"But you can refuse to see Weber for a long time after Randy finishes with him. Luke told me your little scheme. What could make a woman more angry than her suitor getting too friendly with her sister? If Luke's right about Weber, it'll work. Perfect timing is the key, love. Just don't make him think you're spurning him for keeps. I don't want him to think you're contriving an excuse to be rid of him. If Randy leaves with Luke, Weber will know she's out of his reach. He'll then work on regaining your trust and earning forgiveness. I've also come up with another scheme to confuse him. In your state of spiteful rage, you can pretend to sell your firm to someone else."

"Sell the firm?" she questioned, listening intently.

"I can have a friend of mine, a northern shipper, come down and pretend to purchase your company. You can claim you wanted to be rid of the company and its problems. Say you want to live on the plantation or in Washington. Once Weber thinks all's lost to him, he would be foolish to retaliate against you. He wouldn't be able to carry on any of his deceptions because you'll know the true facts. We'll have to wait to use this ploy until he leaves town and we can work out any tangles. The main thing is to protect the woman I love."

"Say it again," she coaxed warmly.

"I love you, Mandy. Soon you'll be mine forever," he vowed confidently, drawing her into the circle of his embrace.

Amanda's hands flattened against his hard chest, then traveled up his muscled shoulders. She snuggled close to him, wantonly rubbing her body against his without realizing how deeply she was arousing both of them. Her fingers pushed aside his shirt so she could place kisses near his heart, then drifted upward to tease at his collarbone. Her arms went around his waist and she pulled him tightly to her.

Reis was trapped in a heady conflict of wanting to remain perfectly still to enjoy this blissful torment and of needing to urgently lay siege to her body and make savagely sweet love to her. Her nearness, touch, and smell drove him wild, and her stimulating actions sent him beyond control. Yet, her movements revealed her inexperience. He flamed with passion just imagining how it would be months from now when her skills were honed and her modesty discarded.

He glanced down at her, eyes dark with desire. "If you have any intention of our honeymoon coming after our wedding, you'd best halt your tempting game, love. I feel like steel in a forging furnace."

Amanda bravely met his seeking gaze and smiled. "If you planned to deny me anything, then you shouldn't have come tonight when I'm weak from illness and cannot think clearly. Surely love is the best medicine for what ails me?" she hinted vividly.

She didn't protest when he removed her gown, or when he eased out of his garments. He lifted her and carried her to the bed. They stretched out, their naked bodies touching from head to foot. When she started to roll toward him, he gently caught her shoulder and pressed her to her back. Bending forward, he warmed the cool peaks on her chest with a moist and

169

fiery tongue.

His lips played upward until they fastened on hers. His kisses tantalized her, sending her soaring above a high mountain of passion. Her head spun madly as his hands danced over her flesh, embracing each breast and enticing each point to readiness. One hand started a titillating journey down her tingling body. It wandered over a flat stomach which tightened with anticipation, then roved over nicely rounded hips to end its thrilling trek in a tawny forest which pleaded for his intrusion. There, he explored gently and leisurely until she was trembling with urgent need.

Passions soared; hearts and bodies united. The sensations which he inspired were achingly blissful. He slipped between creamy thighs which entreated his invasion. With tenderness and caution, he eased into a moist paradise that was his for the taking. He wanted her so much that he feared his control would be lost if he didn't concentrate fiercely on retaining it.

They soared together, higher and higher, until Amanda reached ecstasy's summit. The moment Reis was certain of her rapture, he too surrendered to the all-consuming pleasure.

Rolling to his side, he held her in his arms. Curled against his lithe frame, she lay her cheek against his steadily slowing heart. He cast a possessive leg and arm over her contented body, then trailed his fingers up and down her back. Together they savored this dreamy time so devoid of thoughts or cares.

Amanda closed her eyes and inhaled softly. Reis

smiled into the darkness and briefly tightened his embrace. Whatever lay in their paths, they had each other and a powerful love. He felt so lucky to have found this special woman and to have won her heart. Amanda sighed again, thinking how glad she was that she had found love and passion with this extraordinary man.

Chapter Eight

Amanda was relaxing in a steamy bath Monday morning when her sister burst into the private closet in a flurry of surprise and delight. For the first time in her life, Amanda revealed modesty at being naked before her own sister. Miranda giggled in amusement when Amanda shrieked and tried to cover her ample bosom with delicate hands. Her shyness vanished quickly in the elation of Miranda's return. "You're home!" she declared happily.

"Whatever are you doing bathing so late, Amanda Lawrence? It's almost noon," she teased. "I could hardly wait to get here. You'll never believe what I've learned," she hinted eagerly. "Hurry and we'll talk. I'll make us some tea and a snack while you get dressed."

Amanda finally got a word between her sister's commands and queries. "I'm so glad you're back. Just wait until I tell you my news," she further piqued her sister's curiosity. "I'll be down shortly. Send Mrs. Reed on some errand so we can have total privacy," she hastily suggested. "On second thought, give the dear woman the day off."

Within an hour, Amanda and Miranda Lawrence were sitting side-by-side in the parlor, sipping tea and preparing to exchange facts. Miranda opened the conversation. "Tell me about you and Reis."

"First, there's something I must explain before I start on Reis, for I doubt I would stop any time soon," she mirthfully confessed, bringing a smile to Miranda's face. "Oh, my, where to begin?" she muttered.

"What's been going on here, Mandy?" Miranda interrupted. "That telegram from Reis was perplexing. He said I was to hurry home but to tell everyone I had been visiting friends in Boston. What did he mean: 'W. is dangerous. A. is mine now. L. is helping me. All being watched. Can't meet you at train. Be careful'?"

While Miranda listened with disbelief and horror, Amanda revealed all the events which had taken place. She explained how she had been cunningly deceived by Weber and why she had been acting so terrible lately. She told about Reis's mission for the President and his charges against Weber. Then Miranda told her sister what she had discovered at Morning Star. They discussed this perilous situation, analyzing and speculating about Weber's motives and actions.

"What about you and Reis?" Miranda pressed once more.

Unwilling to keep secrets from her sister, Amanda exposed Reis's kidnapping ploy and its results. Miranda was thrilled by their imminent wedding plans. Clearly they loved each other, and she vowed to do all she could to help and protect them and to thwart Weber's evil plots.

"Don't be so hasty to make such rash promises," Amanda teased her, then told Miranda of Lucas's daring idea to use jealousy between the sisters to inhibit Weber's amorous demands and to foil his wicked schemes.

As Miranda pondered the ruse, Amanda warned, "If Weber discovers we're working against him, he'll be dangerous, Randy."

"More so than he is now?" Miranda debated. "Nothing would please me more than to unmask that vile devil. I think it'll work," she stated smugly, then told her sister how and why . . .

"You're a genius, Randy," she declared, hugging her sister with love and appreciation.

"There's only one thing more, Mandy. Once I encourage Weber, we'll have to find a way to protect me from him," she ventured, half in jest and half in seriousness.

"That's simple," Amanda announced. "But I'd rather let Luke give you his surprise. He's coming over this afternoon. After you and I finish with Weber tonight, we'll both be free and safe," she alleged mysteriously, grinning at her sister.

"What does Luke have to do with this? What surprise?" she eagerly persisted.

Amanda smiled mischievously and refused to say more. "You think we can pull off this adventure?" she inquired softly.

"Positively, and it will be fun," Miranda concluded gleefully. "Now, let's get this stimulating charade planned."

Miranda went upstairs to unpack from her journey. When Amanda came to tell her Lucas had arrived, Miranda was standing before a long mirror, staring dreamily at her reflection. Amanda knew where her sister's thoughts were and smiled in resignation. Lucas was right; Miranda needed to follow her dream and to settle it.

Miranda was wearing a dress of their mother's, an exquisitely beaded buckskin dress which had been made from an albino deer. The dress had been given to Marie Lawrence by her father, Sun Cloud, chief of the Oglala Sioux in the Dakota Territory. The dress brought forth images of their mother as a young girl, a Sioux princess named Morning Star who had sacrificed everything to marry a handsome adventurer named Joseph Lawrence.

Miranda turned and looked at her teary-eyed sister. "She was very beautiful. How she must have loved Papa to marry him and move here. It must have pained her deeply to forsake her family and people to accept Papa's. She once told me she could never

176

return home because she had dishonored her people by choosing a white man. Can you imagine how hard it was to change from a carefree Indian maiden to a Southern lady? Papa taught her well, Mandy; no one would have guessed her heritage. She loved Papa and was happy with him. But many nights I found her in the garden staring at the moon, as if wondering about her family and all she'd lost. Perhaps she sensed danger closing in; perhaps that's why she wanted to go home one last time. Now it's too late. She's gone, and her family doesn't know. Do you suppose grandfather could sense her . . . death?"

"I don't know, Randy. In that dress with your hair braided, you look like she did the last time I saw her wearing it. Where did you find it? Why put it on and torment yourself?" she inquired sadly.

"It was at Morning Star. I went through many of their things, but I didn't move or discard an item. I was going to pack their belongings and store them in the attic, but something stopped me. It was the strangest feeling, Mandy, like they are still alive somewhere. When I found this dress and headband, I could almost hear Mama telling me to take them with me. She was whispering so softly that I couldn't make out where I should take them."

Amanda paled slightly and trembled. "After you talk with Luke, Randy, perhaps you'll understand Mama's message. Yes, it was meant to be," she told herself aloud.

Miranda gazed at her. "What are you talking

about, Mandy?"

"Let Luke explain. But I'll agree with your decision."

"What decision? Explain what?" Miranda questioned, baffled.

"A quest for your destiny, dear sister. You must find yours as I've found mine with Reis. Come and listen to Luke," she coaxed, taking Miranda's hand and pulling her downstairs.

When they entered the sitting room, Lucas jumped to his feet and gaped at Miranda. "My God, Randy, you look just like Aunt Marie!" he cried in astonishment. "I knew you favored her, but not this much. Did you tell her, Mandy?"

"No, it's your surprise and her choice. I'll leave you two alone," she stated, closing the door behind her.

It had never been more apparent to Lucas that Amanda had taken after her father in looks and personality, while Miranda was the image of Marie. Marie had gone so far as to teach Miranda the Sioux language and history and customs, inspiring in her daughter a hunger to experience and witness that vanishing way of life. Now, Lucas was in a position to grant his cousin her lifelong fantasy.

"I'm leaving Alexandria Friday, Randy, leaving Virginia and the South," he began slowly, bringing a look of shock to Miranda's face and a staggering jolt to her senses. "I've been given an irresistible assignment, to write an historical account of the exploits of three men: Custer, Sherman, and Sheridan. The publisher is paying my expenses and a salary of ten thousand dollars. I've accepted the deal."

"You're writing the story of three Yankee destroyers? Why?"

"Because I want the truth published for once, for all time," he declared earnestly, witnessing her distress which would be shortlived.

"But where are you going? What about me and Mandy?"

"All three men are on duty in the same western area, the Dakota Territory. Would you come along as my assistant?" He dropped his news without warning. "I've discussed this with Mandy. She was reluctant at first; now she thinks it's a good idea. She knows what it would mean to you, and this is the perfect opportunity—in many ways," he added, winking at her. "After your charade with Weber, it will get you out of his path with a logical excuse. You and Mandy can have a big quarrel and you can leave home. It should take about three months; then we'll come home to find Weber arrested."

Miranda stood up and paced the room as this information was digested. "But what about Mandy, Luke? We can't leave her alone here with that demon," she fretted nervously. "Reis is leaving too."

"Reis won't be gone but a week or ten days. By the time we leave, she'll have plenty of excuses to refuse his attentions, to play the injured female, to stall for time until Reis can arrest him. In fact, it will be easier for her to fool Web if you're gone. So what do you say?'' he asked.

"You aren't teasing me?" she probed before accepting. He shook his head, smiling at her. "When do we leave?"

"Friday, so get packed and ready. I'll get Mandy so we can tell her our plans." When Lucas left the room, Miranda danced around the furniture, humming and dreaming until they returned to join her.

Miranda and Amanda talked and planned far into the night. After two months of anguish, their lives were changing drastically and happily. Knowing that Reis was aware of Miranda's return, Amanda knew he would not make a nocturnal call on her tonight. Not since they were twelve had the twins curled up in the same bed and chatted the night away until slumber captured them.

To aid their plans, the twins told Alice Reed she could be off until Friday. They told her to rest, to work at her home, and to spend time with her husband. The older woman was appreciative of their generosity, but the girls had always been kind and sweet to her. Mrs. Thomas Reed left their home praying that the bright Miranda could talk some sense into her confused sister, for she felt Amanda had to be foolish to marry that rake, Weber Richardson. Many times lately Alice had bitten her tongue to keep it from running loose to her young mistress. If only Amanda learned a few of the ear-curling tales about that cruel and malicious man, she would flee in terror!

At four o'clock, Lucas delivered a huge crate to the

back door and told Miranda to answer the front door and seat the man standing there in the parlor. Miranda did as he instructed, studying the suit-clad gentleman inquisitively. He smiled warmly but didn't state his business. Miranda left him to question Lucas's weird behavior.

Lucas was forcing open the crate when she returned to his side. He chuckled as he told her to inform Miss Amanda Lawrence that the minister and her sweetheart were here and preparing for their marriage! Speechless, Miranda watched as Reis Harrison stepped from the crate and dusted off his clothes. "Fetch the bride, cousin," Luke commanded, filling the room with hearty laughter.

Miranda raced upstairs. "Mandy, you're not going to believe this, but you're getting married in a few minutes. Reis, Luke, and the minister are waiting for you downstairs."

"What—what did you say?" she stammered.

Miranda laughingly revealed the crafty preparations going on downstairs. "Well? Do you want to become Mrs. Reis Harrison today?"

"But I don't have a wedding gown! Look at me," she panted. "I'm a mess. I can't get married like this. What will people say?"

"Nothing, dear sister; it's a secret ceremony, remember? How about that azure-blue satin gown? I'll get it while you undress."

"How do I look?" Amanda inquired nervously when she was finished dressing. Miranda laid aside the hairbrush and hugged her tightly.

When they entered the parlor together, Reis's blue eyes were for Amanda alone. A look of pride and love flamed upon his handsome face, bringing a flush of passion and pleasure to his cheeks. He looked so elegant in his tailored, wine-colored garments. Amanda's heart fluttered wildly as she stared at him. Never had he looked more handsome.

Her gown rustled softly as she walked into his embrace. "I take it your answer is yes?" he teased her.

"You might have given me some warning, Mister Harrison. I didn't think this ceremony would be such a deep, dark secret," she replied merrily.

"It is," he casually responded. "During the night, the groom can sneak out and none will be the wiser. As for the Reverend Simons here, he knows of our dilemma and will protect our secrets. He is also a doctor and you're supposedly ill; so he has kindly visited his patient today. I'm afraid I couldn't leave on that trip until you were mine, love," he confessed roguishly. "Well?"

"What are we waiting for, my love?" she teased.

With Miranda beside her sister and Lucas beside Reis as witnesses, Reis Harrison and Amanda Lawrence became husband and wife within ten minutes on a lovely Tuesday in mid-May of 1873. The documents were signed and given to Amanda for safekeeping. After Simons's departure, a celebration began.

Lucas teased the couple, "I would take Randy out for the evening, but that would look strange to our observer. After all, if Amanda's sick in bed, she shouldn't be left alone.''

Miranda giggled as she watched her sister blush from hairline to the bodice of her gown. Although Amanda hadn't confessed the prior intimacy between her and her love, Miranda sensed it was there. But Lucas was right. She couldn't leave the house this evening.

The four drank champagne which Lucas had thoughtfully furnished for this joyous occasion. Miranda said, ''I'm afraid the best Luke and I can do for you two is for him to leave and for me to get lost in my room. You can have dinner and . . . talk privately. I do have to pack.''

Neither Amanda nor Reis protested Miranda's suggestion. Lucas congratulated them again, shaking Reis's hand and hugging Amanda. He told Miranda he would come by tomorrow afternoon to finalize their departure plans. Just before opening the door, an outside sound halted his action. He cautiously peered through a slit in the curtains near the doorway. He stiffened as he watched Weber get out of his carriage and unlatch the gate to head up the long walkway.

He rushed into the parlor and warned Reis and Amanda to flee to her bedroom. Lucas and Miranda quickly concealed the evidence of their party, then she rushed to her own room. Lucas abruptly opened the door just as Weber raised his hand to knock, startling him.

"What the hell!" he shouted, glaring at Lucas.

"What are you doing here?" Lucas asked in vivid annoyance.

"Get out of my way, Reardon. I'm here to see my fiancée," he boldly announced, ready to brush past Lucas.

"Hold on, Richardson. The doctor just left. Amanda's in bed. You can't disturb her today," he informed the surly man, amusing himself by telling the truth in such a beguiling manner.

The man whom his spy, Jim, had reported seeing entering and leaving was a doctor? "How is she feeling?" Weber asked, pretending to calm down at the distressing news.

"How do you think since the doctor had to visit?" Lucas scoffed, implying she was very ill.

"Where's Miranda?" Weber inquired, eager to take advantage of Amanda's indisposition to have a pleasant reunion with her sister.

"She's upstairs. Where else would she be?" he sneered sarcastically. "I was just leaving. This isn't a place for visitors today."

"If you don't mind, I'd like Amanda to know I came by," Weber snapped at the infuriating man who was provoking him.

"Wait here," Lucas ordered tersely then went to the base of the steps and called out for Miranda. When she leaned over the railing and responded, he passed along Weber's message, then told her good-by. At the door, he insisted that Weber leave with him.

Convinced of Amanda's illness, Weber left hurriedly. He chided himself for being so skeptical of Amanda, since she really wasn't smart enough to deceive him. But he had feared the stranger was a messenger from that devious and calculating Reis Harrison. At least his foe hadn't made any attempt to get to Amanda! And Lucas was leaving this week.

As Weber drove away in his carriage, he congratulated himself for his cunning and wits. He admitted that Lucas was a good writer, perfect to do the exposé on his despised enemies, the exposé he was supporting financially. But it was a stroke of genius to use that mutual dream to be rid of him! Weber wasn't sure if he was mistaken about Reis's purpose for being in Alexandria, but it wouldn't matter soon. He had picked up hints around the docks that Harrison was leaving town this very day. Weber conceitedly believed that nobody was as smart as he was, for he had covered his tracks skillfully. Before anyone was the wiser, Amanda and her properties would be in his control.

Amanda Lawrence, he sneered to himself, was one bag of trouble, perhaps more than she was worth. But Amanda had things he wanted, needed. It would be a pleasure to conquer that haughty bitch. She would pay for stalling him for two months. He would take and use everything she possessed, including her delicious body. Whe he tired of her, he would arrange a neat accident. Then perhaps he would have a taste of sweet Miranda . . . Miranda . . . yes, she would be vulnerable and pliable with Amanda and Lucas out of the way. She was mysterious and exotic, but so wary and timid. Doubtlessly she possessed more fiery passion in one finger than the arrogant Amanda had in her entire body! The idea of dining greedily on Amanda's treats, then feasting ravenously on Miranda's was wildly intoxicating. It was too bad he couldn't have both at once! Both were beautiful and different. How wickedly erotic to savor two ravishing women. Weber had no way of knowing that the wily twins would use his wanton lust against him . . .

That night, Miranda awakened several times to the sound of soft laughter from her sister's room. How she longed to find a love such as her lucky sister had discovered. But Amanda and Reis's relationship was special, more than physical. The looks which had passed between them almost made her envious. How sad to never experience such wonderful and wild feelings. No one deserved such happiness more than Amanda.

Each time Amanda couldn't suppress her joyful laughter, Reis would cover her lips with his to muffle it, then mischievously seek another sensitive or ticklish spot. Their first union had been swift and savage, their passions starving to be fed. Later, they had made love slowly and tenderly, savoring each touch and movement. But, inevitably, the new day signaled its approach.

"I'll return as quickly as I can, my love," Reis promised between kisses and playful fondles.

"Just be careful, Reis," she urged anxiously.

"You, too," he murmured in her ear before initiating one last joining of their bodies and spirits.

At the back door, Amanda hugged him a final time and vowed, "I do love you something fierce, Mister Harrison, you sly Yankee. If you don't come back safe and sound, you'll answer to me."

Reis trapped her slender and shapely frame next to his hard and smooth body. "If I don't find you safe and sound upon my return home, Mrs. Harrison, you shall do more than answer to me. I love you, woman."

With a parting kiss, they released each other. Reis grinned and winked, then slipped into the gloomy, predawn light. Amanda sighed heavily then returned to her room to sleep until nine.

All morning the twins anticipated and plotted Weber's downfall. According to Weber's habits, they felt he would appear in the afternoon or early evening. Just in case Weber varied his schedule, the girls had an alternative plan.

While they ate a midday snack, Amanda and her sister talked about Reis. Neither mentioned that Reis had slipped out before dawn to catch a ship which was leaving with the morning tide carrying cargo which should unravel Web's evil operation. Nor did the twins discuss Miranda's and Lucas's impending trek west. But both were very much aware of the fleeting time before Friday morning. They had decided to pack Miranda's clothes and possessions for the summer-long journey on Thursday. Lucas came over around three to play his part in their reckless scheme.

If any male besides Lucas had been present, Miranda would have been crimson-faced with embarrassment at the sensual kimono she was wearing. Her courage would be greatly tested when it was Weber standing in this room alone with her! But these trying times called for daring measures. The silky garment in sultry red had two daring slits—one from throat to waist and one from hem to thigh—and provocatively enhanced Miranda's exotic aura. The appealing garment had been sent to Joe Lawrence from Japan by a mischievous friend who was a retired sea captain as a gift for his wife.

Suddenly at four, Lucas warned, "Get ready, cousins; he just arrived. Good luck!" he stated quickly before rushing out, leaving the door ajar as planned. Halfway down the walkway, he halted Weber to exchange taunts and to allow the girls time to settle their nerves.

When Weber approached the front door, he didn't knock when he found it unlocked. He grinned as he decided to surprise either or both girls; he could always say Lucas let him inside before leaving. He eased the door open, sneaked inside, and cautiously closed it. Hearing muffled voices from the sitting room, he furtively made his way to the half-opened door, flattening himself against the wall to listen.

Miranda had been spying on Weber's movements from the narrow slit between the door hinges. As he made his stealthy way toward the parlor, Miranda signaled her sister to begin their charade, one in which she would speak only the truth. She had to be convincing, or else Weber could come after her!

"Tell me the truth, Randy! That's why you ran off to Boston, isn't it! Did you want to hide and sulk or make some plan to get your way? My own sister . . . How could you be so cruel and wicked?" Amanda shrieked at her, wringing her hands as if nervous. "And at a time like this when I'm at death's door," she added pathetically.

"Stop this foolishness, Mandy. I told you I went to see friends and to give you some privacy to think. I'm sorry if you're ill, but you mustn't be so irritable. Whatever's wrong with you lately?"

"You're saying it's only my imagination?" Amanda sneered sarcastically. "I'm neither blind nor a fool, dear sister. I've seen how you watch him— actually drool over him. Always asking questions about my Web, pretending you don't like him. You ran off because I told you I was going to accept his proposal soon. You want to break us apart, don't you? Look me in the eye, Miranda Lawrence, and swear you aren't hanging around like some vulture waiting for Weber's love for me to die!"

"You shouldn't accuse me of such awful things, Mandy. When have I ever flirted with Web or tried to cause trouble between you two? You shouldn't be marrying him if you don't trust him; and if you do trust him, you wouldn't be insinuating I could win him from you."

"How crafty you are, dear sister. I don't hear you denying my charges, only covering your guilt with wily questions. Weber loves me. He wouldn't even look at another woman if she didn't try to wantonly bewitch him. As soon as I'm looking and feeling better, I shall make plans for us to become affianced," she curtly announced.

"I shan't stay in Alexandria after your wedding. I shall go live at Morning Star," Miranda declared soberly.

Weber almost missed part of the devious conversation as visions of having Amanda here in the townhouse and Miranda there on the plantation filled his head. Soon everything would be in his control, and possibly both women. Now he knew why Miranda was so remote and quiet around him; she was resisting her cravings for him! So, the dark beauty with her tightly controlled wildness burned with desire for him . . .

"That sounds like an excellent idea. Then I won't have to worry about you chasing and tempting Weber after we're married," she panted.

"Mandy, please don't say such things. I meant I would leave you two alone for privacy. You're being irrational. I am not trying to steal Weber from you. It's probably the illness talking. Perhaps I should ask the doctor to come over again."

"I don't need to see the doctor again. I'm just tired. I'm going upstairs and take his vile drug. I don't want to be disturbed; the medicine makes me sleep for hours. If Weber comes over before I'm awake, you had best remember he's mine," Amanda warned frostily.

"Don't you want some soup first? I'll get it for you. I gave Mrs. Reed some time off this week." Her back to the door, Miranda winked at her sister.

"I'll eat later, if I'm hungry. I can't remember if Web told me he was or wasn't coming over tonight at eight. That medicine is playing havoc with my memory," she mumbled absently. "Wake me at seven so I can dress before he arrives."

"I'll see you to your room, Mandy; you're drowsy now. I promise to wake you if Weber comes over," she told her sister.

"I'm not a baby; I can make it," Amanda responded.

Miranda stood in the doorway, watching her sister ascend the stairs and vanish from sight. She returned to the parlor and sipped a French brandy as though she needed it to calm her nerves. Miranda withdrew a flower from a nearby vase and smelled its sweet fragrance, whispering, "If only you knew the truth, Mandy . . ."

From behind her, Weber murmured huskily, "And what is the truth, my beautiful Miranda?"

She whirled and gasped in partially feigned surprise. "Weber? Where did you come from? I didn't hear you knock." Miranda observed the way Weber's dark eyes engulfed her body, especially the bare area on her throat and between her breasts. She tried to calm her anxiety as his respiration increased in speed and volume. If lust could become a tangible object, his would encase her thickly at that moment.

He licked his suddenly dry lips and struggled to

conceal her staggering effect on him. His mind was wildly intoxicated by the misconception that she fiercely wanted him as he craved her. "Someone left the door open. You should be more careful, Randy. An intruder could lose his head over a matchless beauty like you."

Miranda flushed a deep red. Weber thought it was from shyness or guilt, but it was from anger. He hadn't even asked about Amanda or her health! While his love lay ill above them, he was trying to beguile her sister! The lecherous rake! Her fury inspired strength and resolve.

"I'm glad to find you home today. I've been wanting to speak to you alone. Isn't it about time we became friends, Randy?" he asked, pulling the flower from her grasp and teasing her bare flesh with it. He watched the astonishment in her eyes as he trailed the flower up her throat and across her lips. "Such pleasures shouldn't belong to a mere flower," he remarked, leaning forward to kiss her.

Miranda tried to twist away, but Weber dropped the flower to embrace her tightly. His lips forced hers apart. When his mouth left hers to wander down her neck, she scolded him, "Weber Richardson! Behave yourself. You're Mandy's beau. She'll be furious if she learns of this."

Weber leaned backward and gazed at her. "You don't care what Mandy thinks. You want me as much as I want you," he boasted. "Perhaps I've asked the wrong twin to marry me. What do you think?"

Not having expected Weber to work so hastily or

boldly, Miranda was stunned. Weber pressed her against the wall, molding his enflamed body against her rigid one. As his mouth covered hers, he ground his hips against her. He moved his chest over hers, almost dislodging the kimono from her shoulders. Miranda didn't respond to Weber, but neither did she urgently battle him as she awaited Amanda's interruption.

When Weber's hands drifted to her bosom, Miranda couldn't wait for Amanda to burst in on them. She shoved his brazen hands from her body and tried to push him away. "You stop this, Weber!" she ordered him brusquely. "How dare you insult me!" Miranda didn't want to scream for help, as that would bring about a drastic change in plans. If he were completely alienated, both girls could become dispensable. She prayed her sister would enter soon.

Weber's gaze was dark with combined passion and anger. He was too enflamed to stop now. After he had possessed her fully, Miranda wouldn't say anything to Luke or Amanda. He wasn't about to let her deny him—now or ever again! Amanda had supplied him with the perfect explanation. She was actually jealous of her sister, mistrusted her, had accused her of chasing him. If Miranda revealed what was about to take place, he would have no trouble convincing Amanda she was lying out of jealousy. He could even tell Amanda that her sister had tried to seduce him while she lay ill upstairs. But it shouldn't be necessary to travel that sacrificial path. He could easily blackmail Miranda into compliance, or sensually enslave her with his magical lips and hands. Once he gave her such exquisite pleasures tonight, she would eagerly be shoving Amanda out of her way; then, he could make Amanda's absence permanent . . . Surely gentle Miranda would be easier to master? Surely exotic Miranda would be more enjoyable in bed? Amanda was a proud and stubborn know-it-all; but Miranda was a thirsty, repressed spirit who wanted to break free, to run wild, to taste life.

Weber seized her around the waist and had her pinned beneath him on the sofa before she could think clearly. His mouth was searing hers, preventing any protests. Miranda was terrified. She couldn't control him! Where was Amanda? What about the timely rescue? It wasn't supposed to go this far! Something was wrong! Something was keeping her away! Surely Amanda wouldn't fail her . . .

Chapter Nine

With a burst of strength borne of fear and desperation, Miranda arched upward and flung Weber to the carpeted floor. She bounded off the sofa and scurried behind it. "If you touch me again, Weber Richardson, I'll scream," she warned him icily. "This isn't any way to behave with your future sister-in-law!"

Weber refused to recognize the fury in her voice. He chuckled and teased, "Come on, Randy, don't play around. We both know you want me," he smugly declared, a lewd grin curling his lips into a devilish sneer.

Miranda saw the peril she was in and the evil which filled this man. Suddenly, she was afraid for both herself and her sister. "You're wrong, Weber. I did want to be friends, for Mandy's sake, but not any more. If you truly loved my sister, you wouldn't be trying to seduce me right beneath her nose. If you don't get out and leave me alone, I'll tell Mandy what you tried to do tonight."

Weber crossed his legs and remained sitting on the floor. He laughed mirthfully, intimidatingly, vengefully—the sound chilled her soul. "She wouldn't believe you," he alleged confidently. "Come here, woman."

"No," she refused flatly. "Leave now, and we'll forget this ever happened."

Weber slowly and purposefully got to his feet. He began to stalk her around the sofa, but Miranda eluded him. "Give it up, Randy; you can't get away. From tonight on, you'll belong to me."

Miranda shook her head, chestnut locks flowing about her shoulders. Her tawny eyes were shaded with rising hatred. Her expression was lined with contempt. Yet Weber saw none of it—he was blinded by lust. He bounded over the sofa and captured her in his arms, her back to his chest. Miranda twisted and fought, but Weber's grip tightened. She stomped his booted foot and elbowed his ribs.

She panted, "Let go of me, you brute!" She jerked her head forward to throw it backward with force into his nose and chin.

Anticipating her impending action, he moved his face aside as her head landed against his shoulder. Before she could lift it, her left ear was imprisoned between his teeth and he gritted out this ominous threat: "Move, and I'll rip it off. No woman teases me like you did. Hold still while I see what you have to offer. You owe me, Randy."

Tears of panic and pain sprung to her eyes as she remained motionless, ready to savagely attack him the instant he released her ear. Before his hands could cover her breasts, the door opened and Amanda walked inside. She came to an abrupt stop and glared at them, shock and fury flooding her features. "I heard Weber's voice, so I dressed to come down. What's going on here?" she demanded.

Weber released Miranda and laughed merrily as he went to her sister. Miranda turned hastily to straighten her clothes and hair. "Randy and I were just having some fun, tussling and playing like two kids. I haven't had so much fun in years. Sorry if we disturbed you, my sweet. We're going to be good friends, a happy family, just like you want. How are you feeling? Randy said the doctor came by, but you weren't doing too well. She said you were napping, so I told her not to bother you," he chatted lightly.

Amanda's frosty eyes went from the grinning Weber to the rigid and silent Miranda who was refusing to turn and look at her. Her skeptical gaze wandered over Miranda's disheveled state and then over Weber's mussed hair and clothes. Her eyes focused briefly on Weber's flushed cheeks and still-cloudy gaze. She noted the misplaced cushions, a rumpled throw rug, and the discarded flower. "Something tells me I should be glad I didn't take that medicine and go to bed," she announced sarcastically. "I asked what's going on in here?" she repeated suspiciously, knocking Weber's hand away from her arm.

"I told you, my sweet, we were teasing around," Weber replied.

"It didn't look or sound that way to me," Amanda refuted hotly.

"Don't be silly. You're just tired and feeling poorly. You go back to bed and I'll come by to see you tomorrow," he cajoled.

"Miranda, what's wrong with you?" Amanda persisted.

"I— Nothing, Mandy. Weber and I were just . . . horsing around. Trying to make friends like you asked," she responded, edging noticeable tension and hesitation into her words.

"Dressed like that?" Amanda scoffed.

"Weber came over right after you went upstairs. I'll go change," she murmured contritely.

"Then why didn't you fetch me instead of entertaining him in that cheap attire? As for you, Weber Richardson, you and Randy are too old to be 'teasing' around," she scolded them both in a scathing tone.

"Don't be such a stick-in-the-mud," he retorted in annoyance. How dare she reprimand him like a child!

His reference to mud reminded her of Reis. She eyed Weber intently. He could actually stand here playing the innocent after trying to attack Randy only moments ago! He was worse than she had imagined! "I suppose you two think I'm gullible. I've seen enough passion to recognize its after-effects. Look at you two. Eyes glazed. Mouths red and puffy.

Clothes and hair mussed. You both have guilt stamped all over you! How could you do this to me? Especially you, dear sister! Tell me, were you going to make love right here on the floor like rutting animals? Or perhaps sneak up to Randy's room?"

"Amanda!" her sister shrieked in distress. "It isn't like that!"

"She's right, Mandy," Weber injected hastily.

"Be quiet, Weber! How long have you two been scheming behind my back?"

"Don't be ridiculous!" Weber snarled. "Randy and I have never been intimate. I suggest you get off that mind-weakening drug!"

Amanda let her tears flow freely. Weber glanced at Miranda and motioned for her to keep silent. "Randy, why don't you leave us alone so I can explain to Amanda," he suggested softly.

"But . . . ," she started to protest.

Weber had pushed Amanda to the sofa. He caught Miranda's arm and led her to the door, saying, "I'll get her settled down." He winked at Miranda, then grinned conspiratorially. "I'll see you later," he promised, licking his lips and winking at her.

Miranda looked over his shoulder at the superb actress on the sofa. She nodded and left, eager to learn how Weber would extricate himself. She poured a sherry to calm her distraught nerves, then concealed herself behind the archway into the dining room to make certain Weber left after his devious talk with Amanda.

Miranda didn't have to wait long. Soon, the double

doors opened and Weber headed for the front exit. After opening it, he cast a longing glance at the stairway before disappearing outside. Miranda rushed to the door and bolted it. She hurried to the parlor.

Amanda looked up and grinned. "Did you lock up?" she asked.

Miranda nodded and sat down. "Well? What did he say? What took you so long to come down? He was about to rip off my clothes! He's more dangerous than we imagined, Mandy. I was terrified."

"I'm sorry, sis. I didn't think he would pounce on you so fast! I thought you two would talk, get cozy, then he would make his play for you. After I was dressed and came down, I couldn't believe what I was hearing. I had a time controlling my temper! I wanted to tear him apart! But it would spoil things. Our plan's in motion and we know what he's really like. Heavens, Randy, I'm glad you're leaving," she blurted out in panic. "His kind of lust is scary. Are you all right?" she inquired worriedly.

"Fine now, but I was petrified," she confessed then revealed what had been between them. "Maybe we got him too worked up; he was all over me before I could think. What did he tell you?"

Amanda laughed. "He tried to cajole me and prove I was deluding myself. He wanted me to feel remorse for my suspicions. He told me how much my mistrust pained him. He wanted to convince me I was acting out of jealousy. He even scolded me for embarrassing you two. He said I should be ashamed of myself for being so ugly to you. What enormous gall and ego!"

"He just implied you were mistaken? He didn't try to insinuate I had tempted him?" Miranda asked in surprise.

"I have a feeling he'll use that ploy when he sees I didn't fall for his charm and lies. The moment you're gone, he'll fall at my feet and beg forgiveness. He'll blame you for everything. If it weren't so grave, it would be hilarious. You know what truly alarms me? If this weren't a ruse, he could take advantage of both of us," she speculated.

Miranda hugged her sister affectionately. "No, Mandy, you would never believe me capable of such betrayal. But you're right; I can't imagine trying to explain tonight if it truly took place. It's so incredible; he would have ravished me right here!"

"Make sure you avoid him until you leave," she warned.

"What about you, Mandy? Luke and I will be gone in less than two days. And Reis won't be back until the end of next week. I'm afraid for you. Weber's so strong and persistent when he's aroused. What if he tries to . . . seduce you?" Miranda fretted anxiously.

"I can handle Web's passions. It's you I'm worried about. He finds you more desirable than we realized. He might go after you and Luke. He could hurt Luke to force you to come home! I feel so duped. It's you he wants, not me. He only settled for me because he couldn't get to you. I could kill him!"

"Don't say such things, Mandy. It isn't me or you

he wants; it's all we own. He just wants to enjoy us while he's stealing everything we have. I'm not sure if he's crazy or just greedy and desperate. Maybe I should stay here and help you stop him."

"No, you must go with Luke. We'd both be in peril if you remained here. If Weber believes he could have you and put me out of the way . . ." She faltered at that staggering reality and shuddered. She prayed Reis would return soon. This drama wasn't so simple; it was petrifying. She instantly berated her cowardice, reminding herself she was smart enough to outwit and foil Weber.

"Then I'll persuade him I despise him before I leave. He'll be convinced you're his only hope for success," Miranda vowed with fierce determination. "I know!" she shrieked in elation. "I'll catch the train tomorrow above Alexandria. Luke can leave from here Friday, then join me in Baltimore. That's where we take the train to St. Louis. You can tell everyone I left for Charleston for the summer. That should throw him off our path. Even if he searches for me, he'll come up empty-handed, except for you."

"That should work," Amanda concurred. "If he goes after you, that will supply me with another excuse to rebuff him. He won't risk hurting me until he's positive he can have you. I'll ask Mrs. Reed to stay over the weekend. Then, next week, I just won't open the door unless she's here to protect me."

"Perfect. When Reis gets back, you drop this game. If you can't announce your marriage, then go to his home like he suggested. Or go visit friends where you'll be safe. You can always tell Weber that I exposed his attempted assault. Or, better still, that I confessed to his forcing me to carry on a secret affair. I was so humiliated by your discovery of our torrid rendezvous that I ran away," she jested. "That should give him plenty to fret over! I can see it now; ailing Amanda trying to decide who's honest and what's the truth."

They joined in nervous laughter. "I think I'll wait to see how he reacts to your absence. He might just ignore tonight. Naturally I won't let him. I shall play the offended, betrayed maiden," she stated in a thick Southern drawl. "I shall waver back and forth, tormented by doubts, harassed by suspicions."

"Just promise me you'll be careful," Miranda entreated.

"We shall both be wary and alert," Amanda concluded.

When Lucas came over the following morning, he found the girls packing frantically. They quickly related the events of the night before. Lucas was furious; he wanted to beat Weber senseless. The twins had a difficult time pacifying him, telling him to be satisfied that his contempt and hatred had been justified. They had to be content with the knowledge Weber would eventually get his due.

They went over their new scheme to get Miranda away before Weber realized she was gone. "We need you to find some way to lure that guard from his post for an hour," Amanda said. "I can take Randy and her luggage to the station outside town. When you catch the train to Baltimore tomorrow, everyone will see you leave alone. After disguising myself as Miranda, I can purchase a ticket to Charleston, board the train, then sneak off and come home."

"That sounds very clever," he complimented them. "Now, all we have to do is pull it off. Let's see . . ." He lapsed into deep thought, then grinned as an idea came to mind. "I can disguise myself as a widow, sneak up on the guard, club and rob him, and escape. Old Weber won't think we had anything to do with the daring robbery of a spy we didn't know existed. While the devil is out cold, you two can sneak out with my help. Considering the train schedule, we have to be ready to act at two. Think we can make it?"

Amanda continued to pack Miranda's possessions while her sister took a carriage to the bank just before noon. It was Weber's custom to eat lunch at noon in the Telford Inn, near the bank. After withdrawing money for her trip, Miranda lingered near the doorway until she saw Weber round the corner to head her way. She gritted her teeth, inhaled and exhaled slowly, then stepped outside into the bright sunlight.

Weber saw her immediately and hurried to intercept her. "And whom do we have here? Are you alone?" he inquired, glancing around to see for himself. "Join me for lunch, Randy; we need to talk about last night. What did Mandy say after I left?"

Miranda jerked her arm free of his light grasp. She glared at him. "Touch me again, Mister Richardson, and I'll cut off your hand. I loathe you. How my sister has stomached you this long, I'll never know. I've tried to avoid you; I've tried to endure you. Then, I even tried to make a truce with you. You sicken me with your lewd mind and repulsive groping. As far as I'm concerned, last night was only a nightmare, and I'm fully awake now. You stay away from me."

Weber actually looked stunned by her harsh tone and cutting words. "What game is this?" he asked skeptically. "I know when a woman entices me, and you did last night. If you're worried about upsetting Mandy, I'll handle her gently. I can make her happy to spurn me. If I frightened you with my overwhelming desire, I'm sorry. I lost my head when I realized you felt the same way about me. It won't happen again, love. Just let me prove it's you I want to marry."

"You're insane, Weber. You're the last man alive I would love or marry. I have never found you desirable, and I despise you. If I hadn't been worried about my sister's health and happiness last night, I would have clawed out your eyes. But you needn't fret over my tattling to Mandy; she'll eventually see you for what you are. I must have been a fool to think we could become friends."

"You didn't act like a friend last night. Not the way you were responding to me," he sullenly protested.

"Think again, Weber. I tried to get away from you, remember? You trapped me against the wall, then chased me around, then pinned me to the sofa. I was not yielding; I was battling you. What is a helpless woman's strength compared to a violent man's? I would have reacted immediately if I hadn't been so shocked by your words and conduct. Remove your egotistic blinders and take another look at what truly happened between us."

"If you have no romantic feelings for me, then why does Mandy think you do? Why do I believe you do?" he debated wickedly.

"Perhaps she's hoping someone will come along to take you away from her. She's been confused lately, perhaps realizing her true feelings for you. There are plenty of rumors about you and women. Also, she's on a medication which clouds her reason. She doesn't honestly think I would pursue you, and I wouldn't. Bother me again, and I'll tell all."

"It won't matter. After I finish telling my side, she'll trust me, not you. She isn't as bright as you, Randy. She's vain and foolish. Of course you won't repeat that because you're too sensitive to hurt her feelings. You're a prize, Randy, one I intend to have," he boldly stated.

"You're a fool, Weber! There's no way you can have me," she declared angrily.

"I wouldn't be too confident, love. By next week, you'll be coming to me and begging me to forgive your nasty rejection. In fact, I'm willing to bet you'll become Mrs. Weber Richardson by May 30."

Miranda stared at him. He looked utterly serious. "Just how do you plan to blackmail me into such a position? What about Mandy?" she probed as if intrigued.

"When a huge debt is made and owed, Randy, someone has to repay it. I've simply decided I want you to clear the ledger, not her. As for Miss Amanda, she'll be taken care of; you needn't worry."

"What kind of debt could I possibly owe you?" she inquired.

"You'll see" was all he would say. He grinned satanically.

Weber didn't realize that Miranda knew exactly to what he was referring with his threats. She had thought he might fall for their ploy, but not this quickly. "What would people say if you suddenly dropped Mandy to marry me? What about the gossip, the scandal?"

Weber laughed in amusement. "Since you vowed you'd never marry me, why speculate?" he teased her.

"You just said I wouldn't have any choice. Why not?" she pressed.

"For one reason, you love your sister and you wouldn't want to see her troubled in any way. I have the feeling you would do anything to make her happy," he hinted between chuckles.

"Why should I be responsible for her happiness? I have my own life to consider. Since you're her sweetheart, how will she be happy if you marry another woman, especially her own sister?"

"Oh, she might rant and rave for a while because of bruised pride, but she'll come around to our way of thinking. We both know Amanda isn't in love with me; I doubt she could love anyone besides herself. I'm just the best suitor she's ever had. Since she has to marry, it might as well be to the superior choice. I was marrying her for the same reasons. But I'd rather have you. And I will," he vowed nonchalantly. "You're a beautiful, sensual creature, Randy. And you don't have any other suitors."

"Only because I don't want any at present. And you're wrong about Mandy; she has plenty of love to give, to the right man. You don't bring out her best qualities. Marriage isn't a business deal, Weber."

"Sometimes, it's the most important deal a man can make. Think it over, Randy. Don't be too hasty to spurn me."

When Weber turned to leave, Miranda called his name. He halted and turned. "Weber, why do you really want to marry me, knowing how I feel about you?"

He came to stop within inches of her. For her ears alone, he murmured, "In spite of what you think, Randy, I love you. And despite how it will anger you, I will force you to marry me. In time you'll forgive me for doing so. I won't frighten you or hurt you again. Once we're wed, I'm looking forward to finishing what we started last night. I will be the man to unleash those passions I sensed in you last night. I want you as I've never wanted any other woman. I can make you happy, Randy; I can make you feel emotions and sensations you never dreamed existed. No matter how much you try to deny it, you want me. Go home and consider my words. I want an answer Sunday afternoon. When I come over, I'll explain everything to you and Amanda. Both of you will agree to my demands, or, shall we say, my wishes."

He left her standing there staring after him. Alarm

raced through her as she decided he was insane, cunningly insane. He was convinced she secretly wanted him. He even believed he felt the same way! That was the most terrifying realization of all. If she had any doubts about leaving town, they were gone now.

Miranda hurried home, anxious to get away from that lust-crazed madman. But the more she saw and learned about him, the more fear she had for her sister's safety.

At home, Miranda told her sister about the shocking meeting with Weber. Amanda's fury rose by the minute. "That despicable vermin! Just wait until I—"

Miranda grabbed her by the arms and shook her. "Listen to me, Mandy!" she shrieked in panic. "Don't you say or do anything to antagonize him until Reis gets back. If you push Weber into a corner, he'll strike out at you. Your safety lies in feigned ignorance, and don't you forget it! You can let him know he didn't fool you after he's arrested. When he realizes I'm gone, he'll be furious. But if you let him discover you know the truth and he realizes he has lost everything, there's no telling what he'll do. Promise me you'll be silent," she pleaded.

"He thinks he is so damn clever! How dare he use me like this! I can't stand the thought of him getting away with this a day longer! Maybe he isn't as dangerous as we think. Maybe he will turn tail and flee if he thinks we're on to him. I'm not afraid of him!"

"Just who's going to protect you with all of us gone? My God, Mandy, he *is* that dangerous; he's crazy! Even if you file charges against him, you have no proof. He's a powerful and wealthy man. He would be released the same day. And aren't you forgetting something else? What about Reis? If you issue a challenge, Reis will be the one to fight it for you. Weber would think nothing of having him murdered. Pride and revenge are costly, sister."

Amanda grew silent. She paced the floor then relented. "You're right. I'll behave myself. It just makes me so angry. I should have listened to you long ago and dropped Weber. I'm sorry I got you into this mess, Randy. We'd best get the carriage loaded before Luke comes," she suggested, forcing a strained smile.

"Are you sure you don't want me to stay?" Randy asked gravely.

"No. This plan is best for everyone. Just make sure you write every day. I'm going to miss you terribly. Three months is such a long time." She suddenly hugged her sister.

"When I return, Weber will be in prison, and you and Reis will be sharing a happy marriage. Just be extra careful," Randy coaxed again.

"I will. I promise you Weber won't suspect a thing."

They loaded the carriage which was waiting in the enclosed yard to the rear of their townhouse. Just before two Lucas arrived grinning and chuckling. He told them his plot had worked beautifully and

Weber's spy was snoozing behind bushes across the street, his pockets emptied by a daring old widow in black. All was ready. The three mounted the carriage and drove away.

There was no time to waste in reaching the small depot outside of town. Miranda and Amanda hugged each other and cried. The whistle blew and Miranda boarded the train, pondering how long it would be before she saw her cherished sister again, wondering what would happen to each of them before that day arrived. From her window, she waved until she lost sight of Lucas and her sister. It was done. She would ride to Baltimore, then wait for Lucas to join her. They would take another train through Cincinnati to St. Louis where they would switch to a river steamer for the remainder of their journey.

Miranda settled back in her seat, dreamy thoughts filling her mind. She felt a mixture of nervousness and exhilaration. She was on her way to the Dakota Territory. Amanda was married to a wonderful man who would protect and love her. She couldn't believe this was really happening—that she was going to see her mother's family and experience her lost way of life . . .

Lucas drove Amanda to the Alexandria station. With a veiled hat covering her face and concealing the color of her hair and eyes, she purchased a ticket to Charleston under her sister's name. She boarded the waiting train and spoke to the conductor as he claimed part of her ticket. She went to her private compartment, leaving the hat on the bench there to insinuate her presence. When the man was busy with other passengers, she sneaked off the train and joined Lucas. By five, Amanda was home again; this time alone.

That night, Amanda wandered around her room in the shadowy moonlight. Never had she felt so alone or so lonely. Miranda was gone, gone for at least three months and so far away. She didn't want to think about her parents, further away than her sister, who could never return. Lucas would be leaving before noon tomorrow. And Reis was somewhere for another week. At least Mrs. Reed would be returning to work in the morning . . .

Weber was propped lazily against a post at the train depot by nine-thirty on Friday morning. He was speaking with one of his henchmen. "Just make sure Thomas Reed has a nasty accident today, one which forces his wife to stay home with him for a good spell. I need a little privacy over at the Lawrence's. Don't kill the poor fellow; just drop a heavy crate on his leg or foot."

The man nodded and left to carry out Weber's orders. Weber observed Lucas Reardon when he arrived with his belongings. He was curious as to why Miranda hadn't come to say good-by. Weber had anticipated escorting Miranda home after Lucas's train departed. Perhaps Lucas had bid them farewell yesterday afternoon while his careless guard had been unconscious. Once Lucas was gone, all of his worries would vanish. By Sunday, the twins and their properties would be in his control.

Lucas noticed Weber watching him and strolled over to where he stood. "Making sure I leave town, Richardson?" he taunted.

"Yep," Weber readily admitted. "Is it true you'll be gone until fall? Can Fate shine so brightly upon a poor Southern Reb?"

"I'll be back in a flicker if you hurt Amanda in any way," he warned icily to mislead Weber. "I love her like a sister, and she deserves better than you. I hope she changes her mind about you before my return. If not, then you'd best take real good care of her."

"No concern for Miranda?" Weber mocked him.

"No need. She hates your guts. Besides, Miranda's in Charleston until September. She left yesterday at four. I should beat her home."

"Why would she leave when Amanda's so ill?" Weber questioned, vexation starting to grow like a vicious disease within him.

"I'm not sure, but she was acting mighty strange, anxious to leave town. You two didn't have a quarrel, did you? She was a mite edgy yesterday when I drove her here. What did you do? Tell her you were moving in so she had to move out? When is the lucky wedding day, Richardson?" When Weber remained silent, Lucas frowned at him. "It sure is gonna be great to miss your face for months. See you around," he stated flippantly then turned to board the train.

Weber waited until the train had left the station, making certain Lucas Reardon didn't change his mind. He breathed a sigh of relief then tensed. He made several inquiries with the ticket agent and station manager, then headed for the Lawrence townhouse to check out this disastrous mystery.

From her bedroom window, Amanda mastered her irritation when she saw Weber arrive out front as expected. Alice Reed had been given orders to admit no one, even friends. First, Weber asked to speak with Amanda, then Miranda. Alice convincingly gave the false story she had been told—Amanda was still recovering from illness and Miranda had left on an extended holiday. When pressed for Miranda's location, Alice told him she only knew her final destination was somewhere in Charleston. As Weber scoffed at her ignorance, she indignantly vowed she was telling the truth.

When Weber demanded to see Amanda, Alice politely and firmly refused. She explained that Amanda could not be disturbed. When Weber persisted and even threatened to go upstairs, Alice told him Amanda had taken a sleeping medicine to calm her distraught nerves because Miranda had left suddenly without revealing her plans. She tried to appease him by confiding. "She's terribly worried about Miss Randy. It just isn't like her to do such a rash thing. She did promise to write Miss Mandy as soon as she's settled.''

"Did they quarrel, Mrs. Reed?'' he inquired, softening his tone, observing her for the slightest hint of deception.

In spite of the unspoken betrothal between her lovely mistress and this imposing man, Alice demurred with, "I don't tell about the goings on here, Mr. Richardson. All I can say is she packed and left yesterday. You'll have to ask Miss Mandy when she's feeling better.''

Weber scowled at her then suggested, "If you wish to continue working here after our marriage, Mrs. Reed, you'd best hide your dislike of me a little better else I'll hire Mandy another housekeeper. In fact, I might hire someone to take your husband's place at work. I'm sure it will be hard to survive with both of you out of work. If she's distressed over something that happened between her and Randy, I have the right to know. They will be my family and my responsibilities soon. Now, I'll ask again. Did they quarrel before Randy left?''

Alice grew pale as she realized the power this man had over her. If Weber had her husband fired, he would be devastated. Good jobs at his age were difficult to find. She loved the twins. She had been loyal to the Lawrences for years and would never hurt them. Still, she was forced to yield to the demands of her future employer. "I suppose it's all right to tell you what happened this morning.''

When she frowned and faltered, Weber pressed

215

eagerly, "What happened this morning? I thought Randy left yesterday. Get on with it, woman. I have to return to work."

"When I came in this morning, Miss Mandy told me her sister had gone to Charleston for a holiday with friends. Miss Mandy said she tried to get her to go to Morning Star, but Miss Randy refused. Miss Mandy said her sister didn't want anyone to know where she was. But when I was cleaning her room, I made a terrible find. She—Miss Randy—left a note saying she had moved to Charleston and wasn't coming back." Alice's eyes lowered in sadness as she repeated her discovery. She had no way of knowing it was all a pre-arranged charade.

"Moved? What are you babbling about, woman?" he shouted. "You're daffy! She wouldn't dare leave here. What did the note say?"

Panicked by his fury, Alice said, "Miss Randy said she wanted to move far away from here to start a new life. Since you and her sister are marrying soon, she said she didn't belong here any more. She wanted to go somewhere and forget the past. She said it was best for all if she left and never came back. Miss Mandy's upset because she thinks her sister might be angry with her about something. She's hurt because she thinks she forced Miss Randy out of her home . . . by marrying you," she stated carefully, unsure of his reaction to that statement.

"Why would our marriage force her to leave home? We wouldn't live here. That's silly, Mrs. Reed.

Where's the note? Show it to me, or I'll have to get Mandy out of bed to question her."

Alice eyed him curiously, then boldly asked, "Why are you so mad about Miss Randy moving? She's a grown woman with no boss."

From her tone, Weber realized he was acting too possessive. "I thought the note might give a clue as to why she left mysteriously. If so, I can find her for Mandy. I can try to get her to come home so we can help her if she's in some kind of trouble."

Alice's heart thudded with uncertainty. Suddenly she was afraid for Miranda; why, she didn't know. "I told you all the note said. Miss Mandy read it to me, then crumpled it and burned it in the kitchen stove. If you rush upstairs and prod her with questions, she'll be more upset. You know she isn't well. She didn't know Miss Randy wasn't coming home. And she doesn't know why Miss Randy left."

Weber couldn't force answers from an ailing Amanda without arousing suspicion. He smiled at Alice and turned on his charm. "Randy's a special lady. She loves Mandy; I'm sure she'll come home."

"I don't think so, Mr. Richardson. She took most all her clothes and belongings. That's why Miss Mandy knows she's gone for good."

"What did Lucas have to say this morning?" he probed warily. "Did he help Randy run away? Didn't he know this would hurt Mandy? Surely he didn't leave without revealing Randy's location?"

"He didn't come over this morning. He said good-by yesterday. When I found the note, I asked Miss Mandy to let me go fetch him, but she said no. Miss Mandy knows how much this trip means to him, so she kept mum. She didn't want him running off to Charleston. Now Mr. Luke is gone and that poor child is alone. It isn't right for them to leave her when she's bedridden and still suffering about her parents. Now don't you go adding to her troubles today. You let that child sleep and get stronger."

"I won't disturb her this morning. You tell Mandy I came by to see her. If she needs anything, you send for me, understand?" he told her sternly.

"I'll take care of her. When she wakes, I'll give her your message," she agreed reluctantly, watching him hurry out the door.

Outside the gate, Weber motioned for his furtive cohort to join him, unaware of the piercing blue eyes which were observing him through the translucent material of the lacy drapes. Amanda couldn't hear their words, but she could see Weber's fury. From where she stood, it appeared Weber was calling off the spy and giving him new orders. Why not? Everyone was gone but her.

Weber was indeed issuing new orders. He had wanted to make sure Lucas didn't get off the train outside town and sneak back to Amanda's, and he had wisely put a man on Lucas's tail early this morning. When the man reported to him later, he would know all Lucas had done before leaving town. He would hire a man to pursue Miranda, and bring her to his home as quickly and secretively as possible.

He was determined Miranda wouldn't escape him. Weber was positive Miranda hadn't confided in her sister or cousin, and he concluded she was merely running from her emotions. Just to be on the safe side, he wouldn't deal with Amanda until her sister was locked in a room at his home . . .

Chapter Ten

In Baltimore Friday afternoon, Miranda was bewildered when a telegram was delivered to her hotel room under the phony name only she and Lucas knew: Marie Starr. She nervously read its contents which stated, "Not to worry. Have brief tail. Use Cin ticket. Meet in Louis. Coming via Chicago. No contact home."

Miranda comprehended the message between the lines. Obviously Weber was having Lucas followed which wasn't unexpected. As prearranged, she would take one train through Cincinnati to St. Louis and wait there. Lucas would take a decoy train to Chicago, then travel down to meet her when he lost his shadow. From St. Louis, they would journey to Omaha on the Missouri River where a steamboat would be the next step in their trip. If Amanda were in danger, Lucas would have come directly to her here. Both knew it was folly to send word home from her secret location. She wondered if Weber or his men were seeking her in Charleston. She wasn't afraid to travel alone; she would have a private compartment all the way. Still, she couldn't help but wonder what was taking place at home. She could hardly wait for Lucas to join her and to relate the news. She was glad that Lucas had a friend in Charleston who was going to mail letters from there to Amanda.

While Weber awaited his men's reports, he continued with his plot to take control of the twin's properties and to locate Miranda. He sent flowers and notes to Amanda, who shredded the papers and tossed out the flowers. When Alice questioned Amanda's curious actions, she told the woman she was annoyed with Weber and herself for inspiring her sister's departure. She went so far as to hint that Weber might have driven Miranda away and that she might reconsider her relationship with him. She pretended to get stronger and better each day.

Weber canceled the ordered accident for Thomas Reed, as it would be unnecessary until he had Miranda under his roof. When Weber hadn't called on Amanda by Monday, she fretted at his inexplicable absence. Since Miranda was lost to him, shouldn't he be wooing her again? The notes and flowers were nothing but wily deceptions. Tuesday, a message arrived telling Amanda he had left on a business trip and would see her when he returned Thursday. Amanda prayed he was heading south, not west.

The weekend had passed without trouble but now odd things were happening. Weber had left town. On Tuesday a telegram arrived from Lucas, from St. Louis. Thomas Reed broke his leg in an accident on Wednesday, and Alice had to stay home with him for a while. A letter arrived from Miranda on Thursday, posted in Charleston. No message, coded or otherwise, came from Reis.

For two nights, Amanda slept restlessly, worrying about Weber's strange actions and praying for Reis's safety. But at least she knew Lucas and Miranda were safe. She had destroyed Miranda's lengthy letter but kept the false one to use on Weber when and if he ever came around. She also kept Lucas's telegram lying on the parlor table. She wished Reis would write or return. She needed to know he was all right. She needed to see him, to touch him, to love him.

Friday afternoon, Amanda paid the Reeds a brief visit. Upon returning home, she found Weber waiting for her on the porch. As she approached him, he stared at her oddly.

"I thought you were too ill to be up and around," he stated sullenly. "I come home to find you traipsing all over town. Would you mind explaining yourself, Miss Lawrence?"

Amanda stiffened with outrage and resentment, then reminded herself to proceed with caution. "I beg your pardon, Mr. Richardson," she retorted in a similar tone of peevishness. "How would you know my state of health, seeing as you haven't called since last Friday—a week past? How long does it require for one to get well? To get jittery lying abed or confined to one's home? And since when must I explain myself to you or anyone? But to answer your insulting and nosy question, I went to visit the Reeds. I take it you're unaware of his terrible accident?"

"What accident?" he queried in confusion, wondering if his man had misinterpreted his order. He had seen Amanda Lawrence in many moods, but never one laced with such anger and rudeness.

Amanda briefly informed him of Thomas Reed's situation. "If that's all, sir, good day to you," she added snippily, unlocking her door. At that moment, she was too mad to be afraid of him.

"That isn't all, Mandy," he hastily informed her, seizing her arm and turning her around. "I came over to check on you as soon as I returned. Why are you being so hateful? Have you heard from Miranda?" he inquired, trying to sound casual.

He didn't fool Amanda in the least. Apparently he hadn't found a trace of Miranda and was seeking clues from her. "As you can see, I'm doing fine now. As to my behavior, I give as I receive. It would have been more pleasant if you had merely sent another note or bouquet of flowers. As you can also see, I'm not in the proper mood for company, thanks to you."

"I'm not company, Mandy," he playfully corrected her. "What inspired this disagreeable mood? Surely I can help change it?" he offered, his tone a mellow and husky sound.

"I doubt anyone possesses such magic, Weber. You can't change what ails me. Everything seems to be going awry these days," she murmured sadly.

"Things can't be that bad, my sweet. Tell me what has you so down, and maybe I can help," he coaxed beguilingly.

Amanda studied him for a moment, then said, "Perhaps we should have a serious talk, Weber. I'll prepare some refreshments."

She entered the house and walked into the parlor. She tossed her cape on one end of the sofa, then invited him to be seated while she made the tea. Unless he sat on her cape, he would have to sit nearest the table which held the telegram and letter. Although a book was partially concealing them, Amanda felt certain Weber would notice and read them.

Weber dropped to the sofa and sighed heavily in fatigue and annoyance. As he plotted his strategy, his gaze touched on the edge of a telegram. He moved the book aside to read the signature and found the letter beneath it. He went to the door and glanced down the hallway. He could hear Amanda moving around in the kitchen. He returned to the table and snatched up the two papers, reading them swiftly and closely. He promptly replaced them and went to stand before the front window.

He mentally went over his dilemma. His men hadn't been able to find a single track leading to Miranda, yet she was definitely hiding in Charleston. He would send word to them to search harder; she must be located with all haste. His aggravation with both females was increasing, and his lust for Miranda was rapidly turning to a desire for vengeance. She would pay for leading him this merry chase! He was beginning to think she was playing him for a fool, that she was only trying to cause a split between him and Amanda. On the other hand, perhaps she was afraid of him.

The riddle lay in Miranda's silence about the episodes between them. She hadn't mentioned either battle to Amanda. She had offered no explanation or excuses in her note or letter. She had begged Amanda to forgive her for running away and encouraged her not to worry about her. She had written she was safe and happy, staying with friends. Yet she refused to give her current address and she repeated her vow never to return to Alexandria. Was she afraid Amanda would pass the address on to him? Did she suspect he would come after her? Whatever Miranda's motives, she didn't seem to want Amanda to know about them. The question was why.

But there was a perilous hitch to this matter—what if Miranda decided to reveal the truth in a future letter? How long should he hold out for Miranda without jeopardizing his chances with Amanda? If he was forced to settle for Amanda, it wouldn't matter what Miranda exposed after their marriage. If Miranda didn't feel guilty, she wouldn't be holding her tongue.

He recalled Lucas's telegram; his foe was leaving St. Louis for Omaha. The telegram had asked

Amanda to forward Miranda's new address when she was settled for the summer, implying Lucas was alone and uninformed. His man had followed Lucas to Baltimore where Lucas had taken another train west. His man had reported nothing suspicious. From the telegram Web knew Lucas would take a boat into the Dakota Territory. At last, Lucas Reardon was out of his hair, far away.

A wary man, Weber was not often taken off guard. Tonight, Amanda surprised him when she returned to the room. He seemed to be engulfed in pensive thought, lost in some dreamy world of dark schemes. Before he came back to reality, she risked a glance at the table to find that he had taken her bait. She suppressed a smile as she placed the tray on an oblong table behind one of the matching sofas in the center of the room.

Weber actually jumped and balled his fist when she offered, "Tea, Weber?" She couldn't contain her laughter at his guilty reaction. "You're awfully jumpy," she teased mockingly.

Weber's cold glare was quickly replaced with a merry grin. "I was just about asleep on my feet. I didn't realize I was so exhausted. Maybe that tea will enliven me."

"Perhaps you should go home and rest. We can talk another time," she stated flippantly as if it didn't matter if they ever talked.

"I've been worried about you, Mandy. You're looking marvelous, but you sound dejected. Surely Miranda's contacted you by now?"

"What are you talking about, Weber? Miranda's away on a holiday. She's having too much fun to write," she jested, acting as if nothing were wrong.

"You don't fool me, Mandy. Mrs. Reed told me what happened last week with Miranda. I know you're worried about her." He strolled forward to accept the cup of hot tea then casually took a seat.

Amanda gaped at him. "Just what did Mrs. Reed tell you?" she asked angrily.

Weber told her of their conversation. "I see," Amanda muttered frostily when he finished his confession. "In the future, you will kindly refrain from discussing me and my sister with the hired help. I'm sorry she was the one to find Miranda's note, since she obviously can't be trusted. When Mrs. Reed returns to work—if I allow her to do so—she will be severely reprimanded for such disloyalty. Why Miranda left home is no one's business except hers and mine."

"Why did she leave, Mandy?" he questioned brazenly.

"I was hoping you could answer that question for me," she stated sarcastically, fusing her challenging gaze to his guarded one.

"I'm just as shocked and confused as you are, perhaps more so. Why would you think she might confide in me?"

"What happened between you and Randy last week while I was ill? Since that night I found you two 'horsing around' in this very room, she's acted strangely. Then, she came home from the bank the next day in a mood I can't even explain, much less understand. She packed and left home that same afternoon. Oh, she tried to convince me this trip had been planned for quite some time, but I knew she was lying. You know how, Weber? Because she lies badly. Just like she lied that night I caught you two in here. Then I found a note saying she'd moved and wouldn't tell me where! What is going on between you two? Something happened to make her leave. And you're involved!"

"Listen to yourself, Mandy. You sure you're off that medicine? Just what are you trying to suggest?" he demanded glacially.

"My head has never been clearer, Web. You know how close Randy and I have been since birth. But after you came around, things never were the same. It isn't my imagination! Both of you have been acting strange for weeks now. Were you two having a fight in here, or what?"

"Are you blaming me for her departure?" he snarled. "What could I possibly say or do to make her disappear?"

"Tell me what happened in here that night. Then tell me what happened the day she left town. You did see her while she was out?" she inquired, sounding as if it were a statement more than a leading question.

"I don't believe what I'm seeing and hearing. If I'm right, you're accusing me and Randy of having an affair behind your back. Is that what you think, Mandy?" he probed, placing the cup on a table.

Amanda jumped up from her chair and paced the

room. Pretending to search her heart and mind for an honest answer, she deliberated her next move. She could not go too far too soon.

Weber used her confusion and hesitation to further her doubts. "I swear to you, Mandy, I've never made love to your sister. How can you hurt me with such charges?"

Amanda ceased her aimless wanderings and looked at him. "Can you also swear you haven't wanted to? Can you also swear you haven't tried to get her into your bed? Can you swear you have never held her in your arms, never kissed her? Swear those things, Weber; prove I have no reason to doubt your love and fidelity. Prove you have nothing to do with Randy's actions."

"You actually expect me to respond to such accusations!" he thundered at her, infuriated by her astute perceptions and the fact that she would dare to interrogate him. "I do believe your fever seared your brain, Amanda Lawrence! It's bad enough you charge me with such vile conduct, but to vilify your own sister like this . . ." He cunningly left the statement unfinished. "By damn, woman, what's gotten into you? I think you'd best call that doctor over to check your head. I'm not going to sit here and defend myself against such crude and foolish insinuations. Why would I court you if I wanted Miranda? Do you realize how crazy that sounds?"

"You're awfully tense and defensive, Weber. It's really rather simple to end this matter; just tell me the truth."

Weber rushed to her and grabbed her, shaking her as he shouted, "Damnation, Mandy! That's why she left! You've been badgering her with such trash, haven't you? No wonder she ran off! You've been accusing her of these same things. Did you call her filthy names and accuse her of such lewd behavior? Mandy, Mandy, what have you done? Randy and I are innocent. You've deluded yourself about some secret love affair between us. You drove her away with your cruel accusations and wild jealousy," he informed her angrily.

Amanda jerked free and glared at him. "All I want to know is who's at fault, you or she or both of you. Damn you, Weber Richardson! I'm not a blind fool. I saw the way you two acted that night. If nothing happened, then why did she leave?"

"I wish to hell I knew!" he rashly stormed at her.

To his consternation, she stated softly and firmly, "I think you and I should end this, Weber. Things haven't been right between us for some time. I've been trying to ignore it, even deny it, but I can't. A marriage between us wouldn't work."

For the first time, Weber panicked. Miranda might be lost to him, and now he was losing Amanda and all she represented. He couldn't permit that. He would deal with Miranda when she was found. Right now, he would have to persuade Amanda she was his one and only love. "I love you, Mandy; I want to marry you. Now or whenever you say."

Amanda shook her head. "You love what I have to offer, Weber, not me. I doubt you ever loved me or ever will. If Randy were here and willing, you would take her in my place. Why pretend?"

Weber felt secure in his schemes and used them. "You have nothing to offer but yourself, Mandy. Your father made some terrible business decisions. Everything you have is mortgaged past keeping. I've been supporting you and your sister for the past two months. If not for me, you and Randy would be in the streets today. I've been slaving to hold things together until we were married. I didn't want you to feel obligated to marry me. You have nothing but me, Mandy."

Now that he was heading blindly into her trap, she encouraged him to go further. "What nonsense is this?" she scoffed.

"If I hadn't made the payments on this house for the past two months, the bank would own it right now. As to Morning Star, I couldn't save it. It was losing too much money and too heavily indebted. And your firm has been on the verge of bankruptcy for months. If you doubt me, check your father's books and ask Daniel McVane. Maybe these burdens troubled your father so deeply that he was reckless that day at sea," he speculated maliciously.

Tears blurred her eyes as she comprehended the extent of Weber's cruelty. How could she have been so wrong about this man? To think she almost married him. What menacing plans he must have had for her . . . "Are you saying you own me?" she murmured.

"Don't be silly, woman. I'm trying to spare you

hurt and humiliation. But I can't stall the inevitable much longer. Too many of your clients are demanding payment. I can't allow my company to sink by keeping yours afloat. Think of the embarrassment, Mandy. Do you want people saying you married me for survival? We've got to do something quick. After we're married, I'll hire a detective to locate Miranda, if you wish. I don't want either of you hurt, Mandy. And both of you must be suffering from this misunderstanding."

"I wish I could believe you, Web," she murmured quietly.

Weber tensed. "Then go to your office and check the books."

"I don't mean about my finances. I mean about Randy. I'm sorry, but you'll never convince me nothing happened. Randy was asking too many questions about you and us. She wanted me to break it off with you. She kept telling me she didn't like you or trust you. Then I find her in your arms."

"I told you, Mandy, we were calling a truce. We were talking and got carried away. We started teasing each other. She's like a child, Mandy," he lied unconvincingly.

"Then why did she act so funny when I caught you two? And why did she spout scorn and mistrust for you the next day before leaving?"

Stunned by that revelation, he shrieked helplessly, "What?"

"I find that your story and hers contradict each other. That makes me skeptical of both tales, Weber.

She runs away, then you vanish on business," she stated sarcastically. "Did you go after her, Web? Did she refuse to come home with you? Did you decide to settle for me since you can't have her? Randy isn't for you, Web. She's a wild creature, a creature of the land like my mother was."

"All right, Mandy," Weber muttered as if to himself. "If you want the truth, then you'll have it. I was hoping to spare you such pain. But I can't remain silent if it's going to destroy us." Weber knew he had to make an irrevocable decision to regain Amanda and punish her sister.

Amanda sensed what was coming and mentally prepared for it. Weber was exceedingly smart and daring, but he was greedy and desperate. Such traits inspired rashness.

"I think you should sit down, Mandy. I wish I could avoid delivering so much bad news in one night." Weber took a seat, but Amanda remained standing by the front window.

Those stubborn lines on her face caused ripples of spite to wash over him. He would fix her—her and her treacherous sister! "I've been a bloody fool, Mandy. I'm sorry. I haven't outright lied to you, but I have misguided you. I thought it would be best for everyone if I forgot about the other night. I've tried to accept it as a misunderstanding. I was so excited and pleased by her change of heart about me that I didn't realize what she was doing. Frankly, I'm still not sure about her motives, but they couldn't be honorable."

Amanda didn't take her eyes off his face and she

didn't debate his allegations. "Continue," she coaxed impassively when he hesitated.

"I let myself be flattered by Miranda's attention. It's rare to have one beautiful woman after you, but to have two . . . She caught me by surprise, Mandy. I've never seen Miranda like she was the other night. Laughing, teasing, smiling, dancing around the room. We were just talking and making peace—at least I thought so. From nowhere she flung herself into my arms and kissed me. At first I didn't think anything about it; I mean, it was just a little kiss. But she didn't move away; she started caressing my chest and sending me a look which was so much more than friendly. Tarnation, Mandy, she's your sister; I was bewildered. Then she rubbed against me and kissed me again. I'm not a saint, Mandy; so I won't deny I had flames nipping at me. There I stood, nailed to the floor, mindless with astonishment, and she was dancing around me. Her hands were tickling me and her mouth was all pouted up, sort of inviting. I didn't know what to do or think."

Weber paced nervously and lowered his gaze contritely. Still, Amanda didn't move or protest. "I don't know what got into her that night, Mandy, but she was a powerful witch. I can't explain what I was thinking, if anything. Lordy, a man can't control his body under trying times like that! I asked her what she was doing, and she just smiled at me. I patted her on the cheek roughly and asked her if she was drunk. She took my hand and moved it down her chest. When I tried to pull it away, she put it inside that nothing dress she was wearing. Lord's my witness, Mandy, she didn't have anything under it, and she clamped my hand over one of her breasts. By then, I was half crazy with worry. I was trying not to tear her dress but get my hand out of it. It was hard not to be affected by what she was doing.''

Weber did more pacing and hand-wringing. ''By then, I was trembling and sweating. Lord, I was afraid you'd walk in before I could control her. I grabbed her hands and pinned them behind her back. I started scolding her something fierce. I don't know if she wanted me, or if she was doing it to split us apart. I think she was hoping you'd find us like that. But I'm still not sure why. She wasn't herself, Mandy; she was like some wild and hungry vixen on the prowl.''

He flopped to the sofa, groaning as if exhausted from the exertion of this confession. ''I talked my mouth dry to your sister, Mandy. She seemed to relax. Then when you came downstairs unexpectedly, she went pale and funny. She could have changed her mind about making me look bad. When I didn't respond, maybe she realized she was wrong. Or maybe she thought you wouldn't believe her lies about me. Who knows, Mandy, maybe she was looking for a good reason to leave home. You said yourself she's different; she has a wild and mysterious streak. You can't ever tell what she's thinking or feeling; it's frightening.''

Finally Amanda spoke. ''You're telling me that my sister enticed you to seduce her that night? Miranda

Lawrence acted like a harlot to the man who belongs to her own sister?''

"I've been flirted with plenty of times, Mandy, and invited to share passion. Randy wasn't being an innocent flirt, and she wasn't trying to become friends. She was tempting me, trying to bewitch me. If there's one thing I'm positive about, Randy was trying to coax me into her bed. As to why, only Randy knows. Maybe she did think I was bad for you; maybe she hoped to prove it that night.''

"You think she left because she was embarrassed? She was afraid you'd tell me everything? Or do you think she left because her seduction failed and she couldn't bear to watch us together?''

Something about Amanda's surly undertone piqued Weber. "When I saw her Thursday, I told her we would forget it ever happened. She acted as if she didn't know what I was talking about; she looked at me like I was crazy. When I kept talking, she accused me of being insane. I don't know if it was an act or not, but she behaved as if the whole episode never happened. Has that ever happened to her before?''

"If you're wondering about her sanity, it was fine until last week. I'm not convinced you're innocent in this matter. Randy wouldn't play the slut to prove a point to me. And if she has secret longings for you, they must be buried deep from the way she talks. Perhaps you got a bit too friendly and scared her. Randy is very sensitive, very giving. Maybe she left because she didn't want to hurt me with the truth— that my future fiancé was chasing her. She dislikes you, Weber, and she doesn't want to live with us if we marry. Maybe she thought I was too enchanted by you to believe her version. Right now, I'm confused; I'm hurt and I'm worried. Until I'm convinced it was an innocent mistake I think we should spend time apart. I'm not accusing you of lying; I'm not charging you're wholly to blame. I need time to sort out my feelings. I've been through so much these past months; I can't take more pressure. I hope Randy will write or come home soon; then we can calmly discuss this mysterious misunderstanding."

"Why are you punishing me, punishing us for Randy's strange behavior? I was afraid you'd react like this if I told you about that night. By damn, I should have lied! What about the firm, Mandy? I can't support two homes and businesses much longer. Marry me tomorrow, and we'll work out everything. We'll find Randy and bring her home with us. Whatever the problem—real or imaginary— we'll help her, I promise."

When Amanda didn't seem moved or touched by his pleas, he beseeched her, "If we stop seeing each other, you'll brood over this and maybe paint me guilty of something I didn't do. Please, Mandy, you must understand and forgive me. I love you. I need you."

Amanda felt she was pushing too far, too hard. She sighed wearily and relented to a mild degree. "I want to believe you, Weber, but my whole world is coming apart. My parents vanish and I'm told they're dead. You, my family, and property were all I had left. Now

Randy and Luke are gone. You say I'm nearing a penniless state. I just recovered from an illness. It's too much at once. Can't you see how I feel? I'm drained and I'm frightened. If you truly love me, give me some time to adjust."

When Weber attempted to embrace and comfort her, she moved away. "Please don't. Not now, not today. Come to see me Sunday afternoon; we'll talk then. Bring Papa's books and we'll decide what's to be done. Just allow me breathing space to recover from these setbacks."

Weber failed to notice his reflection in a mirror on the opposite wall, one which exposed his satanic grin of satisfaction which Amanda was observing intently from the corner of her eye. Her ruse had worked; Weber believed she was utterly confused, vulnerable to his lies. The bastard actually thought he was winning this game!

"You're right, my sweet. I am being selfish and thoughtless. You've had too much dropped on you lately. Rest and think, Mandy. By Sunday when we talk, you'll know I only want what's best for you and us. Don't worry about anything. I'd never let you be hurt by a scandal. If you need anything, send for me."

"You're very kind, Weber. I'm sorry about this mess. You probably think I'm the most ungrateful woman alive. Considering all that's happened, you can't blame me for having doubts. I've just never felt so alone, so insecure, so helpless! Maybe I'm not myself yet. Can you imagine Amanda Lawrence without money; the topic of idle gossip; the butt of amusing or cruel jokes?'' she murmured as if horrified by such visions, planting the seeds for her next entangling vine.

"Don't forget you have me and all I own, my sweet. I would never allow anyone to laugh at you," he claimed smugly. Weber relaxed, fooled completely. He might as well purchase a wedding ring, he thought, for we will be wed by next Friday! Amanda Lawrence would never risk poverty and ridicule. She could be his adoring and grateful wife until he found Miranda . . .

After Weber left, Amanda fumed and paced with the tension and bitterness which engulfed her. Did the bastard think her so stupid? Did he think her so dazzled by him that she would believe every word that left his lying lips? Did he think her so desperate that she would obey him without question or protest? Her fury mounted.

As she returned the dishes and tray to the kitchen, she burst into ecstatic laughter. "I wonder if you're as dangerous as you are evil and greedy? I shall enjoy my revenge on you, Weber Richardson. No one makes a fool of me. No one uses me. You thief! You liar! You traitor! You've met your match, dear Weber. Now that I have you trapped like the vermin you are, I shall torture you and tease you before you're arrested. I shall come to the jail and laugh in your face when this is over. You'll regret the day you set your sights on me and my sister," she vowed confidently.

About ten, on Saturday night, Amanda tossed

aside the book she had been trying to read. She checked the lights and doors and slowly made her way upstairs to her lonely bedroom. She closed her door and leaned against it, sighing dejectedly. Suddenly her gaze widened with astonishment, then she burst into gleeful laughter.

Lying upon her bed was her irresistible love. His chest and feet were bare, his lower body clad in snug jeans. His ebony head was resting upon two pillows as his virile frame reclined seductively. His expression said "come here." But he didn't speak or move. He just grinned.

She ran to her bed squealing. "Reis! You're back. God, how I've missed you. I was so worried," she confessed, spreading kisses over his face between words.

Reis captured her in his arms and pulled her down atop him. "Not half as much as I missed you, love," he murmured huskily then kissed her with such intensity that it took her breath away. He rolled her over him and covered her body with his as his mouth savored hers.

She hugged him fiercely as she responded to his lips, her hands gently kneeding the supple flesh upon his back. After several heady kisses, he leaned back and visually devoured her beauty and smoldering gaze. "You have a potent hold over me, woman. I couldn't wait to come home to you," he stated thickly.

"Is it over, Reis? Did you get the evidence against him? I've been so lonely and miserable without you.

Don't ever leave me again. I've been crazy with fear,"
she told him, snuggling into his arms.

"I learned plenty, but I need a few more facts. I
should be able to wrap up this case in a week or two.
First, I need to get inside your warehouse and his.
Late at night, if you catch my drift."

"But that's dangerous!" she protested instantly.
"Surely he has both guarded. What if he sees you?"

"I'm good at my job, love. Did you see or hear
anything tonight? Yet, here I am," he jested
playfully, tugging on a blond curl.

"But I'm not surrounded by guards," she refuted
his smugness.

"But you are, love. There's one out front across the
street and one out back at the rear gate," he disclosed
to her shock.

"I don't understand. Weber called off his spy last
week. Why would he replace him, then add another
one?" she fretted nervously.

"Why don't you tell me what's been happening
here while I was gone? Are you all right, love?" he
inquired tenderly, possessively.

Amanda gradually revealed the events which had
taken place during his absence. Although he didn't
interrupt her detailed explanation, she watched the
ever-changing emotions which swept over his face.
When she finished, he remarked gravely, "Don't you
think you went a mite far? You were supposed to act
suspicious, not come right out and say it. Now that
he's laid his cards on the table, he'll be more

dangerous than ever. I'll have to move faster. He'll be working to get you two married quickly. There's a lot at stake here, love. I wouldn't put anything past him to get his wishes. I know him, Mandy; I witnessed his cruelty during the war. He would die or kill before losing again. Why didn't you stall him until I returned?" he asked.

She lowered her gaze when she replied honestly and remorsefully, "Pride and vengeance. I'm sorry, Reis. It was foolish."

He smiled and hugged her gently. "I know it's hard to play a simpleton when you're not. But retribution has to wait a while, love."

"Are you angry with me?" she asked quietly.

"Yes, and no," he teased, tightening his embrace and kissing her forehead. He sat up on the bed, pulling her along with him. He lifted the chain from beneath her dress and removed the gold band from it, slipping it on her finger. He smiled and whispered, "But right now, I'm too distracted to think about anything but my wife. Can we skip the talking for tonight?" he inquired roguishly, cupping her chin between his hands, then passing his left thumb over her parted lips.

An enticing smile flickered over her face as she nodded yes. He rolled off the bed to strip off his jeans, leaving himself naked before her intoxicated senses. He reached for her hand, pulling her to her feet. He removed her clothing then rested his quivering hands on her shoulders. She was so soft and sleek. In the dim light, her hair seemed a blaze of golden shades. Her eyes sparkled like rare blue diamonds.

He shifted his dark head to scan her entire body. She lifted her chin to meet the appreciative gaze of those deep blue eyes. His hand deserted her shoulder to trace lightly over her cheeks and parted lips, causing them both to tremble. His finger leisurely trailed over her nose, around her alluring eyes, and poised on her dainty chin. His hand was like an explorer, one who not only mapped out territory, but also claimed it as his.

Amanda was content to stand mesmerized by him, to allow him free rein over her body and will. She felt like a rose petal floating peacefully on an azure sea. Finally, her hands went upward to caress his chest. As her flattened palms moved over the tanned, muscled flesh, she was aware of the thudding of his heart.

Reis's head lowered ever so slowly and his mouth deftly covered hers, their tongues touching and teasing. Amanda was ecstatic that she didn't have to worry about where this unbridled behavior would lead. Never had she felt freer or more confident; she could do or say whatever she pleased. Reis was what she wanted and needed; and he was here with her. She felt so comfortable with him. She felt alive and happy again. She felt wild and wonderful.

His hands eased to her breasts, each capturing and tantalizing a firm mound. There was no need for embarrassment or shyness or resistance. They were married; they were in love; they could do anything which pleased them.

Her body accepted his tormentingly sweet invasion and her hand slid down to encircle his erect manhood, which felt so silky and hot. Recalling the wonders this firm flesh could work within her body, she yearned to feel it driving wildly and urgently into her womanhood.

Reis lifted her and pressed her to the cushiony bed. As if he had forever, he made unhurried love to her. It didn't take long for his lips and hands to have her writhing beside him. He worked skillfully and eagerly, increasing her feverish desire for him. He gently drove his aching shaft into that moist paradise which greeted him ardently.

He didn't move for a few moments, mastering the urge to ride her fast and hard to end his own painful hunger. He was sorely pressed to drive into her body again and again, having dreamed of this night for days. And she was just as ravenous and greedy. He thrilled to the wanton way she responded to him, the way she encouraged and tempted him to devour her, body and soul.

As he set his rhythmic pattern, her legs engulfed his lower body and locked around him. She worked in unison with him, arching to meet his delightful entries and sighing breathlessly each time he slightly withdrew. She struggled against the sweet tension which possessed her, attacked her, taunted her. Her nerves tingled with fierce cravings; her body burned with scorching desire.

Spasm after spasm attacked and shook the very core of her being. For an instant, colorful lights danced before her darkened vision. Reis dashed aside his restraint and raced along with her as she fought and found a blissful path to rapture. When all was spent, they relaxed into each other's arms. Still he kissed her and caressed her. Then he rolled to his side, carrying her along with him and she snuggled against him as their pounding hearts and ragged respirations returned to normal. Tenderly and lovingly his hands trailed lightly over her silky body as if memorizing this enchanting moment.

As they lay entwined and calmed, Reis realized the depth of his love for this woman. He couldn't imagine a life without her, but he surely could envision future days and nights with her at his side.

As Amanda's hand teased over the damp hair on his firm chest, she wondered how this vital and masterful man had remained single so long. He was arrestingly handsome, enormously virile, and skillful in bed. He was fearless, intelligent, confident, and roguish. He was gallant and charming; he was witty and genial. He was a treasure above price and she loved him beyond words.

Just before drifting off to sleep, Amanda murmured softly, "Reis, do you think Luke and Randy are all right?"

"Without a doubt, my love. I think this trip will be good for both of them. Don't worry. We'll be seeing them again before you know it," he replied, nuzzling her ear.

Laughter trickled from her parted lips as she nestled closer to him. "Now that I think about it, I'm glad we're alone. If anyone can take care of herself, it's Miranda Lawrence."

Reis's mouth seized possession of hers, and sleep was forgotten for the next hour . . .

Chapter Eleven

Miranda Lawrence and Lucas Reardon stood at the railing of the steamboat which was carrying them along the Missouri River from Omaha to the next stop which would be Fort Randall. From there, they would visit several military posts including Fort Sully and Fort Pierre. After Pierre, they would take an overland route north to Fort Rice and Fort Lincoln; Fort Abraham Lincoln was reputed to be the new location of George Custer, one of the objects of Lucas's journey.

Miranda had anticipated a leisurely, perhaps boring, trip by water. But she quickly discovered there was little time for personal worries; there was always something to hold her spellbound. She hoped Amanda had received their messages so she wouldn't fret over their safety. By now, Reis should be at her side, insuring her happiness. Lucas had mailed another letter from Omaha, but Miranda couldn't risk writing home yet. In a few weeks, she would send a detailed account of the trip.

Along this awesome stretch of water, Miranda viewed many sights. Huge cottonwoods grew beside the water's edge, standing tall and proud as if guarding this wild land from intruders. Joining them in beauty were lovely chokecherries and wild plum trees in full bloom. Along the banks, bushes with heavy foliage frequently concealed the inland from eager eyes and offered protection for the birds and animals. She heard tales of how pioneers had dreaded challenging this mighty river. Many days and nights the ship's passengers and crew recounted suspenseful sagas of crossings, some victorious and some disastrous. The river was said to have devoured boats of all sizes as well as the banks which tried to contain its force.

She noticed many trading posts and small settlements along the way, each supplying an exciting tale of its own. At sunset, everything appeared gold except the dark outline of trees in the distance. The tawny heavens reflected upon the water and cast a golden aura. Sometimes the air was so still and quiet it seemed eerie, but on moonless nights a mixture of sounds could be heard above the singing and laughter of the passengers, as the steamer halted its trek to avoid unseen dangers in the darkness. On such nights, Miranda enjoyed the throaty croaking of frogs, the soothing calls of bobwhite quail, and the gentle murmuring of the water as it moved along peacefully.

Miranda was relieved to have missed the most terrifying event of all: the breaking up of the frozen river in the spring. She learned that settlers along the river made bets on when "she would go." Cattle were moved to high ground when the intimidating snapping and cracking began sending warning signals from the ice-locked river. It was said the Missouri could go "raving mad" two times each year, and the people sighed with relief and offered prayers of gratitude when March and June passed uneventfully.

That news didn't sit comfortably with Miranda. She had missed the March floods after the melting snows dumped their contents into the river. But the June rains which brought the threat of more flooding were knocking on the calendar's door. Yet the heavens were clear and blue; they even seemed larger than back home. Miranda prayed they would reach their destination before Mother Nature loosened her powers upon the land.

The Missouri was tricky, often hazardous to navigate with its shifting channels, and pilots and captains cursed her yet respected her. Due to the perils of this river and the importance of its location, the riverboat pilots or keelboat captains were highly paid, and their cargo reaped large rewards. Furs, gold, foods, military ammunition and supplies, and Indian annuities were the main cargoes. Sometimes, passengers were just as important: miners, farmers, soldiers, and traders. But with the railroads closing in, steamers were not as crowded as they had once been.

Sadly, the day of the steamer and keelboat was vanishing. By the time Miranda and Lucas were ready to go home, the railroad would be finished to Yankton at Fort Randall. Before long, supply crafts would only be necessary between settlements or into areas where the railroad hadn't yet come.

For a while longer, these crafts and their adventures would continue. Many of their perils and hardships lay in submerged or floating trees or shifting sandbars. Others lay in striking sunken vessels which rested on the shallow bottom with snagged hulls or burned shells. At present, the greatest danger was low water. The spring rush from melting snows had passed and the rise from June rains hadn't come yet.

Miranda watched the river in fascination and tried not to think about her run-ins with Weber. She concentrated on envisioning her sister smiling and walking beside Reis Harrison. Miranda was confident that Reis was more than capable of protecting Amanda, solving the case surrounding Weber, and making Amanda extremely happy. Having seen Reis and Amanda together, Miranda longed for a love that powerful and unique. But she would not avidly search for love and passion, not even among the numerous males on the steamer who had vied for her attention in vain. She would let love and passion find her when the time and man were right.

Halfway between Omaha and Fort Randall, the

steamer ran aground on a sandbar. The *Martha Lane* had previously had contests with smaller sandbars, which had been won quickly and almost easily. But the heavy spars used to free steamers seemed of little use this time. With a full moon to guide them, they had continued long past dusk. The sandbar seemed to have "appeared from nowhere" as the pilot claimed when they were brought to an abrupt stop, one which flung the supper dishes and several passengers to the wooden floor. As if Fate was against the voyage, the moon then vanished behind ominous clouds, preventing the crew from dislodging the boat until morning.

The following day dawned cloudy and dim. When the damage was assessed, the pilot cursed under his breath. Clearly they were too heavy to "grasshopper" off the bar without unloading the passengers, animals, and heaviest cargo. To make matters worse, the rudder had been cracked, and had to be repaired on the spot. It required over an hour to empty the craft.

Lucas was chatting amiably with some of the passengers, in particular two intriguing soldiers from Fort Rice. Miranda was allowed to stroll along the riverbank, taking in the sights and sounds. She admired the wild beauty around her and plucked several colors of pasqueflowers to put in her cabin. She watched squirrels playing in the trees and listened to birds singing joyfully.

As if to seek solitude of its own, a narrow stream

departed the banks of the "Misery"—as Miranda had heard the river being called this morning by a harried pilot—and made a winding path inland, which she followed. She wasn't far from the river and the other passengers, but she felt encased in a private world, concealed from their view by leafy trees and bushes. Growing beside a fallen tree was a lovely patch of wildflowers, seemingly anxious to be the first land decorations this spring. She headed toward it to gather a few to add to those in her grasp.

As she bent forward to reach for the first one, an arrow swished past her outstretched arm. With a thud, it buried its sharp tip in the head of a rattlesnake which had been about to strike Miranda. The serpent thrashed wildly in the verdant grass and fallen leaves as it struggled against inevitable death, its ominous tail sending forth a belated rattle. Finally it was still and silent.

Miranda stared at the arrow with red-and-black-tipped feathers on one end, recalling that her mother had told her long ago that each warrior or tribe used certain feathers and colors for identification. She didn't know who was standing behind her; but there was only one way to find out if it was a white man or an Indian, a rescuer or an enemy. She turned and opened her mouth to speak, but couldn't. He was standing so close to her that she wondered how she failed to make contact with that powerful bronze body while turning. He was an Indian, doubtlessly a warrior, judging from his stance and painted face. In less than an instant, she knew she was in no danger from the virile and handsome man who entranced her with his magnetic gaze.

They merely stared at each other, both surprised and held spellbound by the other. Even though Blazing Star had been watching her since last night when the boat he was shadowing had run aground, he now saw she was even more beautiful than he had imagined. He had been trailing her since she had left the steamer and had defended her without a second thought.

Her hair was like smoldering wood, dark with shining flames. Her eyes were as golden brown as a doe's, and their expression as gentle. Her skin was shaded like a baby otter's, and he knew that it would be just as soft to his touch. He was astonished to read no fear or hatred within those expressive eyes, and more astonished to detect her attraction to him. He wasn't sure if she was white, for if dressed properly, she could pass for Indian. He couldn't seem to move or speak, as if he were in a vision trance.

Miranda warmed all over. Never had she seen such a tempting male. What a superior vision of power, self-assurance, and potent masculinity! Tingles traveled over her body as she took in his appearance. His hair was ebony, falling free down his back, but for two braids on either side of his arresting face. The braids were secured by rawhide thongs with small feathers dangling from them, again tinged with red and black. He wasn't wearing a headband as in the political cartoons by Nast in *Harper's Weekly*; nor was he savage or ugly in appearance or manner as were the Indians in Nast's works.

Other than her mother, Miranda had never seen or met an Indian. But Marie Morning Star Lawrence had told her daughter much about them, especially about her people, the Sioux. Miranda wanted to know to what tribe this man belonged. His coppery flesh was smooth, firm, and hairless. His muscular chest was bare, except for the silver star which hung from a leather strip around his neck. His lower body was clad in buckskin pants and moccasins, and around his biceps and wrists were leather, beaded bands, the loose ends of which dangled from his powerful arms. A quiver of arrows and a bow were slung over one shoulder and rested at his hip.

But it was his face which mesmerized her. Although the upper portion of his face was painted with red from hairline to below his eyes, then banded from side to side with black and white strips to the end of his nose, the design could not distract from his handsome looks, and the paints couldn't conceal them. Again, the color scheme of red and black registered in her spinning mind. His dark eyes shone like polished black jet; their expression was probing and compelling. His nose wasn't large or small, but fit his face perfectly, and his lips were wide and full, inviting Miranda's gaze to linger over them. His jaw was squared, with a slight indention in the middle of his chin which Miranda yearned to touch with her fingertip.

Blazing Star was the one to end their hypnotic drama. He shook his head as if to regain mastery of it. He hunkered down and severed the rattler tail from its body, handing the row of noisy rings to her. The smile he gave her came from his eyes, not his lips. She accepted the unusual gift and smiled up into his controlled features, causing his intense gaze to shift to her mouth. He watched it for a time, then lifted his dark eyes to fuse with hers. Miranda thought he was going to kiss her and was disappointed when he didn't.

Miranda was confused when he used his sharp knife to cut off the lower end of one of her curls. He looked at it as it wound around his finger. He grinned, then placed it inside a pouch at his waist. He couldn't decide if he should be annoyed or relieved he couldn't take a captive on this manhunt, for she appeared too special for such a life. If only his body didn't urge him to take her, or suffer denial's agony . . .

"That isn't how you take scalp locks. What does it mean?" she inquired softly in puzzlement and pleasure.

For an answer, he squeezed her hand which was holding the rattler rings, then patted his pouch, as if indicating a swap of some kind. When he heard Lucas calling her name, the warrior came to instant alertness. She could almost envision those keen instincts and skills coming to full readiness. Lucas's

257

intrusion was unwanted, ill-timed.

"Coming," she responded to Lucas's call. She looked up at the warrior and smiled again. "Thanks for saving my life and for this gift. I shall never forget you or today. Good-by," she murmured sadly.

Blazing Star sensed her reluctance to leave him, her powerful pull toward him. He grinned, for he knew they would meet again. They were both heading in the same direction.

Lucas called her name louder. She turned toward the sound and replied, "I'm coming, Luke. Just a minute." When she turned to ask the warrior's name and to give hers, he was gone. She looked around, but she could find no trace of him. He had vanished as soundlessly and mysteriously as he had appeared. If not for the object in her grasp, she might believe the episode never had happened. To make certain, she shook the object and listened to the musical rattle. She concealed it in her pocket; why, she didn't know. When she joined Lucas, she didn't mention the warrior.

Miranda remained close to Lucas as the repairs were completed and the steamer was freed from the sandbank. But she paid little attention to Lucas's conversation, for her thoughts were of the nearby woods and the fascinating warrior.

The steamer was reloaded. Until they were out of sight, she remained at the railing, staring at the area where they had gone ashore. Her spirits were heavy, for she felt no returning gaze. But as the journey continued, Miranda couldn't forget the imposing Indian. She felt denied of something vital to her life, to her heart. The feelings she was experiencing were tormenting. It might be wrong, but she would pray for their paths to cross again.

As the days passed, Blazing Star had a difficult time pushing the girl called Miranda from his thoughts. He berated himself for dreaming of her, for desiring her above all women he had met, for allowing her to ride with him each day and to sleep with him each night. He berated himself because she was white and he was Oglala Sioux, and the two bloods should never join again. For two such blendings in his distant past had cost him much honor. If two of his ancestors hadn't mated with white captives, he would be chief of the most awesome and powerful Indian tribe ever to rule the open Plains. Because of the love of Gray Eagle for a half-white captive and that of his son, Bright Arrow, for a white slave, the line of chiefs had passed to Bright Arrow's brother, Sun Cloud, who had wisely joined with a Blackfoot princess, Singing Wind, daughter of Chief Brave Bear and Sioux maiden, Chela, herself a daughter of a medicine chief. To make matters worse for the line of Gray Eagle, Night Stalker—son of Chief Sun Cloud—had been slain in a massacre when his only son, Bloody Arrow, was only five winters old, too young for the chief's bonnet. Now, the joint chiefs of their tribe were Sitting Bull and Crazy Horse, leaders with fame and skills to challenge those of the legendary Gray Eagle.

After having made certain the two enemies he had been assigned to kill were aboard this boat, the warrior traveled rapidly toward the steamer's next mandatory stop, the next lengthy stop which would entice the girl to leave the boat once more. He was glad he was on this raid alone; he didn't want the girl injured or slain during a battle, and certainly not captured by another warrior. After he sated his curiosity, he would seek a lofty bank in an area where the river narrowed to send two arrows toward the boat, one aimed for each enemy's heart. Then the matter would be over, for Blazing Star never missed a target.

In spite of the impossibility of the situation, he wanted to see the girl again. He would have one last chance to study her up close when the boat halted to cut wood just below Yankton, the only spot where fuel couldn't be purchased from "woodhawks," where the crew would have to cut and load it themselves. At such times, passengers left the boat to stretch their legs and relieve their boredom and tension. Riding alone and not requiring the numerous fuel stops of the steamer, the warrior could make better time. His fatal attack would come between Yankton and Pierre, on the last leg of this craft's journey.

In his stealthful trek northward, Blazing Star

did not bother to slay anyone along his path. There was so much killing and fighting these days, but not for honor as in olden times. He hated the scars he observed upon the face of Mother Earth, the nakedness of cleared land for farms and settlements, the cutting of all trees in some areas, the signs of careless fires, the fences which blocked trails, the many offenses of the whiteman. These intruders had grown strong and numerous, while sentencing Indians of all tribes and nations to prison camps the white man called "reservations." Many tribes had yielded to the white man's superior weapons and ample numbers, yielded because they had grown weak and dispirited from losses, yielded because continued fighting seemed futile and costly, yielded because of the whiteman's promises and treaties which were broken before the ink dried upon the meaningless papers. But the Sioux had not and never would be conquered. The Sioux would fight against the evil and greed which were destroying their lands and peoples to the last warrior.

Miranda didn't confide her brief adventure to her cousin Lucas, but she included every detail in her letter to Amanda which couldn't be mailed for two weeks. That momentous day and the next day, she was content to remain in her cabin, dreaming of the warrior left far behind, pining for a man she would never meet again. She couldn't forget him, for he invaded her thoughts during every hour. Why had he made such an impression on her? Why did knowing she would never see him again cause such grief and loneliness?

On the fourth morning after leaving Omaha and two days after Miranda had encountered the unforgettable warrior, the *Martha Lane* halted her engines for the crew to chop wood. At first, Miranda was tempted to stay aboard, but Lucas coaxed her ashore for a leisurely walk and invigorating exercise.

Some of the men who were playing cards remained on the boat. The two soldiers were locked in a cabin having a critical conversation which Lucas would have traded a month's pay to have heard. Other men helped the crew cut or haul wood. When the few males who had come ashore and didn't offer to help ogled Miranda, she asked Lucas to stroll with her at the edge of the woods. Out of sight, they sat down to relax and talk.

Time passed as they chatted about Amanda, Reis, Weber, and their destination. When it was nearing noon, Lucas grinned as he said he was going to fetch food and wine for a picnic. Miranda laughed gaily and agreed, waiting there for his return.

She leaned against the gray boulder at her back and closed her eyes briefly. She inhaled and exhaled deeply, capturing the fragrant odor of flowers and the spicy odor of woods. When her eyes opened, she couldn't believe the sight before them. She instantly sat straight, then curled her folded legs behind her.

"How did you get here?" she asked ecstatically, gazing into the dark eyes of the unknown warrior who was squatting beside her. A surge of joy rushed over her body.

From her tone of voice and expression, Blazing Star knew she was glad to see him again, as delighted as he was to see her. He stood, then extended his hand to her in invitation, which she accepted without hesitation or fear. He helped her up, then nodded toward the forest, implying he wanted her to go with him.

Miranda glanced over her shoulder toward the river. When her cousin returned, he would worry if she wasn't here. Was it rash to take a walk with a stranger who wore war paint? Her consternation was evident to him. He smiled again, holding out his hand enticingly. She longingly stared at it, perceiving no threat from him. If he wanted to abduct her or injure her, he could easily have done either. He wanted to see her alone. Should she go along with him? It seemed safe, but was it wise?

Blazing Star removed the decorative wristlet which displayed none of his *coups*, just lovely and colorful designs. He handed it to her as a sign of friendship. Miranda accepted it, noting its beauty and artistry. He motioned for her to take his hand and follow him. When she remained rigid, he smiled as if comprehending her reason for refusal, then turned to walk away into the forest.

Miranda panicked. She rushed forward, whispering, "Wait. Who are you? Why do you keep appearing to me in secret?"

He turned and looked at her anxious expression. He smiled once more to relax her tension, then reached for her hand. He led her only a short distance into the forest, just enough for privacy. When he halted and turned, Miranda nervously backed against a tree, suddenly wondering if this were a mistake.

In a voice which touched her very soul, he murmured, "*Kokipa ikopa*, Miranda." His hand came up to caress her flushed cheek, his touch as gentle as if she were a newborn infant. He was amazed and pleased by her show of trust in him, by her total lack of fear.

Surprise brightened her eyes when he told her not to be afraid, but the warrior didn't know she understood his language. Before Miranda could respond in the Sioux tongue which her mother had taught her, his mouth closed over hers, then she was a captive of his steely embrace. If Miranda had been the sweat of his own body, she could not have been closer to his flesh. He was astonished, and yet not shocked, when she responded to his kiss and embrace. Knowing this would be the last time they met, Blazing Star had the overwhelming need to hold her, to kiss her just once, to test her feelings for him.

Their thirsty lips joined, and his strong arms banded her so tightly she skipped several breaths; yet she clung to him fiercely. It was crazy! He hadn't meant to kiss her, even to touch her. It was as if he had no power over his emotions or actions. He felt he would die of hunger if he didn't feast on her lips. But the more sweetness he devoured from her lips, the more ravenous his starving body became, until it begged to feed upon hers. His weakness and her power stunned him, for such feelings should not exist. Yet, she shared this fire which burned within him.

When Lucas returned to where he had left Miranda, he called her name in concern. Miranda never heard him; she feverishly kissed the warrior before her, mindless of all else. But the warrior's senses were keen, and he heard the summons. He knew the man would come looking for her. For a wild moment, he was tempted to slay the man and to capture the girl who inspired such passion within him. But the time was wrong; he had something vital to do for his people.

He ceased his intoxicating assault upon her lips and emotions. "Miranda *ya.*" He informed her that she must leave his side, nodding toward the direction from which Lucas was calling her. He cupped her face between his hands and seemed to memorize it. Such uncommon indecision filled him. Surely it was wrong to desire an enemy so much.

Assuming Blazing Star couldn't speak or understand English, she responded to Lucas, "Just a moment, Luke, I needed privacy."

If she had known he caught each word, she would have flushed a bright scarlet. "Will I see you again?"

she asked eagerly. Unfortunately, she asked in English, not Sioux.

"Miranda *wilhanmna wincinyanna*," he stated huskily. "*Ya*."

Before she could question his order to leave or why he was calling her a "dream girl," he kissed her urgently and clamped his hand over her mouth afterward, fearing her words might influence him.

When Lucas's voice called out loudly to her, the warrior turned her body toward it. Determined he wouldn't get away without giving his name this time, she whirled to ask it in Sioux. He was gone! Just before shouting in Sioux for him to return, she mastered the impulse. How could she explain sneaking off with a warrior, a stranger, a dreaded and feared Sioux? How could she excuse her wanton behavior, even understand it herself? Most whites despised Indians; the passengers would hold her in contempt for her actions. What a tangled web! Who was he? To which Sioux tribe did he belong? She knew there were seven tribes with many bands. Would they meet again? she mused dreamily.

She called out to Lucas, saying she was coming to join him. She wondered about the warrior's appearance here. Was he following her? Or was it merely coincidence? Was he watching her this very moment? There was only one way to find out for sure. She would leave something behind for him and see if he had it the next time they met, if they ever did. She stuffed the beaded wristlet in her pocket, then removed the lacy scarf at her throat. She pressed it to her lips, then draped it over a bush before leaving.

Three days later, the *Martha Lane* made a two-day stop at Yankton, near Fort Randall. Little did Lucas and Miranda suspect what peril was in store for them, just as Amanda and Reis little suspected what evil was confronting them in Alexandria . . .

Chapter Twelve

After his much-awaited return to Alexandria, Reis spent all day Sunday with his wife. They talked, planned, joked, and made love. Later in the day, Amanda watched in disbelief as her dark, handsome husband transformed himself into a blond sailor in grimy clothes. Checking his new image in the mirror, he smiled and complimented himself on his crafty disguise.

"Now, if old Weber or his scum see me, they'll never guess who lurks beneath this golden hair and these dirty clothes," he remarked between chuckles. "All I have to do is sneak in both warehouses this week, make some notes for Grant, then close this case."

To conceal her apprehension, she asked, "What's Grant like?"

As if exposing a national secret, he whispered softly, "He likes to dress in old, baggy clothes—he would love this outfit. He smokes big black cigars that stink up a whole house. After you leave him, you smell awful for days. But he sure knows how to win a fight. If he hadn't captured Richmond, the war might have gone on and on."

"Do you like working for him more than you did for Lincoln?"

"Both are good men, love, but Lincoln was special. It was a dark day in our history when he was slain. He could have done so much for both sides. Did you know Lincoln offered your Lee the head of the Union Army, but he refused it? If not for Lee, the war wouldn't have lasted two years. A shame all good men can't be on the same side—war wouldn't have a chance of getting started. But one always leads to another, it seems."

"What do you mean, Reis?" Mandy asked.

As he put away his supplies, he talked with ease and intelligence. "The last one we fought started with the one in '12. The New England area got real nervous when we made the Louisiana Purchase; they threatened to secede and rejoin the British Empire. The President was smart; he prevented trouble with those *New Intercourse Laws*. You know what the Northern concession did? Riled up the Southern shipping interests. Lord, you just can't please everybody at once. The South was really suffering from lack of trade; they took heavy losses in cotton and tobacco markets. It was the Southern states that voted to go to war with the British Crown. The Northerners voted not to protect their ships and supplies. From then on, every little cut festered into one big sore until the wound burst open and spilled its vile contents. It's tragically ironic: the North threatens to secede to get her way, then goes to war when the South carries out her same threat.''

The topic was depressing and Amanda changed it with a question. "How did you get in last night? You said Weber has guards out front and back.''

"I sneaked into your neighbor's garden, climbed a tree near the wall, and flipped over. Considering the height of the wall around your yard, no one could see me. Whoever built this house certainly loved privacy.''

"Now that you've accomplished the easy part, how do you plan to get out? I don't have a tree near the wall. Of course, you could remain prisoner here with me," she hinted, smiling provocatively as she eased up on tiptoe to kiss him.

That night, Amanda snuggled into her husband's arms and inquired, "Reis, where will we live when this is all over? What will we do about Morning Star and Lawrence Shipping?''

"I think it should be a mutual decision, love, that we make after my tour of duty is finished. Until October first I am still under orders from President Grant. Our next decision will be whether or not you go on my next assignment with me or remain here until it's done.''

Amanda sat up in bed and stared at him. "There is

271

no decision; I'm going with you, husband dear. Even if you do look like a stranger," she teased him about his blond hair. "I'm glad it's dark, or I would have trouble making love to the man in my bed."

Reis chuckled as he propped himself up on two pillows. "I should tell you, love; I have no idea where or what my final assignment will be. When I get the news, you might change your mind."

"No," she vowed confidently. "You go; I go. You could get lonesome and forget you have a wife."

"Only if I lost my memory," he retorted playfully. "I'm glad Randy and Luke got away safely. And I know I shouldn't say this, but I'm glad your housekeeper won't be around for the next week or so."

"Does that mean I shall enjoy my wily husband's company every night?" she asked seductively, twirling her tongue on his chest.

"Every one possible. I'm suspicious about Reed's accident and those new guards outside. Weber's plotting something. There's no way I'll leave you alone at night unless I can't avoid it."

"You worry about me too much, Reis. I'm fine now that you're home. Besides, I know how to shoot and fight. I'm not as good as Randy, but I can defend myself," she declared proudly.

For a while they spoke of Miranda and Lucas. When she fretted over the safety of her sister and cousin, Reis reminded her of the letter of protection they were carrying from President Grant, one he had personally acquired and given to Lucas. Then Reis told her to go to sleep, that he would be stealing out before dawn. He added he would be late tomorrow night, if he came at all. He was planning to check out her warehouse, then Weber's the next night. She teased him about his recent vow to stay with her at night. He laughed and tickled her until she was squirming and breathless. He became serious when he warned her not to speak to him or show any recognition if they met on the street during the day. He took her office keys so he would be able to study any new and false information which Weber might be putting into her books.

Amanda tensed in fear when he told her he would also be analyzing the books of Daniel McVane and the ones in Weber's private office. He even hinted at breaking into Weber's home to see if there were any records of importance there.

"I'll be careful, love," he tried to calm her. "The sooner I solve this case, the sooner you can be Mrs. Reis Harrison in public," he tempted beguilingly, then pressed her to her back as he began a leisurely and stirring bout of passion.

Monday night was one of the longest nights for Amanda, for Reis never came home. She dozed little and paced until she was exhausted, but still she couldn't sleep. Tuesday passed as sluggishly as the day and night before, and her tension increased. By two in the morning, Amanda was beside herself with anxiety. Not only had Reis been gone since dawn on Monday, but Weber had not appeared as he had warned.

She wondered if the two absences were connected. After witnessing such evil in Weber Richardson, she feared for her husband's life. She could not tell Reis, but she was now willing to lose everything and leave with him this very night! She knew how deeply he despised Weber for his cruelties during the war. She refused to press him about those times because of the unusual coldness which froze his expression and the fires of revenge which burned in his eyes. Perhaps she feared that powerful hatred in him as much as she feared for him.

Shortly after noon on Wednesday, Weber paid her a call. She was dozing when he dropped by and it took a while for his knocking to arouse her from her heavy slumber on the sofa. She felt groggy and wanted to ignore the persistent summons, knowing it could not be her husband and finding any company undesirable at the moment.

The caller pounded loudly on the door. Weber called out, "Open this door, Mandy, or I'll break it down!"

When she unlocked the door, he shoved it open, almost snagging her toes beneath it. "What took so long?" he demanded angrily.

Amanda rubbed her sleepy eyes and moistened her dry lips. She fluffed her tousled hair and straightened her rumpled clothes. Then she looked at him and snapped, "I was asleep. I'm exhausted. I haven't been sleeping well with Randy and Mrs. Reed gone. Don't start on me, Weber! I'm not in the mood for a scolding." She sighed wearily then rubbed her eyes once more. "What do you want?"

"I was called away on an emergency. I just returned. When you didn't answer the door, I was worried. I thought you'd taken ill again, perhaps passed out," he declared petulantly when she didn't appear glad to see him.

"I surely am glad you didn't break down my front door. I could have been out visiting for the day," she informed him sassily, knowing how he knew she was home. "If you don't mind, Web, could we visit another day? I'm truly fainting from fatigue. I've gone for days without sleep or rest; the moment I finally slipped off, you came barging in, screaming at me. Was the emergency with my firm or yours?" she inquired, failing to offer him entrance.

"I was checking out a lead to Randy," he announced casually.

"What!" she blurted out in fear which passed for disbelief.

"I thought we could settle our problems quicker if I located your sister and brought her home. One of my hired men thought he recognized her on the street and followed her home. When I got there, it wasn't Randy. We searched all over. I'm sorry, Mandy, but we couldn't find her. Would you like me to hire a detective?" he inquired.

"No!" she yelled at him then explained heatedly, "I don't want my sister hunted down like some animal. Randy will come home when she's ready. If not, we'll both have to accept her decision, for whatever reason."

He studied her oddly. "Mandy, are you sure you're all right? You're awfully nervous, even a bit evasive."

"What the hell are you talking about?" she scoffed crudely. "How would you feel after days and nights without sleep? My sister's run off. I have a million worries. Then my best friend attacks my every word. Damnit, Weber, I'm a wreck!"

"Then marry me and let me take care of you," he offered.

"This is no way to begin a marriage, attacking each other every time we meet. Besides, I want the biggest and finest wedding this state's ever had. When I get things settled with the company, then I can decide what to do about you and your terrible moods."

"Another excuse to stall me?" he accused sullenly. "I can handle any problem while you plan our historical wedding."

"I promise to give you an answer this coming Sunday," she stated.

"There can be only one answer, Mandy. Your choice is me or the streets. Surely you don't need to weigh one against the other?"

"But you aren't my only choice, Weber," she told him rashly.

"You have another proposal? Who?" he snarled furiously.

"I meant work, not a man," she teased him.

"Just what kind of work can you do? I can't imagine Amanda Lawrence slaving anywhere," he playfully mocked her.

"Is that a fact, Mister Richardson?" she sneered as if insulted. "I daresay I can do many things to earn a living. I'm honest and loyal, and normally full of energy. And, no doubt, I could have five marriage proposals by next week, if I put my mind to it."

"I don't wish to sound cruel, my sweet, but how long would they remain extended if your loss of wealth and station were revealed?"

"You sound as if that's the only reason a man would court me!" she panted at him. "Since you know the truth, why not withdraw your offer?"

"Because I love you and want you, not what you have," he lied.

"Well, you certainly don't sound like it or behave like it of late! All you do is harass me, or scold me, or insult me. You act as if you enjoy demeaning me," she charged peevishly.

"Then why not get dressed and I'll take you out to dinner and the theater? We could ride to Washington and make a holiday of it. Why not elope?" he suggested eagerly. "That would be exciting and romantic. Just imagine the envy of your suitors."

"Elope!" she shrieked. "Don't be absurd, Weber. You know what people think of couples who elope. I won't have people thinking me pregnant. They would stare at me for nine months!"

"Amanda Lawrence, my patience is wearing thin. I demand an answer this minute," he declared stunningly, attempting to panic her.

Amanda's mind raced wildly toward a scheme to extract her from this precarious situation. "Unless your proclaimed love is also wearing thin, you will not mind having your answer Sunday. If such is the case, there is no need to consider your proposal. Love and marriage are not contests where points must be made to prove one's feelings. If you have no respect for my suffering, you are not the man to share my life. Shall it be Sunday, or never?'' she presented her own ultimatum.

"You're serious, aren't you?" he inquired in surprise.

"I have never been more so in my life," she told him smugly. "I will not discuss such a vital matter as marriage in this distraught state. I cannot make critical choices which will affect the rest of my life when I am torn by troubles and doubts and I am assailed by fatigue! If you find that unacceptable, then I bid you a permanent farewell."

"Then I shall wait until Sunday for your decision. But I must know you still want me."

"Your conduct and my numerous worries make it impossible for me to assess the depth of my feelings. I can only say they have not changed of late. Perhaps a trip would be a good diversion—give me time to relax and think. Perhaps the new owner of Morning Star wouldn't mind if I made a last visit. I do so regret losing it," she baited him.

"I don't think that's wise, Mandy. It would remind you of the days spent there with Randy and your parents. I don't want you to go so far alone," he gently protested her alarming suggestion. "If you wish to visit later, then I will escort you there."

"I suppose you're right. It would be too painful to go there again. But someday soon, I'll need to retrieve our personal belongings. Surely the new owner has packed and stored them for us. Perhaps I only need sleep," she hinted innocently.

Delighted he had changed her mind, he smiled and agreed. "To prove I'm not pushing you, I'll stay away until Sunday afternoon. If you promise to send for me if you need anything," he added jovially.

His words were like sweet music to her ears. She smiled to show her gratitude. "I promise. I don't know why you fret so, Weber; whoever could I choose over you?" she teased coyly. "Thanks for being so understanding and kind; I shan't forget it. Until Sunday," she hinted.

"Until Sunday, my sweet," he replied. He kissed her hand, then left whistling.

Amanda knew why he was so elated. He was glad he wouldn't have to see her for days and relieved not to have to play this game where he might make a wrong move. He was so cocky! Without a doubt, he believed she would say yes on Sunday. If only he knew she was already legally wed, and to a man she loved above life itself.

Relief flooded her. Surely he didn't know about Reis. Else, he would have tried to entrap her with enticing hints or blunt statements. Surely Reis would come home tonight. With that conclusion, she rushed upstairs for a nap. "I'll be wide awake and full of energy tonight," she said aloud with a happy giggle.

When she awoke, she warmed water for a bath in the private closet near the kitchen. After a leisurely soaking, she was about to don a lovely dress but decided upon a sensual nightgown instead. Just as she was brushing her golden tresses, she sniffed several times. She shook her head, telling herself she couldn't smell food cooking. How could she? She was alone, and Mrs. Reed didn't have a key. Except for coffee and water, she hadn't used the stove today. When the fragrant aromas increased, she went to investigate, her bare feet treading soundlessly on the floor.

As she peered around the doorframe, she was astonished and delighted to see her husband standing near the stove working contentedly. Deep in thought, he didn't seem aware of her. She watched his profile for a brief time, pondering his intense concentration.

She wondered over his odd behavior. He had come home and started cooking without even saying hello! "Reis Harrison, whatever are you doing?" she questioned as she entered the room.

He jumped and whirled around, his hand automatically going for his concealed weapon. He swiftly mastered his poise and expression. "Making us some supper. I'm starved. It's about time you joined me, wife. I've been exceptionally good to let you nap and bathe before showing you my splendid face. I fully expect to be rewarded for such generosity," he jested mirthfully, confusing her.

He focused his gaze on his cooking, rather than showering her with kisses and hugs. He seemed reserved, distant. Yet, she watched him cover that inexplicable mood with contrived gaiety. "I don't understand," she murmured, coming to stand beside him at the stove. She wanted to fling herself into his arms and to kiss him feverishly, but something about his manner prevented it. He seemed so different.

"While old Weber was trying to beat down the front door, I was sneaking in the back. You certainly did some mighty persuasive acting, love. I surely am glad you're on my side. I would hate to imagine those charms, wits, and courage working against me," he jested roguishly, removing the fried salt pork from the skillet.

"You've been here since noon? Why didn't you show yourself after Weber left?" she asked in confusion, hurt by his actions. That statement meant he had overheard her talk with Weber. It also meant he had been hiding from her since his furtive arrival. Why?

He excused his actions by saying, "You sounded as exhausted as you looked. I knew that part of your colorful tale was true. If you hadn't gone right to sleep, I would have joined you in bed," he stated huskily, slipping an arm around her waist as he worked with the other hand. "I took a short nap in Randy's room; I was dead tired too. I straightened the covers, but you might want to peek in there before Mrs. Reed returns to work. We don't want her discovering our little secret. How do you like your eggs cooked?" he inquired casually.

Amanda simply stared at him as he began cracking

eggs and dropping their contents into a bowl. "What's wrong with you?" she asked.

He looked up from his task and questioned, "What do you mean?"

"You vanish for days, then appear without bothering to explain. Do you know how worried and frightened I've been? When you do come home, you're more interested in sleep and food than your wife!" she charged, provoked by his indifferent mood and lack of affectionate greeting.

"Can't business wait until later? I'd prefer to spend a quiet evening with my wife. Have supper and . . . turn in early," he hinted seductively. "These last few days and nights have been terrible, Mandy. Am I being selfish to want you as my only thought for tonight? Isn't it better this way? I only wanted to surprise you."

"Well, you certainly did," she informed him crisply. "I can see why you would let me take a nap, but why wait so long afterward?" She wanted to demand he tell her why he was being so remote, but she didn't. She fretted mutely over this new side of him.

Passion danced within his dark blue eyes. His mood mellowed, and he smiled contritely. "To enjoy what I'm seeing right this minute." His appreciative gaze moved over her shiny hair and enticing nightgown; then, he inhaled the freshness of her skin and the sweetness of her cologne. "I'll confess I heard what you planned for me as you raced upstairs, and I controlled myself to wait for my surprise."

He chuckled when her cheeks flushed crimson. "It isn't often a husband gets seduced by such beauty and eagerness."

"How would you know? You are new at this role, aren't you?" she responded coyly as she noted a half-grin tugging at his sensual lips.

"Yep, but I've heard plenty of tales which could inspire any male to avoid marriage. Evidently I made a wise choice," he told her, pulling her into his arms. He didn't kiss her immediately. He just held her tenderly, caressing her back and inhaling her fragrance.

Her dreamy gaze touched on a small leather case on the floor near a chair. She was puzzled when he stiffened at her question, "Were you working? Does that satchel contain evidence against Weber?"

He released her and returned to his task. "I thought we agreed business could wait until later. Let's eat and relax."

"You agreed; I didn't. Did something happen you don't want to tell me?" she asked suspiciously.

"All right, have it your way," he stated a little brusquely. "I was making out my report. I obtained some evidence, but not enough. I couldn't get home or send word without tipping my hand. I did warn you our relationship was secret and my mission might require my absence on occasion," he reminded her moodily.

"You don't have to sound so hateful," she chided him. "What evidence did you get? How much longer will it take? Weber is pressing me again, as you heard," she added snippily when he scowled.

"I told you I wanted our discussion to wait because I knew you'd get angry and upset by it. That was a foolish thing to tell him, Mandy. What if I can't solve this case by Sunday; what then? He's going to get suspicious. As to the evidence, I can't tell you. That way, you can't drop clues when you play your reckless games with Weber."

"What was I supposed to do?" she flared back at him, rankled.

"For starters, agree to his idea about Randy. That should keep him occupied for a while, maybe distracted from what I'm doing and from wooing my wife. What new excuse do you plan to use Sunday?"

She was shocked by his suggestion. "You want him to search for her? Heavens, Reis, what if he found her? I would be in danger!"

"I doubt he or his hired thugs could find any trace of her. And even so, you could always play dumb; you could act tricked by her and Luke. There's no way Weber could prove you were involved in their scheme, even if he suspected it. Aren't you forgetting he knows why she left, but he thinks you don't? He can't harm Randy. I'll know if he leaves town and heads that way. I can warn Luke. If he thinks there's the slightest chance of finding her, he won't be pushing you so hard."

"You sound as if I'm his last choice!" she pouted petulantly.

"Stow that pride, Mandy, or it'll get you into trouble. He wants her because he thinks he can manage her more easily than you and because she's unobtainable, the irresistible temptation."

"What do you mean, she's more manageable?" she probed.

"You are one bullheaded, outspoken female. You're smart and willful. Randy's quiet and reserved, and gives Weber the impression she isn't as intelligent as you. Also, you know the business and like it; she doesn't. Her lack of knowledge and interest in the firm would protect his schemes. And you don't seem easily intimidated or misled; Randy's shyness implies she can be. Weber has vastly underestimated her, and you should use that ignorance and conceit against him. Don't be so damn friendly with him," he declared possessively, his jealousy and vexation born of worry over her.

Amanda wanted to argue against his statements, but she couldn't. She sullenly acquiesced. "I'll correct my errors tomorrow."

"While we're at it, we might as well cover all points. I want you to stop taking such rash chances. I can handle the case against Weber, so stop trying to assist me. How can I concentrate on success if I'm worried about you and what you're doing? I can't promise to be around every night, and I can't risk sending a message. And I can't confide my plans to you. There are others involved now, and I won't risk endangering more lives. I don't think you realize the importance of this mission. You're being childish and selfish, Mandy. This isn't the time to prove you can outwit Weber or gain revenge on him. I take chances every time I come here. Hellfire, I risked death and defeat by confiding in you and marrying you so I wouldn't lose you! What more do you want from me?'' he thundered.

Amanda determined she wouldn't cry, but it was a battle to control her tears. Why was he being so mean, so defensive, so secretive? It wasn't jealousy. "You know where I am, but I have no idea where you go or what perils you confront! For all I knew, you could have been lying dead somewhere! You're my husband, Reis. I love you. I was so frightened I almost contacted President Grant.''

"You what!" he stormed at her, his eyes chilling at the vision of what her loose tongue could inspire. "Don't you ever contact him or anyone about me! You want to get me killed? Or in deep trouble? If anyone knew about us . . ." He fell silent, then struck the table forcefully in unleashed fury. "It was a mistake to marry during a critical mission. Damn, I gave you credit for more sense. All you want to do is play amateur detective, and damn the rules and consequences! Why can't you stay out of trouble and mischief? What have I gotten myself into? You could ruin everything, Mandy. Lives and national security are at stake. If you loved me and trusted me, you'd do as I asked.''

She was devastated by his insults. Her chin and lips quivered and tears blurred her vision. A lump came to her throat. He had dropped into a chair and was staring blankly at his clasped hands, musing over how to handle this complex female. When she could force words from her throat, she said in a trembly voice, "If this is any indication of what marriage to a spy is like, then it was a mistake for us to wed. Perhaps we shouldn't see each other again until this 'critical' mission is over, or else we might ruin our relationship all together. I wouldn't want to jeopardize it or any lives, especially yours and mine. Don't feel obligated to check on me; I'll be just fine. As to Weber, I'll follow your orders, sir. After you feed your starving body, feel free to sneak out at your leisure. If you think you've made a terrible mistake by marrying me, then by all means correct it as quickly as possible," she stated, then fled the tormenting room, slamming and locking her bedroom door.

Reis propped his elbows on the table and rested his forehead on his palms, berating himself for taking his frustrations and fears out on his innocent wife. It wasn't fair; he had been cruel. He couldn't tell her he was distressed because one of his agents had been killed last night, for she would worry over his survival too much. Now, he must write a letter of condolence to Bill Hayes's family.

He couldn't blame her because Weber had tightened the security around both warehouses before he could complete his investigations. He was further disturbed because he and George Findley hadn't been given the time to sabotage the illegal weapons they had located in Weber's crates. And he had discovered that a Ku Klux Klan meeting had been arranged for next week, a meeting to plan violence to black voters and several carpetbaggers, and to discuss the possible assassination of Jefferson Davis to rile up the South.

He had taken an oath of silence and loyalty to America for the President. He shouldn't have become so angered by her fear for him, but he couldn't allow any contact with Washington. Grant had many enemies in his administration. Grant had made some terrible errors in judgment, in special-interest legislation, and in patronage. There was much corruption and scandal surrounding the President, and he was trying to correct it and redeem himself with Reis's help. Only Grant knew of his missions. If Amanda dropped clues into the wrong ears, all could be ruined. But if he couldn't trust her, he couldn't trust anyone! Why hadn't he simply explained that no one but Grant knew of this mission?

He couldn't admit to irrational jealousy this afternoon. It wasn't her fault her life was in danger. It wasn't her fault that he had almost been caught by Weber because he had been distracted by thoughts of her! She hadn't seduced him or tricked him into a wedding. She hadn't married him for fear of poverty. It wasn't her fault he wanted this mission over so they could be together and she could be safe.

She had become like an obsession to him, a perilous weakness, a deadly distraction. Yet, those were his problems, not hers. How could he have said such hateful things to her? Hellfire, he hadn't even shown or told her how much he had missed her! What was he doing to her, to them?

Weber Richardson—he was the evil force in this matter. God, how he wanted to kill that man barehanded! Each time he saw Weber or overheard him plotting, it became more difficult to restrain his hatred and desire for revenge. But if he killed Weber, the trail to the others involved in these crimes would be lost. This case was so complicated and demanding. He stood and stretched to relax his taut muscles, then headed for Amanda's room to beg her forgiveness and understanding.

As Reis mounted the steps wondering how to explain his mercurial moods, he knew the only way to show his love and trust was to tell her everything. He had never been this edgy or indecisive. But he had never had someone more precious than life to fret over, to protect. Amanda was right; if he died while carrying out this mission, she wouldn't even know why she had lost him. No one would even know to contact her with such grim news! He sighed heavily, thinking how glad he was that Miranda and Lucas were safe and happy . . .

Chapter Thirteen

It didn't take long for Lucas to realize that wild Yankton wasn't the place for him and Miranda, and neither was their second stop, Fort Randall. They would continue toward Pierre on the *Martha Lane* tomorrow morning.

With two railroads joining in Yankton soon, the town was overflowing with workmen, "ladies of pleasure," and a variety of opportunists. Two mills were being built near town: a flour mill and a lumber mill. A packing plant and foundry were under discussion for imminent construction. Several rowdy saloons were ready for use, with numerous others under construction or planning. Headquarters for freight companies and stagelines had blossomed in and around Yankton. The town was full of crime and violence and Lucas felt they should move on, as the area offered nothing but trouble.

But their brief stay at Fort Randall provided some

grim and interesting insights. Miranda and Lucas
were both surprised by the boredom and hardships
which filled the average soldier's life. They had been
led to believe the soldiers and settlers in this area led
exciting, profitable, and pleasant lives. But the
colorful adventures printed in newspapers and books
were fantasies or fictionalized accounts.

Lucas was fascinated by all he saw and learned,
and made careful notes for future stories or articles.
He questioned almost everyone he met about three
men in particular. His pouch grew fat with information, facts and figures which he was only too eager to
share with Miranda.

True, the Army did protect the trails and railroads,
the miners and settlers, the cattlemen and sheep-
herders, and the traders. The Army did do surveys for
railroad lines and telegraph lines or protect the crews
which carried out such necessary jobs. The Army did
battle "hostiles," as the Indians were labeled.
Sometimes, the Army did the work for companies,
such as building roads or clearing land. Yet, the
majority of time was spent with arduous chores in
or around the fort.

One thing which Miranda found intriguing was
the Army's contradictory views on marriage amongst
its enlisted men. The men were lonely and miserable;
yet families were discouraged. The men's carnal
needs were met in several ways. At some forts, whores
were permitted to live and ply their trades. At others,
women who served as cooks and laundresses also
served as whores for the men who could afford such

luxuries. At still others, wagons arrived every few weeks with prostitutes, games, and whiskey for sale; at such times, some men spent their entire month's wages in one day. Sadly, in some cases, widows or daughters were forced into such professions when left alone and penniless. Many soldiers used Indian women from the nearby reservations to sate their lusts. At those forts which existed near settlements, saloons offered the soldiers their three desires: drink, women, and gambling.

It seemed to Miranda that a happily married man would make a better soldier. Clearly the US Army disagreed. But those men who were fortunate enough to have wives had private homes and relief from boredom and sacrifice; they were in better health and were better fed. Miranda quickly learned that a female, especially a pretty one, was flooded with proposals of all kinds. After a few days in this territory, she was beginning to wonder if she should pretend to be Lucas's wife rather than his sister to dissuade so many men from pursuing her, including the men on the ship!

Before leaving on the steamer, Lucas sent Amanda another telegram, revealing their next destination. He asked her to contact him at Pierre, for he intended to be there for quite some time and needed to hear how she was. To continue their charade, he told Amanda to pass along his greetings to Miranda in Charleston. He stated he would write a lengthy letter from Pierre to relate his adventures there.

Lucas gradually uncovered facts which deeply

distressed him. General William T. Sherman, who had terrorized and destroyed much of the South and boasted loudly of his atrocities, was the commanding general of the Army and was in charge of this territory. Lucas discovered he was operating out of Fort Richardson in Texas. President Grant had given Division of Missouri command to Philip Sheridan, who was working the middle area near Fort Dodge in Kansas.

The Division of Missouri was an immense tract, an area which included the Dakota Territory, stretching from Canada to the coast of Texas and from the Rockies to the Mississippi River, and comprising over a million frontier miles, including sacred and hunting grounds of nearly one hundred tribes. Several tribes which were causing major problems for the Army were the Sioux, Cheyenne, Apache, Comanche, and Kiowas—all known for fiercely defending their homes, lands, and people.

Added to those powerful forces was George Custer, known to have executed seven Rebels during the Civil War without a trial, and now assigned to the Seventh Cavalry at Fort Lincoln. During the Civil War, Custer had risen to the rank of general; here in the Cavalry, he was ranked a lieutenant colonel. But from all Lucas had heard, Custer was rapidly working on improving his rank to general once more. As Sheridan told Custer, "Kill or hang all warriors." This statement appeared to epitomize the thoughts and actions of all three men. Lucas had learned so much about Indians from Marie Lawrence, and it alarmed him to realize the Army's strategy was the annihilation of all Indians, male and female, old and young, especially the awesome and influential Sioux, Marie's family and people, and Miranda's relatives.

After mutually devastating the South during the war, all three leaders were now here trying to do the same with the Indian in the West. No success could be had until they realized this terrain, these battles, and this enemy were vastly dissimilar to those of the Civil War. Lucas's blood raced with elation at the thought of not only exposing the vile war deeds of these three men, but of revealing their grisly actions here in the West. Surely the combined revelations would be detrimental to their careers.

As the steamer made its way toward Pierre, Lucas spent as much time as possible with the two soldiers aboard who had been transferred from Sherman's troop to Custer's. Having a weakness for whiskey and suffering from boredom, the two men accepted the drinks purchased by Lucas, in exchange for colorful tales and intriguing facts about both men and their campaigns. Led to believe Lucas Reardon was a famous writer, the men boasted of exploits in which they had participated, hoping to become as well known as Custer and Sherman.

A wily reporter, Lucas found it easy to extract information from these men. His only problem was in separating fact from fiction. Lucas's genial personality and boyish mien aided his quest for truth. Lucas learned about the notorious "Indian

Ring" of corruption and fraud. He discovered that Sherman was on the rampage once more, now that Satanta of the fierce Kiowa Indians had been released from prison. He listened to grisly tales of massacres which sickened, repulsed, and saddened him.

Both soldiers had shown a strong interest in Miranda, and Lucas cautioned her to watch her step around them. But she had to walk a fine line between silencing them with haughty rejection and inspiring a steady flow of confessions with cordial behavior. The day before they were to join their new troop, the two soldiers ceased their heavy drinking. It was time to sober up minds and clean up appearances. But clearer heads offered trouble for Lucas and Miranda. When the two soldiers began to compare mental notes on the cunning pair, they realized the couple had been asking too many questions about their leaders and exploits. Suddenly they feared Lucas might be a government agent investigating war crimes.

Ignorant of the danger they faced, Lucas went over his impending strategy with Miranda. "One of those soldiers told me our old friend, Thomas Baylor from Virginia, is assigned to Sherman. If we can catch up to him before going home, with luck Tom can get me a personal interview with the beast."

"And what if Sherman guesses what you're trying to pull?" she speculated fearfully, imagining what that man alone could do to her cousin, not daring to envision all three villains at his back.

"He won't; I'll be careful. With the egos of those

three, they'll think I'm glorifying their famous names. Or should I say infamous. Besides, the way things are going out here, the settlers are starting to hate the soldiers more than the Indians. I heard a group of them bragging at Fort Randall about foraging on settlers between pay periods. They made it sound like a common practice for the entire territory."

"What's our next stop?" she inquired anxiously.

"After we load fuel once more, we're supposed to halt at the Lower Brule Reservation to drop off supplies—Indian annuities they called them. We'll only be there a few hours, then head on to Pierre. Good thing we're staying there because that's the termination point for this steamer. The pilot said we could either take another steamer or go north by stage. From the hints I've been gathering, Pierre sounds like a good place to linger," he stated, piquing her curiosity.

"Why?" she quickly probed, eyes bright and wide.

"You'll see," he teased mysteriously, playfully. "You get your letter finished to Mandy and we'll mail it in Pierre. I surely hope we have word waiting for us from her and Reis. It surely would help my mood knowing Weber had been put away for keeps."

"Me too," she concurred.

When the steamer halted its engine, Lucas wondered why Miranda was so eager to go for a walk. She looked as excited as a child on a birthday. She was even more elated when she learned there was no "woodhawk" here and the crew must cut wood—it would be a lengthy stop.

Once ashore, the two soldiers joined them for a talk and stroll, vexing Miranda for more than one reason. She didn't like these two males or trust them. She preferred to be alone or with Lucas. Still, she couldn't keep sneaking off without arousing suspicion. She was anxious to learn if the handsome warrior was still trailing her. And she didn't want to spend time with the two soldiers who made her uneasy, especially today. She sensed something different in their moods, their expressions, their tones.

Anson Miller and Jim Rhodes chatted with Lucas for five or ten minutes, but Miranda paid little attention. A provocative word here and there brought her to alertness. She listened as Jim told Lucas about an old reservation within walking distance. Since Lucas and Miranda had shown such an interest in the Indians, Jim suggested they walk there, hinting they might find arrowheads or such for souvenirs.

Anson remarked, "Surely you've heard of Spotted Tail, the famous Sioux chief? They even named the agency after him, Spotted Tail-Whetstone. The old chief went to Washington in '70 to see Grant himself. Told him the area was trouble 'cause of whiskey traders. Had to have somebody to blame when his warriors got falling-down drunk," he stated between chuckles. "Old Spotted Tail was powerful and Grant didn't want him on the warpath again, so he let them move near White River close to them sacred Black Hills. Didja know Spotted Tail's sister is Crazy

Horse's mother? You do know who Crazy Horse is?" he teased.

Before Lucas or Miranda could reply either way, Jim quickly inserted, "They probably don't want to see no remains of savages—you know there's still bones in some of them trees from that crazy burial practice afore it was outlawed—just old fires and raggedy teepees."

"Luke here's a writer, Jim; he needs to see things like that. Don't you, Luke?" Anson argued as they set their trap for an unsuspecting Luke and Miranda.

"Well, I'm sure Miss Miranda don't care to gaze upon such ugly sights," Jim remarked. He grinned and muttered, "'Course she does seem the brave, adventurous type. You got a good helper, Luke."

Lucas glanced at Miranda and asked, "You want to see it?"

Miranda didn't know which she wanted to see more, the old campsite or . . . Suppose this was that mysterious warrior's old campground; he had spoken Sioux, and the soldier had stated that Spotted Tail was Sioux. Suppose he had returned to his old territory or ancestral grounds for a special reason. She mentally chided herself for centering her plans around a man who might be days away from here. If the warrior wanted to see her again, he would find a way, as he had twice before. She smiled amiably and nodded trustingly, taking Lucas's hand to walk near him.

Anson and Jim talked freely as they guided the two out of earshot of the steamer. Finally, Lucas asked,

"This seems a mite far, Jim. Maybe we should head back. We don't want to get lost."

Anson stopped and informed them, "Let me check the marker back there. Maybe we took a wrong path. We should be there by now." He walked past them, then suddenly turned and struck Lucas on the head with its pistol butt, rendering him unconscious.

Miranda screamed, dropping to her knees to check on her cousin. Lucas was out cold and blood was wetting his hair. Alarmed and stunned, her head jerked upward as she shrieked, "Why did you do that?"

Anson leaned over and seized her around the waist. He flung her to the grass and straddled her. He stated ominously, "So I could do this," then kissed her.

Miranda struggled in his tight grasp as his slobbery lips refused to leave hers. From above their tangled bodies, she could hear Jim's laughter and jests, encouraging Anson to hurry and to give him a turn with her. As Jim verbally planned his coming actions ahead, she cringed in terror as she comprehended their plan—rape!

Miranda knew it was useless to plead, and she didn't. It would only be amusing to them. Considering the distance they had walked, she also knew it was futile to yell for help. Lucas was injured, and she had no weapon. She was at their mercy. If only she were standing, she could use the Chinese defense movements taught to her. She thrashed wildly on the ground, but Anson was strong and heavy. When she tried to claw at his face, he told Jim to tie her wrists.

The other soldier delighted in tearing a strip from her dress then binding her hands tightly. "You want me to tie her feet?" Jim asked when she continued to kick at Anson.

"Hell, no!" Anson shrieked. "How would I get twixt her legs, fool? You just hold her still while I shuck these pants."

With Anson standing between her parted thighs, Jim straddled Miranda's middle. Anson wiggled his pants down to his boots. Jim laughed when she beat at his leg with tightly bound hands and tried to twist free. "You ain't gonna git undressed?" he asked when Anson merely lowered his pants and unfastened the crotch of his longjohns to free a thick shaft which was taut and drooling with hunger.

"Ain't got time. I'm hurting as it is. This big stud needs a fast mating," Anson replied crudely, fondly caressing his aching manhood. He knelt, seizing her imprisoned hands and throwing his confining body on hers as Jim lifted his weight.

By that time, Lucas was stirring and groaning. Anson laughed satanically as Jim struck him again, this time harder. "I'll tie that sly fox whilst you have your turn with her. You ain't gonna spoil our fun, boy. You just lie still 'til we git some relief."

Miranda prayed Lucas was alive, but she feared he wasn't. He was so still and his chest didn't appear to rise and fall. There was so much blood running down into his brown curls. For a time, she had more concern and attention for Lucas than for herself. But with his groin exposed and hardened, Anson's forceful and lewd grinding against her private region refreshed her peril.

When she screamed and fought with renewed energy from fear and fury, Jim asked if Anson wanted her silenced. Anson laughed coldly and said, "No need. Can't nobody hear her. 'Sides, she'll be sighing in pleasure real soon. You know how them women from Newman's wagons fight over who's gonna take care of this boy. Hell, most of the time they don't even charge me!" he boasted falsely. "You tie that youngster, then git ready to follow me. Let's get some relief, then we'll have some slow fun. These two'll pay for tricking us. Luke there won't make no reports to nobody. As for this little filly, we might find somebody willing to pay hefty for 'er, if they's anything left."

There wasn't time for Miranda to ponder his odd words or ominous threat. While she tried to resist the demands of Anson, Jim bound Lucas with his belt and rolled him into the bushes, saying he didn't want no kin staring at him while he enjoyed a "good balling."

Jim started undressing, hopping around on one foot as he removed the boot from the other. Unable to pull his eyes from Anson as he fumbled to find the waistband of her bloomers, Jim pulled off the other boot and his pants, tossing his clothes and gun in a pile. He unbuttoned his longjohns and was attempting to yank them off.

The air was silent but for the heavy breathing from three people and Miranda's grunts as she attempted to keep Anson from removing her bloomers. Unable to stop herself, she yelled at him, "You bastard! You'll pay for this! Get off of me! Touch me and I'll kill you!"

Suddenly, loud and ferocious growls offered more noise and threat than a violent thunderstorm. Anson ceased his attack to shout, "What was that, Jim?" Both men stiffened as small trees to their left moved violently as something awesome headed in their direction.

"I hope it ain't what I think," Jim replied hastily, frantically trying to free his arms from his last garment. He lunged for his discarded weapon, wishing he had his Springfield rifle from the boat.

Jim tossed clothes and boots in all directions and located his Army-issue revolver, but it jammed during the panic of the moment as he fired wildly into the trees. He cursed as he fumbled feverishly to get it working. If only he had that new Colt he had been promised.

Anson made a rolling dive for his weapon, but it was too late. A large, dark blur had surged from the concealing trees, heading for Anson who had tripped on the pants around his ankles. Still fully clothed, Miranda scrambled to lower her skirt and to avoid attracting the bear's attention. She hastily pressed herself against a large rock and attempted to control her noisy respiration.

Miranda had never seen a bear so large. His head and body were massive. When he growled, she could see long, sharp teeth, as well as the saliva which drooled from his mouth. Although his eyes appeared very small, he seemed to have no trouble locating his prey. He moved swiftly and formidably, not at all like the clumsy performing bears back east. His furry coat was a thick yellowy brown. As he agilely ambled toward the two men, Miranda froze in terror.

The creature suddenly raised himself to his full height of over seven feet, seven feet of powerful muscle without fear. She realized his arms nearly reached his groin. At the ends of those forelegs were two sets of claws longer than her fingers!

During the initial flurry of action, the two soldiers had shouted back and forth. "Forget the gun and clothes, Jim! Let's run, run. It's a grizzly." But Anson had fallen forward as his trembling hands couldn't pull his pants from around his shaky ankles. The grizzly was on him in a flicker of an eye. Those gaping jaws ripped flesh and clothes, sending bits of both flying in all directions as the beast viciously mauled him.

When Jim tossed the useless gun aside and was about to leave all behind to flee to safety, the monstrous animal left the severely wounded Anson to pursue him. The man didn't get far before the grizzly came to full height again, waving his paws and growling. Jim made a fatal error when he turned to see how close behind the bear was. With a lightning flash of one paw, the bear made a lethal slash across Jim's throat. Jim was dead before the silence returned after his agonizing scream.

When the groggy and pain-riddled Anson began to

moan, the bear's attention became focused on him again. The smell of blood overwhelmed the fresh air, and the stench of slaughter gradually joined it. Miranda's brain was too dazed to order her to flee this ghastly sight. With a rolling gait, the bear nonchalantly returned to Anson's scarlet-covered frame. Anson screamed and sobbed, rolling to his stomach to protect his face and vulnerable belly, forgetting to play dead until the bear lost interest and left. As Anson shuddered and wept, fear permeated the air, an emotion which encouraged and pleased the enormous animal.

The grizzly rolled Anson to his back with one forceful swipe, tearing flesh and clothes with those sharp instruments of death and destruction. Miranda was grateful the fuzzy body prevented her view, as she seemed unable to look away.

How she wished she couldn't hear the sounds of torture and death. Her heart pounded so forcefully that her chest and throat ached. Nausea churned her stomach and assailed her throat. Her gaze seemed to go out of focus, and lightness filled her head. Her mouth was dry. She was so cold, her body felt like stone. She feared she would faint, yet she couldn't scream in terror, or cry in fear, or even babble in hysteria. All she could do was sit petrified, unable to move. She, or Lucas, would be the next victim.

A warm hand clamped over her mouth and shifted her head. Her eyes enlarged and misted as they took in the most beautiful and encouraging sight she had ever viewed. Blazing Star pressed his finger to his lips, commanding silence. His keen eyes glanced at the bear whose attention was on the dead soldier. Without making a sound, he took his knife and severed her bonds.

Uncontrollably and ecstatically, she flung herself against his coppery chest and burst into alerting sobs as her arms encircled his waist. For a moment, the warrior's arms embraced and comforted her. Instantly the bear's attention was seized and the massive head turned in their direction. Blazing Star stiffened, coming to full alert. As the animal slowly lumbered their way, the warrior gently shoved Miranda aside and shifted his knife in his grip.

The bear was considered a warrior of the forest by the Indians, a symbol of wisdom. A bear was never killed lightly. When necessary, it had to be done with skill and daring, in hand-to-paw combat. Only a warrior who had slain a bear could wear the claws around his neck. The warrior didn't wish to slay his brother of the forest, but he had no choice. He could easily flee danger, but the girl couldn't.

To draw attention from Miranda, Blazing Star jumped to his feet and rushed to a small clearing, sending forth Indian whoops. The warrior crouched and awaited the answer to his challenge, one which was sure to come. The grizzly headed for the warrior, ignoring the girl who was gaping in sheer terror.

Miranda knew she was to blame for endangering their lives. But no power could enable her to take back her rash mistake. She prayed as she had never prayed before. But what could a knife do against such imposing strength and ten lethal claws? Should she run? Was the warrior only distracting the beast for her to escape? But what about Lucas? What if her escape movements attracted the bear's attention? What about the man who was risking his life for her?

She watched the intrepid warrior and the large creature as each sized up the other. She couldn't suppress a scream when the bear swiped at the warrior with those deadly paws. But the warrior was agile and quick, and the bear's attack was unsuccessful. As they moved and slashed at each other, it became a deadly dance of death. She wondered how long the warrior could avoid those destructive weapons. Surely his six-foot frame was no match for such height and weight.

If possible, Miranda's terror had increased with the warrior's involvement in this drama. She saw blood on the knife; yet the warrior's virile body revealed no cuts. She witnessed confidence and determination in the warrior's expression and movements. He exuded physical prowess. Was it possible he could win such a fierce battle?

Weapon . . . She recalled the soldier's guns. She forced her wobbly legs to crawl toward them, desperately trying to keep her gaze off two grim sights. Her eyes darted around as she failed to locate either pistol. It was as if they had vanished. But Miranda hadn't seen the bear's paw fling them into the bushes during his two attacks.

She hurried to Lucas's prone body, placing her ear on his chest to find his heart still beating. She struggled to free him, finally succeeding. But she couldn't arouse him. With luck and prayers, the bear might overlook him, so she left Lucas where he was.

When she entered the open area once more, screams of horror were torn from her throat as the warrior fell backward to the ground and the grizzly charged at him with claws curled ominously. Miranda shouted and stomped the hard ground, trying to pull the bear's attention from the warrior until he could regain his footing and balance. She avidly sought items to seize the menacing foe's eye, tossing rocks and small limbs at the huge body of dark fur. The bear ignored her and continued his charge on the fallen and weaponless Indian. Unable to witness this man's death, she screamed an echoing "no" and slipped to the ground as protective and merciful blackness engulfed her.

Blazing Star was given the split second needed for victory when the bear whirled toward the loud noise. The bear was fatigued from his previous killings and the battle with the warrior. He was distracted and sluggish. Already weakening from a speedy loss of blood from the wounds in his chest and throat, the animal was doomed as Blazing Star sent his lethal blade home. The bear staggered and slowly sank to the blood-spattered ground.

Blazing Star rushed to Miranda's side, dropping to his knees to pull her into his arms. Clearly she had tried to draw the creature's attention and attack to her, to save his life. She had been willing to die for him. That reality stunned his senses but thrilled his heart. She was so pale and cool. Blazing Star sat down and cuddled her in his embrace. He placed kisses on her face and lips. He thanked the Great Spirit for bringing him here to save her life. His mission was over; the two soldiers were dead. For some inexplicable reason, he was glad he hadn't been compelled to kill them before her lovely eyes. It was time to return to his people. He fretted over the feelings he was experiencing: loneliness, desire, and indecision.

Miranda's eyes fluttered and opened. She was bewildered. She was lying on her back in the forest, gazing at the movement of leaves overhead as the wind slipped through them. But for the singing of birds and the soft rustle of leaves, it was so quiet and peaceful. She sighed tranquilly and stretched her limp body. Abruptly she bolted to a sitting position and looked around her. Lucas was lying near her, his head bandaged with strips from his shirt. They were alone, in a different spot!

Voices caught her attention in the distance. She realized they were near the river, near the anchored steamer, near help. But who had brought them here? Where was the warrior?

Her heart thudded with suspense and hope. Did this mean he wasn't dead? She tried to awaken Lucas but couldn't. She had to go back to see if the warrior lived! Whatever the danger, she had to know his fate!

Breathing raggedly, she burst into the small clearing where the rank odor of violent death stung her nostrils. Her hand flew upward to cover her nose and mouth. She inched past the mutilated Jim and Anson, then halted in disbelief. The bear lay dead, without his furry coat and lethal paws and massive head. There was no sign of the warrior who had saved her life and removed her from this grim setting.

Clamping her hand over her mouth to keep from retching, she commanded her feet to take her back to Lucas. She had her answer; he had survived, survived with the strength to take a bloody trophy. As she fought against fainting again, she leaned against a tree to regain her control and wits. She murmured softly, "Thank God, you're alive. I couldn't live with your death on my hands. Will we ever meet again? I don't even know your name. I didn't even get to thank you."

She cried for a long time, releasing her anguish and tension. When she walked away, she was unaware of the somber black eyes which followed her. He mastered the impulse to capture her, for she offered great danger to his emotions and pride. It was wrong for him to take a white woman, so why was he tormented by such desire for her? Why did her sadness and tears pain him more than a knife wound? Why did it take all of his control to keep himself hidden from her, denying both a farewell? Who was this girl with such potent magic that she could have such stirring and forbidden effects on him? Why did he want her at his side under the sun as much as he wanted her beneath him at night? These were new and baffling feelings, feelings he must conquer and forget.

Forget, he scoffed to himself as she vanished from sight. How he wished he had never seen or touched her, for he could never forget her now. But it would be worse if he had shown himself, if he had joined her body to his. Would he be as stirring and haunting to her? If only she weren't so rare, he would take her prisoner and sate his lust for her! But she was, and such treatment would destroy her. For a few moments beneath the sun, they had touched and kissed. He could allow nothing more, for she was more dangerous than any peril or foe or beast he had ever confronted.

At Lucas's side, Miranda tried to arouse him once more. When she failed, she cried out for help, which came swiftly. When Lucas was carried aboard the steamer to a doctor who was heading for Fort Sully, Miranda told him they had been attacked by a grizzly and that she and Lucas had been rescued by a strange trapper dressed in buckskins. After slaying the bear which had killed the two soldiers, the man had helped them get this far and then returned to skin the bear before someone else found it. She added that the trapper said he would see to burying the two soldiers. She didn't know what she would do if they checked out her story and found the two soldiers nearly nude. What if there was evidence it was an Indian warrior? They would force the humiliating truth about the foiled rape from her. They might even suspect she knew the warrior.

One man shook his head and informed the others, "Them grizzlies are known to travel in pairs. I ain't going in there after no mauled bodies. Let that trapper bury 'em like she said."

One of the crew members said the wood was cut and nearly loaded, and they needed to get underway. Several others agreed there was no need to fetch the bodies or to waste more time. Before noon, the steamer was moving again, with one last stop before Pierre.

Miranda was sitting beside Lucas's bunk when he came around, his head freshly bandaged. When he groaned and touched the sensitive area, Miranda caught his hand and warned him to leave it alone. When he was fully alert, she revealed the events which had taken place, confessing her other meetings with the Indian warrior to him, all except the kisses and embraces which they had shared at that second stop. She also related the false tale she had told their fellow passengers.

Lucas was astonished by her behavior. "You mean he's been following the steamer to meet with you?" he asked incredulously.

Miranda replied honestly, "I don't know, Luke. He just appeared each time. If he hadn't, we'd be dead now," she reminded him.

"Considering the tales I've been told about these warriors, it sounds crazy. You don't know his name or tribe?" he probed.

"Neither. He always came and went so quickly and

secretly. As I said, I fainted before the fight with the bear was over. I assume he wasn't injured because he brought us near the river to be found." She explained the precarious riddle as best she could.

"But why did you go back?" he demanded.

"I had to know if he survived. He could have been wounded. He could have used his remaining energy to help us. He saved our lives, Luke. He was kind and gentle. He never harmed me and I wasn't afraid of him."

Lucas couldn't debate her statements. But he fretted over the identity and motives of the warrior. Still, the man had spared her innocence and saved her life. He cautioned himself to watch her more closely. He had almost gotten her raped and killed.

"I'll be fine, Randy. Why don't you get some rest or write Mandy and Reis," he suggested to distract her from her thoughts of the warrior.

"I wonder what they're doing right now," she murmured aloud. She would have cringed in renewed fear if she had known the answer to that question, for matters were just as complex and dangerous back in Alexandria . . .

Chapter Fourteen

After Reis persuaded Amanda to unlock the door, he poured out his soul to her, telling her nearly everything he knew or felt. Comprehending how important she was to him and how much he loved her, Amanda's anguish and doubts fled. He ended his confession with a declaration of love. "I love you and need you as no other person in my life, Mandy. What would I be without you? My life would have no joy or meaning. Please forgive me for hurting you. I promise to do my best never to hurt you again."

Tears sparkled in her light blue eyes. "I love you too, Reis. I suppose this situation is difficult for both of us, a new marriage and a critical mission at the same time. I'll try to be more understanding and patient," she vowed softly, smiling into his expression of relief.

"That's a good suggestion for both of us. But I don't want to mislead you. Until this case is over,

there will be times like this week when I can't get to
you, love, and times when I can't explain what's
happening. But I will be as open with you as
possible."

"Now that I know more about this case and your
duties, I'll accept your rules. I don't have to like
them, but I will try to follow them," she added with
joyful laughter. "You were right, my darling; there
was so much I didn't know. But I love you and trust
you."

Reis's mouth closed over hers in a tender kiss of
love and commitment. When his lips brushed back
and forth across hers, she murmured hoarsely, "Make
love to me. I've missed you so."

Reis discarded his boots and clothes, then slipped
the gown straps from her shoulders and let the
garment slide down her silky flesh to the floor. His
smoldering eyes flickered over her tawny curls and
touched each feature upon her face. His gaze became
as a warm liquid flowing down her trembling frame,
from face to bare feet, over curves and planes that
ached to be sensuously invaded. He placed his hands
on her shoulders, then leisurely moved them down
her arms to grasp her quivering hands. He pulled her
toward him, their nude bodies melting together
before they sank to the bed behind them.

As they fell entwined into the arms of love, they
were oblivious to all but each other and their
cravings. Their love and passion were rich and deep,
given and returned. He murmured words of endear-
ment into her ears, inspiring feverish responses to

him. Her hands caressed his firm, smooth body, and she touched him gently, then almost savagely as her hunger increased. He pulled her closer and tighter to him.

He nibbled at her lips, favoring the fuller lower one. He fondled her in daring new ways, touches which enflamed her to a matching boldness. He seemed to explore and conquer each part of her body, as she did his. He teased and tantalized her with lips and hands until she was tensed and warmed all over, begging to be sated.

She moaned in desire. She was certain she could climb no higher on love's spiral, but she did. Fires leaped and burned within both as they meshed together upon the soft bed. Her head rolled from side to side and she breathed erratically as his mouth feasted upon breasts which were swollen and firm with passion. For a time, she lay mesmerized by his actions and the sensations they aroused.

She discovered the stimulating thrill of bringing him intense pleasure with her bold caresses. Shamelessly and greedily, she gave and took with unbridled desire and new courage. When he entered her, she arched and engulfed his manhood with an urgency which surprised and pleased him, crying out in blissful rapture at that first inner contact.

They moved in unison, Reis whispering instructions into her ears, all of which she eagerly followed. Although each thrust and response inspired ecstasy in both, their needs flamed into one roaring blaze which demanded to be extinguished before they were consumed.

They soared toward passion's peak together, the heights they were reaching bringing a lightness to their heads. They touched, kissed, and mingled bodies and spirits until they could no longer restrain themselves. Fulfillment burst upon them and shook them with an intensity unknown before. Scaling the peak, they gradually eased down into a tranquil valley. They lay locked together, relishing the power and pleasure of this joining. They kissed and embraced tenderly as slumber claimed their exhausted bodies.

On Thursday and Friday, Reis remained with Amanda during the daylight but ventured out both nights to meet with George Findley and carry out his investigation. Amanda could sense his dismay over the accumulating evidence, but she didn't pry. Before dawn on Saturday, Reis slipped out of the house to head for Washington—eighteen miles from Alexandria—to discuss his findings with Grant.

When Reis returned home late that night, he told Amanda the decision had been made to entrap Weber and his men the following week. He didn't tell her that the arrests would come during a meeting of the illegal Ku Klux Klan, or while he was confiscating revealing pages from the books in both firms, in McVane's office, and from letters hidden in Weber's home. Timing was essential to success and survival. To prevent discovery or suspicion, Reis couldn't steal those pages and letters until the last minute. It would be a perilous climax to weeks of work and determination, and it would be a beginning to his new life with Amanda Lawrence Harrison.

Reis was concealed from view when the unsuspecting Weber called on Amanda Sunday afternoon. Reis had warned Amanda he would attack Weber on the spot if that villain offered any threat to her safety, no matter the cost to the mission. Amanda had cautioned him not to react too hastily or rashly or show himself unless Weber physically assailed her and she screamed for help. They agreed on their signals and actions, then waited for Weber to appear.

Wanting this foul matter settled quickly and without trouble, she immediately came to the point the moment Weber was seated. "I have made a decision, Weber. I told you I would respond to your proposal today, but I cannot." When he started to protest, she hastily silenced him. "Wait! Hear me out first. I think you'll agree with my conclusions."

Weber sullenly leaned back against the sofa but remained attentive. She informed him calmly, "I want you to hire someone to find Randy. That distressing and puzzling matter needs to be resolved before you and I can make plans for us. I don't mean to imply I don't trust you, but I must make certain you had nothing to do with her departure. I'm sorry, but I feel there is something I don't know. I want you to locate her and bring her home. If there's nothing between you two, then I'll marry you on any day you choose. If there is love between you two, then I will step aside for Randy to marry you. If the feelings are on her side alone, it should be settled before we wed.

If you have even the slightest desire for her, it should be faced and dealt with before you make a mistake by marrying the wrong woman. I hope you agree this is a fair solution for all concerned. Well, what do you think? Can you find my sister?''

She inhaled and exhaled to release her tension. Stunned by this unexpected proposition, Weber couldn't speak and had difficulty thinking clearly. In his hesitation, she added, "I won't lie to you, Weber. I am not madly in love with you and I won't pretend I am. I'll even admit to being selfish and conceited. I will do whatever necessary for survival. Is that honest enough for you? I shall set a time limit of two weeks.''

Weber probed her incredible suggestion. "I told you I couldn't find her when I went there. What if she can't be found, ever?''

"Perhaps this will help your detective," she stated, handing him a brass oval frame with Miranda's miniature portrait inside. "She can't simply vanish without a trace. Tell your man to work harder, or hire a better one. Someone in Charleston must have seen her by now. If I get another telegram or a letter from her, I will make it available to you." She went on to tell him about the first one, knowing it was unnecessary. "I'm warning you now, Weber; don't marry me with any desire in your heart for my sister. I don't demand love, but I will demand fidelity. If you have any doubts at all, end them in the next two weeks. If Randy is suffering from unrequited love for you, then she will never return home after we wed. Surely it is best for all of us to make peace first. Do you agree?"

Weber rose and faced her. He needed privacy to study this turn of events and time to make some plans. Whatever happened now, he would come out the winner. He smiled and nodded. "I'll locate Randy for you, then you can vanquish any doubts you have about me. If she has any fantasy where I'm concerned, we shall deal with it."

Amanda came to her feet and smiled faintly in return. "Unless there is some pressing business to discuss, I would appreciate your getting to this matter as quickly as possible. I feel it would be best to settle our private lives before we discuss our business affiliation."

Weber concurred and left without even attempting to kiss or embrace her, which suited Amanda perfectly. He was too busy thinking that now that he didn't have to be so furtive with his search, he could pull out all stops in order to locate Miranda and finally decide whom to marry and whom to slay.

Amanda turned to smile at her husband as he entered the room clapping in admiration for her performance. "Excellent, love, excellent," he complimented her, then swept her into his arms and danced her around the sofa as she giggled happily.

When he halted and gazed down into her upturned face which shone with such love and joy, he kissed the tip of her nose. "All we have to do now is pray Weber doesn't come across any clues to Randy's whereabouts," she remarked, slightly worried about this brazen ruse. "You did mail my letter to Luke and

Randy from Washington yesterday?''

"It's on the way to Pierre right this moment, love,'' he replied. "But I'd be willing to bet my boots, comfortable as they are, the case will be over before Randy has it in her hand,'' he alleged smugly.

But at that moment in the Dakota Territory, Miranda had her hands full with another matter, an injured and stubborn cousin. The steamer was lingering at its last stop, unloading supplies at the Lower Brule Indian Agency, before heading for its termination point.

Determined to carry out his own investigation, Lucas insisted they visit the agency to see what they could learn. He assured Randy he felt fine as they left the steamer for a few hours on land. But they observed and discovered things that shocked them. Life on the reservation was not what it was reported or promised to be . . .

The once proud and energetic Indians appeared spiritless, weary, and poor. Many were in rags, small children naked. Most looked hungry and unhealthy. It was a pathetic and depressing sight.

Wagons of supplies from the steamer were being unloaded at the wooden structure which housed the agency. Indians in tattered clothing dejectedly waited for their meager portions to be doled out. She could hear complaints about the moldy flour, the spoiled meat, the flimsy materials for clothing, the injustice of this beggarly practice, the humiliations they were helplessly subjected to by corrupt white men, and the despair all felt at being unable to change their new destiny—a destiny which demanded either an acceptance of degradation or the total destruction of their families.

As Lucas questioned several traders and workers, Miranda learned of the children being forced into schools where they were forced to wear the white man's clothes, where they spoke only the white tongue, where they had to accept the white man's customs and ways over those of their own people. The young boys were required to cut their braids to show obedience to the white man's rules, an act which robbed them of what little pride remained. She discovered that many places used boarding schools to keep the Indian children away from the influences of their parents and tribes. There was a look of bewilderment and sadness in those small faces and somber eyes and it pained Miranda to view such cruelty.

The entire Indian culture was being destroyed. Indians were stripped of their customs, their religion, their language, their pride and dignity, their very reason for existence and happiness. Tree and scaffold burials were outlawed. Leaders and chiefs were often slain or imprisoned to subjugate the remaining members of their tribes. The males were refused guns or horses for hunting and were forced to depend solely on the whites for food, clothing, and shelter. Unable to seek medicinal herbs, many Indians grew sick and died. It was almost as if the sadistic plan was to starve, freeze, or sicken the remaining Indians until they died or were compelled to escape, only to be tracked down and killed as dangerous renegades.

She learned of the demoralizing action of constantly moving reservations from one place to another. The Indians had difficulty settling down, for they were whisked away before teepees were barely in place. They were commanded to become farmers, when they knew nothing but hunting and when the reservation lands were unfertile.

Treaties and promises had been broken or changed as frequently as the white men wished. Randy caught hints of the "Indian Ring," in which dishonest agents or suppliers to government contracts stole part of the goods or shipped inferior ones. Although whiskey was outlawed on reservations, traders were allowed to camp nearby and entice the spirit-broken and restless braves to drink themselves into stupors. It was heartbreaking to witness and hear of such evil and cruelty, to see a proud race trampled and destroyed.

Now she understood why so many tribes and leaders refused to make peace with the white men. She could see why the Indians didn't trust them, why they continued to make war. The whites didn't want peaceful coexistence; they wanted to take and have everything here. They wanted to subjugate these noble people into demeaning slavery. Where was their Lincoln? Who would bravely sign their "Emancipation Proclamation"? Who would battle to free them?

When Lucas and Miranda returned to the *Martha Lane*, both were too gloomy to discuss what they had encountered here. Lucas was also dizzy and lay down to rest, falling asleep quickly. Miranda paced the floor of her small cabin, trying to forget the sights and sounds of this day. If her father hadn't come here years before and eloped with Princess Morning Star, her mother could have been one of those miserable people she had seen today. It stunned and alarmed Miranda to realize her mother's old tribe was now imprisoned and slowly dying near the Red Cloud Agency. Miranda was relieved her mother had not returned here to view such anguish and devastation. All she could do was pray her grandfather and other relatives were alive and safe. She tried to push such haunting knowledge from her troubled mind, but found it impossible to do so.

Nor could she forget the warrior who had saved her life. She knew he must be one of those "renegades" who refused to stop fighting and settle down on one of those despicable reservations. She couldn't imagine that fearless and strong male confined to those conditions. Why had he defended her and followed her? Why didn't he hate her and all she represented? Apparently, fierce warriors made no distinctions between male and female enemies. If that were true, how could she explain their relationship? She couldn't.

Upon arrival in Pierre, Lucas discovered this settlement was worse than Yankton, if that were possible. He refused to remain there a single night, gaining passage on a keelboat heading for Fort Sully. He could only hope the conditions there were better and he was beginning to regret bringing Miranda along. If not for the danger in Alexandria and along the way, he would have been tempted to send her home or somewhere safe. He had not imagined any place could be worse or more perilous than being near Weber. But it was too late to stop this journey, and he was too driven to change his plans. At least Miranda was holding up excellently under these arduous circumstances.

Lucas was delighted to find that Fort Sully was indeed better. What fences existed were low stone ones to separate the officers' quarters or homes from other sections of the fort; there was no tall outer wall to protect the inhabitants from enemies. Lucas and Miranda found this strange in light of the continuing skirmishes between whites and "hostiles." The only barrier of any height surrounded the ammunition and supply sheds and yards, for soldiers were rumored to be as prone to thieving as renegades or white drifters.

The structures were made of varying materials from wood to adobe. There were barracks, stables, a guard house, trader shops, sutler stores, an infirmary, a chow hall, assorted privies, private homes, small cabins, and supply sheds. There was one oblong building which they learned was a recreation hall, complete with tables and chairs for games and reading. Fortunately, Fort Sully boasted of a library of nearly a thousand books and several periodicals.

The fort structures were in close proximity to each other, with officers' private homes nearby. The military compound was designed like the hub of a wagonwheel, with businesses radiating like its spokes and settlers encircling it as an outer rim. From there in three directions, other cabins and structures were built haphazardly. Some brave and solitary types had put up their homes and barns at a farther distance away, toward the Missouri River east from Fort Sully. It appeared few people found the western area desirable, for it edged on proclaimed Sioux Territory. In the military surroundings, trees and bushes were scant, grass even sparser. But as the semicircle increased, so did the amount of greenery. There was an abundance of trees, bushes, grasses, and wildflowers. North of the civilian and military encampments was a small Indian village where workers and scouts lived.

Wanting to keep his real assignment a secret, Lucas decided not to use the letter of protection and introduction from President Grant unless necessary. With so much corruption and fraud in this area, some men might be suspicious of him and his job. After all, those two soldiers had behaved as if there was something important to conceal.

Lucas found a sturdy log cabin to rent near the fort, one recently vacated when the fort sutler's brother had died from a snakebite. Unknown to Lucas and Miranda, it was uninhabited because it lay west of the fort and was one of the most distant structures.

Aware that Lucas Reardon's sister was a real lady, the sutler was glad he had cleaned and repaired the cabin, completing his tasks just that morning in hope of renting it to an incoming and ignorant officer from the fort. When the sutler escorted them to the cabin, Miranda was relieved to find it freshly scrubbed and in excellent condition. She thanked the man who in turn offered any assistance she needed. While she remained behind, the man helped Lucas fetch their belongings from his store, where they were under strict guard.

Before dusk, they were unpacked and settled into their new home. Lucas had assisted Miranda with the sweeping and dusting, and he had opened the windows to allow fresh air to flow through the cabin. Miranda had scrubbed all the dishes, even though they had appeared clean when she began her mandatory task. Lucas had purchased enough wood from the sutler to last until he could join a woodcutting crew and furnish their own. As they dined on the meal which she had prepared, they relaxed and chatted about their new home. The cabin had two rooms: one was a combination kitchen and living area; the other was a small bedroom. It was agreed she would have the private room and Lucas would sleep on a cot purchased from the sutler.

The next week passed swiftly in a blur of excitement. Lucas's injury healed nicely and ceased to trouble him. He spent his days making friends with the soldiers and settlers, observing and questioning everything he saw or heard. It was a simple

task for someone with Lucas's jovial personality
and good looks. The people in this rugged area
admired artists and writers, people who could put
life into words or capture it in oils or photographs.
Each person was eager to play a part in the making
and recording of history. Every time Lucas lazed
around the sutler's shop, men lingered to "talk off his
ears." As for those from the fort, the bored soldiers
were eager for any source of diversion and talked
freely and rashly with the cheerful young man.

Miranda was full of questions when Lucas
returned from a visit to the whiskey wagons which
were camped nearby in a grove of cottonwoods for
one week, pay week. He described what he had seen
in colorful details for her, including the prostitutes
and two musicians who traveled with the group.
Miranda jestingly inquired if Lucas had partaken of
either trade. He grinned and shook his head.

Miranda spent most of her time with Lucas; she
hadn't made many female friends. The upper
officers' wives seemed to be waiting until they were
assured of her social station before offering their
company or inviting hers. The lower officers' and
enlisted men's wives, what few there were, felt it was
improper to approach her and kept their distances.
On fear of penalty from the commander, the lowly
"laundresses" made it a point to avoid her completely, as was required of them where all "proper"
females were concerned. The social system was rigid
here, and Miranda didn't know where she belonged.
She concluded that she, as the stranger and new-

comer, should be approached first by whoever wished to become her friend or acquaintance.

There was one female who Miranda and Lucas found fascinating and colorful, Calamity Jane. Martha Jane Canary was a large, strapping woman who was widely known for her foul language, hard drinking, expert horsemanship, skilled shooting, and men's attire. She was reputed to be the most famous female in the entire Dakota Territory, and often teased about being continually drunk and broke, even though she worked at several jobs normally held by males. She rotated between being a driver for supply wagons and stagecoaches, and a scout for the cavalry. Of course most people said she spent her money buying drinks for all present when she entered a new town or saloon, for that was her way of making friends and gaining attention. She boasted of knowing every legendary male in the West, good or bad. But most of them denied knowing her.

Miranda and Lucas met this rustic character in the sutler's shop one afternoon. Despite her mannish appearance in looks and clothing, both were taken with her vivacity and genial nature. Jane had been many places and had faced countless dangers, or so she claimed. Her independent and obstinate nature caused many people to avoid her or to gossip about her. It was sad and unfair, for Jane simply wanted freedom and adventure, things which the present age didn't allow even a strong and smart female. Jane was so interesting and charming that Lucas and

Miranda didn't care if her tales were true or not. After that day, Jane became a welcome visitor in their cabin whenever she was at Fort Sully. It did not take long for Lucas and Miranda to realize that being Jane's friend meant she would defend them with her life if need be.

But there was a sadness about Jane, for she knew that the present society would never permit her to reach her potential and to carry out her dreams. Miranda decided that Jane used her boistrous and comical manner to conceal her disappointments and bitterness. At twenty-one, the Missouri born Jane Canary could probably outshoot and outride most scouts, soldiers, Indians, and outlaws. Yet, few were willing to let her prove it. Only Custer and Miles were appreciative of her skills and courage; they had discovered she was an excellent scout, when sober.

Most women here viewed life as dull and arduous, but Miranda thrived on the excitement which surrounded her. Due to the confiscation of Indian horses, animals were in abundance at the fort. Lucas would frequently rent two and they would go riding, never straying far alone unless in the company of the soldiers until they could learn their way around the rugged terrain.

Each night, Lucas would record the day's events and store his notes in a leather pouch. He hid the precious packet under a loosened board beneath the table. Miranda also started a journal about her own adventures. She wrote Amanda several long letters but held them until news arrived saying it was safe to contact her sister.

One morning, Lucas rushed to the cabin to tell Miranda he was riding out on patrol with a small troop from the fort. Later, Calamity Jane came by for a visit. Miranda's chores were done, so she was sitting at the table, writing another letter to her sister to pass the time. Jane asked her to go for a ride, but Miranda was reluctant. When Jane convinced her there was no danger, for Indians believed her "touched by the evil spirits" and left her alone, Miranda promptly accepted and quickly changed into her riding habit.

They rode for a time with Jane pointing out sights and telling Miranda tales about the area's turbulent past. When Jane spotted smoke curling up in the distance, she ordered Miranda to wait while she checked it out, for the cavalry paid her high prices for valuable information. Miranda pleaded with her not to go or to allow her to tag along. Jane blatantly refused, saying she could escape swiftly if there was any trouble. She told Miranda to ride hard and fast for the fort if she fired shots into the air.

Miranda watched Jane gallop off toward the hills. She tied her reins to a small bush and walked to a large boulder. She climbed upon it and sat down to wait, tucking her flowing hems beneath her legs. She was apprehensive about the possible dangers Jane might face out there, but she wasn't terrified of being left alone. Yet as time passed and solitude closed in on her, Miranda had the strangest feeling she was being watched. She scanned her surroundings in all directions, seeing nothing and no one. But the sensation persisted.

She waited about twenty minutes before she saw Jane coming her way at a steady pace. She sighed in relief and headed for her horse. As she mounted, she glanced around, finding and hearing nothing. The warrior's image flickered before her mind's eye and she studied the harsh landscape, wondering where he was at that moment.

At home alone, Miranda reflected on the strange episode, scolding herself for not checking out the mystery. She had not felt peril or evil but she had sensed a sadness and longing. She had actually warmed and tingled! Was she fantasizing, dreaming, hoping? Had it actually been the unknown warrior's powerful gaze on her, his forceful magnetism, his heady allure? Her heart soared with pleasure and her mind raced in confusion. Who was he and where? Recalling her cousin's reaction to her last confession, Miranda couldn't tell Lucas about this intriguing event and she couldn't ask anyone about the warrior, but inwardly she felt elated by this delightful mystery. Miranda danced around the cabin, then caressed the white buckskin dress which had belonged to her mother. She had brought it along to wear the first time she met her grandfather and uncle. If she braided her hair and dressed in her mother's Indian garments, she would appear more Indian than white. Surely that would inspire him to accept her.

Days passed as the June weather grew warmer. A letter arrived from Amanda, posted in Washington.

When Lucas and Miranda read it together at supper, he grimaced and she paled. Their gazes met as Lucas exploded, "Are they crazy! Of all people, Reis should know a good detective can uncover clues and track us down! Doesn't he realize Weber will go to any expense for revenge?"

"Do you think he knows yet?" she asked shakily, the emphasis on "he" telling to whom she referred. She panicked at the thought of being thwarted in her quest when so close to victory. "Help me, Luke; I must get to grandfather before it's too late. Find us a guide," she coaxed, eyes tearing and voice quavering.

"I know how much this means to you, Randy. You've been patient while I rushed around chasing my dream. Don't worry; I'll find some way to get you to Sun Cloud this very week." He checked the postmark and chuckled, then commented, "This letter got here quickly. I doubt Weber has discovered any tracks yet. I'll bet Reis has him arrested and imprisoned before he can sniff out the right trail. At least Mandy and Reis are safe and happy."

But things had gone awry in Virginia, perilously awry. The night before the climactic raid, Reis had overheard something which he couldn't share with his wife. The accident involving her parents had been ordered by none other than Weber Richardson. As Weber spouted off to Daniel McVane, neither was aware of the man who hid outside McVane's office door, listening to Weber smugly discuss his many schemes. But Weber made one statement about Joe and Marie which sent surges of hope through Reis;

he would hire a search party in the morning then pray with all his might.

That following evening, Reis and George made their rounds, collecting all the books and letters relating to the case. Not far out of town, the men assigned by Grant converged on the meeting of the Ku-Klux-Klan and arrested all present. Because a business meeting between all partners was to have been held afterward, every man involved was present and apprehended with the exception of Weber Richardson.

A tense week passed as Reis failed to locate and arrest the leader of this menacing group. A friend of Reis arrived to manage Amanda's shipping firm and to appropriate Weber's property for the American government.

Reis fretted over Weber's disappearance and his inability to find his enemy. Grant had already decided on Reis's next assignment, but they couldn't discuss it until Weber was apprehended and this case was closed. Reis had turned the evidence over to Grant, who locked it in his safe until the trials could commence. The case was in limbo as long as Weber remained free. Reis was infuriated by the man's actions; it seemed as if the Devil himself was guarding his servant!

Amanda cried in fear and tension, speculating that Weber was probably on his way west to harm Lucas and Miranda or lurking nearby with the hope of slaying Reis. To ease her worries, Reis sent Lucas a telegram to warn him of Weber's disappearance and the results of the case so far. Reis told them to be careful and alert, to notify him if Weber appeared there, and to have the Army arrest and hold Weber for the U.S. government and President Grant.

It wasn't Weber's cunning or a warning from anyone which had kept him from that meeting; it was lust for Miranda and for vengeance, and a quirk of fate. His escape had nothing to do with a premonition of danger or capture. Word had arrived that afternoon that Miranda had been located and was being held prisoner by his detective. Weber had placed McVane in charge of both meetings to rush to Charleston by train. But, ironically, McVane had been robbed and killed by a common thief as he left his office that evening, preventing him from canceling the pernicious meetings, exposing Weber's location, or contacting and warning Weber after the raid.

Upon arriving in Charleston, Weber went wild with rage and frustration, for it was the wrong girl again. He was in such a frenzy by then that he yanked his gun, a small knuckle-duster .32, from its belt holster and shot the innocent female in the heart. It happened so swiftly and unexpectedly that the girl never had time to suspect her fate. Petrified, the queasy and frantic detective fled the scene when Weber laughed satanically and hysterically as he watched the blood saturate the front of her yellow gown.

When he was settled, Weber calmly strolled over to the girl. He seized her auburn hair and jerked her head backward. She did favor Miranda greatly. As his wintry gaze eased over her body, he decided he had slain her too quickly, for pleasure should always precede pain. He left her as she was, laughing sardonically as he mused on the authorities puzzling over this brutal and mysterious crime.

Before Weber could catch the next train home, one of his men met him with the dire news from Alexandria. His fury was limitless; his hunger for revenge boundless. He sent his man back to Alexandria to spy for him, and each following report increased his hatred and madness. Miranda had better pray to every known god that he wouldn't find her. If he did, he vowed he would do unspeakable things to her before mutilating her lovely body and face! As for Amanda and Reis, their punishments and deaths would be far worse, for he had heard the announcement of their secret marriage. Clearly he had been duped, and they would pay in blood!

Chapter Fifteen

While Lucas was trying to figure out how to get into the Sioux camp without arousing suspicion, an eye-catching officer arrived at Fort Sully from Custer's Seventh Cavalry Regiment. He was there to escort ten recruits to Fort Lincoln, as Custer liked a full report on his new men before they arrived in camp. Major Brody Sheen was Custer's most trusted officer.

Although cavalrymen rarely wore their sabers except for ceremonies, Brody Sheen was in full dress upon arrival. He cut a most impressive figure in his dark blue and sunny yellow uniform, an outfit which looked custom tailored for his well-muscled body. His brown hair was shorter than most men's and very curly. He had hazel eyes which concealed his thoughts and feelings, unless he chose to expose them, and he wore a neat mustache. Six feet tall and twenty-nine years old, Brody was well toned and darkly tanned from his active, outdoor lifestyle. He was dashing in looks and immaculate in dress. Among such rough men who gave little care to their appearance and to amenities, Brody's conduct and charm shone. But while outwardly he was considered handsome and virile, Miranda Lawrence was to find him less than perfect.

Once he learned that Brody was Custer's right arm, Lucas promptly made his acquaintance, thinking that when they eventually headed to Fort Lincoln, Brody's friendship would be a valuable asset. Brody seemed to take an instant liking to Lucas, who was as jovial and bright as he was and of similar breeding and education. Brody was from a wealthy and prestigious Northern family, and he had served loyally with Custer during the Civil War. For that reason, Custer had personally requested him as an officer in his regiment. A hard man to admire and like, Custer needed someone with him who held him in high esteem and affection.

Major Sheen introduced Lucas to the officers at Fort Sully, strengthening the writer's position there. While waiting for the recruits to arrive by keelboat, Brody had time to spend with Lucas and Miranda. The second evening of their meeting, Lucas brought him to their cabin for supper. Brody made no effort to hide his strong attraction to Miranda, entertaining her with tales of bravery and daring, pleasing her with his wit and charm. At first, Miranda found him appealing and stimulating company, a delightful conversationalist. If Miranda's mind and heart had not been already claimed by a mysterious warrior, she might have fallen under the disarming spell of this dashing soldier. And, after that night, Brody spent as much time with Miranda as with Lucas.

They would take walks together, alone, or with Lucas. They went riding and shared several meals, including a picnic on a pond near the river. One night, there was a dance in the yard around the flagpole. Hardly three songs had been played before the men there realized Brody had staked a claim on this beautiful stranger. Knowing of Major Brody Sheen's reputed prowess with the ladies, no one dared challenge him.

If Miranda and Lucas had not been present to occupy his time and attention, Brody would have been furious with the delay in the recruits' arrival. The June rains had failed to come as yet, and the Missouri River was treacherously low. The recruits had been compelled to leave their stranded craft before Yankton and come overland to Fort Randall to take a keelboat, requiring ten days more than anticipated. The men were fortunate that Major Sheen was too busy with a delightful and enchanting Miranda Lawrence to notice the lost time.

The day before Brody was to leave Fort Sully, he made a terrible error in judgment. Feeling Miranda was as enamored of him as he was of her, he showered his romantic attention on her. He tricked her into a private stroll, then attempted to kiss and embrace her. When she tried to reject him without embarrassing either of them, he didn't realize she was serious. When he playfully tripped her, then caught her and rolled upon the grass with her in his tight grasp, she was angered by his boldness and persistence. Still, the arrogant Brody believed her to be coy and timid. He couldn't imagine any female would spurn him. After all, he had given her plenty of time, more than any other woman who had caught his eye. He continued his roguish siege, until she frostily scolded him and made her refusal very clear. Although Brody apologized for his misconception and behavior, Miranda noticed a glow of insincerity and impatience in his eyes. Clearly, Brody found her desirable and was resolved to have her!

As Brody left, he encouraged Lucas to hasten his trip to Fort Lincoln, telling him there was much more going on in that area for the reporter to record. Lucas told him they would be along in about three weeks and politely refused Brody's escort this trip. Brody responded with courtesy but felt annoyance. He told Lucas he would notify him if a mission called him back this way.

Miranda had learned many facts about her mother's people and other Indian tribes from Brody. He had made no secret of his hatred for several warriors, chiefs, and leaders: Sitting Bull, Crazy Horse, Gall, Red Hawk, Bloody Arrow, and Blazing Star of varying Sioux tribes, and Two Moons of the Cheyenne. She listened intently, learning all she could about these men.

Two names in particular had brought fiery lights of rivalry and antagonism to Brody's hazel eyes:

Crazy Horse and Blazing Star. Several times Brody had made comments about the feud between those two men. Brody had seemed to think that if Crazy Horse did not exist, Blazing Star would be war chief under the direction and influence of the imposing and powerful medicine and spiritual chief, Sitting Bull. Brody had laughingly remarked one night that he hoped they killed off each other over the chief's bonnet. Brody had not seemed to fear those powerful warriors, but he clearly respected and envied their skills and ranks.

After Brody departed, Miranda gave him a good deal of mental study. Now that he was no longer present to use his charms and good looks to sway her, she mused on his personality and disarming appeal. He was unlike most men she knew. But she realized something she hadn't noticed before; Brody had a beguiling way of making a person feel a particular way about him—his way. It was as if he possessed a magical power of suggestion. Now that he was gone, she could see certain things more clearly.

She thought about the way Brody had handled himself, and treated others, and she was astonished to conclude that Brody was arrogant and obsessive but covered such traits when it suited his purpose. Visibly, he was a man used to giving orders, to having his way or else. Qualms filled Miranda as she decided Brody could be pleasant when he gained his way or was after something, but she sensed he could be dangerous if crossed or denied. She felt sure Brody had shown his real self that last day and she shuddered as she found herself comparing Brody Sheen to Weber Richardson.

Miranda didn't mention her concern to her cousin, but she was glad Brody was gone. She didn't trust that contradictory man. Besides, her thoughts were claimed by another, as were her dreams. A strange loneliness and hunger chewed at her, and a feeling of loss assailed her warring senses. Slowly the truth dawned on Miranda, and she chided her foolish behavior. Perhaps she had given Brody the wrong impression—that she truly cared for him. Had she unknowingly been using Brody as a needed diversion? Had he perceived her loneliness and genial overtures as romantic signals?

Again, she pressed Lucas to help her reach her grandfather. Lucas was working on a safe solution to that problem with Calamity Jane, as she knew this territory, its people, and its dangers.

Three days had passed when word arrived by special messenger from Brody. Two days from Fort Sully, near the Cheyenne River Agency, his troop had joined his notorious leader who was waiting there before heading west to Fort Phil Kearny. There, a meeting was to take place of the commanding officers from this immense area. The entreating letter informed Lucas of the possible historic importance of this talk, for General Terry, Colonel Gibbon, and General Crook would be present—three of the most successful and destructive officers in the cavalry. Colonel Custer had left Captain Benteen behind to guard his fort and had ordered Major Reno to ride with him. But the name which irresistibly drew Lucas was Philip Sheridan—he, too, was alleged to be heading for this parlay.

Lucas read the message over and over, his excitement mounting each time. He was so eager that his hands shook, causing the paper to crackle noisily, and his green eyes danced with elation. Unable to restrain himself, he gave a whoop of victory and joy. He was mentally applauding his good fortune when Miranda entered from the other room to question his merry behavior.

He revealed his incredible and exhilarating news, but it did not have the same effect on her. Her smile faded and her heart skipped several beats, for she knew he would accept the invitation to ride along and her dream would be forced to yield to his. Miranda could not share his exuberance and zeal, but she comprehended what a priceless opportunity had been dropped into her cousin's lap. She was too dejected to care about his work, too nettled to consider its importance for history or the South. For weeks, everything had gone her cousin's way; was it selfish to demand time for her dream, to obtain her desires? They were so close to her mother's people; the new fort would put them hundreds of miles from her goal.

Miranda also realized that if she tagged along as invited, she would be in the company of untrustworthy, cunning Brody Sheen and many squadrons of rowdy men. Evidently there was no peril in this trek, or she would not have been invited. She wondered how Brody had gained approval for her presence from Custer.

Caught up in his own world, Lucas did not notice the staggering effect this "golden opportunity" had on his cousin. A resentful shadow dulled Miranda's brown gaze; anger enticed little creases around her mouth and near her eyes. Defiance began boiling within her.

Lucas turned to ask, "How soon can you be packed and ready to leave, Randy? Brody sent a written order for an escort to take us to meet him. There won't be any danger," he stated smugly.

With a clear and calm voice, Miranda replied nonchalantly, "I know, because I'm not going. I'm staying here. If at all possible, I'll find a way to get to my grandfather. You go along with Major Sheen. I'm sure you'll obtain enough material for several books."

Shocked by her icy demeanor and incredible announcement, he shrieked frantically, "You can't go into a Sioux camp alone! Be patient until this trip is over, then I'll take you there. I promise, Randy."

"I have been patient, Luke, patient and unselfish," she declared accusingly. "Do you realize how far away this parlay is? Afterward, we'll be forced to remain with those troops for safety. They could ride in any direction and for any length of time. It could be months before we return here. By then, my people could be gone to their winter grounds, out of my reach. Besides, with all of those infamous killers joining forces, it could be a conference to plot a new war against the remaining Indians. If so, the Sioux won't let a white within ten miles of their camp, or they'll go into hiding until spring. I can't risk losing this chance, Luke. I'm sorry, but I'm not going with you. If I can't find a path to grandfather, I'll be fine here in our cabin."

"I can't let you stay here alone," Luke stated obstinately, believing he could change her mind. "This is the moment I've been waiting and working for, Randy; please don't take it from me," he beseeched her.

"I can say the same thing, Luke," she told him sadly. "Please don't ask me to leave when I'm so close to my people. I wouldn't ask you to sacrifice your one path to victory. I have plenty of company and protection here, and I promise I won't leave the fort unless I know it's safe. At least by remaining here, I might have the chance to send word to grandfather. If I leave and trouble begins, my dream could be lost forever. Jane told me sometimes Indian chiefs or leaders come to forts for talks. If I leave, I could miss a visit. Don't you see I have to stay?"

"This is dangerous and crazy, Randy. I could be gone for weeks or months."

"I know; that's the problem. Time could be against me, Luke. Besides, why would I want to tag along with countless men. Surely you realize what kind of harsh conditions I would face on such a lengthy journey? In some barren spots, there would be no privacy at all. It's no place for a woman—a lady. I should wait for you here where I'll be comfortable and happy."

Lucas noted that defiant glimmer in her eyes, that fierce determination which told him he could not change her mind. Either he had to leave her here alone or remain himself. Neither choice was pleasing. After all, he could not force her to ride with him. And in a way, she was right about being safe here in the rented cabin. But he tried one other approach. "Brody Sheen would be your protector."

"That's another reason to stay behind," she answered. "Perhaps the best one," she added sullenly.

"What do you mean? He's loco about you, Randy. I'd bet he's asked me just so he can see you again. I thought you liked him," he stated probingly, eyes and ears alert.

"He's your friend, not mine. I don't like him or trust him. And I can think of nothing more disagreeable than enduring his company and pawings for weeks on end," she brusquely announced. Wisely, she didn't say he reminded her of Weber; for she didn't want to refresh that threat in Luke's mind.

"You mean you were just pretending to be friends?" he asked, that revelation coming as a complete surprise.

"I was merely being polite to your company. You made it clear he could be important to your work, so I did nothing to offend him. I was delighted when he left and I prayed he wouldn't return. In case you didn't know it, I had to scold him severely that last day when he practically forced his intentions on me.

I'm surprised he's asking for another chance to be rejected. If he issued his invitation because of me, then he is out of luck. I see you failed to notice that streak of ruthlessness in him. Didn't you see the look in his eyes or hear the coldness in his voice when he boasted of bloody victories, when he vowed to tack the scalps of Crazy Horse and Blazing Star on his wall? He's dangerous and conniving, Luke. If I were you, I would guard my back around him. Most assuredly I would guard my journals. If he or Custer even slightly suspected what you were after, you would find them more of a threat than . . . Sherman was to Georgia," she panted breathlessly, having the wits to alter her comparison from the grizzly. She didn't want Lucas recalling the warrior who might have trailed her for days; after all, he was long gone.

They debated their dilemma until both were weary and depressed. Neither would give in to the other. Realizing he might never have another chance such as this one, Lucas could not bring himself to refuse it. And knowing each of Miranda's arguments was valid, he still encouraged her to go with him but with less conviction. The matter was settled when Calamity Jane came over with some news of her own, news which would displease Lucas and delight Miranda.

Jane revealed she was "unrollin' my bedroll in the rear of the sutler's shed," and she would be staying around for several weeks. She told them she would be working with a friend and fellow scout, Tom Two-Feathers Fletcher. The two had been assigned to check on the camps of Indians who had refused to sign treaties or live on reservations, several of which were Sioux and Jane thought might be of interest to Lucas and Miranda.

Before Lucas could relate his new plans, Jane told them about the other scout. Tom was half white and half Cheyenne. He had scouted for the cavalry for years but refused to join any troop. He came and went as it suited him, or when he needed money for supplies and weapons.

When Jane settled her roughly dressed and ample figure in a chair, Lucas told her about his plans and Miranda's refusal to accept them. Jane, who was in her early twenties but looked forty-five, glanced from one person to the other as she mused on their conflict of interests. She felt she could protect and assist Miranda while Lucas was away, and, besides, Miranda appeared a woman of mettle.

Jane removed her floppy hat and dropped it to the table, shoulder-length dark hair tumbling from its confinement. "Don't you be worryin' none, Luke. I'll watch'er like a mother hawk. She won't git three feet without me tailing her backside," Jane vowed fondly. "Me and ole Pete will guard'er," she added, affectionately patting the butt of her pistol in the holster swinging from her thick waist.

"You don't know her like I do, Jane. She could talk a bandit out of his weapon if she had the mind to. She's willful and stubborn. I'm not sure I should leave her here to get into mischief," he protested.

"Watcha gonna do, Luke? Hogtie'er and throw'er

cross yore saddle," Jane teased mirthfully, winking at Miranda. "She don't wanna ride with them ruffians. Ain't narry a good man 'mongst'em; at least, ain't a one who can outride er outshoot Calamity Jane. Miss Miranda's a lady, Luke, my boy. You git'er out there where they ain't no trees and rocks fur miles; how's she gonna shuck her bloomers and have privicy? And ya knows she cain't go fur days with no bath like us'en."

Lucas threw up his hands in a gesture of surrender. "All right, you two. Randy can stay here," he acquiesced reluctantly. "But I'll warn you now; one speck of trouble and I'll hightail it back and redden two behinds. Savvy?"

That was Lucas's last warning before packing and riding off under the escort of five men from Fort Sully. It would require several days for the small group to catch up with Custer's regiment and for Brody to learn of Miranda's startling rebuff. Once there, Lucas would be in for many surprises and perils.

Jane and Tom ate supper with Miranda that night. They planned their outing for the next day, telling Miranda they needed to ride out at dawn to avoid being noticed by the commander of the fort. He would not have approved of her spending time with the scouts.

Miranda was so ecstatic about her quest the next morning that she could hardly sleep that night. Miranda felt that both Jane and Tom were trustworthy; both had been told of her goal. Jane had teased that the North Pole would melt before either of them betrayed her to a single soul. Both found her secret intriguing and stimulating. It was rare to have a daughter of an Indian princess and granddaughter of a famous chief as a friend. Miranda recalled how Tom's dark eyes had glittered with excitement, and she was very aware of his rugged good looks and powerfully built frame. Finding Tom charming and bright, Miranda wondered why he was called "that half-breed trash," and why the soldiers found Tom repulsive. If Tom was such offensive and undesirable company, why had the Army hired him? As she lay in bed, Miranda's mind wandered back to tales her mother had told her . . .

Joseph Lawrence had come to this wild and rugged territory in 1850 to seek adventure before taking control of his family's shipping firm on the Potomac River. Soon after his arrival, Joe met and fell in love with a Sioux princess named Morning Star. She was the daughter of Chief Sun Cloud, second son of the legendary and powerful Gray Eagle. Joe won the heart of Morning Star, a beautiful girl with doe eyes and ebony braids. When neither side would accept their love and Joe was called home because of his father's death, Joe convinced Morning Star to elope with him to Virginia.

Those first years in "civilization" were made easier for Morning Star by Joe's mother, who adored the young girl from the first. Joe gave his new wife his mother's middle name, Marie. Before Annabelle Marie Carson Lawrence died, she taught Marie all she could about her new role in the white society. While Joe traveled between the Alexandria townhouse, the shipping firm, and the plantation which he considered his home, the two women stayed on the plantation—later renamed Morning Star—to complete Marie's cultural training.

Marie learned how to converse and to conduct herself as a lady. She fooled everyone she met; most thought her of Spanish descent, for they never would have accepted an Indian. Her broken English flowed correctly after the months of Annabelle's gentle tutoring. Secretly Marie was taught to read. She was taught geography and history, and she was trained in manners and customs. She learned about theaters, plays, literature, and politics. She was shown how to dress properly and how to wear her flowing dark hair. She was trained in household tasks and instructing servants. Marie Morning Star Lawrence was bright and quick; she learned enough to join her husband in Alexandria after Annabelle's death in '53, sliding smoothly and unsuspected into the elite society there.

And now, if all went as planned, Miranda would finally be meeting her mother's people and observing their way of life in a matter of days. She tried to recall all her mother had told her about her Indian family. Marie had had one brother when she left her people; his name was Night Stalker. He had married a Brule Sioux called Touched-a-Crow and they had had a male child. As far as Miranda knew, she had a cousin here whose name she could not recall. But since the time for his "vision quest" must have already passed, he doubtlessly had taken another name. Her grandfather, Sun Cloud, had had a brother named Bright Arrow who had wed Rebecca Kenny, a white girl; both had died before Morning Star's birth. For that reason, Sun Cloud had assumed the chief's bonnet after Gray Eagle.

Gray Eagle—that name stirred memories for Miranda of tales of immense bravery and cunning. He had wed Alisha Williams, a girl he believed to be white and his captive. But the Oglalas discovered her to be the missing Blackfoot princess, Shalee. Their love story was beautiful and bittersweet, and it thrilled and warmed Miranda's heart when she reflected upon it.

She wondered if the Oglalas would accept her, for her mother had dishonored herself and her people by choosing a white man over a Sioux or other Indian warrior. She had been banned from the tribe. As the hostilities between whites and Indians increased over the years, she had realized her people would never forgive her.

Miranda could not imagine what she would confront within the next few days. But as she drifted off to sleep, visions of a tall, lithe warrior with a silver star around his neck stayed with her.

Miranda was dressed and waiting eagerly when Jane and Tom appeared before dawn. Beneath its shadowy protection, the three rode away from Fort Sully toward the Sioux camp, galloping swiftly across the terrain. Their stops were brief, merely to rest and water the animals. To avoid trouble, they wanted their trip to be as short as possible.

It was the end of June and the days were longer and warmer. Miranda did not know she was entering the Sioux territory during the same month Alisha Williams had in 1776. Neither could she know what tragedy had struck her mother's people in the year of her birth. Nor could she imagine what horrors this same month would bring in 1876 . . .

At dusk, Jane and Miranda hid while Tom rode into the Sioux encampment under a white flag of truce. They were to wait two hours for him, then ride for the fort if he had not returned. Jane attempted to draw Miranda from her silent and apprehensive state, but she failed to do so because Miranda was feverishly praying her grandfather would not refuse to see her. To prove her identity, she had sent a locket to him, one which contained a miniature painting of Morning Star in the white doeskin dress, matching moccasins, and headband which Miranda was now wearing. For years, Joe had kept the locket hidden, fearing someone would find it and guess his wife's secret.

Miranda paced back and forth in the coulee while Jane reclined on the grass. Scattered thoughts floated across Miranda's mind. She tried to imagine her mother living in this vast and arduous territory. She tried to picture her parents riding across the Plains. She could not help but recall the mysterious warrior had spoken Sioux. Yet, there were seven divisions and numerous tribes and bands. The unknown warrior could belong to any of them . . . Miranda forced herself to concentrate on meeting her relatives.

It seemed hours before Tom returned alone, but it was actually less than one. His solemn expression and lax stance said everything. Miranda cupped her face and cried. She had known this could happen but had refused to consider it. Her weeping ceased abruptly and her head jerked upward as she questioned Tom. "You explained who I am and why I must see him? You showed him the locket? He refuses to see me?" Tom nodded after each question, then shook his head at her next two. "Can I disobey? Can I ride into the camp as you did?"

"It is not done. When you make a request under a truce flag, you must honor the answer. To defy it would make you look foolish and arrogant, not brave. It would stain your honor in their eyes. Let him think on this matter for a time, then we'll try again. You must accept his refusal, at least for now," Tom replied.

Miranda inhaled raggedly. It was her moment of truth. Did she leave without meeting Sun Cloud, or did she dare to defy his wishes? She fused her gaze on Tom's face and asked seriously, "Will they shoot me if I go there and demand he speak with me?"

"He forbids you to come. He says his eyes must not touch upon the evidence of his child's betrayal. He says he no longer has a daughter; he denies you are of his blood. If you go, others will prevent you from seeing him. They will be angry with you for forcing yourself upon their old chief. They might order you from the camp or ignore you until you leave. But I don't think they will harm you. I could be wrong.''

His meaning was clear to her. Anger and courage flooded her. She had come so far and faced many dangers; he was cruel to reject her without an explanation. Could he do so if she personally presented her request? Without thinking twice, Miranda willfully declared, "Let's go. I will make the selfish coward disown me to my face. After I've come so far, let him reject me himself.''

Before Jane or Tom could protest her actions, she was racing toward the village, muttering to herself, "Mandy wouldn't yield to such a crushing blow, and I won't either!" But if she had known what was happening in Virginia, she would not have made that statement.

Chapter Sixteen

Two weeks had passed since Weber's band of daring and misguided traitors had been arrested. When it appeared their leader was long gone, Grant called off the extensive search for Weber Richardson, assuming someone had warned the villain to flee the country. Reis was positive a vengeful Weber would return, and he was furious to think that Weber was still free after committing so many crimes. But he had received his new assignment and would soon have to leave.

When Reis told Amanda where his next mission was, she could hardly believe her ears. They were going to the Dakota Territory where Grant's civilian son, Frederick, was working under George Custer, a man who was rapidly becoming another thorn in Grant's tender side. If Grant had merely suspected what menacing role his own son would play in the tragic history of this territory, he would have summoned Frederick home as hastily as possible. Reis explained that this investigatory mission was also secret, so Amanda did not question her husband further.

Actually she was delighted to be heading for a reunion with her sister and cousin, as they were in the same area. That very night, she wrote a letter to them, telling of their plans. All they needed to do was make arrangements for the Alexandria townhouse, the plantation, and the packing. Amanda Lawrence had learned that social status, wealth, and beauty did not compare with love and happiness. She knew she would sacrifice all she owned and would challenge any danger to be at Reis's side, for he was the only man to stir her heart to overwhelming love and her body to fiery passion.

Reis's friend was already managing her firm, so she felt content with the plans to leave home and Virginia. Since Weber was still on the loose, she was thrilled to be traveling so far away.

During the next week, Reis completed his reports and took care of business matters for his wife. Amanda kept busy preparing for their exciting trip. When Reis was not home by seven one night, Amanda fretted. It was not like him to be late without sending word. When the meal was beyond saving and serving, she placed the pots on the sink, biting her lower lip in mounting worry. She was alarmed when a note arrived from George Findley at eight-thirty which stated her husband had been injured and she was to come with the messenger at once. She left everything as it was to accompany the man to her warehouse.

Upon entering the large structure, she was seized from behind and held tightly. Her captor laughed satanically as he whispered, "I bet you're glad to see me, my sweet. Did you think I'd forgotten about my fiancée? It was wrong of me to leave you in that Yankee's grip."

At the sound of that familiar voice, Amanda nearly fainted in paralyzing fear. After her hands were bound, Weber flung her aside where she tumbled over cotton sacks and landed on the hard floor, bruising and scratching herself. She hurriedly came to a sitting position and leaned against another pile of sacks, gazing at him through shock-filled eyes. Her hair was in wild disarray and her clothes were mussed and soiled.

"Weber? Whatever are you doing in Alexandria? Don't you know there's a warrant out for your arrest, for treason? Where have you been all this time? Why did you send that note? Where is Reis?" she asked fearfully.

"Your beloved husband is fine for the moment. You could say he's a bit tied up, but fine," he joked devilishly. "I didn't know your blood was so hot that you needed two men to cool it. You amaze me, woman; romancing two men at once. Before I decide what to do with you two, I might show you what you've been missing."

Comprehending his lewd meaning, she warned carefully, "You're in terrible trouble, Weber. Surrender before they kill you on sight. McVane's dead, but you could find another smart lawyer to help you." *Let your mind work faster than your mouth*, she told herself.

"I never surrender, my sweet. Ask your husband. After I killed his family and burned his stinking ranch to the ground, he chased me for months, but I was too fast and clever. Too bad my aim wasn't truer. As to them killing me, you needn't fret about my safety, my sly vixen. I've managed to avoid them thus far. And if I still wanted you, I could take anything I please. In fact, you'd be begging to comply to spare your love from torture. Might be educating to that Yank to watch how a Reb pleasures a woman."

"You wouldn't," she murmured hoarsely.

His sardonic grin sent shivers over her. Weber thrilled to her terror and fed ravenously on it. He sought to increase it by saying, "I can promise you'll have a man to compare with old Reis, but I haven't decided if it's to be me or one of my men. I'm not sure if you're worthy of my touch. Of course, afterward, you'll have plenty of comparisons. I'm selling you for a pleasure slave. I don't really have the stomach to murder you, so I'll find other ways to enjoy revenge."

He strolled around her, nudging her with his boot when her attention seemed to stray. "I thought about killing Reis, but I changed my mind. Death would be too quick, too merciful. Months and years of suffering will be much better punishment. He'll blame himself for your sorry fate. He'll search the world for you, but he won't find you. As for our firms, nobody will profit from them. I'm burning them down before I start my search for Randy. Don't look so surprised," he jested cruelly when she paled. "That damn Union won't steal anything more from me! After I'm rid of Luke, I plan to enjoy Miranda for a long time."

"So, I was right to suspect you craved her more than me. She hates you, Web. She'll kill you first," Amanda spat at him before she could prevent the rash words from spilling forth.

"She won't have the strength, my sweet. No woman can resist me for long."

"My God, you're mad," she cried.

"Mad, yes; but crazy, no," he argued between chuckles which chilled her flesh. "I'm afraid you'll have to pay for siding with our enemy, the Yankees."

"The war is over, Weber!" she shouted at him.

"Far from it, my sweet. When we assassinate Jeff Davis, the South will rise in defiance and beat the North this time. They caught us unprepared last time but not this time. I've seen to it myself."

"Davis is a Southerner, the ex-Confederate President, you fool!" she shrieked incisively to pierce his veil of madness.

"Then he won't mind being a martyr for his cause. Life isn't the most important asset, unless you have the best," he debated nonsensically, his dark eyes rolling wildly.

Amanda was becoming frantic trying to find a way to reach him. She tried a different approach. She asked softly, "You mean the South will become powerful and free again? Is it truly possible, Web? How can you do it without your money and men? They were all arrested. Surely anyone else involved will be too frightened to help?''

At her softened tone and curious questions, he eyed her strangely. "Why'd you marry that damn Yankee spy?" he snarled. "Only a whore would choose a Yank over a Reb!"

"What was I supposed to do? You disappeared, and everything went crazy here. You left me at their mercy. You don't understand, Web; I had no choice. He was blackmailing me. He threatened to kill Luke and Randy if I didn't do as he demanded. I was stalling until Luke could get away. Reis was having me and Randy watched; he was even spying on the men you had watching me! Every time you came over, he was hiding in the house and listening to everything I told you. That's why I acted so crazy! Damn you, why didn't you help me!''

When he stiffened and squatted to pay closer attention, she continued her cunning tale. "Until I received a letter from Randy last week, I thought he was holding her captive somewhere. I knew why she ran away; she left because of the way I was treating you. She knew I was seeing Reis, but she didn't know why. And I dared not tell her or refuse to follow his strange orders. When I called his bluff with her letter, he told me if I hired anyone to warn her he would have one of his men slay her that very day—that he knew where she was.''

When she halted to catch a breath while thinking

what to say next, he snarled coldly, "What kind of lies are you feeding me?"

"Reis was gone that day I asked you to search for her, but his men were lurking outside. I was afraid your actions would warn them had I confided in you. Reis told me they had orders to shoot both of us if I betrayed him to you. I thought if I dropped some crafty hints, you would track her down and rescue her. But I was trying to get you to search secretly to protect all of us. He said he was a government agent. How could I refuse to cooperate? He told me he was after some notorious ring of ex-Rebels who were buying and stocking arms for another war. He said they were using your firm and mine, but he didn't talk like he thought either of us were involved. When he said you were the leader, I couldn't believe you were guilty of treason. Heavens, Web, how could you do something foolish like that?" she asked angrily.

When the befuddled Weber did not respond, she wearily continued. "If I didn't obey his orders or if I warned you, he said I would be arrested as your accomplice. Me—Amanda Lawrence—arrested and imprisoned for treason! Do you have any idea how female prisoners are treated inside those stone walls? I do; Reis vividly described it. I was so confused and frightened, I didn't know what to do. He told me everything would be over in two weeks. But everything went crazy. He said you would be arrested and hung for treason, that he possessed positive proof. I couldn't understand why he forced me to marry him then kept it a secret. During the raid on your meeting that night, he explained why. He was using your fiancée to punish you, to gain something for what you took from him. He wanted your woman and a wealthy position and business, in exchange for that family and ranch you boasted of destroying. Like you just did, he threatened to take whatever pleased him; if I resisted or defied him, he vowed to find a way to implicate me in your traitorous schemes. I didn't want to go to prison, Web. When you escaped, he was furious. When I told him it served him right for all he'd done to me, he said you would kill me when you came back because you would never believe me innocent of helping him trap you. Look what you've done to me, to my life. How can you say you loved me after hurting me so much? Oh, Weber, are you really going to kill me?"

Weber watched the fragile creature as she focused those innocent and entreating eyes on him. He listened to her pitiful voice and he was consumed by confusion. "Surely you don't expect me to believe all this?" he debated, his eyes exhibiting his doubts. "You tricked me, woman. You nearly got me killed. You lied to me," he declared, opening the door for some valid charges from her.

"I *tricked* you? I nearly got *you* killed? I *lied* to you?" she sneered, stressing his ridiculous accusations. "Reis showed me the books and letters he confiscated from the firms as evidence. He was boasting about how much he owned now, compliments of his wife and you. You lied to me about the firm, Weber! You lied about the townhouse and

Morning Star! I wasn't going broke; I'm a wealthy woman. Or I was until that spiteful Yankee took control of everything! You were using me, duping me all along! It was a cruel game to steal all I owned. Oh, he enjoyed showing me how you had been deceiving me. Now you accuse me of betrayal? What a stupid, blind fool I was. I thought you were my gallant knight, saving me from all of life's dragons, when all along, you were the fire from their nostrils; you were the enemy trying to consume me. You were even spying on me! Why? You know what's so ironic and tragic? You didn't have to trick me at all. If not for your crimes bringing that Yankee here to ruin both our lives, we would be married now and our mutual firm would be thriving. And Randy would be safe at home. She's in Dakota with Luke," she added desperately to win his trust. "All this time she's been safe. If only she or Luke had told me . . ."

Weber was staggered by her vast knowledge and accusations. She seemed to know everything and she was blaming him for this defeat and danger. She had seen the evidence, so he could not deny it. She appeared bitter and angry, vulnerable and sad. He had planned to kill them both and burn the businesses, then vanish. Did it change things if she were innocent? It was too late to correct his mistakes, too late for Reis's death to alter his dire situation.

In a way, his revenge on Reis could still take place. Reis wanted Amanda and her lucrative firm and holdings. He could make certain Reis gained nothing and he could burn the townhouse and the plantation. Once again, all the Yankee would have would be a scorched parcel of dirt and charred trees. The kink in his plans was Amanda. Reis had been using her like he had. It would not matter to Reis if he killed or sold the haughty bitch. In fact, as her husband, Reis would gain everything without having to endure Amanda. It irked Weber to realize his plans were being usurped by his enemy. Even with a few fires here and there, Reis would win.

"You never loved me, did you, Web?" she asked somberly, as if that realization pained her deeply.

"I wanted you because you were wealthy and beautiful—and because you were desired by so many men," he replied calmly. He went on to confess his lust for Miranda and what had happened between them.

"You mean she left because of you, not Reis?" she shrieked as if surprised by that statement. "I was only using that jealousy argument to stall your proposal. I never suspected you actually wanted her. I honestly thought I was hurting you, insulting you. You tried to attack her in our home! You tried to force her to marry you in my place! She despises you. My God, Web . . ."

Suddenly Amanda jerked her head toward him. She seemed to brighten with a new thought. "Reis knew! Randy must have told him and Luke. Of course—that's why they helped her get away. That's why she wouldn't confide in me. You tried to ravish her, so naturally she turned to chivalrous Reis! Reis probably told him you were the one blackmailing and threatening me. They were all three in on that plot. How could Luke and Randy side with him?" she wailed. "Don't tell me he's in love with her, too. I wonder if Reis is planning to get rid of me before she comes home! That devil! I hate them all! There's no telling what that Yankee said to them. You don't think Reis convinced them I was working with you, that I'm a traitor? Merciful heavens, Randy doesn't know it was Reis making me so jittery and secretive, not you. Your lust tossed her right into Reis's lap and plans!"

Weber did not realize Amanda was filling his head with doubts and suspicions, hoping to drive a wedge between his madness and his desire for vengeance. If she could persuade him she was on his side, that she also wanted revenge . . . If only she could disarm him . . . If she could entice him to trust her, to untie her . . .

Amanda sensed he was wavering as he gave this matter new study. She murmured, "My own sister and cousin . . . How could they do such evil to me? Is there no one I can trust? Am I so terrible that everyone hates me? If only Mama and Papa were here—they wouldn't let this happen to me." She began to cry.

Her last statement reminded Weber of what he had done to Joe and Marie. Their missing bodies did not matter now, for all was lost. Just before cruelly breaking her heart by disclosing that final secret, he changed his mind. "You do have a way of bringing out the worst in people," he informed her sullenly.

"Besides everything else, must I take the blame for

the wickedness and greed of others?" she scoffed tearfully. "That isn't fair." One last and desperate plan to save her beloved entered her mind. "There is one way to spite them, Web," she hinted.

"How, Miss Lawrence?" he sneered sarcastically, yet his curiosity was piqued. She looked so tantalizing, all tied up like that. She probably still wanted him, the foolish tart.

"How could a jury convict you without evidence?" she asked. When he perked up with interest, she went on, "Why not force Reis to steal it for you? If you destroy it, they can't touch you legally."

"How do I accomplish such a feat?" he scoffed, eying the soft swell of her breasts.

Amanda tried to ignore the dreadful reason for the flush on Weber's face, the passion glaze over his dark eyes, his harsh breathing. As consternation flooded her, she pretended to think of a plan. "I doubt using me as bait would work. He doesn't care what happens to me. He would probably thank you for removing me for him. And you can't threaten to burn down all he owns; he would merely place guards around the buildings. Besides, with my money under his control, he can rebuild everything with no problem. Luke and Randy are out of your reach, so you can't use . . . That's it!" she squealed. "Randy! That's how to get to him. Sweet Randy will lure him into our trap."

"What?" he growled in befuddlement. "She's in Dakota."

"You know how much we favor each other. What

if we use soot or something to darken my hair? Perhaps use a blindfold to hide my blue eyes. If he glanced at me at a distance in the shadows, he would think you had Randy captive. He would steal the evidence to save her. You could dress one of your men to pass as Luke. If you keep us in dim light and at a distance, with mouths gagged, he would be fooled. I can hire a lawyer to prove he blackmailed me, then I'll be free of this repulsive marriage. We'll make certain we obey every American law and give them no new evidence or suspicions for a new case; agreed? After he lowers his guard, you can get rid of the beast."

"And just how did I capture Randy and Luke?" he queried.

"You've been missing for weeks, Web. You've had time to locate them and bring them back as prisoners," she snapped in frustration, as if irritated by his lack of intelligence.

"And what if he asks to see you?" he added, finding another inconsistency.

"Must I think of everything!" she exploded in fury. "You were clever enough to trick me for months and to almost pull off a second civil war! The least you can do is help me figure out how to defeat them and save both our lives and fortunes! In case you're not thinking clearly, I've just as much to lose as you have! I don't want to be Harrison's showpiece! I don't want him commanding me! I want to come and go as I please. As long as he's in control of me and my wealth, I'm helpless; I'm like a prisoner! You can

371

show me bound in one area of the warehouse. Then surely you can find some way to taunt and delay him while I disguise myself and sneak to where you're supposedly holding Randy and Luke for exhibition,'' she suggested.

"Why would you help me?" he questioned skeptically.

"As I said, for a price," she replied hastily, glaring at him.

"What price?" he inquired, piqued.

"Everything I just told you and my escape. After the ruse is over, you destroy the evidence against you. Then you must help me get free of Reis, either by his death or an annulment. In exchange for my help, I'll sign Lawrence Shipping over to you. I'll sell everything else, move to another state, and begin a new life—perhaps in New Orleans or New York. When my traitorous sister returns, she'll be at your whim because I won't be around. And neither will our property and money for her protection and support. Since you find her so pleasing and desirable, you can rescue her from poverty. But I don't want her beaten or killed; is that understood? You can make her your mistress or wife, whatever suits you and her. As for Reis, you can do as you please with him. That way, we'll both have what we want.''

Just as Amanda suspected and prayed, Weber agreed to go along with this scheme to obtain the crucial file. But she knew he would attempt to delude her into believing he would free her and help her afterward, which he would never do. Despite his hazy madness, Amanda was reading him clearly. Yes, Weber would try to use her one last time, but he would fail!

The plans were made. Weber untied her but placed a guard on her. She frowned at him, mocking his mistrust. "Prove yourself, my sweet, then I'll trust you with my life," he teased her. "In fact, I might do all I can to persuade you to marry me. We would make a fine team, Mandy. We could both come and go as we pleased, discreetly, of course. I would enjoy having your sister as my mistress for a while, if you didn't mind." She shrugged nonchalantly as if agreeing.

When all was prepared, Amanda was nervous. All she could do was go along with her scheme as she awaited a moment to attack him. She hoped Reis would see through this farce. If he did not, he would be offered a chance for escape and to summon help. For the first time, she knew what it meant to be willing to sacrifice her life for that of someone she loved. But to think this could be the last time she saw her love was staggering and tormenting.

Amanda was bound and gagged, then placed in a corner. Her guard concealed himself and she was ordered to feign unconsciousness. Weber went to get Reis. He brought her beloved to the center of the immense room, then had another guard come and stand near her. A flaming torch illuminated her limp figure, revealing her disheveled and dirtied state. She remained still and silent.

Weber warned Reis she would be killed instantly if

he made any moves or called for help. As they headed for the office, she could hear Reis threatening to slay Weber with his bare hands if she were harmed in any way. It ripped at her heart to note the anguish in his voice, the pain and fury which she prayed Weber would ignore or think false. His hands bound, Reis could help no one, including himself. And with her as a prisoner, her love feared to escape or resist.

The guard untied her the moment Weber and Reis were out of sight. He was already dressed to resemble Lucas. Amanda sealed herself in a closet to change dresses, then the two of them sooted her blond hair until it appeared dark. They hurried to an adjoining warehouse to take their places. When the guard leaned over to move a crate to partially shield them, she furtively seized a crowbar. Refusing to feel any remorse, she slammed it across his head, then quickly bound and gagged him. She grabbed his knife and stuck it into a cotton sack near where Weber would stand while pointing them out. She took the guard's gun and her assigned place, calculating that there would be Weber and another armed guard against a bound Reis and herself. All she could do was wait with her stolen gun, and pray Reis noticed the shiny knife.

She went rigid when she heard the door open then close. She ordered herself to relax yet remain alert. She could hear Weber's voice, but could not make out his words. He halted near the center of the structure, telling the guard to show Reis "their little surprises."

Amanda knew their lives were at stake but

wondered if she could actually pull the trigger and shoot a man. Her arms were in a position to indicate she was bound, and she had remembered to gag herself. The other man moved the torch back and forth over the couple as Weber referred to them as Miranda and Lucas. Reis was unprepared for the sly ruse and was briefly deceived at that distance.

As Weber issued his demands, Reis snarled, "How do I know the three of them are still alive? All I've seen are limp bodies. I want to talk to them."

As pre-planned without Amanda's knowledge, Weber signaled the guard who instantly shot the man playing Lucas. It did not surprise the other guard or Weber when the unsuspecting man did not move or scream, or when Amanda jumped in astonishment. Weber casually informed the stunned Reis that he could only bargain for the two twins now. If he refused Weber's orders, both girls would be murdered tonight.

"You son-of-a-bitch!" Reis stormed at him, causing Weber to shove him backward. Miraculously, Reis's hands made contact with the knife, and he hastily closed his fingers around the handle.

Then everything went wild. Amanda panicked and shot the guard, the thunderous roar of her gunfire drawing Weber's attention from Reis. The wounded guard tried to get his gun out of his holster, but she closed her eyes and fired once more. This time he stopped permanently.

It was evident to Weber that he had been duped by her again, and that both of his guards were now dead or seriously injured. With a loud yell of hatred, he jerked out his concealed weapon to kill her. Reis yanked the knife from its place and whirled around. There was no time to sever his hands. He slammed himself into Weber's back, driving the knife into his demented body. Both men fell to the floor. With speed and agility, Reis pulled the bloody knife free and rolled away. He instantly came to his feet and raced to where Miranda was hiding.

When he turned to ask if she was all right, he was shocked; the woman beside him was his wife. She ripped off the gag and smiled at him, then hugged him tightly. Weber's agonized voice returned her anxiety. Reis told her to cut him free, which she did with some effort. She handed him the guard's gun, then he smiled at her, and stole a brief kiss of encouragement.

"I'll kill you, you bitch!" Weber shouted in pain and fury.

"It's over, Richardson," Reis announced confidently, shoving Amanda's head down when she tried to peer over the crate.

She understood the precaution when Weber fired shots at them. Reis attempted to talk Weber into surrendering, but he adamantly refused. Spouting how he was going to "roast them alive," Weber staggered toward the only unsealed exit. From his wild rantings, it appeared he was planning to barricade the door and set fire to the building. Reis could not allow him to escape or give him a chance to trap them. He fired at Weber's legs, one bullet shattering a knee. As Weber screamed in pain and clutched at a stack of crates for balance, the heavy pile tumbled down crushing him. Weber Richardson would threaten them no more.

Finding the guards dead as well, Reis left the bodies while he took the trembling Amanda home. Later, in each other's arms, they compared stories. At last their ordeal was over, the anguish of the past and present. They nestled together, sharing comfort and joy.

Before leaving Alexandria, Reis hired a crew for the desperate search which Weber's boastful words had inspired. Only in the event that his men were successful, would he tell his wife anything about it. Soon they would be in Dakota to challenge new adventures. But they would also confront perils as yet unknown, perils more numerous and lethal than any devised by the late Weber Richardson . . .

Chapter Seventeen

Calamity Jane and Tom Two-Feathers Fletcher had no choice but to mount hastily and follow the impulsive and courageous girl toward the Oglala camp. Tom caught up with Miranda and cautioned her to conduct herself with patience and respect. He warned her not to make trouble if Sun Cloud refused a second time to meet her.

Tom witnessed the look of fierce determination and resentment which were visible in her tawny eyes and upon her lovely face. This audacious and exquisite creature would be a sensuously wild vixen to tame, an assignment he would relish. What more could a man who survived in the wilderness desire than a woman who was beautiful, brave, sturdy, and keen witted? He could easily envision the type of wife and mother this half-girl, half-woman would make in some lucky family. And luck was something a clever man created for himself in this barren, onerous territory. With her half-blooded heritage, Miranda was a perfect match for him.

They reined in before the colorfully painted teepee of the famed war chief, Crazy Horse. Tom and Jane gingerly dismounted and Tom assisted Miranda down to the ground. Miranda stood poised and guarded as Tom spoke with the leader who had left his teepee at the commotion outside.

"Tashunka Witco," Tom addressed the chief by name in Sioux, then related that the girl with him wished to know why her grandfather refused to see her after she had come so far and faced many dangers.

Crazy Horse eyed the beauty at the scout's side, a female who looked as Indian as the women nearby. His sweeping gaze surveyed her manner of dress: she was wearing the garment and headband of an Oglala princess! Did the proud creature think she had the right by birth to commit such an offense? She was *hanke-wasichun*, half blooded!

No one approached the small group or dared to speak without their leader's permission. But all observed the strange sight. Miranda remained alert and silent while Tom reasoned with the chief. From the expression and tone of Crazy Horse's voice, she knew he did not realize she spoke his tongue and understood his cutting words. Forewarned by Tom, she held her anxious tongue as her anger increased.

Miranda observed the masterful warrior who was rumored to be dauntless—a powerful man who challenged any force or obstacle, an intelligent man whose cunning was feared and respected, an heroic man whose influence and prowess were held in awe and dread. *Tashunka Witco* was said to be a seasoned leader who rode before his band, always putting himself in the first line of danger. And he was known also for his military tactics and expertise, a "Plains soldier" unsurpassed. He was a proficient warrior of such enormous mettle and skill that others envied him but feared to challenge his rank. So immense was his valiance that he had become a member of the *O-zu-ye Wicasta*, the Warrior Society, before reaching his sixteenth birthday. It was as if Crazy Horse had been trained from birth for his rank in history, as if no person or nothing could prevent him from being thrust into the role of the Sioux's most powerful warrior. It was true that he trusted no white man, and with just cause. Believing himself protected and blessed by the Great Spirit, he could endure intense pain without flinching. It was alleged that the intrepid warrior "dreamed" himself into an aura of invincibility and matchless valor before every battle, seeing a vision in which his horse pranced eagerly and crazily, and from this dream the illustrious warrior took his name. Just over thirty, Crazy Horse was a growing legend amongst both whites and Indians.

One thing which surprised Miranda was the lightness of his hair and skin. He possessed bold features and piercing eyes on a face which could be called ruggedly handsome. He was the son of the sister of Spotted Tail, the noted Brule chief confined to a reservation. The defeat and humiliation of his

once-great uncle inspired and encouraged Crazy
Horse to make certain he and his people never shared
such a despicable and degrading fate.

Another curiosity for Miranda was the physical
size of Crazy Horse. She had expected this legend to
be tall and muscular, as was the unknown warrior
she had met several times. But Crazy Horse was of
medium height and lean, with the lithe build of a
swordsman. Yet, strength of body and character were
emblazoned upon his face and frame. As the two men
talked, Miranda admired both the mental and
physical attributes of the war chief.

The warrior chief speaking with the half-blooded
scout knew the story behind this girl's birth and the
shame and betrayal of her mother. Although he had
been only ten years old at the time, Crazy Horse could
recall the day when Princess Morning Star deserted
her father and people to marry a white man. He
respected the past skills and prowess of Sun Cloud,
now seventy-five and growing more eager each day to
seek the Great Spirit, and he could understand why
Sun Cloud refused to meet this woman. He was
keenly aware of her intense study of him, and her
conclusions. But perhaps, he silently reasoned, he
should change the old warrior's mind; perhaps she
offered solutions to several problems.

Miranda thought it was best to keep her knowledge
of the Sioux tongue a secret in order to discover all
she could, unaware that her great-grandfather, Gray
Eagle, had used this same ploy to learn the white
man's secrets. She asked the scout to translate her

words. "Tell my grandfather that his daughter, Morning Star, and my father were killed; they now live with the Great Spirit. Tell him I have come a great distance alone to meet him. Ask him to forgive the pain and sadness which my mother brought to him. If she had not been taken from my life-circle, she would be here this sun speaking these words. She longed to see her father once more and hungered for peace in her heart and mind."

She waited while Tom interpreted her statements. "Tell him I am not my mother; tell him I should not pay for her acts which brought shame and sadness to the teepee of Sun Cloud. Is it not the Sioux way for each man to earn his own honor and to pay for his own evil? Why must I pay and suffer for the deeds of my mother? If he will not speak with me, I will never return. Will he deny himself my love? Can his bitterness and hatred of my mother and her child be so great that he denies I carry his blood? Will such a denial remove that blood from my body? He was a great warrior, a worthy chief. Where is the wisdom and logic in rejecting me?" she reasoned candidly in a tremulous voice.

Those words were translated for the Sioux chief, even though he comprehended most of her English words. Miranda selected her next words carefully and brazenly. "Surely such a great man has no reason to fear a mere woman? Have I denied that an Oglala Indian is my grandfather? Have I rejected him because he is Indian? Have I refused to travel through great distance and danger to see him only one sun?

Does this mean I hold more courage, generosity, and wisdom than your former chief? If a man or woman cannot steal another's good or bad shadow, then how can he use my mother's dark shadow as the reason to deny me sight of his face and the sound of his voice? What man of honor and bravery cannot speak for himself? Can he not find the courage and generosity to share but one hour with me?" She knew she had cleverly used two of the most respected Indian arguments, tempering her tone with appealing frankness and honesty.

Crazy Horse's expression softened with appreciation, but he did not smile. To her surprise, Crazy Horse told them to wait while he spoke with Sun Cloud. Miranda's gaze trailed him to a teepee in the second ring. He ducked and entered. Tension increased within her as she waited. When he finally returned, she was prepared to hear another refusal. She could not hide her astonishment and pleasure when Crazy Horse related the summons of her grandfather, to share "one hour" as requested.

Miranda's hands were trembling and her heart raced as she followed the chief into her grandfather's presence. Complying with the instructions from Crazy Horse to Tom, Miranda seated herself on a buffalo skin before the older man, three feet away. Jane had been ordered to wait with the horses, which she reluctantly did.

Sun Cloud's hair was mostly gray with only traces of ebony. His stoic face was lined from the passage of time and exposure to the elements. Even after so many years, Sun Cloud still radiated courage and greatness. Such wisdom, pride, and intelligence flickered in those age-glazed eyes. His once strong body was now slim, having lost its firmness and power. He was sitting cross-legged on another buffalo hide, erect and silent, watchful and wary.

The unnecessary translations began. Her grandfather asked why she had come to him, his voice vital and clear despite his age and increasing weakness. A twinge of sadness and disappointment assailed her, for he did not inquire about his deceased daughter or even hint he was glad she had come. He appeared untouched by her arrival and identity. She struggled to contain the tears which threatened to expose her turmoil. Whatever happened today, she would show great courage and control.

Before replying, she quietly asked permission to begin her tale where it started, here in 1850. She waited for Sun Cloud to object. His response was for her to choose her own words. If either warrior was moved by her narrative, it did not show on their impassive faces. Fearing her time was limited, Miranda revealed only the major points of her and her mother's pasts. Sun Cloud did not react to the news of her twin sister or to the perils they had faced recently. Only Crazy Horse perked up when she exposed her cousin's assignment here. Knowing Tom hated the blond-haired Custer, she felt no qualms in revealing it.

When she finished telling of her history and motives, her grandfather asked if she had spoken all the words she wished him to hear. Miranda wondered if her heart truly stopped for a moment, for it sounded like a dismissal. When she nodded, Sun Cloud asked if she had completed her quest and was ready to leave. Miranda stared at him, for she could not respond in the way she felt he wanted her to. She wondered if Sun Cloud possessed any feelings of affection or loyalty or respect for her. She was disheartened by what she did not see in his eyes or perceive from his mien. At least she had made the effort.

Miranda rose slowly and stood proudly before Sun Cloud, sealing her fathomless gaze on her grandfather's face, ignoring the others present. She stated with false calm, "My hour has passed, Grandfather, and I will leave as promised. I pray you will seek and find understanding and forgiveness before you join my mother with the Great Spirit. Do not blame her for loving and choosing my father, for she answered the call of her own destiny. If joining with my father was wrong for her, the Great Spirit would have prevented it. Perhaps it was not the wish of the Great Spirit for Morning Star to marry a white man, but He allowed her to follow her heart. I will not trouble you with the telling of their love story and happiness. It is not for you or me to judge her actions; only the Great Spirit has that right. Goodbye, Grandfather. Until you look into the face of the Great Spirit and learn all things, I wish you health and happiness." With that, she turned to leave, unable to bear the weighty anguish of this moment any longer.

Just before she ducked to exit the teepee, Sun Cloud stated she had not answered his last question. Miranda inhaled and exhaled several times before turning to face him. In a clear and compelling tone, she replied, *"Hiya. Cante ceya,"* saying no and that her heart was weeping in sadness. She went on to tell of her desire for peace with him. *"Wookiye wocin."* Both warriors stared at her as she spoke fluent Sioux with ease.

The elderly man told her to come and sit once more. Miranda hesitated. Sun Cloud's expression warmed and relaxed as he coaxed again, *"Ku-wa, cinstinna,"* calling her "little one."

When she did as he had requested, he stated evocatively, "You speak my tongue. How is this so? Why do you leave without fighting words?"

"My mother taught me to speak Oglala. She loved you deeply, Grandfather. It pained her heart to leave you and her people; it pained her more never to return. She missed you and longed to visit you. She spoke of the Sioux history and her life here. She spoke of you, telling me what a great warrior and chief you were. She told me why her love and marriage were wrong in the eyes of her people. For many years I have hungered to come here, to know you, to know this life. When she was taken from me, the hunger increased. It was as if I had no power or wish to resist the summons of the Great Spirit, as if He were calling me home. I belong here, Grandfather; I am more Indian than white. She taught me your customs and ways and that is why I knew it was wrong to beg or resist," she explained.

"But you resisted my command not to come," he refuted astutely.

Miranda lowered her gaze in guilt. "Yes," she admitted. "But I did not feel it was right for you to reject me from a distance, to reject me for another's deeds. I was drawn here by a force too powerful to resist."

Sun Cloud observed the girl who returned his daughter's image to life. Morning Star had always been different from other Oglala maidens. She had been willful and daring, yet gentle and unselfish. This girl was much like his own. Seeing her made him feel younger and his spirit freer. Morning Star had left of her own will; Miranda returned in that same way. After the death of Night Stalker, his loneliness for his only child had increased. He had feared and prayed for her safety, though he never mentioned her name after her departure. His body had survived many winters and hardships, his heart had known many emotions, and his eyes had seen many changes in his life and lands. His children had reached the Great Spirit before him. All he had left were memories of past glorious days, and two grandchildren who differed as much as day and night. He mentally corrected himself—three grandchildren.

"To speak the truth takes great courage, little one. You will stay in my teepee for five suns then return to your sister," he calmly informed her, then asked Tom to return for her on the sixth day.

Tom gazed at Miranda. "What if someone learns your secret?" he asked.

"I want to stay, Tom; I need to stay. Please help me. If the truth leaks out, I'll face that problem when it arises. Jane can say she took me to visit friends downriver while Luke's away. Who could doubt us?" she reasoned aloud. "Please," she urged him.

"That sounds good," Tom agreed, smiling at her.

Miranda told her grandfather she would stay with him. She said she must bid her friend, Jane, farewell, and she left the teepee. Jane agreed to live in the cabin while she was in the Sioux camp, then return with Tom for her.

While Miranda and Jane were exchanging their stories, Sun Cloud was asking Crazy Horse, "Has she earned a *coup* feather, for she stole this old warrior's heart? Did I speak and act like a foolish old man?"

"You spoke as a wise, unselfish man. She carries much of the blood and spirit of Sun Cloud. She will make no trouble. She will bring you peace and smiles," the youthful leader concluded. He added mischievously, "Perhaps she will remind Bloody Arrow why he does not wear the chief's bonnet. Perhaps she will soften his anger and bitterness."

Sun Cloud nodded gravely. "Each moon I pray the Great Spirit will remove his pride and greed. It was the will of the Great Spirit for you to guide us. In time, my grandson must see and accept this."

Sun Cloud was relieved when Crazy Horse did not mention another warrior in the distant line of Gray Eagle, the great-grandson of Bright Arrow. If the white man's evil took the life of Crazy Horse, there was only one warrior to take his place, Blazing Star. But Sun Cloud and others knew that Blazing Star would not challenge Crazy Horse for the chief's bonnet, or vainly try to rival their leader's *coups*. Surely a smart and intuitive man like Crazy Horse realized as well that Blazing Star posed no threat to him. In many ways, Blazing Star was more like a son or grandson to Sun Cloud, and he was anxious for Blazing Star to return to him and his people. Sun Cloud was determined not to permit Bloody Arrow to plant any more seeds of doubt in his mind about the absent warrior, and he trampled his grandson's malicious suspicions within his heart. He hoped Crazy Horse had not ordered Blazing Star on so many dangerous raids just to be rid of him.

Crazy Horse left Sun Cloud and Miranda alone to talk, which they did for a short time as it was nearing the hour of the evening meal. Although Miranda had not noticed her, there was an Indian slave preparing their meal beside the teepee to allow them privacy. Miranda learned about a ghastly massacre during 1854, the year her mother had given birth to twins. Besides many people in the tribe, others in Gray Eagle's bloodline had lost their lives to the bullets and sabers of treacherous bluecoats. She learned of the slaughter of her grandmother, Singing Wind, daughter of Oglala maiden, Chela, and Blackfoot chief, Brave Bear, and of her uncle, Chief Night Stalker and his Brule wife, Touched-A-Crow, from Sun Cloud's line. From Bright Arrow's bloodline

Tashina was lost, youngest daughter of Bright Arrow, along with her husband, Soul-of-Thunder, and their son, Soaring Hawk, both his wives, Talking Woman and Sapa Ista, and one grand-daughter called Bitter Heart, who was the twelve-year-old half-sister of Blazing Star. She listened as Sun Cloud revealed that Blazing Star was the only survivor in Bright Arrow's bloodline, and that Bloody Arrow—her first cousin—and she and Amanda were the only ones to carry on Sun Cloud's line.

Having heard the name of Blazing Star so often from the whites and now the Indians, Miranda inquired about him as their food was served by the sullen girl. Because men, especially Indian men, did not consider physical appearances, Sun Cloud talked only of the immense prowess and accomplishments of the awesome warrior. As she listened, she realized that Crazy Horse and this mysterious Blazing Star were very much alike in strength and courage. In the days to come, Miranda would hear a great deal more about this warrior.

After the meal, Sun Cloud left her to attend a council meeting. Miranda relaxed on her assigned pallet to ponder this momentous day which had gone extremely well. Her drowsy thoughts were of her eagerness to meet her cousin, Bloody Arrow, and the legendary Sitting Bull tomorrow. She was disappointed that the intrepid Blazing Star would not return to camp before her departure. She snuggled against the fuzzy hide, inhaled deeply, and totally relaxed as a pleasing odor assailed her hazy senses. She smiled and pressed her face closer to the hide, inhaling again. Her mind floated toward a warrior whose face and body she knew, but not his name. Perhaps she would describe him and seek his identity after she had been here a few days, she mused dreamily. Contented and fatigued, she was soon sleeping peacefully.

When Miranda awoke the next morning, she felt wonderful. She ate with her grandfather, again served by the unfriendly girl of about twenty. Afterward, Sun Cloud guided Miranda around the camp, introducing her to everyone who caught his eye or ear. She smiled each time he called her his granddaughter, *Tamaha*, which meant "Rising Moon." When she asked him why he had selected that name, he said it had been Sitting Bull's suggestion. When she probed deeper, he told her that Morning Star was the name for the moon rising during the day to cast a faint white image upon the blue sky, just as she had arisen in her mother's image.

She was touched and moved by the significance behind the lovely Sioux name which sounded like she was saying, "Ta-my-ya." Sioux was a difficult and guttural tongue, but her name sounded soft and flowing like a gentle stream, as warming as the spring sun. She thanked him.

Later, she met the man who had chosen her Indian name. Sitting Bull, *Tatanka Yotanka*, was a medicine man and spiritual leader. She wondered why the soldiers thought he was a chief. Said to have great mystical powers and immense courage, Sitting Bull was very perceptive and intuitive, a prophetic man to rival the Biblical Isaiah. His silvery tongue had reached the minds and hearts of Indians and whites. Little did Sitting Bull or Miranda realize that many of his letters and speeches would become historical readings, revelations of the dark blot upon humanity and American history.

Around forty, Sitting Bull was a tall and powerfully built man. His broad shoulders seemed capable of taking on the burdens of his tribe, or the entire seven-tribe Sioux Nation. Only the skills and prowess of Crazy Horse or Blazing Star could rival those of Sitting Bull. He possessed piercing eyes which seemed to cut through one's body and view the very soul. Upon his chest were the marks of courage and sacrifice, the scars of the Sun Dance. If ever a man embodied and exemplified stoic greatness, fierce courage, keen intelligence, and stamina of mind and body, here was that man—Sitting Bull.

All Indian tribes knew of him and respected him. His words could be trusted. Sitting Bull, like Crazy Horse, had no respect and feeling for those who condemned themselves to reservations. Sitting Bull called them fools who would enslave their souls for rotten food and ragged blankets. As long as he had breath, he determined to remain free on the lands given to his people by the Great Spirit, *Wakantanka*.

Miranda was greatly impressed by this unique man. How she prayed he could keep his people free and alive. Having seen how they lived off the land in such harmony and tranquility, it pained her to envision their defeat. She could not imagine these proud and vital people lazing around a reservation. The Indians were the epitome of courage and strength. Why couldn't they be left in peace? Hadn't the whites taken enough land and lives?

Sun Cloud had told Miranda how the chief's bonnet had left the bloodline of Gray Eagle. When Gray Eagle was fifty-five, he was wounded critically. The chief's bonnet was passed to his son, Night Stalker, but only for two years until the grim 1854 massacre. With Bloody Arrow only five and Blazing Star only eight, Sun Cloud resumed the chief's bonnet until Crazy Horse won it at age twenty-six after his successful and daring victory over Captain William Fetterman and his troop. Seventeen at that time, Bloody Arrow had been too young and rash to become war chief, too inexperienced, too distracted by shameful pride, and too hot tempered. Since then, her grandfather had confided worriedly, Bloody Arrow had been unable or unwilling to accept his loss.

Sun Cloud had just been served his evening meal when Bloody Arrow swept into the teepee like a conquering hero returning home after a victorious raid. As was the Indian custom, Miranda had been waiting for her grandfather to finish eating before she was served. Bloody Arrow's audacity shone like a bright beacon on the darkest of stygian nights. At first glimpse, he seemed intense, moody, and rebellious; such traits were unusual for a warrior. Clearly, here was a force she would have to reckon with before this day was over. The warrior halted instantly when his eyes touched the beautiful Indian girl sitting near his placid grandfather. His gaze took in her features quickly, then shifted to his grandfather as he decided he would enjoy this new slave.

Bloody Arrow took a seat near Sun Cloud and was served by the Crow captive. His gaze was cold and his demeanor forbidding as he ordered the slave to see to the freshly slain deer outside. His dark eyes settled on Miranda as he commanded her to help the other woman, warning her of punishment if she disobeyed or made any mistakes.

Startled by his wintry stare and mood, she did not know how to respond. Was she supposed to help with chores in the teepee? Could she skin and cure a lovely deer? She swallowed with difficulty. Was she subject to her cousin's orders and whims? Wasn't she a guest?

Sun Cloud suppressed laughter as he revealed her identity to the astonished warrior. Bloody Arrow's gaze narrowed and clouded as he gaped at his cousin. "You are Tamaha, my cousin?" he asked in disbelief.

"*Sha*," she cheerfully replied yes in Oglala, although he had spoken in English.

He came to full alert at her use of his language. "Tell me why you came to the teepee of Sun Cloud and Bloody Arrow?" he inquired oddly.

Miranda allowed Sun Cloud to relate her story and his invitation. She noticed the increasing coolness in the younger warrior as he watched and heard the warmth and pleasure in their grandfather's eyes and voice. Surely a blind person could detect the jealousy and bitterness in Bloody Arrow at her arrival and treatment, Miranda thought to herself.

Bloody Arrow asked question after question until he felt he knew everything about this girl and her visit. Miranda sensed there was something peculiar about his interest; it certainly appeared to be more than curiosity about a new relative. He seemed particularly interested in how she had been received by Sitting Bull and Crazy Horse. At the end of their talk, he asked if she had met Blazing Star. Sun Cloud told him that Blazing Star had not returned from his scouting mission and probably would not return before she left. That statement caught his attention, and he looked pleased to learn she would be leaving soon.

At bedtime, Bloody Arrow did not attempt to hide his irritation when he was told to go outside while she changed for sleep. He was more vexed to discover he would have to sleep in his breechclout while she was there. He teased her about not knowing the ways of their people, telling her if she remained here long she must cast aside her modesty and accept them. Miranda could not imagine sleeping nude even with family!

As she lay on her pallet listening to the heavy breathing of both men, she comprehended several dismaying realities. She had recognized the antagonism in her cousin's voice and eyes when three names had been mentioned: Crazy Horse, Sitting

Bull, and Blazing Star. Having met two of the three men, she could not understand this leashed hatred and envy. Clearly her cousin did not want her around, and it would be difficult, if not impossible, to win his friendship and acceptance. She pondered how much contention or unhappiness he could bring to her. But she had discovered another fact which Sun Cloud had not mentioned, a fact which would force her to end her visit as planned, for she now knew that she could never take up permanent residence in this abode. Blazing Star also lived in this teepee and would be home soon.

Now she understood why there were three prayer pipes and so many weapons, items she knew females were forbidden to touch. Certainly she could not live with three men. And she and Blazing Star were so far apart on Gray Eagle's ancestral chart that they could hardly be called relatives. If they had been children, living together would not have made a difference; but they were adults.

And there was another factor. Since Bloody Arrow's return, the atmosphere in the teepee had changed drastically. It seemed intimidating and unfriendly now, and that plagued her. Did her grandfather feel this chilling atmosphere? She admitted that hearing about Indian life and living it were vastly dissimilar. Having Indian blood did not necessarily make her suitable for this existence. No matter how much she wanted to fit in, she wondered if she could, or if her cousin would permit it.

Miranda asked herself why her cousin disliked her

and why he was anxious for her to leave. He had seemed delighted by her presence when he thought her a helpless captive. There were many conflicts and ill feelings in that skilled warrior. Why could he not accept his role in life and in this camp and be happy? He had accused her of being ignorant of Indian ways and customs, but his attitude and behavior were wrong for a warrior—despicable! Her first impression had been accurate; he was trouble and anguish for her. But did it matter when she had only three days left here? She had fulfilled her dream, but now she was so confused. Did she belong to this world? Was she more Indian or white, or neither? She drifted off to sleep with these poignant questions haunting her.

When she awoke the morning of the third day, Sun Cloud was gone; Bloody Arrow was sitting cross-legged on his mat, watching her intently. She rubbed her eyes and sat up, holding the light blanket before her. She smiled faintly and told him good morning. His stare unnerved her, as he no doubt intended.

He suddenly grinned and teased, "Do you enjoy sleeping on the mat of Blazing Star? Be glad he has not returned and joined you. His prowess upon the sleeping mats is known by many females."

Miranda paled then flushed a deep red at his crude insinuations. "The lust of Blazing Star does not interest me, dear cousin. Nor does your childish dislike of my visit," she told him brazenly, hoping her chilling displeasure and brave words would prevent more insults.

He scolded her mischievously. "It is not the way of Indian women to speak so rudely to a great warrior."

She promptly retorted, "Is it the way of a great warrior to insult his relatives? Is it acceptable for a warrior to be rude and hateful to the granddaughter of Sun Cloud?"

"Your wit is keen and your tongue is quick, Tamaha. But they are scornful. Perhaps it is because you have more white blood than Oglala," he mocked.

"Your wit is black and your tongue sharp, Bloody Arrow. Perhaps you have more hatred and envy in your body than pride and intelligence."

"You possess great courage or stupidity to speak so boldly to me. I will think more on you before we talk again," he declared sullenly, then quickly left.

"And I will think more on you, too, cousin," she scoffed softly.

Later that morning, Bloody Arrow watched his cousin as she walked and talked with Crazy Horse, unaware the chief was probing her about the defenses at Fort Sully and things she had perhaps overheard which might inform him of the soldiers' plans. He observed the easy and genial manner of the envied war chief, then noticed the sullen way the Cheyenne wife of Crazy Horse was furtively observing the two. Bloody Arrow grinned as he envisioned the warring teepee of their leader if Crazy Horse revealed too much interest in this beautiful girl.

Bloody Arrow needed time to think and plan, things he did best while hunting. He called several

braves together for a hunt for the widows of slain
warriors or the families of those warriors who were
away from camp. This was a common practice but
not usually suggested by him. He rode out of camp
with rising pleasure at the game he was plotting, a
sport to defeat more than one rival.

Before leaving, Bloody Arrow commanded the
Crow slave to loan Miranda one of her best dresses,
the one she kept folded inside a leather parfleche for
the day of her escape and return home. The girl was
filled with anger and defiance at this cruel order. Her
feelings altered, however, when Bloody Arrow told
her he wanted his cousin looking her best until she
left their camp, and he promised to bring her a
beautiful doeskin for a new dress in return for her
services to Tamaha. The prisoner sensed spite in her
captor, spite toward the chief he had been secretly
watching all morning and spite against the half-
white girl who now shared his grandfather's affec-
tions. She also wanted revenge on the Sioux, and
agreed to do as commanded. Her captor's scheme
would come to light, and she would enjoy his
punishment.

Miranda was surprised and pleased when the
captive offered her a clean buckskin dress and
undergarment to wear. Her astonishment grew when
the girl suggested a bath and hairwashing with her
assistance. The slave smiled shyly, craftily, as she said
it was to please Tamaha's family, to perhaps inspire
her release for kindness. Of a gentle and trusting
nature, Miranda smiled and accepted the captive's

devious words. She followed the girl to the stream where she bathed and scrubbed her hair. After the sun dried it, the Crow woman brushed and braided it, then secured Miranda's headband around her forehead. Donning the fringed and beaded dress, Miranda looked exquisite. The girl told her to return to camp while she washed her dress for tomorrow.

The Indian custom was to rest after lunch, but Miranda was too excited to take a nap. Her grandfather was in a council meeting, discussing the reports of two scouts who had returned during her bath. She decided to stroll around the camp to study the artistic adventures painted on the teepees while the village was still and quiet. Within an hour, she was at the edge of camp. She strolled to a large tree and leaned against it, her contented gaze sweeping over the sight of her grandfather's immense village.

The thunderous sound of many hoofbeats seized her rambling attention. Panic filled her as she recalled tales of surprise raids on Indian camps. She rashly jumped from behind the tree, stepping into the path of a band of returning warriors. She screamed as she was knocked face down to the hard and dusty ground by the leader's horse.

In their elated and distracted mood, the leader and his band almost raced over the reckless and inquisitive girl who had stepped from behind the tree. He was relieved to see she had been thrown aside before being trampled by the pounding hooves of seven horses. The startled warrior agilely bounded off his horse to check on her. He was scolding her furiously as she lifted her head to present his stunned senses with the same beautiful face which filled his dreams!

Both were silent as they stared at each other. His astute gaze flashed over her tawny eyes and sun-kissed skin, and the unmarred flesh which had been soiled by her fall. Her hair was as soft and dark as a bearskin, braided neatly. Having been about to speak, her lips were parted, displaying a mouth which was provocative and whose taste and softness he recalled too well. Her wide gaze revealed her astonishment at seeing him again. Yet, there was another emotion emblazoned there, an emotion which caused his loins to flame with desire, a response which made him forget where he was or who he was!

Miranda could not pull her captive gaze from the magnetic attraction of this man who had haunted her dreams for many weeks. Here he was before her once more, here with his arresting features and strong, virile body. He was like an intoxicating blend of stormy black and molten bronze. Her mouth was suddenly dry and she could not speak. Her heart was racing madly and she could not think. Her eyes were glued to him and she could not free them. Intense desire flooded her as she stared at this embodiment of manhood, this savage and powerful warlord of the Plains, this captor of her heart and inspiration of her fantasies. In her wildest imagination, she had not thought of finding him again, and surely not here in her grandfather's camp! How fortunate he had come to visit before her departure.

The mutual trance which seemed to hold them was broken when the other warriors dismounted and surged forward to demand the identity of the beautiful Indian maiden. Miranda watched the mood of the handsome warrior as it changed rapidly, confusingly. His face was unpainted today, giving her a clear view of his mounting fury and resentment, reactions she could not understand. With feet planted apart in an arrogant and forbidding stance, he glared at her, refusing to offer her assistance in rising. He merely gaped at the hand she extended entreatingly for his help, gaped as if it were leprous.

For a brief time, she had presumed he was glad to see her. Now, he was acting as if they were strangers, foes. She had watched coldness cover the warmth on his face and freeze his eyes. Why? She slowly and gracefully stood up and dusted off her clothes and bare arms. The other males were laughing, teasing, and ribbing each other as they watched her closely, watched her and the curious behavior of their leader. Miranda did not know what to say.

He stood tall and erect, recalling the day he had secretly watched her riding with the female scout from Fort Sully. He berated himself for not capturing her that day or one of the other times they had met. He knew where she lived, in that small wooden teepee near the fort. He knew a white man shared that teepee, the one who had traveled with her to his land. Now she was the captive of another warrior, out of his reach forever. He cursed his pride which had prevented her capture, his ego which had wanted to be spared the teasing and taunting of other warriors at his taking a white slave. In the back of his mind, he had known he would fall prey to his desires one day. He had known he would attack that cabin during the night and ride away with her bound to his body, to become his slave. Now that was impossible; he could never take her after another man!

The instant that thought left his tormented mind, he knew it was a lie. She could not be blamed for her capture, or any treatment afterward. He had seen the way her eyes lit up with joy and relief when they touched upon him. Whatever price her captor asked, he would pay it. He had to pay it and have her. Yet, his honor had to remain intact. He could not reveal love and desire for this white girl. He silently prayed she had not been injured, then realized how exceptionally clean and healthy she appeared. Surely she wasn't Indian or half-blooded? Surely she wasn't some warrior's wife or willing whore!

Miranda and the others were stunned and baffled when he sarcastically demanded to know whose captive whore she was. Before she could recover from the staggering insult to respond, others questioned his words to her. He coldly revealed she was a white girl from Fort Sully who had come to this land recently. He told them she had been on the boat he had trailed while stalking the two soldiers he had been ordered to slay. He related how they had been killed by a forest warrior while trying to rape this very girl.

Unaware she understood his words and the degrading meaning behind them, she was speechless in disbelief and anguish. She did not realize the warrior was infuriated by his stupefied reaction to her, angered in his belief that she was out of his reach, nettled by his weakness toward her before his band. Miranda's watchful and wary gaze shifted from warrior to warrior as they stared at her differently now, disdainfully.

When he cruelly asked again in English whose whore she was her wits and words returned in a fury of her own. "No man's! Get away from me, you savage beast!" She whirled to leave.

The warrior's hand snaked out and grabbed her wrist painfully, yanking her against his hard chest and rigid body. "Whose teepee holds such a sharp tongue and brazen whore?" he pressed boldly as the others watched his curious actions, for one warrior did not touch another's slave.

Through clenched teeth, she snapped in vexation, "I am no man's whore. I sleep in the teepee of Bloody Arrow and Sun Cloud."

She was determined to yank free of this insolent, smug, and cruel master of her heart. She owed him no explanation! "Release me before I cut off your offensive hand! Don't ever touch me or come near me again," she threatened.

Her previous statements had enticed a strange reaction. "You live in the teepee of Sun Cloud and Bloody Arrow?" he pressed skeptically.

Since he was speaking in English, so did she. "Yes. Sun Cloud will slay you if you harm me," she warned icily.

"You do not belong to Bloody Arrow?" He needed clarification but wondered what he would do if she said yes.

"Of course not!" she sneered as if insulted. "I belong to Sun Cloud," she added vaguely, wanting to flee this painful scene. His grip was as firm and confining as a band of steel.

Sun Cloud was told of the quarrel outside camp involving Tamaha and the warriors. He arrived and demanded her release. Miranda fled into the protective and affectionate embrace of her grandfather, trying not to sob. Sun Cloud smiled at her and patted her shoulder, his gaze settling angrily on the man who had dared such an offense.

One of the younger warriors rashly teased, "Surely our old chief does not take a white whore to his mats at his great age? If she is for trade, speak her price," he coaxed, as others added their bids.

Outrage filled the older man. He drilled his snow-clouded, ebony eyes into the oddly furious leader of this group. With a distinct voice, he informed them, "This is Tamaha, my granddaughter, child of Morning Star, my daughter. Do not ever touch or insult her again, or I will forget I am an old man. I will paint for a challenge with the warrior who dares to dishonor or hurt her, including you, Blazing Star."

At that name, Miranda's head jerked upward and she stared at the man whom her grandfather had called Blazing Star. As if no one else were present, she asked in a trembling voice, "You're Blazing Star?" He had shown astonishment at her identity, but he blinked in disbelief when she spoke fluent Oglala. When he nc ided, she paled, suddenly realizing what distinctive and dream-inspiring odor had assailed her each night, each night upon this man's sleeping mat.

Miranda told Sun Cloud she was fine. She left her grandfather's embrace to flee as if demons were chasing her. When Sun Cloud questioned their strange behavior, Blazing Star asked the others to leave for privacy. He explained how he knew Miranda. Sun Cloud asked him why she had fled in fear; Blazing Star honestly replied he did not know. The old chief asked what had taken place between them today. Blazing Star ruefully repeated his words, abruptly comprehending that she had known what he said. Sun Cloud related her arrival and story.

"She did not know about me?" he inquired anxiously.

"She has heard many tales of the great warrior called Blazing Star, from Indians and whites. She has not asked about a warrior who saved her from the grizzly, who paints his face as you do. She has not asked who shoots arrows tipped with red and black. She sleeps upon your mat each moon. You return before enough suns pass. She is to leave soon. I did not tell her you lived in my teepee," he replied.

He was dismayed she had not inquired about him, since she had understood his Sioux words at each meeting. Her identity explained her previous lack of fear or scorn toward him. Blazing Star was intrigued by where she was sleeping and her reaction at seeing him. She had not expected the man who met her secretly to be the famed Blazing Star. "Did Bloody Arrow tell her I live in your teepee?" he pressed oddly.

"I do not know. Why do you ask such a question?"

Blazing Star deceived the old man by saying defensively, "She will be eager to leave now that I am home and she uses my mat."

"We can borrow a mat for her for two moons," he announced.

"Two moons?" Blazing Star echoed in bewilderment.

"She was to stay for five suns; three have passed. She will return to her people soon," Sun Cloud explained.

"Why must she go?" the warrior asked quietly.

"You know why, Blazing Star. Soon the white waters will try to roll over us and drown us. I do not wish her to find pain and death. She has been raised white; she must return to that world."

"She does not wish to live here with her grandfather?" he pried.

"She has not asked. If she does, I will refuse. I must," he stated sadly, sounding as old and weary as he looked at that moment.

"What of the white man who traveled with her?" he questioned.

Sun Cloud looked at him. "He is as Bloody Arrow to her. Luke puts words on papers for others to read. He comes secretly and cunningly as the fox, seeking to record the soldiers' evil. His eyes are on butchers and Yellowhair. And your eyes speak words I have not seen written there before. Do I see love and desire? Do I read pain and anger? Do I read jealousy and shame? Tell me if these eyes are too old and clouded."

Blazing Star fused his gaze to Sun Cloud's. He replied truthfully, "I cannot explain feelings I do not understand. There is a pull from her as strong and mysterious as the one to our sacred hills. I have resisted its power and magic, for I believed her white. But . . ."

When he wavered in confusion, Sun Cloud smiled and remarked, "But she is not. She is the grand-daughter of a chief, the daughter of a princess, from the blood of Gray Eagle."

"Such truth makes trouble for us, Grandfather," he concluded aloud, using the endearing name he called this beloved man. He chuckled as he said, "I hurt her with cruel words, yet she fought as a wildcat, Grandfather. Can she be tamed?"

"The answer is, who should be the man to try?" he jested slyly.

"Has another warrior cast hungry eyes upon her?" he asked worriedly, wondering if he must battle for her.

"Many," Sun Cloud replied mirthfully. "But none

have brought the lights to her eyes as you did," he whispered devilishly.

Blazing Star recalled their past meetings and smiled happily. The smile quickly faded as he recalled his behavior today. "I must speak with her," he declared, dreading her reaction.

A lone rider approached with a message from Bloody Arrow, telling Sun Cloud the band had joined with one from the Cheyenne camp. They were heading into the Black Hills to make raids upon the camps of white trappers who had intruded upon their sacred ground. The message stated they would be gone for one or two moons. The rider mounted up again and headed to join his friends on their blood-thirsty trek.

Blazing Star smiled and remarked roguishly, "We have no need now to borrow a sleeping mat, Grandfather."

The two exchanged smiles and matching thoughts. At Blazing Star's request, Sun Cloud headed for the special council meeting. Blazing Star returned to their teepee to find Miranda sitting on the ground near the stone pit used for cooking. Lost in thought, she failed to hear his approach. It was a stirring voice which had become familiar to her that broke her intense concentration.

"I spoke too hastily and cruelly, Tamaha," he told her.

Miranda battled to keep her gaze from him as he spoke a sort of apology. She wanted to scream at him, to refuse it. He had hurt her, embarrassed her. She did not want to behave childishly or reveal her turmoil, so she let him know of her anger by ignoring him completely. How she wished she had something to occupy her hands and attention! It was alarming to be alone with him, to know his name and rank.

He saw she was not ready to listen or forgive. "So be it," he informed her calmly. "When your temper cools, we will talk."

Her head jerked upward and she glared at him. "I have no words for you, now or later. I will leave in the morning."

"Do you run from me or yourself, Tamaha?" he inquired in a husky tone. "A girl who challenged the eye and claws of the grizzly to save another's life showed more courage than I see in you this sun."

"I was not the one who came and went in secrecy, Blazing Star. I'm leaving because there is no room in my grandfather's teepee," she explained, trying to excuse her hasty flight from his closeness.

"I am glad you are here, Tamaha. Bloody Arrow will not return for two moons. You will sleep on his mat, unless you wish to stay on mine," he murmured seductively. "I wish—"

"I wish to share nothing of yours, you arrogant beast!" she panted at him as he teased her playfully, cutting off his tender words.

"I did not say share, Tamaha. Sleep where you will; it matters not to me," he stated flippantly to goad her.

"It matters to me," she vowed sullenly.

"And to me," he contradicted himself, grinning at

411

her. "It matters, if it is not alone, or with me."

She was about to take his beguiling bait when his grin alerted her to his ruse. "I have heard you rarely sleep alone," she sneered before thinking, then blushed at her shameful boldness.

He warmed to the spark of jealousy in her. "The speaker of such words is a liar. For many moons, I have craved but one female, one female I have denied myself," he stated suggestively, meaningfully.

Miranda did not know how to respond to such a statement, so she remained silent. She dared not ask the name of the woman, fearing she was wrong to think it was she.

He hunkered down before her and said, "Grandfather has gone to council. I must join him. We will talk later," he stated firmly.

Their gazes locked; neither moved. His hand reached out to run the back of it over her flushed cheek. "You are beautiful, Tamaha. I feared you were another's captive. You should not put such conflict in me," he murmured mysteriously, his dark eyes glowing strangely.

"Conflict?" she echoed hoarsely, her anger a thing of the past.

His thumb rubbed over her lips very gently, noting her erratic breathing. "You have caused my mind to war with my body."

"I do not understand," she responded naïvely.

He was disappointed by her words. "If you do not, a battle does not rage within you. We will return after the moon passes overhead."

He was gone before she could ask for a clearer explanation. How she wished he had embraced and kissed her! Was she a wanton creature? Her mind was spinning in confusion and her body ached with a strange . . . Conflict? Battle? Did he mean what she was thinking?

Chapter Eighteen

Blazing Star had spoken accurately; it was long past midnight when the two men returned from the meeting. She had tossed and turned for hours, trying to understand this complex man and this new situation. Their reunion had been most unexpected; his reaction, most disturbing and distressing. Try as she did, she could not get this afternoon off her mind. She was deeply concerned over his chilly and almost brutal conduct at first sighting her today. Before, he had not seemed to care that she was white. But in front of his people, particularly the other warriors, it had made a vivid difference. Was it so essential, so significant that she was proven Indian or half Indian? From what she had heard and witnessed, it was worse to be half-blooded! She fretted over his treatment when he had viewed her as white, a slave. She could not help but wonder how he would feel and act if she had appeared in his life again as another's "captive whore," white or Indian. If he had seen her being abused by a cruel master, would he have done anything to help her? It was the contradictions in his behavior which plagued her. His affection and desire had been shown only in secret, and the complete change in him when he understood her relationship to Sun Cloud confused Miranda even more. She reflected, too, on his seductive behavior and stirring words when they had been alone in this teepee. She cautioned herself to be still after they entered quietly, hoping they would not realize she was still awake.

But the moment Blazing Star lay upon his mat, he smiled into the darkness. Her fragrance still clung to it, a scent which aroused his body to sensual hunger. He should have known she would change mats after learning whose she had been sleeping on for nights. He could not stop thinking about how close she was to him; yet she was so far out of his reach.

What he did not know was that she had absently claimed his mat at bedtime, then quickly gone to her cousin's. She sighed heavily and rolled to her back, staring up into darkness. How would she ever get to sleep knowing Blazing Star was within a few feet of her!

His senses keen, he knew she was awake and restless. What was worse was the fact that he also knew Sun Cloud was deeply entrapped by slumber. He did not even stir when a violent thunderstorm attacked the lands. But Miranda jumped and gasped at several bolts of lightning which struck too close to camp, then shook the earth with rumbling echoes.

"Do not be afraid, Tamaha," he whispered tenderly across the dark span which separated them, telling her he was also awake.

She was too unsettled by the turbulent weather to recall how angry she was with him. And it was easier to be annoyed when he was not so near. Perhaps he had responded from jealousy and pride this afternoon. Surely he would be furious to find her the captive of another, if he truly cared about her. And surely under those circumstances, he would be embarrassed by their reaction to each other in public? When the winds whipped at the teepee and heavy rain poured upon it, she asked softly, "Are the storms always this bad?"

"When they come so late," he replied. "The rivers and lands are thirsty; they require much rain to refresh them."

Miranda hid her face as another streak of lightning seemed to invade the teepee itself. Blazing Star went to her side and pulled her into his arms. "It will be this way for a long time. Sleep, Tamaha. I will guard you from all harm."

When he made no romantic overtures, but simply offered her the comfort of his arms, she relaxed and nestled against him. He stretched out on Bloody Arrow's mat and curled her against his side. He did not move or talk again. He felt her body going limp and her respiration becoming steady. Soon she was asleep in his arms. As if feeling completely safe, nothing more troubled her.

Just before dawn, he eased from her side and returned to his mat. He was baffled by the fact that he had slept next to the most beautiful and desirable woman he had ever known without making love to her. There was a strange contentment and great pleasure in being near her. He had not felt such emotions before. How could a smile warm him? How could a touch make him happy? How could a voice stir his soul? How could a gaze steal his thoughts? If such was true, what would it be like to make love to her? How could he lose her? Yet, how could he keep her here in the face of such death and destruction?

Agony chewed at him. Sun Cloud was right. She must not remain here. If he enticed her to fall in love with him, each of them would be hurt. It would be easier for both to forget if nothing happened between them. She was so trusting and innocent, so vulnerable to the feelings he inspired within her. To reject her would be the fiercest battle he had ever fought, but he knew it would be wrong to take her to his mat and to love her wildly and freely, then force her to leave him. It would be cruel to encourage her love and desire when there could be no more between them. She must be sent away.

He slipped from the teepee. He would have to find the strength and courage to resist her. If he were right, why did this unselfish act torment him? The white man was like a mighty eagle, its talons ever closing around his people, preparing to rip them to bloody pieces. So many battles and lives had been lost. The white man's forces and weapons were many and powerful. One by one, they were destroying or conquering each tribe. No matter how smart or brave the Indians were, they could not last forever against such an enemy.

He had never thought to see the sun when his lands were owned by foes. He had never envisioned such crushing defeats, such wanton slaughter of his kind. Never had he dreamed the sun would come when he doubted the survival of a single Indian. But the white butchers were slaying women and children to annihilate the entire race. Why was the Great Spirit allowing such evil to breed, to grow larger? Why must he find his true love when it was too late and dangerous to claim her?

It rained all morning, forcing Miranda to remain inside the teepee. To pass the time, her grandfather taught her a game played with small pebbles. Sun Cloud napped for several hours during the afternoon, and Miranda stood at the teepee entrance, gazing out at the teepees in the first circle. She wondered where Blazing Star had gone; she wondered why he had not returned for their talk.

He had confessed he was glad she was here. If she inspired such "conflict" in him, why didn't he confront her and discuss his feelings, feelings she shared? He had not gone hunting, and there was no council meeting. She remembered again how he had held her and comforted her. She glanced in all directions but could find no trace of him. She instinctively knew he was avoiding her. But why?

The evening meal came and went without Blazing

Star's return. She wanted to question his absence but was too proud to do so. What was he trying to prove? Was this some joke or test? Why waste such precious moments? It took her a long time to fall asleep that night. She realized, as she knew he must, there was only one day left of her visit.

When he was certain she was asleep, Blazing Star sneaked into the teepee and slept restlessly. He was up and slipping out at dawn when she saw him. She sat up and cleared her throat, the noise drawing his attention. When he turned, she motioned for him to come over to her. Concealing his love and turmoil, he scowled as if annoyed by her and her request, then shook his head and left.

Miranda stared at the waving flap. Why was he doing this to her? He was making it clear he did not want to speak with her or see her. Sadness gripped her heart, and panic tugged at her mind. She would be leaving in the morning. Was that why he did not want to start anything between them? That speculation warmed her.

At rest time that afternoon, Blazing Star was still keeping his distance. Once when he sighted her watching him, he began flirting with a lovely Indian maiden. From her tortured expression, he knew she understood his message. He could not allow her to linger here, not after learning of the white war council.

While her grandfather slept, Miranda left the teepee to walk near the stream. She found a lovely spot and sat on a rock studying the newly green foliage. She was about to continue her stroll when Blazing Star came into sight. She called his name. He glanced her way then headed in the opposite direction.

Miranda jumped up and raced after him. They needed to have a talk. He owed her an explanation. There was no time for modesty or manners. She caught up with him, but he quickened his pace to prevent their confrontation. She ran forward again, grabbing his arm. She panted breathlessly, "Why don't you talk to me? I'll be leaving tomorrow, and we have so much to say to each other. Why are you avoiding me? Why are you being so distant?"

"There is nothing to say. Return to your people, Miranda. You do not belong here. You are more white than Indian," he stated coldly.

"But, why?" she beseeched him. "I thought we were friends," she murmured in a quavering voice. He had called her Miranda. He was clearly rejecting her. He was trying to hurt her. She must know why.

"If you wish to be my friend, do not chase me as a she-dog with mating lust. When a woman steals my eye, I will chase her. Why do you trap a man who wishes to escape?" he asked insultingly, hoping to encourage her to leave, for this necessary game was hurting both of them.

His words were as physical blows. Tears welled in her golden brown eyes, and her face became the color of fire. "You need not be cruel, Blazing Star. I've never chased any man, and I surely won't start with one who despises me and deceives me. I didn't mean

421

to give you the impression I was the whore you called me. But I can understand why you would think such evil of me after the way I behaved when we first met. I don't need or want you as my friend. I won't inflict my repulsive company on you again or trouble you further," she told him then fled.

Before Miranda reached the teepee, Tom Fletcher met her, saying he needed to escort her back today as he was leaving on a scouting mission tomorrow at noon. This timely rescue was welcomed, and she told him she was ready to leave and would fetch her belongings. When she entered the teepee, her grandfather was still asleep. She decided it would be better to leave without awakening him, for he might read her turmoil, and she wanted the painful matter between her and her tormenting love kept private. She took the small bundle of her possessions. She wondered who could give her farewell message to her grandfather. She could not ask Sitting Bull or Crazy Horse, as both had left camp. Whom could she trust to be kind and gentle?

Yellow Bird, wife of Fox Eyes, was the perfect choice. She took one last look at her grandfather, love and sadness filling her. It was best to avoid a painful good-by, and it was vital to avoid Blazing Star. Perhaps Fate had kindly provided this gentle departure. She left the teepee, clutching the little burden under her arm. She explained to Yellow Bird why she wished to leave secretly, to spare her grandfather's feelings and hers. The woman did not concur, but agreed to pass along the message when it was too late to follow or stop her. Yellow Bird sensed there was more to her hasty and furtive departure, but she did not feel she had the right to pry.

Miranda and Tom walked to the edge of camp to mount their horses and ride away. She suppressed the anguish which plagued her. She told herself she was doing the right thing for everyone. She wished Blazing Star had remained a mystery, a lovely fantasy. They set out in the direction of the tree-lined gully where she had awaited the response from her grandfather a few days past. She would never regret riding brazenly into his camp. It was done; her quest was over and her dreams had vanished. Perhaps she would visit her grandfather briefly again before returning to Virginia.

For two hours, Yellow Bird fretted over the girl's departure. Finally, she could restrain herself no longer. She went to find Blazing Star, as she dreaded to tell Sun Cloud of her part in this matter. When the warrior heard her tale, he told her not to repeat it to Sun Cloud, that he would explain Tamaha's actions. It was too late to catch up with her, to change her mind.

After repeating the astonishing tale to Sun Cloud, Blazing Star revealed that he was going after her. He said he would sneak to her cabin during the night and speak with her, to make sure she was home safely and nothing was troubling her. Sun Cloud could tell that the warrior was concerned for his granddaughter. It almost seemed as if Blazing Star suspected another motive behind her secret departure.

He did. Blazing Star could not forget the look on her face or the sound of her voice when he had scolded her. He had not meant to make it sound as if he despised her, scorned her. He had to see that she was all right. He quickly mounted his horse, knowing he could not allow her to leave this way. He must have hurt her deeply.

To prevent the discovery of their trip, Tom and Miranda rode hard and fast until they neared the outskirts of the fort shortly after midnight. They dismounted and spoke for a few minutes, as talk had been impossible along the trail. Miranda did not realize the effect she had on Tom when she caught his hand and thanked him as she smiled genially and gratefully. It had been an innocent and friendly gesture for her, but one which stirred Tom's blood and passion. As she sneaked to her cabin, Tom guarded her. He had sensed a sadness, a conflict within her, and he wanted to comfort her, but he was afraid of alarming or offending her. At that moment Tom knew he must have her, and knew a path to such a victory was near.

When Miranda was inside, he left with no one the wiser about their actions. Miranda was relieved that Jane had left yesterday for a scouting trek southward and would be gone for several weeks. Once Tom left tomorrow, she would be alone for a time. Frankly, she didn't care; she was glad to have solitude. She secured the door, went into the small bedroom, and began to unpack her belongings.

As she lifted her nightgown, she felt something hard and heard a strange noise. She opened the bundle to find a tormenting and baffling gift. It was a *wanapin*, a special necklace. There was a long, sharp bear claw suspended on a leather thong, and there were five rattler-rings separated by six sets of blue beads between twelve white beads, strung on either side of the unforgettable weapon of the grizzly. It was evident who had made the necklace and hidden it in her bundle. It was also evident who had taken her first souvenir, though she had presumed she had lost the rattler-ring from her dress pocket that awesome day.

But why had he made it, and why had he concealed it so she would find it after their separation? Did he want her to have a remembrance of their meetings, of him? She began to cry softly. If he cared about her, why had he been so cruel and cold?

Miranda placed the haunting necklace on the table near the bed. She changed into her nightgown and flung the covers aside. Before she could get into bed, she heard a soft tapping at her door. At first she tensed in panic then decided it must be Tom with a message. She went to the door and called softly, "Who's there?"

Knowing she would not open the door to him, Blazing Star muffled his voice and said, "Tom," in an undistinguishable whisper.

When she asked what he wanted, he muffled his

voice so that she was compelled to open the door to hear his words. She stood behind the thick door and peered around it as she said, "I couldn't hear you."

"Tamaha," he called her Indian name as he pushed the door aside and entered. "I must speak with you."

Miranda turned and stared at him. "What are you doing here? Get out before I scream for help. As I recall, we have nothing to say."

He stepped forward, pinning her between his iron-muscled arms and the door, which he closed and locked. "Why did you sneak away like a cunning fox in the night? Sun Cloud worries over this behavior."

She looked up at him through tear-soaked lashes. This time, she did not want to see him or talk with him. She did not want him maliciously toying with her emotions again. She should not have trusted Yellow Bird. How dare he come here to torment her! She pushed his confining arm away and walked into her bedroom to retrieve something. He followed her to the doorway. She snatched up the necklace and flung it at him, sneering, "I don't want your gifts! I don't want anything to remind me of you! Just stay away from me, you beast!"

He had ducked to avoid the forcefully thrown necklace. He came toward her, closing the short span which separated them. When she attempted to flee past him, he lunged at her and reached for one wrist. She fought him wildly, cursing and berating him in a quiet tone. When he attempted to imprison her arms, she shocked him by seizing his arm and whirling and flipping him to the floor with a thud. As he scrambled to his feet, she kicked him in the abdomen. Unprepared for such a blow and action, he was knocked backward to his seat in the middle of the doorway. He stared at her as she assumed a crouched position, ready to ward off his next attack. As he grabbed the doorframe to rise, he observed her stance and hand positions.

"Where did you learn to fight this way?" he asked warily. No one had ever thrown him, not in a contest or battle! How could this fragile girl do what no warrior had done? "You are a trained warrior in skills many men cannot master. But if you continue this battle or scream, others will know of my presence here. You will be trapped by danger and shame, and I will be captured and killed," he advised her, hoping to settle her down so they could talk.

"I know skills which can bring a quick death or a slow one. Come near me, and I will show you," she warned. "Return to your camp. Don't waste time on a white girl with whorish ways," she sneered coldly. "And thank Yellow Bird for her betrayal."

She was full of anguish and fury. He had to deal with her carefully. "Your grandfather is sad you left this way. Will you return?" he asked, trying to distract her from their personal battle.

"It was not wrong to refuse to say farewell to his face. Perhaps I will try to visit him before I return home. But I will never return while you are there," she vowed, relaxing when he did not retaliate.

"Then I will go away to allow your grandfather

this time with you," he offered seriously, for the white war council meeting to the west might prevent it later. "I accept your terms. Let us go swiftly."

"No. I haven't decided if I will go back to his camp. When and if I do, I won't need your escort! You were right; I should not have come or remained. It is better for both of us that I left this way."

"I will tell him why you left. I will speak the truth, Tamaha," he informed her. "He will be hurt that I drove you from his side. I spoke falsely and cruelly," he confessed contritely.

"To you, my name is Miranda Lawrence. But if you're really concerned about him, you'll lie to spare his feelings. You've certainly had plenty of practice at deception! Explain how the scout came for me. I didn't run away. He doesn't have to worry about me. I can defend myself, and I have a gun."

"I will tell him all that happened between us," he declared.

"No! I want you out of my sight," she told him. "And take your gift with you. I don't want anything you've touched and nothing to remind me of you. I wish you'd never come home while I was there. I would rather have remembered you as . . ." She halted the confession and cried, "Go away! I hate you, you bloody savage!"

Her icy tone and expression alarmed him. Had his game succeeded beyond his wishes? How could he tell her that his words had been meant to free them from this trap they faced? How could he say there could be no love between them, when they both felt such an emotion now? How could he claim their lives could not mingle, when they already had many times? "My words were harsh, Tamaha. I was angry when I heard you pulled the eyes of Crazy Horse to you many times. Why so after you showed desire for me? It is dangerous to desire you when you have offered your heart to our chief. Return to camp. I will not hurt you more, but I cannot remove the pain I have inflicted."

"That's ridiculous! Crazy Horse is a stranger; he's married. We've only talked a few times. I would never flirt with him. And I didn't go there searching for you. I never expected to see you again, and I wish I hadn't!" she vowed angrily, but her revealing gaze belied her words. She scoffed, "What makes you think I have such feelings for you, you conceited rogue? And the only reason you caught and held my brief interest was because you enticed it! What female wouldn't be curious about a handsome and mysterious stranger who saved her life two times? But I'm not a she-bitch in heat! I never asked you to desire me! I never asked you to do anything for me!"

Her voice altered as she confessed, "Yes, you did hurt me. You hurt me because I thought we . . . were friends. First you said we must talk; then, you claimed there was nothing to say! You offered friendship and comfort; then you behaved as my enemy and tormented me. I don't understand you! Play your games on someone else, Blazing Star. You're a wicked devil; I'll never . . . like you again."

When he did not respond, she asked sarcastically,

"Would you explain a few things? Who told you I was chasing after your chief? And why would you believe such lies? I'm not in love with him and never could be. You sound as if it's a crime or a sin to find me desirable. Even so, why punish me for your feelings? I didn't try to entrap you. I only wanted to know why you were avoiding me and being so cold after behaving so differently the other times we met."

He inhaled deeply. "The wife of Crazy Horse and others think you desire him and he desires you. To become his second wife would cause much trouble in his teepee and much trouble in camp. Perhaps envy blinded their eyes to the truth. When I said I must not desire you, it was for your happiness and safety, and mine. You were to leave on the new sun. If you desired me as I believed, it would be wrong to take you to my mat knowing our union would make you think I was claiming you as my woman, my mate. If you yielded to me, it would change nothing between us. When you learned this, you would hate me; you would think I used your desire to trick you to my mat. You are beautiful and rare, Tamaha. You strip a warrior's mind of reason and place wild thoughts in his head. You cause a man's blood to run swiftly and his body to hunger. I cannot help wanting you. I thought it wiser to cool the heat which burns within us."

"You think I'm a whore, Blazing Star? You think I would sleep on the mat of a stranger? That you and I would . . . Even so, when does a man unselfishly reject a woman he finds desirable? Besides, I would never sleep with a man I didn't love," she told him bluntly.

"I have not and do not see you as a whore, Tamaha. Desire is a powerful force, one which can defeat or control the strongest person. It would be wrong to let you believe love and desire are mates."

Something in his tone of voice during his last statement snared her attention. "I do not understand the difference between love and desire, Blazing Star. How can a person desire someone they don't love?"

"You are much too pure in mind and body, Tamaha, or you could answer your question. For you, they are the same. For me and others, it is not so. It does not take love for a hungry body to feed on another's. If you were not the granddaughter of Sun Cloud, I would take you this moon, or I would try. Each time I saw you, I craved you. I did not take you because I thought you white. When I learned of your Oglala blood, I could not take you and hurt Sun Cloud or you. A body that burns with such a fire is dangerous and hard to master. But to master two wildfires would be impossible. My cruel words and actions were to put out your fire for me. If I could anger you, you would not let me near and your temptation would be removed. But though I did not wish to hurt you so deeply, I could not lead you to think there could be love after such a union. Do you understand, Tamaha? Your dream does not match mine," he lied desperately.

She lacked experience and knowledge about men, but his meaning was clear; he felt passion for her but not love. Even so, he cared enough to spare her anguish and shame by spurning her. Could she leave forever without knowing him, without having him? "You hurt me and angered me, Blazing Star, but you did not put out the fire within me. I have never known such feelings for a man. I swear there is nothing between me and your chief. I cannot return with you, for the temptation you present is too great. I would make your words true, for I would coax you to my mat. I know a real lady wouldn't say such things, probably not even feel such things; if she did, she would never confess them aloud. I have been so confused since I met you. Even that first day, I felt a powerful pull toward you. Whether it's wrong or not, I can't help how I feel. But I wouldn't want you to think badly of me after I left. So I must remain here and never see you again. If I had known you were beyond my life-circle and you were in Grandfather's camp and teepee, I would never have gone there. Please find some way to comfort Grandfather; I love him very much. Would it be too difficult to hold me and kiss me good-by?"

He was as taken by surprise at her request as she was to hear herself issue it. She flushed but did not back down. "I could not promise to stop with a kiss, Tamaha. I have wanted no female since my eyes touched upon you. I hunger for you like a starving man. To touch would cause smoldering embers to burst into a roaring fire. Such flames could consume us. You must not tempt me; you must free us from this forbidden spell. You cannot be my woman."

"Why do you speak of what cannot be? Why can't you admit to what is there between us? I need to feel your arms around me, our spirits touching. I need to sense you share my feelings. I need to understand why it cannot be for us. I need you, Blazing Star." She showed all her feelings in those few words. She loved this man, and she was about to lose him. She had told Amanda to pursue Reis boldly and brazenly. Should she not take her own advice? Time was fleeing, and so was he.

She earnestly offered, "For a short time before we must part forever, can't we forget everything but us? Can't we be man and woman, Tamaha and Blazing Star, for a short span? Must we part as white and Indian, as Miranda and a Sioux warrior? I swear I will let you leave when the time comes, but must you go away like this? Surely no pain can be greater than never having you?"

"I fear you would not let me leave after we joined, Tamaha. Once you have known me and our union, the fires would burn brighter and higher. You do not know the powers of passion. I do not speak from pride. I speak from the lights I see in your eyes and the defiance which I have seen in you. You should not love me, Tamaha; you cannot have me. I will take you to Sun Cloud, then ride away."

"Are you so weak and cowardly that you cannot control your body and mind long enough to give me a single kiss?"

Blazing Star was aware of her coaxing ploy and took no offense at her clever taunt. Despite his

433

expertise at concealing his inner emotions, turmoil was exposed in his gaze. "It takes all my strength and courage to master my hunger for you. Do not sway me, Tamaha. Do not ask for the forbidden."

Miranda knew she was flirting with emotional peril, challenging Fate. "You say I should not love you; but I do. You say I cannot have you; yet I want you more than life itself. You say I cannot be your woman; yet, in heart and soul, I belong to you forever. You say I must free us, but I have no strength or will to do so. You say I should not tempt you; yet you have tempted me many times. Even when you aren't standing before me in temptation, you visit my dreams and encourage my surrender. You say it cannot be; yet it is and always will be," she murmured raggedly as tears slipped down her cheeks.

"Go, Blazing Star. I'm not holding you prisoner. Take the *wanapin* with you; its memories are too painful to bear. Why did you enter my life-cycle if you can't become part of it? Why did you keep appearing to me, imprisoning my heart and soul? There is no other man to compare with you. I could never desire and love another after knowing you. You shouldn't have come after me. It was less cruel to let me leave in anger. It was so much easier when I thought you despised me. But knowing you want me as I . . ." She could not finish, for tears choked off her words. She turned and walked to the bed and flung herself face down upon it. She had never imagined the day when she would be enticing a man to seduce her! The sacrifice of Blazing Star was too much to endure, and she wept at her loss.

He watched her for a time, then went to sit beside her. He stroked her silky hair as he pondered what to do. He stretched out beside her, moving his hand up and down her back as his dilemma increased. He encircled her body with his arms and pulled her against him. "Do not weep, Tamaha. It is as a sharp lance into my body to see you suffer this way."

She turned her head and locked her gaze with his. There was no need for words; her eyes said it all. She rolled to her back, her hand caressing his tanned cheek. His head came down to seal their lips, to fuse their destinies into one. Her arms went around his neck, and they sank entwined to the bed where their bodies would join in rapture in a dreamy world shared only by lovers.

When his lips left hers and he leaned away, both read the passion blazing brightly within the other's eyes. Right or wrong, dangerous or wise, this moment could take no other course. When she smiled up at him, it drove every doubt or restraint from his mind and body. His mouth returned to hers, exploring and tasting the sweetness of her response. He crushed her so tightly in his arms that she could hardly breathe, but she did not care.

For a long time he held her tenderly, and his gentle kiss became more savage. He knew this time could not be rushed, for it would exist only once for them. His lips touched every inch of her face and throat, then each hand. His body surged with new life and joy. He could as easily stop the seasons as this joining.

Never had Miranda known such excitement and happiness as here in his arms. His warm breath caused tremors to sweep over her tingly flesh. As his tongue swirled about in her palm, she shivered with delight. When he removed her gown, she made no attempt to halt him. Nor was she embarrassed when he removed his own garments, dropping them to the floor upon hers.

His gaze was so loving as he murmured huskily, "If you wish to say no, Tamaha, now is the last moment."

She smiled and replied, "There is no such word for you."

As it should be between lovers, there were no reservations, no inhibitions; it was right and natural between them. There was no modesty or shame, only pure love and its mate, desire. His hands were careful as they claimed her flesh, roaming her sensitive body as each area responded instantly to his contact. His touch was skilled and masterful. Soon, there was no spot upon her that did not cry out for him to conquer it and to claim it as his own. Flames licked greedily at their bodies, enticing him to hasten his leisurely conquest of her body.

When he bent forward and captured a compelling breast with his lips, she groaned in pleasure. As his tongue circled the taut point, she watched with fascination, wondering how such an action caused her body to quiver and warm. Wildly wonderful emotions played havoc with her thinking; it seemed she could do nothing but surrender to pure sensation. One hand slipped down her flat stomach to claim another peak, and he teased both simultaneously.

Her hand wandered up his powerful back into the ebony mane. Each time his mouth left one breast to feast upon the other, it would protest the loss of warmth and stimulation. His mouth drifted upward to fuse with hers. Between kisses, moans escaped her lips, moans which spoke of her rising passion, moans which proved all she had said was true.

His own passion straining to be freed, he moved over her to feel her warm moistness against his throbbing flesh. Assured she was prepared for his entrance, he cautiously pushed past the barrier which eagerly gave way to his loving. Her demanding womanhood surrounded his aching shaft with exquisite bliss. He was so consumed by desire that he nearly lost all control, something that had never happened to him before. He halted all movement to cool his molten blood. Dazed by heady passion, he urged her to lie still until his control returned, but she did not.

She was feverish by now, thrashing her body against his. As he began to move within her, the contact was staggering and she cried out softly in mounting need. Her face was imprisoned between his hands as he deftly savored it with his lips. His hips worked swiftly and skillfully as he increased her great need. She heatedly yielded her body to his loving assault, seeking the pleasures and contentment only he could provide.

He dared not free her mouth as he felt her body tense and shudder with her release, muffling the cry of ecstasy which would have alerted anyone nearby. A sense of intoxicating power surged through him just before his own stunning release came forth. He was so shaken by their potent joining and enchanted by her magic, that he almost shouted his victory aloud. He moved rhythmically until the urgency had fled and they were curled together peacefully.

He held her in his arms as he lay on his side. When his respiration returned to normal, he twisted his head to gaze over at her. Sensing his movement, she shifted her eyes to meet his probing gaze. They exchanged smiles, then hugged tightly. There was such an immense sharing of love and joy. She lay her face on his damp chest and snuggled closer to him. He kissed her forehead and sighed tranquilly. It was not the time for speaking; it was a time for touching and feeling, which they did until she was fast asleep with her arm lying across his chest.

Blazing Star knew his time was gone and he must leave. How he longed to stay at her side, laughing and talking and making love for hours. He looked at her, memorizing each feature. He whispered too quietly to disturb her, "If it is the will of the Great Spirit, we will meet again. If we do not, love for you will live forever in my heart and desire in my body, Tamaha."

The valiant warrior recalled what she had said

about painful farewells. She was right. It was easier to leave while she slept, while those lovely eyes of golden brown could not tempt him to stay or to take her along, while those sweet lips as soft as the petals of a pasqueflower could not tease him so he would forget to leave before dawn, while her clever tongue could not plead or argue against their necessary parting.

He arose carefully so as not to awaken her. He slipped into his clothes, cursing the war which was tearing them apart, which would always separate them. She snuggled into the warm spot he had left beside her, inhaling the musky odor from his sated body, stirring his soul to joyful song. He watched a serene smile which flickered briefly on those lips. His dark eyes traveled over her bare flesh, sparking new fires within him, fires which had no time to burn. He must leave quickly!

His gaze fell on the *wanapin*, and he vividly envisioned those two episodes which had supplied the rattler-rings and the grizzly claw. He placed it on her pillow, for she was resting on his. He hunkered down beside the bed, staring into her face. There was so much he wanted to share with her, so much to tell her and so much to hear, so much to enjoy; but he could not. Where she was concerned, there was no difference between love and desire within him. But he dared not confess that to her. More than anything, he wanted to lie down beside her, to make love to her again, to hear her laughter, to see her smile, to hold her tightly, to run his hands over her skin, to spew his seed within her and to let it grow into proof of their love. He wanted to walk beside her beneath the sun in the cool forest, holding her hand, listening to her giggles as the grass tickled her bare feet. He wanted her pressed against his body every moon. It was too late to linger, too late for her to become his wife, but not too late to dream and to suffer for what could not be.

When he recalled how one of the most awesome and grisly massacres of an Indian village had taken place under a white flag of truce and an American flag of submission, he grieved for what this despicable war was costing him. He would rather give up his life than his love! But memories and warnings could not be denied or forgotten. He had been an impressionable eighteen winters on that frosty day at Sand Creek. He would never forget the white butcher named Chivington, that white killer who did not care what Indians he slew, friendly or hostile, armed or weaponless. Blazing Star could not understand the hatred behind a man who could instigate and plan the slaughter of babies and women, declaring, "Nits make lice!" It had not mattered that the Cheyenne Indians at Sand Creek had been friendly, had been camped there under orders of the soldiers at Fort Lyon! It had not mattered that they had surrendered immediately! It had not mattered that the truce and American flags had been raised to reveal their friendship! It had not mattered to the other whites that the soldiers at the Sand Creek Massacre had slaughtered innocent women and children, nor that they had mutilated the slain males, nor that they had scalped any Indian of any age and sex!

Yet, the whites accused the Indians of being savages! They claimed the Indians started the wars and refused to cease the conflicts! *Refused*? he mentally scoffed. All they refused were defeat, death, reservations, and annihilation!

Chief Black Kettle and his wife survived and escaped the Sand Creek Massacre in 1864, only to be slaughtered by a yellow-haired man called Custer four winters later, in 1868, at the Washita bloodbath! It was between those two bloodlettings, in 1866, that the white-eyes called Sherman said on paper to the Great White Father in Washington that the Sioux "must be exterminated." Sherman—said to have tried to destroy half of the white lands in a war not long past—told the white leader that the soldiers would act quickly and harshly to complete the "extermination of men, women, and children" of the Sioux! Now, here in the Indian ancestral grounds and nearby hunting grounds, there were three powerful white warriors with hatred burning in their hearts: Sherman, Custer, and Sheridan. They had joined once before to battle an enemy larger and more powerful than the Sioux Nation, defeating what they called the Confederacy, the South, the Rebels. Now they were joining forces against the Indians, mainly the Sioux. He could not place his beloved in such danger, danger which even a flag of truce or surrender could not halt!

He reached for the locket with her mother's picture, placing it in his medicine pouch. It was Tamaha's image he saw in the picture, an image he would forever hold. Taking one look at his beloved, he turned and left, using a string to close the latch behind him. *"Waste cedake, Tamaha."* He murmured his love for her, then vanished into the shadows.

Chapter Nineteen

The moment her tawny eyes opened, Miranda sensed he was gone, and pangs of loneliness and loss filled her along with a twinge of anger. She did not have to turn over to look around the cabin. She felt an emotional chill in the air. Blazing Star's warmth and vitality had been taken away, and his special scent had vanished. His spiritual aura was missing. She suddenly felt very alone and sad. Why was he determined to prevent their love?

She could not go after him; she could not even visit the camp under the guise of seeing her grandfather. She had promised to part after one night with him. How rashly that vow had been spoken! But she prayed he would miss her, miss her enough to send for her or to sneak back to see her. If not, perhaps she would be compelled to find him once more.

It thrilled her heart when she discovered her locket gone and found the *wanapin* on her pillow. She smiled, then danced around the table. Her heart surged with life and joy, for they had touched in many ways. How could he deny or ignore what had passed between them?

She recalled his warnings: "Once you have known me and our union, the fires would burn brighter and higher . . . You do not know the powers of passion . . . I have wanted no female since my eyes touched upon you." Were those warnings as painful for him as for her, and as truthful?

In the throes of ecstasy, he had said, *"Ni-ye mitawa,* Tamaha," which meant "you are mine, Tamaha." Had he forgotten she could speak Sioux and had understood those words?

She bathed and dressed, then prepared a small meal for herself. Around three, there was a knock at her door. Her heart did not lurch with excitement; she knew her love would not return in the daylight. She opened the door and gaped at the two grinning people standing there: Amanda and Reis. Miranda squealed with surprise and hugged both as she bubbled with delight, spilling forth countless questions.

"Slow down, Randy," Reis teased her. "It's been a long trip and Mandy is tired. Let's catch our breath, and we'll tell you everything. Where's Luke?" he inquired, having much to tell his friend.

When Miranda answered, Amanda could not believe their cousin had been so careless with her sister. "He left you here alone?" she blurted incredulously. "Just wait until I get my hands on

Lucas Reardon! He promised he would take care of you and protect you, yet he ran off and left you at the mercy and lust of these crude soldiers!"

Miranda giggled, then replied mirthfully, "I've been perfectly safe, Mandy. Surely you know I can take care of myself. Remember how many times I had you or Luke pinned helpless to the floor or ground? Remember how many suitors I sent scurrying in fear? I'm so glad you're here; I've so much to tell you," she murmured, mystery and joy shining brightly in her dark eyes. "I'll prepare some coffee and shortbread, then we'll talk for hours."

Reis noticed the same mysterious lights which Amanda observed, sensually dreamy lights which matched the softened tone of her voice, all of which hinted at a change in Miranda's life, a masculine change. Reis grinned and winked at his adoring wife. He excused himself under the guise of looking around the fort, leaving the two sisters to talk privately. Evidently both females had plenty to relate.

Miranda insisted her sister give her news first. She was stunned to learn of the danger they had faced in Alexandria but was relieved it was over. She could not grieve for Weber Richardson, for he had brought about his own fate. She smiled at Amanda, thrilled by her sister's happiness. Clearly her sister loved Reis Harrison deeply.

Miranda did think it slightly odd that her sister knew so little of her husband's current mission. Then again, men could be such mysterious, complex, and mercurial creatures! But Amanda would be safe with him and surely more happy at his side. Miranda was glad to discover this was Reis's last duty and they would be establishing a home afterward. It was easy to picture them with children, herself as a loving aunt. Her heart warmed at such pleasing thoughts. Amanda had found her destiny and followed it.

When Miranda heard they would be traveling around the territory while Reis did whatever it was he had come to do, she warned her sister about the continual hostilities and perils in this rugged area. She revealed all she had learned about the whites and Indians nearby. She told about her episodes with Lieutenant Brody Sheen and Lucas's subsequent journey with him and Custer's regiment. It was evident to Amanda that her sister disliked Brody; she had even compared him to Weber! Miranda talked about Calamity Jane and Tom Two-feathers Fletcher and related how Lucas had found and rented this cabin. When she halted briefly, Miranda had told about everything except her visit to the Sioux camp and her love for an Oglala warrior.

Amanda watched her sister closely, knowing something vital was about to spill forth from those parted lips. Amanda sat rigid and silent as Miranda divulged her exciting trek to see their grandfather, describing him and the camp and her adventures. Amanda was so staggered by this unimaginable and frightening tale that she could not speak. Having heard horrifying tales about certain warriors and events, she could not believe her sister would calmly ride into an enemy camp! Yet, she also could not deny that her sister had returned safe and happy.

Again, Miranda hesitated noticeably, for there was only one drama left to unfold. She realized Amanda was shocked by her conduct, and she could not envision Amanda's reaction to her imminent confession. She waited for her sister to regain her clear head and tongue.

"How could you do such a reckless and dangerous thing, Randy? You could have been killed! Or taken prisoner! Or worse! I should never have allowed you to come here with Luke. Whatever were you two thinking? You just told me both sides are preparing for war."

"I was never in any danger, Mandy. What white would harm a woman with a letter of protection from President Grant? And what Indian would harm the granddaughter of Chief Sun Cloud?" she asserted.

Amanda threw her hands into the air and shrieked in exasperation, "I don't believe what I'm hearing! After all we've been through lately, you think you're safe from all evil? There are Webers everywhere, Randy! If you were captured and slain out in the wilderness, who would know who did it or why? Don't you realize how few females live out here? Haven't you noticed how crude and rough these men are?" she rebutted.

"No one has tried to attack me, Mandy. I carry a gun, and I can fight like Ling taught me. You worry too much," she teased.

"It seems I didn't worry enough. If we leave before

Luke returns, you're coming with us. But if he does show his roguish face, he'll have to promise not to leave you alone again. I doubt he will after I finish with him," Amanda determined aloud.

"I'm not leaving here just yet," Miranda announced defiantly.

"If Luke isn't back when Reis and I depart, you're going with us, young lady," Amanda argued just as stubbornly and firmly. "I mean it, Randy; we're not leaving you in this hellish place alone."

Miranda stared her straight in the eye and stated, "I'm in love with someone who lives nearby. I'm not leaving until I learn if he feels the same. Now that you have Reis, can't you understand my feelings? I love him. I need him and I want him," she vowed earnestly.

"Who?" Amanda probed. "You haven't mentioned anyone to me."

"Yes, I have. He's the Indian warrior I wrote you about, the one I met on the way here by steamer," Miranda informed her softly.

"The Indian warrior? He lives around here? Have you seen him again?" she pressed, a curious qualm chewing at her racing heart.

Slowly and carefully, Miranda related much of what she knew about the warrior, except their intimate night together here in this cabin. She told her sister about their meetings and how she felt. "I can't help it, Mandy; I'm in love with Blazing Star."

Amanda went white and trembled. "Who . . . did you say?" she stammered, that name terrifyingly familiar to her.

"I see you've heard of him," Miranda scoffed as she witnessed her sister's alarm. "He isn't like that, Mandy," she protested, then revealed more facts about him and this racial conflict.

"How could you fall in love with a barbarian, an enemy? Oh, Randy, what's gotten into you? What have you done?" Amanda fretted in a near whisper, recognizing a vast change in her gentle sister.

"During the war, Yankees were considered bloody barbarians, our fiercest enemies. Have you forgotten the horrible atrocities they committed against the South? Even so, you fell in love with one and married him," she retorted cleverly.

"That's different!" Amanda shouted at her.

"How so?" Miranda debated. "If we make peace with the Sioux, our differences will be the same as yours and your Yankee husband's."

"From the way things appear, there will never be peace," Amanda remarked, her opinions colored by false information.

"I believe that same statement was made about the North and South only a few years ago," Miranda reminded her astonished sister.

"But Reis's life isn't vastly different from mine, Randy. You and Blazing Star have nothing in common," she contended.

"Love," Miranda slyly announced, smiling dreamily.

"I doubt even powerful love is sufficient to overcome such complicated differences, Randy." Her sister softened her argument.

"Until I know beyond a single doubt that I can't have him, I'm not leaving here."

"You don't know him, Randy. You've only spent a few days with him. Love takes time; it takes working and being together. You can't love at a distance. You can't love through war."

"Tell me something, Mandy; how long did it take for you to fall in love with Reis? How long before you knew you wanted him beyond caution or wisdom? How long before you knew you couldn't live without him? How long after meeting him did you two marry?" When Amanda sighed heavily at her inability to argue those points, Miranda asked quietly, "Did you make love to him before you wed?"

Amanda went scarlet with modesty more than guilt. She gasped in shock at her sister's bold query. "Miranda Lawrence!" she panted reproachfully. "How could you ask such a question?"

Miranda had gotten her answer. She glued her gaze to Amanda's and made her confession of love and passion. "After experiencing such emotions for Reis, Mandy, can't you see how I feel? He is my destiny, my one true love. Like you did with Reis, I must pursue him, whatever the price or danger. Don't you understand that one day with him is worth any price?"

"But Reis loves me in return, Randy. Sharing passion isn't enough. What about your future, your happiness? What if you can't have him? You can't force this man to love you," she explained sadly.

Miranda considered those words, then replied, "I believe he does love me and need me. I just have to make him realize it."

"How do you plan to do that?" Amanda asked seriously.

"I don't know, Mandy. I wish I did," she admitted hoarsely. "When I think of never seeing him or touching him again, it's like fiery arrows are being shot into my body. It's such an awful feeling of loneliness and pain, worse than when Mama and Papa died," she confessed. "Do you remember how you felt when you thought you couldn't have Reis? Imagine how you would feel if you lost him this very day."

Amanda stood up and went to her sister. She hugged her affectionately and comfortingly. "I wish there was something I could say or do to help, Randy. I'll just have to trust you to do the right thing, as you did with me where Weber was concerned. Will you promise me to act slowly and carefully?" she entreated.

Miranda smiled and hugged her tightly. She had never loved or needed her sister more than she did this very moment. "I promise. Just stand by me, and I know everything will work out fine."

That night, Miranda slept on the cot in the living area while Reis and Amanda used the small bedroom. She could hear them whispering far into the night. She knew Amanda was revealing their conversations to her beloved husband, but that did not matter to Miranda. Later, she ached for Blazing

451

Star while her sister made passionate love to Reis, their muffled cries escaping beneath the closed door. Finally, all was quiet; still, Miranda found it difficult to get to sleep.

Two days passed while Miranda and Amanda shared each other's company. After announcing himself as the liaison from President Grant to the commanding officers in this area, Reis was busy asking questions, making observations, and writing reports, reports which he concealed in the same hiding place which Lucas used for his critical and secret papers.

Each time Miranda remarked on Reis's assignment and curious actions, Amanda would shrug and say it was a covert mission and they should not discuss it. But Miranda caught her sister's longing gazes over the area beneath the eating table several times. When Miranda laughingly suggested they sneak and read the reports, Amanda was horrified. She warned Miranda never to attempt such an unforgivable act. When Miranda asked if Reis's work was dangerous, Amanda grimaced and said she did not know but suspected it was from his dealings with Weber. Even more confusing and intriguing was the second set of papers which he wrote upon, then intentionally left on the table near the bed.

Reis sent a telegram to Lucas, relating their arrival at his cabin. Again, he stated he was here as a liaison for Grant. He asked Lucas to send word of the impending locations of several important officers. When an answer came the next day, Reis informed the two women that Lucas was on his way home. Arriving with their cousin would be Brody Sheen and Custer. Apparently, Custer was piqued with curiosity about Reis and his business.

Miranda did not know what to think when Reis sat her down at the table and began probing her for answers or speculations about the Sioux Indians, especially the Oglala tribe. He seemed particularly interested in learning all he could about Crazy Horse, Sitting Bull, and Blazing Star. He even exhibited a keen interest in the Indian agencies which she had seen, and anything she had overheard about them. She wondered why he did not ask any questions about her grandfather or her Indian cousin, Bloody Arrow. Oddest of all was the fact that he had sent Amanda to the sutler's shop to prevent her from hearing their talk!

Miranda started asking questions of her own, wanting and needing to understand Reis's desire for facts and figures. Obviously, these questions and facts had something to do with his mission. Yet he evaded her probes and went on with his interrogation.

"No more, Reis, until you tell me why you need such information," she eventually declared, eying him intently, oddly.

"Just tell me all you know, Randy, then I'll explain. First, I need a clearer and larger picture to study. This area's like a volcano ready to explode, and Grant wants to know why and who's furnishing the molten lava," he hedged.

"No. Not until I'm assured of your intentions. I can't betray or endanger my grandfather and his people, or . . ." She did not finish.

"Or Blazing Star," he completed the name which worried her the most. "If I'm to help your mother's people, Randy, and possibly avert more bloodshed, I need facts for President Grant. I have to be careful who supplies such information; too many people are profiting from lies and greed. What's so unique about this area? The land isn't that good for ranching or farming. The game is as good anywhere else. There has to be something else to inspire the whites to crave it at any cost. Do you think it's possible to speak with the Sioux chiefs? Would Tom Fletcher take us there without any questions?" he asked shockingly.

"You want to see Crazy Horse and Sitting Bull? Why?" she pried.

"I can't explain my mission right now, Randy. You've got to trust me and help me. Can you get me into the Oglala camp? Naturally it has to be in total secrecy," he urged her.

"You want to spy out their strengths and defenses for Custer!" she surmised coldly. "You expect me to help defeat them?" she sneered.

"I expect you to help save their lives and lands. You know the kind of men in charge out here, the ones Luke is writing about. Custer and Grant aren't friends. You've seen what's taking place at those agencies. There's corruption and fraud here, Randy, and Grant wants to know who's behind it and how to stop it. Evidently there are plenty of reasons behind the continual hostilities. That's all I can say. Will you help me?" he coaxed gravely. "You could see Blazing Star," he tempted in order to sway her. "And I don't work with the cavalry or army," he declared honestly.

"I hope I'm understanding you correctly, Reis. If you're lying to me or misleading me . . ." she hinted ominously. She abruptly asked, "Did you know about this mission before you married my sister? Did you know we were Sun Cloud's granddaughters?"

A frown lined his handsome features. "Please don't even think such things, Randy. But to answer you, no and no. I swear to you I'm no threat to the Oglalas. My investigation isn't for military purposes. Anything I learn is for the ears of Grant alone."

"All right," she finally acquiesced after studying him intently. "Tom seems completely trustworthy. But just in case, I'll take you to my grandfather's camp; I know the way. If anyone sees us, you can say we were out riding and got lost. I can get you in and out, but don't betray us. What about Mandy? She would increase the danger of getting caught. Besides, she sounds afraid of them; she might accidentally insult one of them. Then, we'd be in big trouble."

"This mission could be very dangerous for both of us, Randy. I've already explained matters to her; she knows she can't tag along. She's going to remain here and cover for us. If it appears safe, I'll take her back to visit Sun Cloud later. She's a little miffed, but she understands why we have to leave her behind. I'm glad you agree."

Miranda guessed from her sister's gaze and voice that this idea did not suit her at all, but she would follow her husband's wishes. Just after midnight, Miranda and Reis walked their horses a safe distance from the settlement, then mounted and rode away at a swift gallop. All went as planned until dawn when they halted to water and rest their animals. Miranda had brought along her Indian dress but had not changed into it yet. To avoid being noticed as a woman, she was wearing jeans, a blue cotton shirt, and a floppy hat to conceal her chestnut locks.

Reis and Miranda were strolling around, loosening stiff muscles, when they were suddenly surrounded by ten painted braves. Reis did not have time to draw his weapon, fortunately. It required three men to hold Reis under control as he fought to save Miranda. A fourth brave was standing before Reis with his lance pointing directly at Reis's heart, yet, Reis showed no fear of him or death, gaining the brave's respect.

Miranda was seized and imprisoned between two strong males and lost her hat during her brief struggle. When the leader spoke, Miranda recognized his voice. In Oglala, she shouted, "Bloody Arrow, it's me, Tamaha. We're heading to speak with Grandfather and Crazy Horse."

Her cousin whirled and glared at her. He asked why she was here and who the white dog was with her. She explained Reis's identity and asked her

cousin to take them to camp. A quiver of alarm raced
over her, for she read contempt and reluctance in
Bloody Arrow. Yet there were others around to
witness his actions, to control them and his hatred.

Reis stayed quiet and alert. He assumed Miranda
knew this brave and was reasoning with him.
Although taken by surprise that she could speak
Sioux, Reis waited until she could explain. The
leader appeared to recognize her and to listen to her
words. He wondered if it was Blazing Star, then
hastily concluded it could not be.

Suddenly Bloody Arrow nodded and agreed to take
them to the Oglala camp. Everyone was ordered to
mount up and follow him. Miranda hastily explained the circumstances to Reis, her eyes hinting at
more news to come later. Riding in the midst of the
group, they were escorted to the entrance of Crazy
Horse's teepee.

The noted chief observed this curious sight as
Bloody Arrow informed him of Miranda's words and
actions. The imposing chief looked at her and asked
why she had brought a white man into their camp.
Miranda asked if he would speak with Reis alone, as
his words were important and private. She gave her
word of honor Reis could be trusted. When the stoic
leader did not respond, she actually pleaded, saying
Reis was from the white chief far away.

"If he speaks false or his words are not important
to the ears of Crazy Horse and the council, you may
kill me where I stand. For the lives of all we love, hear

him," she urged.

Crazy Horse agreed to see Reis, in the company of Sitting Bull. The three men went into his teepee and the flap was sealed. Bloody Arrow was furious when she refused to reveal the meaning of Reis's visit. Miranda apologized but held silent. She headed to see her grandfather while the critical meeting took place. Bloody Arrow followed her, to see what she would tell Sun Cloud. When she asked about Blazing Star, Bloody Arrow lied to her, claiming he was off chasing a wife. Her startled reaction confirmed his suspicions.

"So it is true you seek the eye of Blazing Star. It is foolish, Tamaha. He loves honor and battle, not a woman. He takes a wife to give him his teepee and a son. He would not stain the blood and skin of his child by mating with a girl with white blood. Seek your kind, Tamaha; the blood of your mother's dishonor and shame runs within you. Do not come again," he warned coldly. "What does the white man want?"

"I don't know. But if I did, I wouldn't tell you. Don't you think I know you would have killed both of us if you'd been alone today? Why do you hate me, Bloody Arrow?" she asked bluntly.

"Your eyes are clouded with lust for Blazing Star, Tamaha. He joined with Black Buffalo Woman of the Cheyenne. He lies upon her mat this moon. His neck carries the joining necklace to match hers. The white man can do nothing to win Blazing Star for you," he baited her.

"I didn't come here to capture Blazing Star's heart or eyes. Stay away from me; your heart is cold and evil," she murmured softly, to avoid being overheard. Her heart was aching at his news. Could it be true? Or was it a cruel and malicious joke? Dare she ask her grandfather and risk having her very soul lacerated? If it were not true, why would her cousin speak a lie so easy to unmask? Blazing Star had made no promises to her, no commitments, no vows of love and loyalty. He had done all he could to prevent any contact between them. Perhaps that hurt the most; he had not lied or tricked her. She had surrendered willingly, eagerly, wantonly, helplessly . . .

Sun Cloud was ecstatic to see her. He hugged her and kissed her cheek. He scolded her for leaving him without a good-by, but understood her generous motive. She told him that Amanda and her husband had arrived at Fort Sully. She told him Reis had come to parlay with the chiefs and he would learn of the meaning in council later. After promising to visit again if possible, she asked about Blazing Star. It was silly to be a coward; it was silly to allow hazy words or a simple misunderstanding to come between them.

Her grandfather suspected her reason for inquiring. His heart soared with happiness at the thought of his father's bloodline joining and strengthening in Blazing Star and Miranda. But he could not interfere. It must be the will of the Great Spirit. It warmed his aging heart to recall how both looked at each other and how each asked about the other, as it had been with his beloved Singing Wind before the white dogs attacked their village and wantonly slaughtered her and many others. He had lived with sadness, bitterness, and hatred for many winters, but this fresh and gentle creature enlivened him once more. She was the essence of life and joy.

He smiled and stated innocently, "He visits the camp of our brothers, the Cheyenne. He brings a surprise to my teepee," he added mischievously, thinking of the horse which was to be a gift for her from her grandfather, a swift and agile pinto.

Miranda misconstrued his words and excitement, assuming he did not know of her love for Blazing Star. When her smile faded, her eyes teared, and she trembled, he asked if she were ill or distressed. She forced a smile and told him she was simply fatigued.

Sun Cloud was still alert enough to notice the sarcastic and mocking sneer which flickered over Bloody Arrow's face when Miranda glanced at him. The old man did not realize he had aided Bloody Arrow's spite, but he sensed a chilling aura which he did not like. As Miranda was encased in pensive silence, Sun Cloud furtively observed the way Bloody Arrow watched her.

Sun Cloud knew his days were short. He wondered if his granddaughter might choose to remain with his people. She knew a great deal about them, but there was more to learn. Did he have the days to teach her? Would she be accepted? Would she be safe and happy here? If only the bluecoats would leave them in peace.

The unexpected appearance of the beautiful descendent of Gray Eagle and Sun Cloud had sparked great interest and mixed feelings amongst his people, a blend of rejection and acceptance, affection and dislike. The rumors of jealousy in the wife of Crazy Horse had not avoided his keen ears. How sad for such lies to be born, to be allowed to grow. What would happen to his granddaughter after his death, if anything happened to Blazing Star? She would be alone, and jealousy and envy were powerful destroyers.

She was such an uncommon creature, half woman and half vixen. She was as eager for adventure as any brave. She possessed such energy, such daring, such courage. Here, she could be as free and wild as the winds. If only they were not warring winds.

As all three came to attention at the sound of drumming, the call went forth, *"Ominiciye kte lo,"* summoning the leaders to council. Sun Cloud and Bloody Arrow reached for their prayer pipes to leave.

Miranda tensed but did not ask questions. But her heart lurched and beat wildly as Bloody Arrow returned briefly to say, "Pray to your Great Spirit, Tamaha, if they vote to slay the white dog and hold you captive for your offense. If you have helped our enemy, no man can save you, even Sun Cloud. I will vote for your punishment."

Tremors raced over her body, as her malevolent

461

cousin laughed satanically. She mastered her rampant emotions and stated clearly and evenly, "I will pray, Bloody Arrow, but for you. I will ask the Great Spirit to burn the hatred and evil from your body. I will pray He sears away your hatred for me, for there is no reason for it. I will pray for Him to open your eyes to the truth, to honor."

Miranda paced the confines of the teepee until she thought she would scream from anxiety. To pass the time, she removed her soiled riding clothes and donned her Indian dress. The meeting went on for hours while each man had his say in a matter which was unknown to her. Never had she prayed so intensely or swiftly in her life. No matter how Blazing Star felt about her, she wished he were here. He was so intelligent, so influential. His words and power might be needed.

When she felt as if she could not breathe from the tension which was attacking her chest, she left the teepee to stroll along the stream bank. She walked back and forth until she made a path upon the lush grass. She halted and leaned against a towering tree, the evening breeze playing softly through its leaves and small branches. She inhaled deeply, then sighed. She closed her eyes and murmured, "Please let everything be all right."

"What could be wrong, Tamaha?" a stirring voice questioned.

Her eyes flew open and she stared into the arresting face of Blazing Star. A smile captured her features and brightened them. Joyful tears of relief threatened to spill forth. She was about to fling herself into his arms when she recalled Bloody Arrow's words. She clasped her raised hands and lowered them, the beaming smile vanishing before his baffled eyes. She moistened her suddenly dry lips and pulled her tormented gaze from his, trying vainly to mask her warring emotions. "I didn't know you were home," she murmured, turning slightly to lean against the tree as if needing its support while avoiding his piercing gaze. "I was waiting for Reis to finish his meeting so we could leave," she informed him to explain her unwanted presence.

"The meeting is over. He waits for you in Sun Cloud's teepee," he responded, unintentionally giving her the impression he was telling her it was time to go. He witnessed a shadow of anguish and turmoil which dulled her somber eyes. When her chin and lower lip quivered, she caught it between her teeth. He wondered at her strange behavior.

Without looking at him again, she straightened and tried to move past him toward camp. To think of him with another woman seared her heart. She was afraid she would burst into racking sobs at any moment. When he imprisoned her left arm and refused to allow her to leave, she shuddered at the contact. "Please let me go, Blazing Star," she beseeched him in a choked voice, shivering as if cold.

He studied her lowered head and behavior. "Do you hate me so that you cannot face me? You can share no words with me?" he asked worriedly, dreading the reason for her strange conduct.

Stunned by his words, she looked up into his solemn expression. "I don't hate you; I could never hate you," she vowed sadly. "I didn't want you to think I had broken my promise to you by returning here."

Still he did not relax or free her. "I have been in council; I know why you are here. But why do you wish to run from me? Why are your eyes so full of pain? I do not understand, Tamaha. Did the moon which passed between us change your feelings for me?"

She stared at him in disbelief. Was he being cruel without meaning to be? Did he not understand how the news of his marriage would affect her? Did he not know how much she loved and wanted him? Did he not realize she could not accept the Indian custom of having more than one woman or wife? Did he not realize she could never share him with anyone! "I have not changed, Blazing Star; you have," she responded mysteriously. "If my feelings have changed, they have grown stronger, just as you warned me. Please don't torment me."

His bewilderment increased. "Why does it torment you to be with me? Why do you draw away in such coldness?" he probed tensely.

Tears wet her lashes, then slipped down her cheeks. "Because you belong to another. Because you think I am unworthy of your love and teepee. Because

464

I can never forget you or what we shared. I must go,"
she stated frantically, yanking on her arm.

His grip tightened, then he encircled her body with
his powerful embrace. She struggled wildly for
freedom from this agonizing embrace. He would not
let her go. When she accepted her helpless and
vulnerable position, she rested her forehead upon his
chest and cried. He found this action stunning. "I
belong to no other woman, Tamaha. What woman is
more precious than you? If it could be, I would take
you to my heart and mat this very moon. You fill my
thoughts each sun and my dreams each moon. Why
do you speak this way?"

Miranda lifted her head and stared at him. "I know
the white customs differ from yours, Blazing Star, but
you can't have me and her, too. How can you take a
wife, then speak such words to me? It's wrong for us
to be together now that you're married. I can't. And I
hate myself for wanting you so much."

Blazing Star shook his head, trying to clear his
steadily rising confusion. "I have taken no wife,
Tamaha. Explain your words."

Shocked and baffled herself, she asked warily,
"You didn't marry Black Buffalo Woman in the
Cheyenne camp?"

Blazing Star threw back his head and laughed in
amusement. When she punched him in the stomach
and demanded he stop his laughter, he did. Grinning
broadly, he grasped her chin and kissed her nose. "I
have taken no wife, Tamaha, nor any woman to my

mat since knowing you. Black Buffalo Woman has enough winters to be my grandmother. I can think of no woman when my people are at war, when my life is in danger each sun and moon. Your jealousy pleases me, but your head mixed another's words," he jested playfully.

Miranda realized what Bloody Arrow had done. Her eyes narrowed and frosted; she grit her teeth as she planned her revenge.

Observing her anger, he demanded sternly, "Explain the fires of revenge which flame within your eyes, Tamaha."

"I didn't understand about you and her. I was told clearly that you married her," she stated, then revealed the source.

"Bloody Arrow wishes to hurt us, Tamaha. I will watch him closely. Has he been cruel to you another time?" he probed oddly.

Miranda related their capture this afternoon and all other events involving her and her cousin. "Do not turn your back to him," he warned after she finished. "I will settle this matter later. Reveal no sadness or anger when we return to the teepee. Let him believe his words never harmed you or played in your mind. You must trust me, Tamaha. Do not believe such lies. I could take no woman while you fill my senses. When the moon of peace comes, then we will talk of our love and desires." He wisely did not add, if I still live.

She hugged him and spread kisses over his chest.

"Then I shall pray with all my might for the moon of peace to come quickly, my love," she whispered against his thudding heart. "Can I stay and visit?"

"No, Tamaha, it is too dangerous," he blatantly refused.

"But I've missed you so much," she protested urgently, snuggling provocatively against his hard and taut frame.

His voice was strained as he confessed, "As I miss you. We must remain apart until a final truce," he asserted unflinchingly, stubbornly, protectively. "Do not beg, for my mind is as stone."

They were standing so close that she noticed his hunger for her. She smiled enticingly and murmured, "But your body is not."

He glanced at her and shook his head roguishly. "Your tongue speaks too quickly and freely, Tamaha," he jested seductively. "I can control all, except my desire for you. Return to the teepee while I cool this fire you have started." He knew he should send her away immediately. He knew he should not touch or kiss her. He knew he should not be saying such encouraging words to her. But her nearness dazed his senses and inflamed his body.

Her senses were also spinning wildly at his nearness. Their foreheads were touching; his breath warmed her flushed face as he spoke. Their gazes were locked and their needs exposed. He shuddered with loosely leashed control; she trembled with unbridled passion. "You must go, Tamaha; they

467

wait for you.'' He tried one last time to deny what they both wanted and needed.

"I can't," she murmured simply, those words saying much. "I feel no shame or modesty with you, Blazing Star. Our time is too short and precious for such feelings. Is there no place we can . . . be alone?" she asked boldly, revealingly.

"Do you know what you say, Tamaha?" he asked huskily, his manhood throbbing with painful craving.

She needed to prove to him how much he loved and desired her. She needed to show him they belonged together. She needed to break down all barriers between them, all forces against them. He was on the verge of giving in to his emotions, and she needed to assist that blissful defeat. Once he accepted his love and need for her, then he would keep her with him.

There was so much love and desire emblazoned in her eyes when she smiled and murmured, "Yes, I want you. I love you."

Those words rang warnings in his mind, warnings he refused to hear or follow. "What if they come looking for us?" he argued weakly.

She grinned. "I know you can go and come in secret. If you wish to hide us, you will find a way," she replied trustingly.

He debated once more, "There is little time before they seek us. Passion should not run as swiftly as the river after a rain. Such moments should not be rushed."

"Are you saying a treat eaten quickly is not as filling or enjoyable as one eaten slowly?" she teased brazenly, sensuously.

For an answer, he scooped her up in his sturdy arms and headed into the forest. She suppressed her giggles by sealing her lips to his shoulder. When he felt he had put a sufficient distance between them and the camp, he lowered her feet to the grassy earth. The only sounds present were from the birds, a gentle wind, and their erratic breathing. "You are sure?" he asked one final time.

She nodded as she smiled happily. His fingers shook as they unlaced the ties at her throat and removed her dress. His smoldering gaze slipped from her passion-glazed eyes down her throat to heat her breasts with its flames. His hands upon her shoulders eased down her arms with snaillike leisure, halting at her wrists and capturing them gently as he leaned forward to tantalize those firm points with his tongue. She moaned and swayed at the intensity of that pleasure.

He caught the ties of her breechclout and untangled them, to allow the triangular garment to drift to her ankles. He straightened, then leaned away to gain a full view of her. She was so beautiful. His hands cupped her breasts, his thumbs caressing the hardened peaks. When she fused her lips to his mouth, his hands traveled down her sides and encircled her body, grasping her buttocks and drawing her naked body against his shuddering one.

Their tongues touched and explored the taste of the other. The peaks of her breasts were like two coals burning into his chest. He groaned in achingly sweet desire. He unlaced the ties of his breechclout, allowing it to fall to the earth at his feet. They sank together upon the forest floor, their lips and bodies meshed tightly.

As his lips worked between her mouth, ears, and breasts, his skilled, aggressive hands stimulated her womanhood to quivering need. Her hand drifted over his shoulders and hips until it made a discovery which enticed him to feverish pleasure. As if by instinct, her hand encircled the swollen, fiery object which could grant such delight. It felt so smooth and sensual. When her hand moved up and down its length several times, he groaned and writhed his hips, his mouth increasing its feasting upon her breasts and his hand working swiftly at a lower point. An urgency to fuse their bodies assailed them.

They moved together gracefully. Her thighs parted as he slid between them. As his shaft sank into her moist, dark warmth, her legs encased his body. They kissed savagely, greedily as their bodies surged in unison toward a mutual goal. There was no time for leisurely lovemaking; their starving senses were ravenous.

There was no restraint or caution. Their bodies blended time and time again until they were rewarded with rapturous ecstasy. When every drop of passion's nectar had been released, they lay exhausted in a serene bed of love and contentment. Both wished they could remain here like this for a long time, but it was getting dark.

Reluctantly he lifted his head and smiled at her. "We must go, Tamaha," he murmured against her lips, then kissed her thoroughly, wishing he meant they could go to their teepee for more lovemaking.

She hugged him desperately. "I know, my love."

She blushed when he suggested they splash off in the stream to remove the musky odors of sated passion. He cuffed her chin and laughed merrily. "There is some shyness left in you," he teased.

"Perhaps in time you can conquer all of it," she retorted coyly.

"Change nothing in you, Tamaha. I desire you as you are," he stated honestly, kissing her palm. She quivered. "Do not look at me so, Tamaha," he playfully warned when renewed passion glowed within her golden brown eyes.

"You have a strange and powerful effect over me, Blazing Star. When I am with you, you are the only person alive. You've cast a magical spell over me, and I am powerless to resist you or to refuse you anything. What will happen to us if there is no truce?" She spoke her inner fears aloud. "How long must we live separate lives? How long must we steal such golden moments?"

"You will not refuse or resist my wishes; you will stay apart from me and the war which controls my life and destiny."

471

"Please don't ask such a sacrifice of me," she begged him.

"I must, Tamaha. As long as there is war between our people, we cannot share a life or a teepee," he vowed.

"You want me to return home with Reis?" she asked somberly.

"Yes," he replied almost tersely, fearing her defiance.

She sighed heavily, knowing it was foolish to argue. "Let's go," she conceded, feeling she had improved her chances of winning him sooner. Now, she merely had to wait patiently. It would not be wise to reveal she was not as submissive and manageable as Indian women were alleged to be.

He seemed surprised, even suspicious, at her willingness to obey his commands. He watched her slip away to the stream to wash off and dress. He lay there for a time, thinking of her. When he finally joined her, she was ready and waiting for him. She sat meekly while he tossed water upon his body, then dressed.

When he extended his hand to help her rise, she smiled and declined it, saying, "Someone might think we're too close if we hold hands. We wouldn't want anyone to imagine I was your woman." She laughed merrily and raced away toward the camp, wondering if a man was more tempted by a seemingly elusive prize.

Her mood was odd, and he mused on it. Would he ever understand this playful creature? Would he be able to capture her, when she was as carefree and quick as a wild wind? Her mother had left her home during times of war; the conflicts had increased with the passing winters. Tamaha had been born a daughter of two enemy bloods, a daughter who had returned to confront those warring winds.

Chapter Twenty

In Sun Cloud's teepee, Miranda questioned her brother-in-law about the council meeting. Reis told her it was better if she did not know anything; that way she could not drop any clues by mistake. Miranda did not want to imagine Reis betraying her or her people, but she was alarmed by his refusal to discuss his mission. She persisted in asking what was going on between him and the Oglalas. How else could she judge his honesty and sincerity?

Sun Cloud recognized her fears and their reasons. He smiled and consoled her, telling her to trust Reis and to follow his orders. Blazing Star added his encouragement and prodding. Only Bloody Arrow remained silent and watchful.

Miranda's gaze went from one man to the next, sensing all were in total agreement except her cousin. How could she argue against such odds? She relented and kept silent.

When Blazing Star smiled raffishly at her, no one missed the warmth or power behind it. Nor did they miss the way Miranda's eyes softened and glowed when she returned the smile. Reis had to shake her arm to cach her attention. She blushed and listened as he said it was time to go.

She hugged and kissed her grandfather, telling him she would come again if possible. The old man's eyes were moist as he smiled. She glanced at her cousin and politely said good-by. When she turned to Blazing Star, thankfully her back was to the others. Her eyes wandered over his arresting form, mutely asking how long it would be until they were together again. She smiled and caught his hand in a sort of genial gesture, needing that final contact. She told him good-by, hoping her voice did not betray her excitement and turmoil as his thumb caressed the back of her hand.

Outside, Sun Cloud presented her with his "surprise" from the Cheyenne camp. "He's beautiful, Grandfather," she cried, nuzzling the pinto's nose. "But I can't take him with me. How would I explain him?" she fretted in disappointment. "Will you keep him a while longer?"

Reis solved the dilemma by suggesting that he say he purchased the horse downriver. All agreed. After her saddle was switched to the pinto, Miranda was helped to mount. She bid them all farewell, her gaze lingering on Blazing Star. Just before they were out of sight, she glanced over her shoulder and waved.

Blazing Star turned to find Bloody Arrow's wintry

gaze on him. "Why did you lie to her about Black Buffalo Woman?" he demanded.

Even amidst the knowledge of Bloody Arrow's envy and spite, no one realized the extent of his hunger for power and revenge. No one could imagine the heights to which he would reach to obtain his wishes, or the depths to which he would sink if denied. He deceitfully said, "Because you trick her. Because you pull her into your arms when she cannot remain there. What of her feelings, Blazing Star? What of the moon when she learns the truth? What of Sun Cloud when he learns of your deed? Who will kill you for taking her body when you will not share her life-circle, Sun Cloud or Miranda Lawrence? Your lust for her blinds you to your cruelty and evil. Do you forget she carries the same blood as Sun Cloud and Bloody Arrow? Do not force us to protect her from you. I wished to end her feelings before she was harmed by them."

Blazing Star knew he was lying but rashly allowed it to pass. This was not the time or place for a private battle between kin. There was a greater matter at hand. "I will end it when the time is right, Bloody Arrow. I would not harm Tamaha. I have spoken words of truth to her. Do not interfere," he warned ominously.

Miranda and Reis repeated their arduous journey, arriving home near three in the morning. Reis unsaddled their horses and placed them inside the small corral which he had constructed and attached to the side wall of the cabin. He tossed hay into one corner and carried in two buckets of fresh water from the well. Then they went to the cabin door.

When Amanda answered their summons, she hugged each one tightly, telling them how relieved she was to have them back. She wanted to hear everything, but Reis and Miranda were exhausted. Miranda collapsed upon the cot and fell asleep without undressing. Amanda was nettled when Reis gave her a light peck on the cheek and did the same in the bedroom.

Amanda struggled to remove his boots and pants. He mumbled his thanks, then rolled to his side and went limp. Amanda was very quiet that morning, not even building a fire for coffee. She knew they needed to sleep as long as possible. She sat in a chair reading or sewing to pass the time. But as noon came and went, she became anxious to hear about the daring trek. And she was getting hungry.

She went into the bedroom and sat down on the edge of the bed. She watched her husband sleep for a long time, relieved he was home safe. She wondered why his mission had to be kept secret from her. Had he confided in Miranda? A note of discord struck her at that insensitive thought. But how could Miranda help Reis if she did not know what was going on out here? If this case were as dangerous and time-consuming as the previous one, he would damn well confess matters soon!

When would Reis realize that ignorance did not provide safety or prevent worry? Why could others know facts or assist Reis, but she could not? It was almost as if being his wife was nothing but a cover for his assignments! After all, she only had Reis's word that he was a government agent! For all she knew, he could be a sly criminal!

Amanda scolded herself for being so silly and dramatic, but she was tired of secrecy. She wanted to meet her grandfather, too. She wanted to join in the excitement and suspense. She longed to be a part of this mission, and she yearned for Reis to trust her implicitly.

He stirred and opened his eyes, his keen senses detecting a presence. He smiled faintly as he rubbed his eyes, yawning and stretching. He sat on the side of the bed opposite her. He stretched his body several times and massaged his sore neck. "Any coffee left?"

"I haven't made any. I was afraid of disturbing you two. Do you think it's all right to awaken Randy?" she inquired hesitantly.

"What time is it?" Reis asked before replying.

"A little past one," Amanda responded. "I missed you."

He flashed her a smile, then stood up to flex once more. "We could both use more sleep. But I think it should come later. Why don't we fix some coffee and food, and talk? Your grandfather's quite a man. And so is Randy's warrior," he added playfully.

"You met them? You liked them?" she pressed eagerly.

He stretched and yawned a final time, then splashed his face with tepid water. While drying it, he nodded and grunted affirmatively. "What's

Grandfather like Reis?" she probed, coming to stand near him.

He fluffed her golden hair and remarked, "A real chief. Let's get that coffee, then I'll tell you all about him." As she turned to obey, he reached for her, pulling her into his arms. "Don't I get a welcome kiss and hug first?" he jested, grinning beguilingly.

As the kiss lengthened and deepened, Reis drew away and murmured, "I think we should close the door for a while."

His implication was clear, and the feeling shared. But before he could do so, Miranda sat up and caught sight of him, telling him good morning. He responded, then turned to Amanda and stated ruefully, "Randy's awake. We can prepare that coffee and breakfast."

When Amanda came to his side and embraced him, she teased, "I do believe my husband has acquired modesty from some place. The more I lose, the more you find."

Arm in arm, they entered the front room. While Miranda freshened up, Reis helped his wife with their meal, and as they consumed it, Miranda and Reis went over their trip. Both women were perturbed when Reis withheld the motive for his visit. Amanda questioned her sister about this secrecy.

Miranda shrugged and contended, "He wouldn't tell me either, Mandy. Even Grandfather took a vow of silence. I think we're merely decorations for your husband's work. Who would suspect a sinister villain lurking behind two delicate ladies?" she jested mirthfully. "Could it be your love doesn't trust women to have brains and courage?"

Reis chuckled, shaking his head. "I'll never survive this mission with two females picking at me all the time," he speculated jovially.

"We wouldn't have to if you didn't keep us under a basket of secrecy," Amanda teased him, and they laughed. Amanda snickered when she asked her sister, "Did you see your handsome warrior?"

Miranda's expression was a blend of joy and sadness. "For a short time. Too short," she added petulantly . "You should teach your husband about love and romance. From the way he ardently courted you, I believed he was familiar with both. He insisted we leave as soon as the council meeting ended. We were barely given any time alone."

Reis felt it unwise and insensitive to jest about the length of time it took the warrior to retrieve her before they could depart, or to remark suggestively on the telltale signs of the cause of their delay. In fact, he was worried and concerned about Miranda and her choice of sweethearts. What could come of such an impossible match? With Blazing Star's rank and the continual conflicts, he would be lucky to live out this month! Reis feared he could not change the situation quickly enough to spare two lives so precious and vital to his sister-in-law. There was so much greed, corruption, lust for power, and hatred here; and he was only one man with limited time.

After their meal, the sisters helped Reis move aside the table and chairs to conceal a packet of papers, unaware of its critical nature. The packet contained the power to alter history and many destinies if it were used properly. But even as Reis thought about the council meeting which Crazy Horse had agreed to schedule among all chiefs off and on the reservations, the forces and powers of evil were plotting rapidly against him . . .

Reis was so ensnared by his mental musings that Amanda had to call his name twice and shake his arm to gain his attention. "Reis! Whatever are you thinking about?" she asked.

He forced a beguiling smile to his lips and stated unconvincingly, "Nothing to worry that pretty head, love. I think I'll take another look around." With that, he left the two women looking at each other.

"Randy, did something happen to worry Reis so much?" she inquired anxiously. "That's the same look and mood I saw when things started getting complicated with Weber. This entire matter frightens me."

"I know what you mean. But he wouldn't tell me. Do you think we should take a look at those papers? What if he's in danger or trouble? We can't help him if we don't know anything."

Amanda fretted over such a desperate action. She was trapped between concern and loyalty. Reis loved her. How would he deal with such a traitorous act? Would her motives matter to him? She could not understand why this part of his life must remain a black void to her. Yet, he felt it must and was most adamant about it.

"We can't do such a thing, Randy. Reis would be hurt and angry if he felt I didn't trust him completely," she asserted faintly.

"And you aren't 'hurt and angry' because he doesn't fully trust you?" Miranda asked bluntly. When she saw her sister's stricken look, she relented. "I'm sorry, Mandy; I shouldn't have said that. I don't know what's gotten into me lately. Why does everything have to be so complex and difficult?"

"Did you get to see Blazing Star alone?" Amanda inquired carefully. Miranda nodded. "Did he say something to hurt you?"

"He says we can't think about us until this war is over. What if it's never over, Mandy? What if something happens to him?"

Amanda slipped her arm around her sister's trembling shoulders and advised, "Don't worry, sis. You did tell me how strong and brave he is. I'm sure he can protect himself."

"You don't understand, Mandy. There are so many soldiers in this area, so many of them determined to kill him. There's no comparison in their weapons. The Indians don't have someone to provide their ammunition and supplies! They have to make them or hunt them. And while the braves are doing so, the soldiers wipe out villages and tribes! As long as the whites press closer and tighter to Indian lands, the warriors will go forth to battle them. It can't stop unless one side yields. And the Oglalas will never do so as long as they live and breathe. You haven't been to their camp and listened to them. You haven't seen the terrible things the whites and soldiers do. He'll die, Mandy; he'll die before accepting defeat and dishonor."

Miranda locked her gaze with her sister's and explained, "Don't you see? That's why I have to spend every moment I can with him. When the time comes that we're parted forever, I'll have these days and memories. Am I so awful to want all I can have of him before it's too late? Do you see why he keeps pushing me away, back to so-called safety? If he didn't love me, my life and happiness wouldn't be so important to him. He loves me enough to unselfishly sacrifice me. And I love him so much that no danger is sufficient to obey him."

Suddenly Miranda laughed reproachfully. "He's a lot like your Reis. He thinks ignorance provides safety and prevents worry. Do you realize how lucky we are? We both have loves who will do anything to protect us. I'm glad Reis is working with Blazing Star. If any two men can make a difference in this conflict, they can."

Amanda had not comprehended how much suffering and turmoil her sister was enduring until now. Nor had she guessed that her husband was being pulled into a situation which was deadly and uncontrollable, a situation which would alter and destroy many lives. She tried to encourage and comfort her sister. As their destinies overlapped, they were being drawn ever closer.

Around four that afternoon, Fort Sully was assailed by commotion and excitement as the

Seventh Cavalry set up camp in a clearing nearby, under the command of George Armstrong Custer and his favored officer, Major Brody Sheen. Lucas hurried to the cabin to relate this news to Amanda, Reis, and Miranda.

At nearly the same time, in a smaller clearing miles from the fort, another meeting was taking place. A vindictive and menacing Oglala warrior was passing detrimental information to a half-blooded scout whose cunning, vengeance, and hatred far exceeded that of the Indian's. So blinded by his own greed and bitterness, the warrior failed to recognize the traitorous enemy he was supposedly using to gain his own wishes. The aggressive and sinister scout was cleverly plotting revenge on both sides, white and Indian. Once the opposing leaders killed each other, he would take over this area, for he possessed the intelligence and daring to fool both sides. Who better to rule than a man who carried both bloods, who knew the strengths and weaknesses of each. As he watched the treacherous warrior ride off, he sneered at the man's stupidity. For the warrior had just given him the means to accomplish his ends.

When Lucas finished telling of his journey, he told Reis that Colonel Custer wanted to meet him tonight at dinner. Lucas then told Miranda that Brody was eager to visit with her. When she scowled, Lucas added that he had tried to discourage Brody's interest but could not.

"How long do they plan to stay around here?" Miranda inquired.

"It looks as if they'll set up camp and headquarters here. Custer's been ordered to check out the Sioux hostilities and get them under control. He said it would be easier to work out of Fort Sully for a while," he explained to her dismay.

When Reis and Miranda related their eventful tales, Lucas realized why Custer's presence might present a problem. With Brody dogging Miranda, it would be difficult for her to leave home for another visit to her grandfather and Blazing Star. She feared for her love's life and safety with two of his worst foes so near. Perhaps she should find some way to warn him and his people, for she knew Custer was not here for a truce.

When Brody came to call later, Amanda was forced to lie to him. She claimed her sister was not feeling well. After disarming Amanda with compliments and his dashing manner, Brody said he would call again tomorrow afternoon and left.

"Are you sure you have him pegged right? You were enchanted by Blazing Star when you met Major Sheen. Perhaps you've misjudged him. He's quite handsome and charming," Amanda remarked as she watched Brody swagger back toward their makeshift camp of tents.

"Brody is devious, clever, and sinister, just like Weber Richardson was," Miranda sneered sarcastically. "Take another study."

The subject was dropped instantly. The two waited nervously until Lucas and Reis returned from their meal and conversation. Each woman was full of questions for the men who tried to answer them amidst laughter and amusement.

"The President's son, Frederick, wasn't with Custer tonight?" Amanda asked, knowing that was one cover Reis was using.

"Custer says Frederick's planning to join him when he's ready to ride into the Black Hills for that survey," Lucas responded before Reis.

"They're riding into the Black Hills?" Miranda echoed in shock.

"Yep. They claim it's just a mapping expedition, but it's going to cause trouble. I think the military is asking for it, just seeking an excuse to wipe out those renegade tribes," Lucas spoke out again.

"But what about the Laramie Treaty of '68? It makes trespassing on their sacred grounds forbidden. That's the last and most crucial promise to the Indians, to stay out! From the Missouri River past the Black Hills, the land has been declared the Great Sioux Reservation. They've broken all the treaties and promises except that one. They establish reservations until they find a reason to move them another place, but this time it's a lethal mistake. If they ride into that territory, no Indian—Sioux or otherwise—will back down from that challenge," Miranda stated fearfully. "You've got to contact President Grant, Reis. You've got to convince him to stop Custer."

"I plan to do my best, Randy. But you have to trust me and keep silent. If anyone suspects what I'm up to or who I really am, it's all over for us and the Indians.

Just as soon as I get my facts collected and recorded, Grant will know all about the crux of this matter," Reis promised them, revealing more today than he had to date.

"You realize there are people in Washington involved in some of this fraud and corruption, people in high places, people in the Indian Bureau, people close to the President? What's he planning to do about his kin?" Lucas questioned gravely.

"He promised to punish whoever is involved," Reis replied.

"You think he will?" Amanda asked skeptically.

"If Custer's connected to it, yes. There's no love lost between those two. As to his blood, I can't say for sure," he answered candidly.

"But if it's brought into public light, even his kin would be forced to halt such vile and criminal behavior," Miranda surmised.

"That's what I'm working and hoping for," Reis declared.

"When Custer asked why you were here, what did you tell him, Reis?" Miranda probed apprehensively.

"I said Grant sent me out here to look around and see how things were progressing. I made it sound more like a pleasure trip than business. I told him I was recently married and this was a sort of honeymoon. If he mentions that we're looking at ranchland to settle in these parts, don't act surprised," he said with a smile.

"Did he believe you?" Miranda asked merrily.

"Partly. But he did make a joking comment about

first a writer showing up with a Lawrence girl, then a liaison from the President with another Lawrence girl. He remarked on what a potent and curious pair a government ex-agent and a writer made. I hadn't considered him associating me and Luke as some undercover team. We'll all have to be careful what we say and do. It's going to appear strange for me and Luke to be asking questions and making observations. We could be hindering each other's progress."

"Right now, yours seems more important, Reis. You're working on history in the making," Lucas said.

"That's real generous of you, Luke. I know how important this trip and book are to you." Reis acknowledged.

"Not quite so meaningful since I discovered Weber Richardson arranged and financed it—no doubt to get me away from Alexandria and my cousins," Luke ventured in lingering annoyance.

That disclosure gave way to talk of the past. After coffee and pie, Lucas went to sleep on a bedroll and Miranda used the cot while Reis and Amanda were given the bedroom. They tried to protest, but neither Miranda nor Lucas would budge from their positions.

In the camp nearby, Brody was asking Custer, "Do you believe Harrison is just wandering around for no special reason?"

Yellowy blond curls tossed around blue-clad

shoulders as his commander shook his head. "Grant doesn't do anything without a purpose. You keep a close eye on our four friends. See what you can learn about the writer and see if you can get some of his work to me. Let's see which side of the fence he landed on, and how long ago. As for Harrison, get me all the information your contacts can locate. He's a troubleshooter if I ever saw one. I want to know just what he and Grant are pulling," he remarked, then began whistling an aria.

While he clipped his mustache and evened his curls, he told his aide to roll the locks of hair in strips of cloth and give them to his female admirers. After receiving orders to check his horse, Vic, once again before bedtime, the aide left muttering about how glad he was that Custer had not brought along any of his numerous dogs on this journey.

Custer was a strange man, a man either fiercely hated or genuinely admired. He cut a dashing figure as the epitome of a professional soldier, a man obsessed with fame and power, a man who believed he could conquer any force. When the Civil War ended, Custer needed excitement and danger as others needed nourishment for survival. He started his new career with the Seventh Cavalry Regiment in Kansas in 1867. Only recently had he been ordered to take command of the Dakota Territory, operating out of Fort Lincoln.

Considered a proud or vain man, depending on the source, Custer appeared fearless, often charging headlong into the heat of battle. Some called him reckless and vainglorious, but above all, Custer was a military man. He followed orders, even if he resented or disagreed with them. He was often called a brilliant strategist, but others claimed it was merely luck. Custer never drank alcoholic spirits and rarely used profanity. He believed in the total authority of a commanding officer. Although he loved his wife Libby deeply, it was rumored he had a Cheyenne mistress. As much as he was alleged to despise Indians, he felt it his duty to try and uphold the treaties and promises made to them.

Custer was now being thrust into historical events beyond his control. He saw many wrongs but felt his first loyalty was to his country and his men. Often overzealous in his conduct, he was determined to go down in history as a brave and intelligent leader, but Fate was swiftly coloring the pages upon which his personal drama was being recorded.

When Miranda told her sister of her intentions to sneak to the Oglala camp and warn them of Custer's arrival, Amanda was petrified. Miranda angrily declared that her sister could cover her absence by sticking to the story of her illness. They argued for a long time, until Lucas finally intervened and told Miranda she could not go.

"You can't order me about, Lucas Reardon," she snapped.

"If you're caught, Randy, it would spoil everything," Luke retorted, his own eyes glittering frostily. "This time you listen and obey!"

"That's Custer out there, Luke!" she panted frantically. "And Sherman and Sheridan aren't far away. I'm going!" she announced.

"You don't have to! Reis is ... Just wait awhile and things will settle down," he finished, trying to cover his slip.

When she questioned his half-statement, he passed it off nonchalantly. But Miranda guessed what he had been about to say; she relaxed, assuming Reis and Lucas were going to warn her people.

When Brody called again, Miranda could not refuse to see him, for he caught her outside getting fresh air with Amanda and Reis. They chatted for a time, then Brody asked her to go for a walk or allow him to step inside for some coffee. Recalling that Reis's reports were lying on the table, Miranda had no choice but to accept his invitation. Reis smiled at her, knowing why she had agreed, sensing why she disliked this man. He resolved to find a way to keep them apart, even though he could have used her to distract Brody.

As Brody and Miranda strolled along, he asked how she had been occupying her time and why she had not joined Lucas for the trek. Miranda passed off his questions with light remarks and sunny smiles. She tensed when Brody said he wanted to get to know her and her family better. He asked if she would join him for a picnic the next day.

Miranda was not caught unprepared for his romantic siege, but she had not expected the rapidity of his onslaught. Her mind was elsewhere and she was not thinking clearly or calmly. She stammered and fidgeted. "I think . . . we should get . . . to know each other better."

"That's what I just said, Miranda," he teased devilishly. "Do I make you nervous?" he asked, reaching out to take her hand.

She jerked it away and flushed. She tried to recall every feminine wile she had seen Amanda use, every coquettish gesture, every shy expression. "I fear you press too quickly, sir," she hinted in a thick Southern drawl, fluttering her lashes demurely. "I'm unaccustomed to men being so bold and persistent as you Westerners. Now that my parents are . . . dead, I find it strange to choose my own companions and activities. I thought perhaps this trip with cousin Luke would make me a bit more daring and confident, but alas . . ." She sighed dramatically as if disappointed with her progress and modesty.

Brody grinned mischievously and hinted, "No one could doubt your courage or mettle, Miranda. You remained here alone while Luke was with us. Surely you have become less fainthearted," he teased her.

"That was different, sir. I was locked in my cabin each night, and there were soldiers to guard me during the day. A lady could not travel in the company of so many men and under such deplorable conditions. I was greatly shocked that your invitation included me. Surely you would not wish me to face such dangers and deprivations?"

He huskily declared, "I would confront whatever

necessary to be with you. In my eagerness to have you at my side, I overlooked such matters. You are an exquisite treasure, Miranda. I never dreamed of meeting such a divine creature, and surely not in this hellish place."

Miranda's face grew redder with each compliment. "Sir, you should not speak so boldly. But thank you. If you are to be at Fort Sully for an extended period, perhaps we shall have time to become properly acquainted. I should return home now," she stated uneasily.

"Please don't go," he coaxed. "I've thought of nothing but you since we parted. I persuaded Custer to set up command here just so I could be near you. You have me utterly bewitched, and my duties have suffered greatly from lack of attention. Join me for a picnic tomorrow? We can be alone and . . . we can share Cupid's potent spell."

She stared in amazement. "You should not suggest such a thing, sir. It seems our morals and breeding differ immensely. I think it best if you do not call on me again. I fear you misconstrued our relationship and my feelings." Her scheme to discourage him had failed miserably.

Witnessing her reaction, he hastily declared, "I didn't mean to offend or alarm you. Perhaps my manners have dulled in this uncivil land. When a man faces death every day, he comes to live for each hour and to speak frankly. We wouldn't be totally alone, Miranda."

"We wouldn't?" she questioned his meaning,

imagining what she could learn from this man about Custer's plans.

"Not if it made you uncomfortable. I could have an aide serve us and remain as your guardian. I would prefer to have privacy to talk, but I don't want to panic you with my eagerness."

Miranda eyed him skeptically. Something in his inflection told her he was being dishonest. But she could take care of herself. Perhaps it would do Brody Sheen a world of good to be tossed on his ear by a refined and delicate lady! "All right, Major Sheen," she acquiesced. "But only if your aide accompanies us," she added.

He grinned roguishly and agreed to her terms, even as he plotted how to outmaneuver her. "I'll pick you up at noon," he suggested.

She smiled genially and nodded in agreement. Afterward, Brody escorted her back to the cabin. Confident of his sexual prowess, he felt there was no need to rush this delicate flower. No doubt she was confused and dismayed by her wanton attraction to him. He must attack her virtuous, naïve shell with skill and caution. She had been taught to keep those legs tightly locked until marriage. But his fiery passion could melt the moral clamp which prevented his possession.

Once she became his mistress and he observed her closely, then he would judge her appeal and value as a wife. His tour of duty would end next spring; perhaps Miranda Lawrence was the ideal choice for him. If a man had to be shackled to a wife, who better than a beautiful and genteel woman? On the surface she seemed an angel; but her sensuality was earthy and powerful. With a little training, he could have her right where he wanted her. He was a master of seduction and guile; and they would be alone in a romantic setting tomorrow afternoon . . .

When Miranda told Reis of the picnic plans, he was both delighted and dismayed. He revealed that he had vital plans tomorrow afternoon which she could aid by distracting Brody Sheen while Lucas commanded Custer's attention with an interview for his phony book. Reis said he would take Amanda with him to meet her grandfather; his wife's presence would make their journey from the settlement appear a romantic outing for the honeymooners. But Reis warned Miranda to be alert and wary of Brody.

When Miranda pleaded to go see Blazing Star, Reis protested. If she went along, Sheen would be encouraged to ride after them and attempt to join their party. He forced her to realize the importance of misleading Brody Sheen and Custer. He promised to give a message to her love, to try to set up a secret meeting between them. She unhappily agreed before retiring to dream of her intrepid warrior.

While Reis and Amanda made passionate love and Lucas envisioned literary accolades and Miranda dreamed of her copper-skinned lover, Brody Sheen was staring coldly and sardonically at the odious scout who had told him of the upcoming parlay and Reis's covert mission. It did not matter that the scout declared Miranda ignorant and innocent of Reis's mischief; Brody painted her guilty of deceit. That night, Brody dreamed of punishing a girl who had made a complete fool of him, of capturing a savage chief whose name sent shivers of fear through most whites, and of helping his friend and commander by destroying all of his enemies!

Chapter Twenty-One

Despite the vitality of the landscape, death whispered upon the gentle breezes which swayed the verdant grasses and supple leaves, played through colorful wildflowers, and teased the wings of the brilliantly shaded butterflies that danced with the currents. Suspense hung heavy over the settlement that next morning as each person planned his or her day's events.

A pleased Tom Fletcher rode off early to watch his plot unfold from a distance through his field glasses. The drama was in motion, but the naïve actors did not as yet know their roles. The final act had begun on this warm morning, and nothing could save the white and red players from destruction.

Lucas Reardon obtained permission from Custer to ride along with part of his troop to the Cheyenne River Agency to check on rumors of trouble on the reservation. The larger part of his regiment was to remain camped near Fort Sully, under the command of Brody Sheen. Practically ordered to mount up and accompany the departing squad, Lucas was dismayed by the fact that he was not given time to return to his cabin to warn Reis of their destination, where Chief Red Cloud would be found missing if Custer requested to see and speak with him.

Reis and Amanda Lawrence Harrison rode off with a picnic basket, laughing and chatting as if on the way to a romantic tryst. Reis cleverly headed in the opposite direction from the council meeting, planning to skirt the settlement to prevent discovery. He hoped his wife was in excellent condition, as they would be forced to ride strenuously to arrive on schedule after this diversionary tactic. Reis felt no qualms about taking his wife along on this trip. Crazy Horse had promised they would be observed and protected from a distance.

Amanda was glowing with exuberance, delighted to be a part of this monumental conference and thrilled about meeting Sun Cloud and her sister's love.

From surrounding areas, imposing and illustrious chiefs and spiritual leaders headed for the meeting which Reis Harrison had arranged with Crazy Horse and Sitting Bull. Soon to convene were: Two Moons of the Cheyenne; Lame Deer and Hump of the Minniconjous; Sitting Bull, Gall, Black Moon, and Crow King of the Hunkpapas; Crazy Horse, Big Road, and He Dog of the Oglalas; and Red Hawk of another Sioux tribe. The Brule chief, Spotted Tail, and another Oglala chief, Red Cloud, slipped away from the agencies named for them to attend this crucial parlay. Along with these historic leaders came their most legendary warriors, a group which included Blazing Star.

Reis had convinced Crazy Horse, Sitting Bull, and their council that the "Great White Father" did not know of the evil taking place on their lands. He asked that each tribe list their grievances and sign the paper; then he would personally carry the papers to the "chief of the whites and bluecoats." He told them Chief Grant would halt the bloodshed and punish the whites and bluecoats consumed by greed and evil. He tried to convince them that Chief Grant wanted peace, that he had sent Reis here to unmask the evil and correct it. Reis also warned that the meeting and papers must be kept secret, as those evil whites would try to prevent him and the evidence from reaching the "Great White Father."

Crazy Horse, Sitting Bull, and the members of the council had sensed courage and honesty in the white man. The conflicts were increasing. Each time they slew a "white butcher," another would take his place with better weapons, endless supplies, and further aggression. If there could be peace without dishonor or defeat, this was the last chance to attain it. They agreed to trust Reis, to help prevent more war. They wanted to live in freedom and happiness upon their ancestral grounds; they would agree to allow the whites and bluecoats to settle on lands not included in the Laramie Treaty. They wanted to hunt and enjoy their existence close to Mother Earth. They wanted safety and honor for their families and homes.

"Mahpialuta, Sinte Galeska, ku-wa," Crazy Horse greeted Red Cloud and Spotted Tail and invited them to join his campfire as they awaited the arrival of others.

"Tashunka Witco," both greeted Crazy Horse in return, then gave the sign for peace. *"Pizi."* Red Cloud nodded at Gall and addressed him in friendship.

At Fort Sully, Brody Sheen and his aide called on Miranda Lawrence to commence their scheduled picnic. Although Brody was attempting to be outwardly charming and genial, Miranda perceived an intimidating remoteness in him. She wondered why he was beginning their afternoon so sullenly. A shiver of alarm ran over her body, and she wished she could cancel the outing.

As they mounted their horses, Miranda asked about the squads which were riding east and north from Fort Sully. Brody glanced in their directions, then shrugged noncommittally. He said the men were heading for a military exercise. She prayed she was not acting too curious or nervous. She watched the swallow-tailed cavalry guidon as it waved rapidly with the flag carrier's movements and dismissed her fears and doubts. If he were suspicious of Reis's conduct, Brody would not have remained behind.

Brody and Miranda rode to a serene and lovely spot near the river. As Brody helped Miranda dismount, the look in his hazel eyes caused her twinges of forboding to return. Yet she felt there was nothing she could do but carry out this charade. After all, they were not alone. And, she was not helpless. She could fight like a trained wildcat, and she had the small derringer from Reis strapped to her thigh.

"We should have invited your sister and her husband to join us. I noticed they had the same idea when they rode off this morning," Brody commented casually as he spread the blanket for sitting.

"They're newlyweds, Major Sheen. I think they preferred to be alone," she conversed lightly, returning his amiable smile. "Shall we eat?"

Miranda tensed apprehensively when Brody signaled to the aide, who mounted and rode off instead of serving them. She looked at the man beside her whose expression was cryptic. "If this is a joke or trick, sir, I do not find it amusing or pleasing. I shall leave now," she announced haughtily, sending him a frown of reproach.

"No, Miranda, you shall not leave," Brody informed her icily.

"Sir, you are an officer in the United States Cavalry! This is most distressing and repulsive behavior," she criticized sharply.

"And you, Miss Miranda Lawrence, are a half-breed slut," he stated calmly and insultingly.

"You're an enemy to whites—you and your heathen family. I believe the infamous Chief Sun Cloud is your grandpa. Here I was courting Injun royalty. But not for long. Before nightfall, your family and those savage leaders will be dead or captured."

Miranda went ashen beneath her olive complexion. Tremors swept over her body. For a time, she thought her heart had ceased beating, until it began to race frantically. Horror filled her as his words settled into her distraught mind. She decided to call his bluff first, then physically battle him if she had to. "Whatever are you saying, Major Sheen? Surely this is some malicious ruse to spite or frighten me? I shan't deny my mother was Indian, but that gives you no right to verbally degrade or harass me. I am not ashamed of my heritage. Colonel Custer will be told of your despicable and rude conduct when he returns. My family shall demand your apology and punishment. I will listen to no more of this offensive talk, nor shall I see you again. You, sir, are no gentleman!"

"And you, ma'am, are no lady," he satanically sneered, placing his hand upon her chest and shoving her backward to the blanket.

Miranda alertly and agilely rolled aside, landing on all fours, then jumping to her feet. "How dare you touch me, you vile beast!"

As Brody scrambled to his feet, she struggled to withdraw the tiny pistol. Before she could grip it properly, Brody slapped her across the wrist and sent the weapon flying into the bushes. To her rising terror, when she tried to battle him as Ling had taught her, she discovered Brody knew the same tactics and movements but was far superior in skill and strength. And he was not reluctant to physically battle or beat her!

Miranda tumbled backward and landed roughly on her seat when he kicked her in the abdomen. This was the first time a male had returned her attack. But he had wisely controlled the force of his blow, only wishing to stun her. Miranda gasped for breath as he approached her like a stalking beast. When he came within reach, she tripped him with her leg before he realized she retained the strength and courage to do so. His fall sprained his left wrist and enraged him.

As he pushed himself up from the hard ground, he laughed bitterly and sneered, "So, you like to play rough, do you?"

When Miranda continued to battle him with every skill she possessed, his anger mounted to a dangerous level. She had just enough talent and nimbleness to keep him at bay for a time, but he inflicted many bruises. Twice, he struck her across the face, bringing a darkening bruise to one cheek and a steady flow of blood from the corner of her mouth. She started to retreat while panting breathlessly.

For each step she took backward, Brody took two forward, his eyes glittering with lustful intention. He savored relating where Custer and his men were heading after joining forces away from the settlement. He mockingly revealed the fates of Reis and Amanda but claimed that hers was in his hands. As his arm snaked out to seize her, his gaze never left hers, watching for any sign of attack or defeat. But all he saw was the feigned look of terror and vulnerability which Miranda desperately displayed.

She had to escape and warn them. Her booted foot lifted with such quickness that it landed accurately and rackingly in his private region before he could dodge it. Just as instinctively and rapidly, his fist shot out and made contact with the side of her head instead of her jaw as she shifted with her movement. Rather than breaking her jaw or cheekbone, the blow dazed and staggered her. She fell sideways, injuring the other temple when it struck a large rock.

Muffled curses and groans filtered into her hazy mind as she attempted to clear her head and flee. As she pushed upward to a wobbly sitting position, she saw Brody in a crouched stance, his face a mask of grimacing agony and his hands cupping his throbbing groin. She shook her head and blinked her eyes to regain her senses. It was useless; her vision blurred as pains and drowsiness assailed her. She crumbled to the ground, chestnut curls falling over her bloody face. She was weary and groggy; she could no longer defend herself.

Brody mastered his pain and started toward her, drawing his Colt from its holster. Suddenly, a red-and-black-tipped arrow sang ominously through the still air and slammed into Brody's back. He wavered for a moment, then fell dead near Miranda. She could not react, but she roused herself slightly. In the tiny opening between two fiery curls, she could make out two masculine figures heading toward her. Her confused gaze returned to the arrow whose colors and markings did not match the identity of either male. Perhaps she was dreaming. The arrow was her lover's, but it was her Indian cousin and the fort scout who were approaching her prone and limp body. She could not summon the strength to speak or move, but she listened to their words.

"Why did you shoot the bluecoat with Blazing Star's arrow? Why did you not let him slay her?" Bloody Arrow sneered maliciously.

"She is mine. I claim her as reward for helping you defeat your rivals." As Tom kicked Brody in the ribs, he scoffed, "I wondered why he didn't ride out with Custer to attack the parlay. When I gave him your words about the council meeting, he looked strange. What real man would choose vengeful rape over a glorious battle? When they are all dead, Bloody Arrow, you will rule the Indians and I will rule the whites as we planned. If you try to trick or slay me, I will call down more soldiers upon you than I sent to slay those at the meeting," he threatened malevolently. After today's victory, he would slay Bloody Arrow in his own time and in his own way.

"You wish to have this half-breed whore as your woman? I will sell her and her sister to the Apaches as slaves. No white female can survive such torment. She must die. After this sun, only Bloody Arrow will carry the blood of Gray Eagle," the warrior vowed. "Such matchless blood will flow only in my sons."

"You forget, Bloody Arrow, I also carry two bloods

507

within me. Do not insult the man who helps you earn your dream. She will be my mate and slave. Do as you wish with her sister, but Tamaha is mine. You must go and prepare to call the warriors from all tribes together to avenge the slaughter of their chiefs," he suggested coldly.

"In death, they will do more to free and avenge our many tribes than they did in life and battle. Their deaths will spark hatred and unity in all tribes. I will lead the final battle to slay the killers of our chiefs. At last, the chief's bonnet will be mine. Take her; she is yours. But do not let her escape you," he warned.

When Bloody Arrow rode away to observe the results of his careful and daring plans, Tom threw back his head and laughed heartily. "You are a fool, Bloody Arrow. Once all white and Indian leaders are killed, you will join them in death and I will be chief of all Indian and whites. When you and your family are slain today, only Miranda will carry the blood of Gray Eagle and Sun Cloud within her. My sons will carry the blood of the two great chiefs which flows in Tamaha's body; she will pass such honor to our sons." Chilling laughter filled Miranda's humming ears as she lost consciousness.

Tom gathered Miranda into his arms, his rage boundless when he saw her injuries. He laid her down, then scalped the dead soldier. He had told Sheen that Miranda was not involved in this matter. The fool should have listened! He held the bloody trophy high and issued a Sioux war cry, then tossed it into the bushes. When this deed was discovered and reported, all evidence would point to the deceased Blazing Star.

He lifted Miranda in his arms and headed for his horse. He had previously decided where to conceal her until this matter was settled. Once her family and people were all dead, she would turn to him for love and protection; she would be grateful for his rescue and solace.

At the council meeting, another drama was unfolding. Several Oglala scouts had arrived with dismaying news; bands of soldiers were converging on the area from three directions. Crazy Horse retained his self-control and concealed his infuriating suspicions as he ordered the chiefs to disperse quickly and furtively; he told them soldiers were scouting the area and the parlay must be cancelled. He said he would send word when the next meeting would take place. He scolded himself for having been fooled by this white foe.

Reis failed to perceive the danger he now faced. When the others were gone, Crazy Horse and his small band of warriors lingered to capture the white dog who had arranged this trap. Crazy Horse turned to Blazing Star and ordered him to seize Reis and Amanda, to bind them and bring them to their camp for questioning and punishment.

Reis was grabbed by several warriors and bound securely. Initially he was alarmed and bewildered by their actions, since he could not understand the

Sioux tongue. The two small pistols in his suspender holster beneath his jacket were taken; then the Barns .50 boot pistol with its lengthy butt and barrel was yanked from its concealed position.

Amanda screamed in fright as she was bound and handled roughly. Sun Cloud inwardly doubted their guilt and asked to take control of his treacherous granddaughter until this affair was clarified. Reis wished he had brought Miranda along to translate for him. When he appealed for mercy and gentleness for his wife, Blazing Star glared at him coldly and declared that she would be executed along with him!

The situation was extremely perilous. Reis was worried about Amanda, who had fainted in shock. He tried to convince the Indian chiefs that he had not betrayed them, that he knew nothing of the cavalry's plans. He protested against their harsh treatment, arguing that he would not have brought his beloved wife along if this was a trap, reminding them of her Indian heritage. Reis beseeched Sun Cloud to take their side, to protect Amanda; but the old man hung his head in renewed shame and refused. As a last resort, Reis entreated them to wait until they discovered the truth before harming his wife. Clearly, they did not believe him.

Blazing Star took control of the female prisoner, wondering if his beloved Tamaha knew of their treachery and had been unable to warn them. Either way, the Oglalas would never accept her into their village and hearts after this betrayal. As surely as *Wi* arose each morning, these two would die for their evil. But as they rode for camp with Reis and Amanda as prisoners, Blazing Star prayed that Miranda was not involved and prayed that she would not risk showing her face in his camp to defend her family. She had encouraged this situation; she had brought the white dog to camp. She would be slain on sight!

By the time they reached camp, Blazing Star's anger and anguish had been mastered. He was skeptical of Reis's guilt. Obviously the white man felt no fear for himself, no fear of death or torture; his only concern was for the safety and survival of his wife. The white man would not intentionally have endangered his woman's life. The warrior noted lines of anger in the white man's face, anger which indicated he was being falsely accused and bitterly resented it. The look in Reis's dark blue eyes shouted he had trusted the Indians rashly, that he was disappointed by their treachery.

Amanda was held captive in Sun Cloud's teepee. She cried and trembled in fear of her beloved's fate. What did she care about her own death if she lost her love? How could they be so cruel to people trying to help them? She glared at her grandfather and Blazing Star. She had seen her husband bound to a thick post in the center of camp. The signal had been given for the leaders to meet in council to decide their fates. Poor Miranda had been so mistaken about these barbarians!

Before the two men could leave her secured to the center pole, she scoffed at Sun Cloud, "No wonder my mother ran away from you and this vile life!

You're cruel and evil! I'll never understand why she longed to visit you! I wish I had never laid eyes on you. You're not my grandfather; Gray Eagle's son and Morning Star's father could not be a savage coward!''

To Blazing Star, she sneered, "I'm glad my sister didn't come along with us. How could she love an animal like you? She'll hate you both and never come here again. I pray she never learns her cherished grandfather and her beloved killed her sister. I despise you both! If you harm Reis, you'd best kill me too.''

Then she murmured sadly, "You two really fooled her, didn't you?'' Tears eased down her pale cheeks as she whispered in disbelief, "You're killing the only man who can help you stop this war. He's telling the truth. I don't know how the soldiers learned of the meeting, but it wasn't from me or Reis. At least try to uncover the truth!'' she panted angrily.

Blazing Star related her words to Sun Cloud, then disclosed his own misgivings about this situation. Sun Cloud spoke to the younger warrior, then left for council. Blazing Star knelt before Amanda and told her, "Your grandfather is saddened by your cruel words and hatred. He says to tell you he will speak for mercy. He does not believe you and your mate betrayed us. He believes you because, Sky Eyes, you are the sister of Rising Moon and the daughter of Morning Star.''

She exhibited utter shock at her grandfather's understanding. "And what do you think, Blazing

Star? What vote will you cast in council?'' she asked.

Shiny jet eyes fused with misty blue ones. "I will vote for your release," he stated simply, evading a full explanation.

In a quavering voice, she pressed, "My release? Or mine and Reis's freedom? If you slay him, I don't wish to live. He is my life."

"I will vote to free you and your mate," he responded warily.

"Why?" Amanda questioned incredulously. "Because of my sister? Do you believe we're innocent?" Suddenly she was no longer afraid.

"I vote with my head, not my heart, Sky Eyes. You said I have fooled Tamaha. I have not. I have told her she cannot be my woman. I have told her we cannot love each other. I have told her to stay where she is safe and happy. She cannot live here. These things I have told her. When you go free, you must also tell her. Do not allow her to dream of what cannot be. Our people are enemies, and we battle to the death. She must not be forced to choose between her bloods, for she must be white or Indian. Do you understand, Sky Eyes?"

"Yes, Blazing Star. You love her enough to spare her from death. I will do as you ask, if I am freed. You are a very generous and unselfish man. I'm sorry you can't share a life with her."

The look of yearning in his eyes exposed his feelings. As he turned to go, Amanda added, "She loves you very much, Blazing Star. Now, I understand why. If—if the council doesn't vote to free us, will you . . . go to her and tell her . . . what happened? If you don't, she will come to you for answers and comfort. If they kill us, they will kill her too. The truth will be softer coming from your lips.''

He did not turn. He simply inhaled loudly and responded, ''Yes. But if you do not go free, she will hate Blazing Star and Sun Cloud. She will blame us for your deaths. I cannot go against the council vote.''

''Blazing Star!'' she called out to him as he ducked to exit. ''I have a plan! Wait!'' When he came back to her, she entreated, ''Will you go to our cabin and speak with my sister and cousin? Perhaps they can tell you what really happened today!''

''If Crazy Horse agrees, I will go seek the truth,'' he replied. ''I will tell Reis you are safe and unafraid,'' he added, then smiled.

She smiled in response and thanked him. Their fates were probably in Blazing Star's kind, strong hands. Surely he would help free them. But what if he failed? No, she could not think that way!

When Bloody Arrow returned to camp, no one suspected his thwarted plot, or comprehended the true reason for his fury over the near massacre. Fortunately for him, but tragically for others, he had been assigned to scout the only direction from which soldiers did not arrive. He had sat alone, dreaming of fame, while he presumed the attack was taking place. When he went to view his victory, he found the same thing Custer had: nothing! Not a trace!

When Custer checked with the Indian agencies, all

chiefs were present and no hints of trouble were sighted or reported. Custer had no choice but to accept this mission as a wild goose chase, somebody's mistake or clever ruse. He planned to question Brody the moment he returned to camp. He wished now that he had not sent Lucas Reardon back to the fort under guard. Even if that writer had gotten away from his two men, he could not have warned the Indians in time for so many to vanish completely. Perhaps he should interrogate both Reis Harrison and Lucas Reardon, and perhaps the two women with them. Or perhaps that arrogant scout was playing games with him; that was where the information had originated! He would have his answers by tonight, and someone's head! He ordered the regiment back to Fort Sully.

Not expecting Custer to return so early, Tom Fletcher pretended to have found Sheen's bloody body and brought it to the commanding officer just before Custer's stormy arrival. Tom had just identified the arrow and charged Blazing Star with the crime when Custer swaggered into the room. When Tom was asked to repeat his tale about the council meeting once more, he lied again, claiming he had overheard several warriors who had been talking around a campfire. No matter how Custer debated or challenged his words, Tom stuck to his false claims.

Tom was furious when Custer placed him under arrest. He knew he had to find some way to escape, for he was holding the unconscious Miranda prisoner in a place no one could find. If he did not return in a few days, she would die! Yet if he had to, he would sacrifice her life rather than expose his guilt by revealing her location. He was taken to the blockhouse and imprisoned.

Custer headed for the cabin. Lucas was pacing anxiously, awaiting word of Miranda and the others. Custer could not deny the man's shock at the news of Brody's death and Miranda's abduction. Custer related the events of the day, which further stunned Lucas. He told Custer he did not know anything about such a meeting. He asked Custer to send out a search party for Reis, Amanda, and Miranda, for Lucas knew something was terribly wrong.

"You have no idea where they are?" Custer demanded sternly.

"Reis and Amanda went for a picnic; they're just married, you know. The last time I saw Miranda, she was waiting for your Major Sheen to take her riding and picnicking. What's going on here? That scout said Sheen was murdered and scalped, and Miranda is missing. Here it is nearly dark, and Reis and Mandy haven't come home. I'm worried, sir. Something awful is going on out there. You've got to do something; you've got to locate them. Is that scout trustworthy?"

"Frankly, I doubt it, but he's sticking to his story. I'm beginning to think there wasn't any parlay. But you're right about one thing; there's a stench in the air I don't like. If any of them return home tonight, you wake me at any hour. If not, we'll take us a look around tomorrow. A man should know his enemies,

Reardon; I do. Blazing Star doesn't take full scalp, only a small lock. That was his arrow in Sheen's back, but not his handiwork. When you come over in the morning, bring Harrison's papers with you. They could give us a clue.''

Lucas did not fall into his baited trap. He suggested slyly, ''Why don't you take them tonight and study them? If there's a clue in them to help find my cousins and Reis, you can have 'em now. I'll fetch 'em.'' He went into the bedroom and retrieved the false set of papers, then handed them to Custer. ''Just make sure you return them undamaged.''

To the west of the Missouri River, there was a small and narrow cave which had been dug into the side of a hill by miners as a hiding place from the Indians. At one time, large boulders had been used to conceal the entrance. Later, they were left aside and trees were propped before the opening to hide it, being replaced as they wilted. It was in this cave that Miranda regained consciousness.

When Miranda stirred, her entire body ached. Any movement sent pains washing over her. Her head throbbed and her mouth was cottony dry, but she endured the anguish to sit up and look around her.

She was groggy and disoriented but managed to lean against the damp surface at her back. She appeared to be inside a dirt chamber, the oblong entrance to which was sealed by a barrier of crisscrossed ropes. She stood on rubbery legs and struggled with the unusual fence which refused to yield. The confining door was covered with numerous branches, no doubt to prevent anyone from locating her. She pressed her sensitive face against the ropes to discover why they refused to give way. Obviously they were secured around heavy rocks, and all covered by leafy branches. The square openings were too small to allow escape, even for someone as slender as herself. Trying to unsnag the ropes, she yanked until she had rope burns on her palms. She finally ceased the futile waste of energy. Without a knife, the ropes were as strong as iron. Someone had used plenty of skill and time with this confining doorway!

She returned to her former place and collapsed to the makeshift pallet of two blankets over supple branches. Nearby, she discovered a canteen of fresh water and a leather pouch with dried beef strips and cornpones. Inside a square cloth, she found wild berries. She sipped the water but did not eat. There was no knife inside the pouch or any other weapon for defense, but she had expected none.

As she leaned weakly against the moist wall, she surveyed her sepulchral surroundings once more. The cave was seven feet from back wall to sealed entrance; from side to side, it was almost three feet; and from floor to ceiling the walls were between eight and ten feet high. Due to the recent rains, it was musky and damp but oddly clean.

Around five in the afternoon, there was still light inside the dirt prison. She stared longingly at an opening far above her, frustratingly beyond her reach. She tried to suppress the visions of snakes and crawly things that assailed her. Normally such creatures did not frighten her, but she was vulnerable here. She shuddered as she prayed her captor would free her before darkness, or at least come to guard her.

Her captor . . . Why was Tom doing this to her? She had had no idea he was so obsessed with her. He and Bloody Arrow made such an implausible pair of villains. Had they spoken truthfully? Could everyone she loved be dead or imprisoned right now? If not, were they searching for her? How long would Tom keep her here? How long before she had any news about her family and her love?

She had underestimated the hatred and evil in her Indian cousin. Would he get away with this satanic deed? Until Tom killed him? Until he killed Tom? Even if the Indians were warned in time to prevent or respond to Custer's attack, they would hold Reis and Amanda responsible. What if an awesome battle was raging somewhere this very moment? What if Tom and Bloody Arrow were slain? No one would find her; she would die here in this cave alone. What if her love thought she had betrayed him? No, he would never think such evil of her!

All she could do was wait and pray. If they were all dead, she would make no attempt to dupe Tom. If they were only captured, she would do anything to gain her freedom to help them, even kill him. She lay down on the blanket and wept at her helplessness.

In the Oglala camp, a fierce debate was in progress.

Bloody Arrow demanded the torture and deaths of Reis and Amanda as strongly as Blazing Star and Sun Cloud demanded a chance to prove their innocence. Bloody Arrow listed the crimes of all whites during his verbal condemnation. When Sun Cloud used Amanda's heritage as a favorable point, Bloody Arrow disputed it by saying there was no proof that either woman was the daughter of Morning Star. And even if it were true, they would have learned treachery from their mother, who had brought shame and sadness to her family and people.

As the meeting went on, it became clear to all that Bloody Arrow despised his female cousins and wanted them dead. Yet no one could deny the accuracy of many of his arguments. Bloody Arrow asserted that only Reis or Miranda could have betrayed them to the soldiers. How else could the bluecoats have known exactly where to attack? The cavalry had not merely been out scouting; it had been sighted heading straight for the location of the council meeting!

When Blazing Star suggested Reis would not have knowingly brought his wife into danger, Bloody Arrow contended that the two white-eyes had assumed they would be safe because of Amanda's claim to be the granddaughter of Sun Cloud. He declared that Amanda probably had been ordered to sneak away during the talks but had not been given the chance before her capture.

When Bloody Arrow feared his vengeful arguments were failing, he sneered, "Sun Cloud's eyes are blinded by love for the child of his child. The eyes of Blazing Star are clouded by lust for the white girl's sister who came here as Tamaha. I tell them to think and vote with the head, not loin or heart."

Blazing Star stiffened and glared at the insolent warrior. "I do not deny I have love and desire for Tamaha, but it would not prevent me from voting against this white man and woman if I believed them guilty. I do not. Let me go to the wooden teepee of Tamaha and speak with her. Let me see who lies and who speaks truth. A man can die on any sun or moon, but he should die in guilt, not innocence."

"How can we trust Blazing Star to return with the truth he finds? I will go," Bloody Arrow announced. "I claim the right to prove the guilt or innocence of my family. Tamaha and her sister are of Sun Cloud's bloodline, as I am. It is my right."

"Do you think us fools, Bloody Arrow?" Sun Cloud shrieked in unnatural anger and agitation. "Your hatred of Tamaha shines as brightly as *Wi*. I feel shame that you are of my blood. I choose Blazing Star to seek the truth. Who challenges me? Who votes for the child of my blood to be slain and for the death of her mate?"

The ceremonial lodge was deathly silent after Bloody Arrow stated coldly, "I do. I will prove the three white-eyes are guilty."

Crazy Horse's unfathomable gaze went from one man to the next. In a resolute tone, he stated, "We will take the vote. All warriors will accept it or leave our camp and tribe. Do you wish them to go free? Do

521

you say they are innocent? Do we seek the truth?''

In each man's hand were two painted sticks, one black and one white. The pure white was an affirmative vote; the deathly black was negative. As it came to each man's turn, he tossed in the stick which revealed his vote. Blazing Star and Sun Cloud could not watch as the pile grew larger . . .

Chapter Twenty-Two

The Oglala Sioux warrior keenly observed the cabin near the edge of the bluecoat settlement. Soon, the fates of many would be sealed; soon, he would be free of the past. There was no sign of the half-blooded scout or Tamaha, but there was one dark-haired witness who knew the truth! The warrior waited impatiently until all signs of movement ceased. Then, he daringly headed for the cabin to see what the white cousin knew . . .

In the Oglala camp, Amanda nestled as closely as possible to the powerful frame of her husband, whose chest and feet were bare. After the council meeting, Reis had been cut free and imprisoned in Sun Cloud's teepee with his wife. Though this could be their last night together, there was no way they could have a loving farewell, for the hands and ankles of both were bound securely to prevent escape. All they could do was snuggle close to each other and share intoxicating kisses.

Suddenly Reis rolled to his back and lifted his bent knees. He wiggled and struggled, grunting and breathing heavily with his exertions. Amanda watched silently, as it was obvious what he was trying to do. At last, he was successful and knelt before her with extended arms beckoning her into his confining embrace. She worked her way to her knees and slid between those muscular bands of warm flesh. He smiled radiantly at her, lowering his bound arms to encircle her in them.

He sealed his mouth over hers, and as his fingers interlocked with hers behind her back, they savored this contact of bodies and spirits. Reis guided her carefully to the buffalo mat. They lay on their sides, kissing and nuzzling each other.

He murmured earnestly and tenderly, "I love you, Mandy, and I would give everything I own to have you one last time."

She leaned her tawny head away from his hard, smooth shoulders, and smiling at him, she replied, "So would I, Reis. I love you so much. Don't blame yourself for this. I'd rather be here with you, even if it's to die together. I couldn't live without you."

Reis's dark blue eyes sparkled with moisture, and he cleared his lumpy throat to speak. "I could never watch you die, my love. If we must end this way, I pray they show mercy with you but take me first. You see, I'm a selfish coward after all."

A gaze as soft and light as baby blue cotton fused with his. "I wish I could slip my arms around you, but I doubt I'm that limber," she teased, both attempting to lighten the dismal mood and ease the anguish of the other.

"One day, I'll teach you," he promised with a playful grin.

"I hope so," she responded, forcing a cheerful smile. "Reis, do you think he will tell the truth when he returns? What will he do with Randy? What if he captures her and brings her back to die with us?"

"He was ordered to seek the truth, Mandy. Warriors are famous for their obedience and honor," he reminded her.

"But are honor and honesty the same in this affair?" she deliberated worriedly, rubbing her lips over his furry chest. "What if the truth doesn't suit his purposes? How do you suppose Custer found out about the meeting?" she inquired gravely.

"I wish I knew, love. Even if Randy dropped a clue with Sheen today, the timing would be wrong. Custer knew last night or early this morning. But who told him, and why? There's something else, love," he hinted ominously, dreading to mention it.

"What?" she asked, sensing his alarm and reluctance.

"Why didn't Sheen ride out with the others? Blazing Star said the man who rode at Custer's side was missing today," Reis revealed.

"I don't follow your insinuation," she murmured. "Maybe he was left in charge of the fort or other men."

"If Custer knows you and I are involved in this

parlay, I wonder what he's done with Randy and Luke. On a patrol this important, something urgent kept Brody at the camp. By now, Custer knows we're missing, but does he suspect why? I'd bet my scalp he's reading those false reports right this minute," he surmised astutely.

"If they arrested Luke and Randy, they wouldn't harm them without proof, would they?" she fretted at this distressing news. "And they couldn't possibly have any firm evidence against any of us. Besides, you're working for the President. He'll protect us, if we get out of this."

In the vanishing light, Reis observed the unfamiliar shadows in her eyes. He questioned them. Tears began to ease down into her tawny curls. "Randy and I have always been close, Reis. There's some kind of mystical bond between us. She's in terrible danger. I sense such a chill and blackness. It's like she's . . ." Amanda shuddered violently, unable to say, in a grave.

Tom Fletcher angrily paced the dirt floor of his cell. He had demanded his release; he had demanded to go scouting for the facts to exonerate him. He had demanded to be shown any evidence against him. None of his demands had a favorable effect on Custer. It was past midnight, and he was still imprisoned. But he had left food and water with Miranda and she was not severely injured. There was no danger of her dying within two or three days. Surely he would be free by then. Besides Miranda, only Bloody Arrow knew the truth about their daring plot; and neither would ever reveal it. Tom intended to slay the antagonistic Indian as soon as he was free. Then he would take Miranda to another place and begin a new life. At least he had earned one reward from this devastated plot! No one would locate her, for the cave was in an area no one ever visited.

Tom exhaled in vexation as he leaned the back of his head against the window bars. He could not even trick a sentry into giving him freedom, for Custer had not placed one at the stone brig. It seemed Custer had felt no Indian would dare sneak into this settlement with him in command, certainly not to free a half-breed scout!

In the flicker of an eye, a bronze hand closed over Tom's mouth and forced his head backward. A sharp blade slid smoothly and swiftly across his neck. As if to make certain the scout was dead, the intruder forcefully drove the shiny weapon directly into the scout's heart, then twisted it viciously. Before releasing the body to let it sink into the dust of the cell, Bloody Arrow wiped his knife clean upon his victim's clothes and hair. He grinned satanically as he tossed a red and black feather into the brig, then sneaked away. There was one other person to silence tonight . . .

In the cabin not far away, Lucas was pacing frantically, unable to sleep. When he responded to the light tapping at the door, he was astonished to find a warrior standing there. The man introduced himself as Blazing Star and asked to enter and speak with him. Assuming the warrior had either news of or a message from Amanda and Reis, Lucas stepped aside and motioned for him to enter. Lucas hurriedly locked the door and turned to speak with the Indian who had once saved his life, whose face now exhibited a pattern of color designs, as if he were painted for war . . .

Far away, Miranda pushed herself to her feet, her buttocks aching from her last attempt to reach the hole at the top of the cave. It looked just large enough for her to wiggle through to the outside. But her first attempt had failed, sending her crashing to the hard ground, straining one wrist and bruising her bottom.

Her hands and arms were scratched, and her dress was muddy. But she did not curse the mud, for it made the surface she was trying to overcome sticky, sticky enough to aid her treacherous climb. She caught her breath and sipped more water. Tears rolled down her grimy face, for her escape might come too late for those she loved.

She had recalled two occasions at the plantation when a similar situation had existed. Once, a worker had fallen into an abandoned well whose wooden covering had rotted and given way. Another time, a worker had fallen into a well containing several feet of water. Both times, the men had not used ropes or help to climb out; they had eased up the sides by pressing their backs to one side and their feet on the other. Inch by inch, they had wiggled to the top and climbed out. She had heard both tales. But could she do the same?

Concluding she would have more agility and control if her feet were bare, she removed her stiff boots and cast them aside. She had previously removed her petticoats; now, she twisted her skirt hem and tucked it into her bloomers to free her legs. She pressed her back to one wall and lifted one foot against the opposite side then cautiously placed the other foot just below the first one. Seesawing her shoulder blades, she flattened her palms to the semi-hard surface near her buttocks. She warned herself not to rush her movements this time.

She worked upward a short distance, then rested. She held her body stiff, bracing herself between the two surfaces. As she neared the top, she feared she would not succeed this time either. Her injured wrist was throbbing as much as her head. Her thigh and calf muscles were cramping; her knees and ankles were quivering. If she fell from this height, she could be hurt badly. She had to make it! She had to get out before Tom returned, or before he never returned.

Her feet were growing numb from the damp chill and lack of circulation. Miranda was positive her shoulders were getting raw. Her hands were bleeding from tiny cuts and broken nails. She knew she was weakening. She wanted to sob hysterically from exhaustion, pain, and fear. She fiercely overcame that rash urge.

The chestnut haired beauty prayed for one final burst of energy as she prepared to seize the edges of the hole above her. As she gripped them, she cautioned herself not to become careless. She struggled frantically to pull her upper torso into the night air. Her vision began to blur precariously, and her arms trembled ominously. She was so close to victory. But if she passed out now, she could drop back into that entombing chamber. Sobbing, she pushed and shoved desperately to free herself. Gradually everything went black as Miranda went limp . . .

Near Fort Sully in a quiet cabin filled with rising tension, Lucas questioned the warrior with penetrating eyes. "Where are Mandy and Reis? What happened out there? Why haven't they come home? Why the hell did you kill Major Sheen and kidnap Randy this afternoon? Where'd you take her, and why didn't you bring her back tonight?"

"You ask many questions; your words make no sense," Blazing Star ventured curiously. "Why do you ask if I killed the bluecoat and took this Randy captive?" His ebony eyes glanced around for his love. He was bewildered when she did not appear. "Where is Tamaha, Miranda?"

"Miranda is called Randy by her family. What have *you* done with her? Why'd you kill Major Sheen?" Lucas demanded tersely.

"I have not seen Tamaha since she came to our camp with the man called Reis. Why do you say I captured her? I have not slain the white-eyes called Sheen. What do your words say?" he probed, an uneasy feeling assailing his keen senses.

"Where are Reis and Amanda?" Lucas insisted.

"They are in our camp. They are safe. Tell me what happened this sun," Blazing Star pressed. "How did Yellowhair learn of the parlay? Where is Tamaha?"

The two men compared tales and facts until a curious picture formed, one which puzzled and alarmed them. Lucas vowed his cousins and Reis were innocent. He related all he knew, and the more they talked, the darker the mystery became.

Lucas muttered fearfully, "If you didn't kill Sheen and abduct Randy, then who did? And why? Where is she now? They said it was your arrow, one with a black-and-red-tipped feather." Lucas then told the warrior why Custer doubted Blazing Star had killed Brody.

"Yellowhair has the mind of a fox and the eyes of an eagle, for he sees the truth in my enemy's cunning. We must return to my camp. I must get warriors to help search for Tamaha. I do not like the cold winds which blow over my heart. I must seek the face of my enemy, one who dares to steal my woman, one who slays a foe in my name. I will protect you with my life if you return with me and speak to the council. There is great evil playing in our lands. We must stop it."

Lucas and Blazing Star headed for the Oglala

531

camp just before the first streaks of dawn tickled the horizon with pink and gray fingers. At that same moment, Bloody Arrow was scouring the countryside, seeking the place where Tom had concealed Miranda . . .

Dazed and injured, the bloody and dirty Miranda urged herself to keep walking on her sore, bare feet. Often, she staggered and fell to the ground, but stopped only briefly before forcing her body to move forward again. She had no idea where she was, so she followed the angle of the sun, knowing the Oglala camp was in the southwest. But that was from the fort, and that was if she was not already beyond the camp.

She was so thirsty and groggy, yet she had to go on. Time was of the essence, if it was not too late. She tried to control her tears and sobs, for they pained her throat and chest. She was so tired and her body hurt all over. Soon, she was so exhausted that she dreamily wondered if this mental and physical anguish was worth it. When she knew she could walk no further, she sank to her knees and cursed cruel fate with her fleeting consciousness.

Three Oglala warriors hovered over the pitiful body lying on the grass. One nudged the other and asked, "She is Tamaha?"

The second warrior knelt, pushing her tangled hair from her injured face for a closer inspection. "*Sha*," he replied uneasily.

The three warriors who had been scouting the area for signs of Custer's return discussed this problem. They wondered how she had gotten here, who had injured her so badly, and what they should do with her. Her family was being held captive, but these warriors were friends of Blazing Star's; they knew of his love and desire for this half-white girl. What if the council voted for her death? Should they try to warn their friend? Should they conceal her until his return? That was wrong, and she was hurt. It was decided to return to camp with her.

When Miranda was taken to Sun Cloud's teepee, Amanda screamed in disbelief. "My God, Reis, what have they done to her?"

Both Reis and Amanda battled for freedom to help Miranda. Sun Cloud ordered one of the warriors to fetch the medicine man. Crazy Horse entered the teepee and ordered Miranda taken to the medicine lodge. Her strange wounds would have to be treated before she could be questioned. There was a disturbing mystery here. Had the whites tried to beat the truth of the parlay from Tamaha? Somehow, the war chief doubted she would talk even under torture. It was no secret to him that Blazing Star and Tamaha were in love. Had she escaped too late to warn the Sioux?

The warriors and Sun Cloud departed with the limp Miranda. Crazy Horse glanced at the terrified and worried Amanda. He stated clearly, "We have not harmed your sister. She was found injured by the warriors. We will care for her wounds. Then we will have answers."

Shortly, Blazing Star and Lucas entered the teepee. Reis shouted at them, "They have Miranda! I don't know what they've done to her, but she's hurt badly. Help her, Blazing Star," Reis pleaded urgently.

When Lucas tried to go with him, Blazing Star ordered him to remain here where he was safe. He promised to send news after he saw her. The moment he left, Lucas seized a knife to cut Reis and Amanda free. Before he could do so, two of the warriors returned to guard them, but they did not bind Lucas or free Reis and Amanda.

When Blazing Star raced into the medicine lodge, he discovered Crazy Horse and the others staring at Miranda oddly. As his dark eyes moved over her face and body, pain and fury attacked him. He dropped to his knees and pulled her into his arms. He held her gently and protectively. "Who did this?" he asked in icy contempt, his temper and control unleashed. "There will be no vote for her life. I will take her and leave. No one will slay her. I will battle any man who steps into my path to stop me. She is my heart."

Blazing Star lowered her carefully, aware of her numerous injuries. Suddenly he realized some were bandaged. "Why do you treat the wounds you have inflicted? She is as innocent as her sister and the white man."

Crazy Horse locked his gaze on Miranda's face, recalling the look in her eyes when she had awakened briefly and told her incredible tale. Crazy Horse temporarily ignored Blazing Star to ask Sun Cloud,

"Do you think she spoke the truth? Is her mind trapped by dreams or pain?"

The old man sighed wearily. "She did not lie. But I feel shame at his great evil, for I did not see it with these old eyes and weak heart. How could he hurt my little Tamaha? How could he wish us dead?"

"What words do you speak?" Blazing Star demanded angrily.

"Tamaha said Bloody Arrow betrayed us to the scout who betrayed us to Yellowhair," the chief informed him then repeated Miranda's shocking story of treachery.

Blazing Star revealed all he had learned from Lucas. They realized Bloody Arrow had not been present that awesome afternoon. They also knew he had left camp right after Blazing Star rode away.

"Where is Bloody Arrow now?" Sun Cloud wondered aloud, his old heart suffering with this dishonor and distress. "Did he do such injury to her? May *Wakantanka* forgive me for allowing such evil in my teepee."

Sitting Bull, the medicine chief of great power and wisdom, said, "She is weak, Blazing Star. She used all of her fighting spirit to come here. She is very brave. I will try to save her. But she is in the hands of the Great Spirit; He will decide her fate."

Shivers ran over the warrior's bronze frame. "Are you saying Tamaha . . . could die?" His heart thudded painfully when Sitting Bull nodded, his steely gaze exposing his sympathy and respect for the girl.

"She is only tired from her journey and her wounds," Blazing Star protested in panic.

"She has many injuries, Blazing Star. Beneath her garments, there is a blackness here," he explained, touching her left rib area. "Her back bleeds and flames red. She has many bad wounds, my son. We do not know how long she has been without food or water. Look at her feet," he instructed. "Look at her hands. It is as if she dug herself from a grave. The scout did this to her. Bloody Arrow wished to sell her and Sky Eyes to the Apaches, but the scout wanted her for himself. We will prepare for Bloody Arrow's return."

Crazy Horse and Sitting Bull exchanged meaningful looks. The younger chief told Blazing Star to free the prisoners and bring them to Tamaha's side. When Reis, Amanda, and Lucas were shown into the large teepee, Reis spoke first. He told Sun Cloud and Blazing Star that Miranda must be taken back to Fort Sully where the doctor knew how to treat such injuries and had powerful medicines to use.

It was noon before Blazing Star and Sun Cloud convinced Crazy Horse that the whites must leave. If they did not leave, Miranda could die, and Custer would surely start a search for them. They decided to use the story that Tom had captured Reis and Amanda when they happened upon him abducting Miranda. Lucas came searching for them early this morning, but they had been rescued by friendly Indians. They would say Miranda had been injured defending herself after Brody was murdered and increased her injuries while trying to escape the vicious scout. They would blame everything on Fletcher.

It was settled. A travois was constructed to carry Miranda to the fort. Lucas, Reis, and Amanda were given horses. A band of warriors would follow them to the fort, to make certain they arrived safely. But the warriors would also make certain they were not seen escorting the white party home.

When all was prepared, Blazing Star knelt by the travois to say farewell to his love. Soon, Reis and Lucas would leave this land and take both women home to safety before Reis delivered words to the white leader. This would be the last time his hungry eyes fed upon his Tamaha. She had come so close to death, was still challenging it; he could not allow her to remain where it lived each sun and moon. Death and danger could not be averted, for Yellowhair had been ordered to control this region and the Sioux at all costs.

Amanda came to Blazing Star's side. "I'll make sure she gets well. Is there anything you want me to tell her when she awakes?"

Blazing Star did not care who was watching or what they said or thought. He leaned over and lightly kissed Miranda's lips, then her forehead. "There is nothing to say, Sky Eyes. Our lives must take separate paths. You must never let her return to our camp. Take her far away from this death and evil. She must forget Blazing Star and the Oglalas."

"She will never forget you, no matter how much distance there is between you. I'm sorry, Blazing Star," she murmured sadly, her meaning understood.

"She will never love another as she loves you."

"You are kind, Sky Eyes. For as long as I breathe the air of the Great Spirit, she will live in my heart and mind," he vowed.

Reis helped Amanda to mount, then clasped wrists with Blazing Star and Sun Cloud. Reis looked at Crazy Horse and stated, "I will tell Chief Grant what I have learned and seen here. Try to avoid as much bloodshed as you can; that will please him. No matter what happens, Crazy Horse, I will do my best to bring peace to your lands."

Crazy Horse gave the sign of peace and friendship to Reis. But his words were, "It is too late for such dreams. You leave in friendship, but do not come again. I do not wish your blood to stain our lands. You have warmed the heart of our old chief Sun Cloud. It was good you came to us before his death. Go in peace," he dismissed them.

When the dust settled and the small group was gone, Crazy Horse looked at the courageous warrior at his side. "I am sorry you cannot take Tamaha as your mate. You have chosen the right path, Blazing Star, but walking it will be hard for a long time. You will ride as my chosen band leader, at my side. Come, we must decide the fate of Bloody Arrow; he was captured by Gall's band."

Blazing Star's gaze chilled. He declared, "Let me battle him, Crazy Horse; it is my right."

"*Ki-ci-e-conape?*" Crazy Horse inquired knowingly.

"Yes, I will fight him to the death in challenge."

"Bloody Arrow is a skilled warrior, Blazing Star. He is strong and cunning. He battles for his life, with the power of evil behind him. If I allow the challenge, the winner goes free," the chief argued.

"He must die at my hand. If he slays me, then evil is greater than good, then evil is more powerful than the Great Spirit. If such is true, we are all fools to worship Him. He will guide my hand in battle, or I will die as the fool I have been since birth."

"So be it," Crazy Horse agreed. "But if he goes free, Blazing Star, I will be the next fool to challenge him."

As they walked toward the teepee where Bloody Arrow was being held captive, Crazy Horse said, "We must move our camp closer to the sacred hills. Soon the bluecoat with yellow hair rides there. We must go and prepare to stop him. We must defend our sacred grounds. Do you wish to send a message telling her of our new location?"

Blazing Star caught his hint. Shaking his ebony head of hair, he replied sadly, "It is best if she does not know where to find me."

"What if she returns to this place when she is healed?" Crazy Horse speculated.

"She will find nothing. She will not know where to seek us, and she will go home. This is best," Blazing Star remarked dejectedly.

Crazy Horse watched him from the corner of his eye and wondered, Best for whom?

Chapter Twenty-Three

When the small group arrived at the rented cabin, Lucas went to fetch the doctor while Miranda was taken inside by Reis and her sister. She had not regained consciousness. Unaware the sleep had been induced by Sitting Bull's healing herbs, Amanda was terribly worried. They placed her on the bed and waited for Doctor Starns to come.

Amanda assisted the doctor with her sister's examination and treatment. Colonel Custer arrived to question Reis about their curious adventure. Reis gave him the colorful story which had been agreed upon by all concerned. Reis was surprised, but not shocked, to hear of Tom Fletcher's gory murder. He shrewdly guessed it was the foul deed of Bloody Arrow to cover his guilt. But naturally Reis could not reveal his accurate conclusion.

Custer insisted on seeing Miranda and speaking to her sister. When pressed for answers, Amanda corroborated her husband's story. Then Lucas was briefly interrogated. Custer could not be sure they were telling the truth, but they certainly told the same wild tale.

While he awaited his final orders to ride into the Black Hills for an extensive survey, Custer directed his troops to break camp and head for Fort Lincoln. It was said that Custer often raced off to visit with his wife just before a new mission was undertaken, and this new mission would prove to be his ultimate challenge.

The countryside was curiously peaceful. Custer was far away with his regiment, the Oglalas had moved secretly toward the Black Hills, their sacred *Paha Sapa*; Reis was completing his final reports; Amanda was enjoying the serenity of her love, and the new life growing within her.

Lucas wrote several articles and sent them back East. He also slaved over two manuscripts, one he had planned before coming here and one which had been inspired by recent experiences and lessons learned.

Miranda was nearly healed after two weeks of enforced rest and treatment. Only occasionally did a fading bruise or sensitive area remind her of her ordeal. But the more her body healed, the sicker her heart became, until she was in a fever to return to her love.

Miranda argued and cajoled to no avail. Reis and Lucas refused to take her back to the camp, and Amanda protested the idea fervently, relating Blazing Star's parting words to her. When Miranda reached the point of rebellion, Reis told her the Oglalas had moved west, far from this hazardous area.

"He's gone?" she shrieked. "No! He wouldn't leave without telling me good-by!" She desperately refuted the tormenting words. "He wouldn't leave until he was sure I was all right."

Reis calmly and patiently went over the circumstances and events of these past weeks. Amanda told her sister what Blazing Star had said that last day about the impossibility of a shared life. "I swear he's gone, Randy. I'm sorry," Reis said and Amanda concurred.

"Then I'll find him!" Miranda declared stubbornly.

"Do you realize how large this territory is? Do you realize what dangers await you out there?" Lucas reasoned. "I know."

Miranda fled in tears to the bedroom. Amanda looked at Reis, tears in her eyes. Reis shook his head, indicating there was nothing they could do to comfort or help her sister. This was one problem Miranda would have to solve for herself.

A telegram came for Lucas that week from a noted Boston publisher who wanted to meet with him and discuss his articles and the two works in progress. Lucas packed and was gone that same day, promising to contact them with any news, vowing he would become either an illustrious novelist or famed historian.

Another week passed. Reis told Miranda they should begin packing for the trip home to Alexandria. He then told her that after he filed his reports with President Grant, he and Amanda would be traveling to Texas to decide where they wanted to settle and build their home. He said they would sell the shipping firm and townhouse unless she wanted either or both. Miranda told them she did not want anything except Blazing Star.

Even the news of Amanda's pregnancy failed to lighten Miranda's gloomy spirits. What was there for her in Virginia? Or anywhere? She did not want to work. She did not want to amuse herself frivolously. She certainly could not marry. Her heart was here with this land and the love who had deserted her.

Still another week passed. Miranda finally agreed she would leave with Reis and Amanda if she could see Blazing Star and be certain he did not want her. "If he says he doesn't love me, whether it's true or not, I will return to the plantation. You and Reis can have everything else."

Miranda left the cabin for some fresh air and serious thought. She could not force Blazing Star to love her. She could not deny the perils here. But there had been just as much danger back in Virginia, in so-called civilization. She could not intrude on Amanda's and Reis's lives. But no matter what decision Blazing Star might make, she would hear it face to face!

When Miranda returned to the cabin, the sight which greeted her was so totally astonishing that she fainted in shock. When she recovered, she found herself face to face with her parents! After an abundance of joyful embraces, Joe and Marie told the incredible tale of how they had been found and rescued by Reis's search party.

Amanda and Miranda stared at Reis Harrison. He explained how he had learned of their attempted abduction on the sloop and the disappearance of the "bodies" after the shipwreck in the South Seas. He revealed a conversation he had overheard in which Weber worried over the sinking of the vessel which had been taking them to the Far East where they were to be sold as slaves. Weber had ranted at McVane that he had not wanted to kill them mercifully but had wanted them to be tormented as slaves. Knowing how much they loved their daughters, Weber had known they would endure more anguish alive than dead.

McVane had declared that no survivors had been found, and he gave Weber the location of the sinking. On the chance Joe and Marie had survived and made it to an island, Reis had hired men to search the entire area. Joe and Marie had been located and returned to Alexandria where they learned of the recent events concerning Weber Richardson, Amanda's marriage, and these two trips west. They immediately followed their daughters, hoping to find them in order to deliver their joyous news in person.

The five talked for hours, exchanging tales. Every so often, the girls would jump up to hug their parents. It was a happy occasion despite the problems and dangers all had faced. But Marie Morning Star Lawrence was particularly intrigued by the dramas involving them and her people. Again and again, she insisted on hearing them.

Marie tried to envision the warrior whom she had not seen since he was four, the man who caused a mixture of joy and sadness in her daughter's eyes. There had been so many changes since she had left her father's teepee to marry Joseph Lawrence. She was pained by the deaths of her mother, brother, and so many relatives during the 1854 massacre. She asked Miranda countless questions.

Miranda's heart fluttered wildly when Marie asked Joe if she could see her father and her people before their return home. Marie cast her dark eyes upon her daughter's face and smiled. "There are those Randy and I must bid farewell one last time."

Miranda went to her mother and hugged her, for perhaps only Marie could truly understand her inner conflict. There were no words to express her love and appreciation. Marie looked down into the face which so closely resembled her own and teased, "You do wish to go with me? Since my father has smiled upon you, perhaps it will lessen his anger and bitterness toward me. He will be shocked to hear I am alive."

For everyone's protection, Reis suggested that he go to the new camp and bring Sun Cloud and Blazing Star to the old one to visit with them, if the two warriors agreed. Miranda glared at Reis when she realized her brother-in-law had known their location all along. He confessed contritely that he had promised not to reveal it to anyone, including and especially her.

Marie witnessed the devastating effect of Reis's enlightening words and unexpected admission on her chestnut-haired daughter. The tawny gaze which focused on Reis was filled with accusation, anger, sadness, and disbelief. Miranda hurriedly excused herself before she could verbally or physically attack her brother-in-law. When she left, Marie demanded to know the extent of the relationship and the problems existing between the warrior and her child. When Amanda and Reis completed their stories, she knew how Miranda must be suffering.

"Perhaps I shouldn't have suggested she go along to see him. I did not think of the impossibility of the situation." Marie looked at her husband, who smiled at her with love and tenderness. "We know her suffering and confusion, don't we, my love?" she whispered.

Joe nodded, recalling that complicated and arduous path too clearly. "This is different, Marie. You must understand that. War is costly and bloody. We can't allow her to remain here."

"I know," Marie concurred sadly. "It won't be easy for her. Perhaps we should return home in the morning," she generously suggested, her tone exposing her turmoil.

"It wouldn't help her if you sacrificed your desire to see your father," Joe answered. "Should we let her go with us? Won't it hurt too much to see him? You think he'll return to see her?" He addressed this last question to Reis.

"I honestly don't know, sir. He is in love with her. But he loves her too much, too unselfishly. He would lose her rather than risk her life," Reis confided to them. "He wants her to leave as much as he wants her to stay. He could be afraid to see her, afraid of weakening in his decision."

"I can understand the pain of that dilemma," Marie stated softly. "I will speak with her. Perhaps I can persuade her not to go."

The mother-daughter talk failed to deter Miranda from making the journey. How could Marie convince Miranda a mixed marriage would not work when she and Joe were living proof that it could? But times had changed; antagonism had increased. Life was precarious here. But love did not see such obstacles. That night, the women shared the bedroom and more conversation, while Reis and Joe bunked in the living area.

Two weeks later, four people rode from the cabin to the campsite deserted by the Oglalas after the death of Bloody Arrow. Marie and Reis had insisted the pregnant Amanda remain behind at the cabin in safety and comfort. Reis had contacted Sun Cloud and set up this crucial and emotional meeting. When they arrived at the assigned location, there were four men waiting for them. Three braves were sitting around a campfire as protection for the elderly ex-chief, and Sun Cloud was sitting alone not far away. When Marie dismounted, she hesitated only moments before racing toward her father. After embracing affectionately and filling the quiet air with joyful laughter, they sat down upon buffalo hides to talk. Sometime later Reis, Joe, and Miranda joined the reunited father and daughter. After Miranda had had a chance to speak with her grandfather, she insisted on taking a walk alone. Knowing their daughter needed privacy to master her warring emotions, Marie and Joe did not try to stop her. Obviously, Blazing Star had not come; his painful decision was evident to all.

When Reis tried to comfort Miranda, she pulled away from him. "You're the last person who should try to console me. You lied to me, Reis; you used me and betrayed my trust and friendship. It wasn't your right to withhold the truth from me. My destiny isn't in your hands. You can't make my decisions or control my life. I'll never forgive you for duping me. I need time alone, away from traitors. Please don't follow me. I'll return before Mama's ready to leave."

"Please listen to me, Randy," he entreated earnestly. "I promised Blazing Star I would hold silent. What kind of man would I be if I betrayed a promise? I had no right to interfere either way."

"Aren't you forgetting how I assisted your romance and conquest of my sister? When you pleaded for my help and interference, I didn't hold silent or keep my promise to her. You know why, Reis? Because I knew you two loved and needed each other. I doubt you two would be happily wed right now if I had retained my *honorable silence*," she sneered sarcastically. "After all I've done to help you with my people and my sister, you damn well owed me your help! Whether you agree or not, you have interfered in my destiny! You're selfish and insensitive."

When Reis made no attempt to justify his behavior, Miranda fled into the forest to the stream and followed its winding bank until she was assured of privacy. She halted, staring into the swirling water just below a small cascade. He was not coming. Did he even know or care if she was alive; she had left this camp injured and unconscious. He had not checked on her. He had not sent word to her. He had simply ridden out of her life as if she meant little or nothing to him.

Anguish assailed her. Tears silently rolled down her cheeks. She removed the *wanapin* and stared at it. "What a stupid, blind fool you are, Miranda Lawrence. Blazing Star never loved me. He never cared about me. I could have died by now for all he knew or cared. It was all lies to trick me to his mat. How he must laugh at me now. Why did he have to be so cruel? Why did he want to hurt me and punish me? How he must hate me to do this to me. Oh, God, it hurts so much," she cried out, flinging the necklace into the stream.

"Damn you, you traitor! You could have the decency and courage to tell me the truth! You never loved me! You were only using me. You didn't even care enough to say good-by," she sneered sarcastically. "Why, Blazing Star? Why must you punish me for loving you? You owe me the truth. *Damn you, you owe me the truth!*"

She sank to her knees and cried. When the tender word "Tamaha" was spoken, she did not know it was real. Her heart was aching; her world seemed to be ending. "Why did you betray me? I can't live without you," she sobbed raggedly into her palms.

Two strong hands imprisoned her head and lifted it, and ebony eyes gazed into her tormented expression. "Do not weep, Tamaha. Your words are untrue. I told you it could not be between us. Why do you come here to torment us this way? Return home with your family."

"You've been hiding?" she asked angrily as the stunning reality settled into her warring mind. He had come to protect Sun Cloud, but he was not going to tell her good-by! Did she mean nothing to him?

"I thought it best if we did not see each other again. You must go, Tamaha. I did not lie. I told you it was impossible," he stated sadly.

"You did lie! Your lips said no, but your eyes said yes. Your words said it could not be, but your heart shouted yes each time we touched! I thought you loved me, but I was a fool. I don't need your pity! Go back to your wars and hatred! Make love to your pride and *coups*! Just leave me alone. You were right—is that what you want to hear? Will it soothe your conscience? End all guilt? I did chase you like a she-dog; isn't that what you called me? I pursued you because I loved you. Because I thought you loved me too. What a fool I am not to have realized what you've been telling me all along; you don't love me or want me. The least you can do, great warrior, is tell the truth. You owe me an explanation. Say it, Blazing Star! Tell me you don't love me and free me from these golden dreams which you helped create."

Her anguish pierced his soul like sharp lances. How could he end it without pain? "I did not mean to hurt you, Tamaha. I tried to speak in truth to you. I said our life-circles could not join," he reminded her gently.

"But you did hurt me. Was I supposed to believe your words when your loving touch proved them false? How could I have been so wrong about you, Blazing Star? I promised I would go, but for once, tell me the truth. Is it difficult to say you don't love me?"

"I cannot, Tamaha. It would be a lie," he informed her bluntly. "You promised to go, but you have not. Why did you come again? Must you cut my heart with the knifing words of farewell?"

"I don't understand your game, Blazing Star. If you loved me, you would not treat me this way. Love isn't selfish or cruel. If you loved me, nothing and no one could keep us apart." She stood up and turned to leave. "If I could not have your love, why did you tempt me with it each time we met? If you loved me, how could you take all I had to give, then force me to leave with nothing left? If you wished to protect my life, then why have you destroyed it? How can you be the center of my life-circle, then claim it is not . . ."

She could not finish. She just started walking slowly along the stream bank. Finally she stopped and sat down, propping her chin on a large rock. "No, Blazing Star, you are wrong. Love is not cruel.

Love does not punish or destroy. Love isn't sad or painful. Love doesn't betray or desert. Not when it's shared. Not when it's real. No, my deceitful warrior, you do not love me. But I love you with all my being."

"Have you learned nothing here? Do you refuse to see the hatred and dangers around you, refuse to see why we must part? You wish the truth, Tamaha? Then I will tell you, and it will hurt. But it will change nothing. I will make you leave," he declared stubbornly.

He sat down beside her, fusing his gaze to hers. "You are white, Miranda; I am Oglala. I am Indian," he began.

"I am half Oglala, half Indian," she corrected him, noticing which name he was calling her. But something in his tone and expression compelled her to listen, to delve deeper into his meaning.

"You were born white and raised white. You cannot change," he replied. "Even so, it is too late to become Indian. We are at war."

"I am not your enemy, Blazing Star, nor any Indian's. Must I be viewed as one because my father is white?" she implored him. "Must you punish me for what I cannot change? Must you reject me?"

"If you become more Indian than white, you are your own worst enemy, Miranda." He observed her increasing confusion. He tried to explain. "White and Indian are at war, a war for the destruction of one side. You are half of each. What happens when one side fiercely battles the other? Or your heart wars against your mind? To become Oglala, you must become all Indian in thought and action. Ask Morning Star about such a life between two separate people. Ask Morning Star of the pain of such a choice," he challenged gravely. "Ask how her Indian blood felt when she learned her brother and mother were slain by her husband's kind? Ask how she felt knowing whites were slain in retaliation? Ask how she feels when she knows she can never return here, for she has chosen the white world. If you chose my world and love, you could never return to your father's kind. If your white friends come to slay us, I will battle them. How can you endure this?"

"The war must end someday, Blazing Star," she asserted.

"It will not, Tamaha. It will not until all Indians are wiped out or conquered. The whites and bluecoats will not allow it," he refuted.

"But Reis will help, Blazing Star," she argued hopefully.

"What is one drop of rain upon such a roaring fire?" He caressed her cheek as he entreated, "What of your white friends and family? What of their deaths at Indian hands during this endless war? What of losing all you have and have ever known to become Oglala? To choose me and the Oglalas, you must do such things, for we have vowed to battle to the death against the white man's evil and greed. You speak of knowing such troubles; you speak of understanding such a choice. But you do not, Tamaha. When you realize what you have done, what you have lost, it will be too late. You have not seen torture and slaughter. You have not witnessed the draining of pride and strength. We are weary of the fighting and killing, but they give us no choice. They will not accept peace without defeat and dishonor. They demand the surrender of our land, our freedom, our dignity, our spirit, our way of life! Is any peace or survival worth such a price, Tamaha?"

Miranda gazed into midnight eyes which shone with frustration and anger. "Can either side win?" she asked dejectedly. "No, so why must the fighting continue?"

"The whites started this war, Tamaha. They invaded our lands. They spit upon us and curse us. They take and destroy. They attack peaceful villages under a flag of truce, under the colors of the Great White Father. They kill all Indians, even women and children. They call us savages, animals. But they force us to fight this way. They make us live and battle as the wild creatures of these lands. And the soldiers keep coming. The more we slay, the more the White Chief sends. But we have no warriors to take the place of those murdered, for the white-eyes kill the young braves and children who would follow in our tracks. The White Chief sends more weapons, but we are harassed and have no time to make new weapons or trade for them. They burn villages and supplies during the winter when such things cannot be replaced, and many of our people freeze and starve. And you ask me to bring you into such a life-circle?" he scoffed bitterly.

Blazing Star's voice trembled with emotion. "They speak of their honor; they do not understand the word. When your grandfather goes to join the Great Spirit, I will be last in the line of Gray Eagle. Look at me, Tamaha. I was a great warrior; now I must flee like a coward to save my life so that I may fight another sun for a peace which will never be born. They offer truces and the fighting halts for a few moons. But the whites always find another reason to take more land and lives."

He sat down with his back against the rock. He murmured tenderly. "It is wrong for me to ask you to make such a choice, such a sacrifice. It is wrong and selfish to keep you here in danger. It is wrong to make such a decision more painful by showing you my love and need for you. You only see me and our love, Tamaha. You refuse to see beyond that. If I allow you to fall into such a powerful trap, you will suffer greatly. I cannot permit it. You must return to your family and forget the Oglalas. You must forget me. You must not be caught between two warring peoples. This is why it cannot be between us. I cannot endanger your life to have you at my side. I love you too much to watch you suffer or die. Do not ask such of me."

"It's too late, Blazing Star. I'm in love with you. Since the first time we met, you've stayed in my heart day and night. I've wanted and needed you more than anything in my life. There's nothing you can say or do to change those feelings. I don't care about the dangers. I can adapt to your way of life. I will live as an Indian. Please don't ask me to leave you," she pleaded urgently.

"I must. If you refuse, I will force you to go," he vowed.

"You seek to run from the truth, Blazing Star, and cowardice is not within you. Must two hearts bleed from such unnecessary wounds? Why must our hearts and lives be divided? Everyone must die sometime. Isn't it better to do so together? Don't you see it's the will of the Great Spirit for us to share a life-circle? Surely that's why He guided my feet back to the lands of my true people, to the warrior who now rules my heart. With all my being, I love and desire only you among all men of any race. What good is safety if we're both unhappy? I cannot say good-by. And I will depart only if you do not love me and want me. Say it, and I will leave with my family," she dared him desperately.

Blazing Star was fighting his most difficult adversary—himself. Could he risk her life by keeping her? Could he bind her to the cruel lifestyle of the vanishing Sioux? Could she become Indian and side against her father's people when that awesome time arrived, as he knew it would? If he but weakened his stand for a moment, she would remain.

As he wavered, Miranda moved closer to him on her knees, placing her hand on his chest over his heart, detecting its fierce drumming. Tears silently flowed down her cheeks as she challenged, "Say I am unworthy of your love and touch. Say you do not love me or desire me. Say you wish another woman to share your life, your mat, your pain, your happiness. Say you wish another woman to bear your children. Say you can forget me and what we share. Say you would feel no pain in your heart if you lost me forever. Say the war between our peoples has greater power and meaning than our love. Say these things, Blazing Star, and I will walk away this moment. Even if you lie, say them, and I will go. I swear it."

Blazing Star could not think clearly with her so near. He jumped to his feet and put some distance between them. His arm extended, he placed one hand upon a tree and propped himself wearily against it. He gazed into the forest, unseeing. His next words would seal their futures. Could he lie?

Miranda came to stand behind him. She watched and waited, her fears and anxieties mounting. His motives were unselfish but so misguided. He was so proud, so stubborn, so caring. If he said no, could she keep her promise?

His voice seemed distant when he spoke. "The white man's greed, hatred, and weapons are stronger than love, Miranda. Their numbers and powers sprout and grow stronger each moon; with each sun they spread as wild grass over our lands. Ours wither and die beneath their evil and force. I cannot deny your words. But my love cannot protect you from such powerful evil. If I selfishly claim your love, I risk finding your innocent blood upon my hands. You know my rank, Tamaha. Many soldiers are eager for my scalp and life. What will happen if I am slain and you are left alone in our teepee? What will happen if you bear our child, and he is slaughtered by your whites?"

"Then come away where we can live in peace, Blazing Star. Come and speak with our leader; make him see and hear the wrongs our people endure. Reis will help you. If not, we can buy land here, near our people and sacred grounds. I have money. I have a paper of protection from the White Chief. You say the Sioux are not farmers. We can ranch; we can raise horses or cattle or sheep. Or we can pay men to do it for us. You can hunt and fish on your lands, lands which cannot be taken from us. We can have a home and children. We can find peace and happiness. You say the war is futile, a lost cause. Must you die to prove some point which will be forgotten before your blood soaks into the ground? Isn't there pride and honor in the wisdom of change? To begin a new life when the old one is destroyed doesn't show weakness or dishonor, Blazing Star. Amanda has married a white man and weakened the bloodline of Gray Eagle. Only in us can the Great Spirit renew its power. Surely that is why I am here?"

Miranda moved between his stalwart body and the sturdy tree, clasping his chiseled jawline between her hands. "If you were right, Blazing Star, the Great Spirit would not trouble your heart and head this way. Open your senses to understand his wishes. He wants you to live; He wants the line of Gray Eagle to be reborn. Come away with me, my love; come away until we can return here in peace. You said Reis was only one man, a tiny drop of water. So are you, my love. Will your prowess win this war? Will your death change anything? Soon there could be no one to chant your *coups*. I need you—more than your people. The line of Gray Eagle must continue.''

"You ask a warrior to flee as a coward to save his life, to exchange honor for love? You ask a warrior to desert his people when they are at war? You ask a warrior to deny all he is and has learned? You ask a warrior to live and die in a white teepee, in white clothes, living as a white? You ask a warrior to deny his heritage, his duty, his honor?'' he inquired sadly.

"I did not say to flee as a coward, but to walk away proudly and wisely. Your people have warred since the sun was born. If you wait until there is no battle to fight, it will be too late. I want you to protect your heritage, to record it, to make certain it survives this monstrous devastation. Who will be left to lead those who aren't slain? Who will there be to remind them of their customs and history? I'm not asking you to pretend you're white. If I wanted a white man, I would not be standing here imploring you. I am willing to challenge any danger for us. Is it so hard for you to do the same? Isn't a compromise the answer? We can have it all, Blazing Star, if you will reach out and take it with me.''

"You should not have come, Tamaha. You make it harder for me to see my duty and to follow it. You try to blind me with love, as you are blinded. Is it not enough to know I love you, to know the truth?''

Miranda dropped her hands to her sides. It was no use to debate with him, to plead or to reason. She clenched her teeth to control the trembling of her chin and lips as her golden brown eyes filled with tears. His thoughts and feelings were so ingrained that she could not alter them. Her line of vision was directed at his defiant heart, for she could not meet his gaze and do what must be done.

"No, Blazing Star, it is not enough for me. If words are enough for you, then your love is small and unworthy of return. But I will accept your words of rejection and go as I promised. May the Great Spirit protect you in battle. Perhaps you will find another who can share your life this way. I will always love you and remember you. Always," she murmured, then slipped under his arm to leave.

"Will you not kiss me and say farewell?" he asked, needing to hold her one last time. He knew she was telling the truth, that she would leave because he was demanding it. But he wanted her and needed her. Could he let her go? Could he pay the price to keep her?

"I cannot. The pain in me is too great now. You have cut out my heart and spirit, and I can take no more agony. I would rather be tortured than touch you for a last time. If a farewell is spoken between us, it must come from you. I will never say such cruel words," she whispered faintly without looking back at him.

"Tamaha, I love—"

He tried to speak his heart one last time, but she sharply injected, "Say no more! It is over, as you demand."

Miranda turned and fled. Blazing Star's attention was drawn to Reis when he said, "You are a fool, Blazing Star. There are some things more precious than dying heroically in battle. I thought I'd find you lurking around somewhere. Why did you do that to her? Why didn't you show some mercy and tell her lies? Why didn't you say you only felt lust for her? Why didn't you tell her you don't love her? No, you had to play the long-suffering, unselfish hero. Honor—you call what you did just now honor? You're selfish and vindictive. You can't have her, so you made sure she'd never want another man. You wanted her to believe no man alive could compare to you, could match you, could love her so much he would spare her suffering and death!"

"Why do you spy on us? Why do you speak such words?" the warrior snarled angrily at the white man with fiery blue eyes.

"I came to fetch her to leave. Do you hear me, Blazing Star? We are leaving this area at first light, and she will be out of your life forever." Reis realized it was time he gave Randy the help she deserved.

"You do not understand. I cannot have her," Blazing Star argued, then gave Reis all his reasons.

When he finished, Reis explained about the Civil War, his own battle for honor. He told how his family had been killed. He revealed that he and Amanda had been on different sides, enemies. He compared the two conflicts, the two love affairs. Reis told him how he and Amanda had overcome their differences, because of love. "My wife was a daughter of the warring winds, Blazing Star. But that war ended. Many on both sides are still enemies; many say the battle will begin anew someday. But we cannot live for future battles. Life is short and hard. We must take what love and happiness we find, for both are rare and precious. Your life will accomplish far more than your death. Your blood should run in your children, not on the dry earth. Miranda will never be happy again, for she will never be free of your hold."

Observing the warrior's turmoil and anguish, Reis was relieved that he had not met Amanda during the war. He could not imagine how their lives and love would be different if that Southern belle had first looked upon him as a Yankee officer.

Reis clasped Blazing Star's wrist and murmured what Miranda had taught him. *"Wookiye wocin, koda."*

Blazing Star glanced at the white man who had called him friend and wished for peace between them. He said the same, then watched Reis vanish. He slowly and helplessly walked to the edge of the forest to observe their departure. He watched the two women embrace Sun Cloud affectionately, bidding him a last farewell. He watched the two men speak their last words to the old chief. He watched the four mount. He watched Sun Cloud exchange smiles and waves with his child and granddaughter. He witnessed the look which passed between Joe and Marie, a look which spoke of powerful love and total acceptance.

Miranda did not glance toward the forest; she sat alert and poised in her saddle. But Reis and Marie watched the intrepid warrior who was observing them. The white friend waved and turned, but the Indian princess stared for a moment. Then Marie looked at her rigid and somber daughter, so full of pride and resolve, so full of anguish and disappointment. Marie's gaze returned to the warrior, so rigid and somber, so full of pride and resolve, so full of anguish and disappointment. She shook her head sadly and joined her retreating family. Love and acceptance had to come freely, and they had to be felt by both. She could not interfere.

As the love story of Morning Star and Joseph Lawrence echoed in his keen mind, Sun Cloud caught the younger warrior's eye. The days of greatness were past for his people. He had spoken with his granddaughter, the mate of Sky Eyes, the mate of Morning Star, and his own daughter. The old man knew of the raging battle with Blazing Star, one he now understood. Sky Eye's mate was right; such a noble warrior should not die in defeat. His voice rang across the distance like sweet music as he fervently called, "If you are to catch her, Blazing Star, you must ride swiftly. Tamaha belongs here with us until the war's end sends you both to safety. My father's spirit is restless this sun, for he fears his line will die in you. There is no warrior greater than Gray Eagle, and he refused to let white blood and battles take his woman from his life. How can this love and match be wrong when Tamaha carries more Oglala and Indian blood than Princess Shalee?"

Blazing Star hurried over to Sun Cloud. "You think I should go after her? I should join with her? I should endanger her life?"

"Only you know the feelings within your heart. Each moment of life holds some unknown danger, my son. But love and happiness are found rarely. If she goes away, she will take the heart of Blazing Star with her; what good is a fierce warrior without a heart? Unless you love Tamaha more than life itself, do not go after her. But if your love is such a love, you are a fool to lose her."

Blazing Star's gaze shifted from the retreating group to Sun Cloud, time and again. His decision would be irrevocable. Finally his gaze settled on Miranda's back as it became smaller. Soon, his love and heart would be out of his reach. He raced to his horse and mounted determinedly. He galloped after her, shouting her name.

In her pensive state, Miranda heard nothing, and Marie was compelled to shake her daughter's arm to gain her attention. "He pursues his true love," she teased, pointing toward the warrior racing their way. "Go and speak with him. We will wait nearby. Whatever you decide, little one, I love you."

Miranda smiled and hugged her joyfully. She kneed her pinto and pulled on the reins to turn him around. With a radiant smile, she raced toward Blazing Star as swiftly as he was moving toward her, his splendid features lit with love.

When they met, he scooped her off her horse and

sat her before him. He held her tightly in his arms. "I love you, Tamaha. Stay and be my wife, the mother of my children. When the time comes, we will ranch if peace is refused my people. You must not leave me. All you said was true. It will be hard and dangerous for many suns. But you must share those suns and moons with me. I was the one blinded by love and fear for your safety. It was meant to be between us; I cannot deny it or resist it. You are my life and breath, the beating of my heart." Their eyes met, their gazes misty and rapturous.

He had spoke in English, but she vowed her love in Sioux. "*Waste cedake. Ni-ye mitawa.*"

Exuberant laughter filled the air. "Yes, my love, I am yours, as you are mine." His mouth closed over hers as they hugged each other fiercely.

Joe and Marie Lawrence watched the romantic scene, then exchanged knowing smiles. The road to happiness would be rough but the lovers would travel it happily.

Reis was consumed with relief and pleasure at the sight before him, only wishing that Amanda were beside him to witness this delightful scene. He knew that he and Amanda shared a love as powerful as that of Blazing Star and Miranda Tamaha Lawrence. He was eager to complete this last mission and more than ready to settle down with his beloved wife and their eagerly awaited child. He had not decided yet if they would live in Virginia or Texas; that was a choice to be made with his wife. Perhaps a large ranch run by brothers-in-law was an idea to ponder . . . Yes, the twins would be close to each other. And Reis could think of no better partner and friend than the proud warrior. Perhaps he would speak with Blazing Star before he left the Dakota Territory . . .

As Miranda snuggled into her lover's bronze embrace and returned his passionate kisses, Joseph Lawrence grinned and sighed tranquilly. Each of his daughters had faced warring winds from within and without. Each had discovered love and happiness with the one man who could fulfill her destiny and dreams. Watching the compelling scene before him, Joe concluded that his two daughters had chosen exceedingly well. He was proud of them and he loved them deeply.

Joe knew the conflicts between North and South, Indian and white, were far from over. But the raging winds of Fate had swirled into gentle breezes for his two daughters, and for his cherished love, his Morning Star . . .

Historical Epilogue

As many readers are eager to learn more about the lives and fates of real characters used in novels, and often such information is difficult or impossible to locate, the author of this tale will discuss the major historical characters and their roles in history following the end of this story in the autumn of 1873.

In mid 1874, Custer was sent on an exploratory expedition into the sacred Black Hills of South Dakota. In 1875, Philip Sheridan planned and initiated the Plains campaign to finalize the white conquest and the United States Government ordered that all Indians be confined to reservations by January of 1876. Lieutenant Frederick Grant, son of the current President, became a party to the "gold craze" exploitation of the Black Hills; thus, the crucial Laramie Treaty of 1868 was broken when countless prospectors, miners, settlers, and opportunists poured into that area and defiled the sacred and burial grounds.

The Indian/White conflicts and hostilities
mounted rapidly and ominously during 1875 and
early 1876. In June of 1876, Custer and his regiment
rode to the Little Bighorn Mountains in Montana to
attack the Sioux encampment there, little suspecting
the awesome force awaiting them. Custer's regiment
of approximately six hundred men was rashly and
fatally divided into three units—units commanded
by Captain Benteen, Major Reno, and Colonel
Custer. Custer did not wait for the regiments of
Crook, Terry, and Gibbon to assist in what was to be
his final battle. Tragically, Custer rode with only
several hundred men into the waiting arms of
thousands of Indians, mainly Sioux and Cheyenne.
In less than one hour, Custer and his unit were slain.

This monumental battle was led by Crazy Horse
and many other chiefs. Sitting Bull, Gall, Two
Moons, and Hump were a few of the illustrious
warriors present. After the stunning Indian victory
which would be recorded in history as "Custer's Last
Stand," Crazy Horse and Sitting Bull were hunted
with a vengeance. These two leaders held the power
to choose continual warfare or peace, but it would be
peace without honor.

At that historical battle, four of Custer's relatives
were slain: two brothers, one nephew, and a brother-
in-law. Later, Major Reno was court-martialed, and
while he was eventually exonerated for his conduct,
he lived the next ten years under the stigma of betrayal and cowardice.

Crazy Horse and his Oglala band hunted and camped until the next spring when the famed warrior was compelled to surrender to the Cavalry to save the lives of his remaining people. His camp had been attacked by Col. Nelson A. Miles, but Crazy Horse and his band had escaped. Crook had then offered the warrior chief a favored reservation, among other promises. Without food and weapons and with his people dying, Crazy Horse gave himself up to the Cavalry at Fort Robinson in May of 1877. When the Army feared the warrior was going to escape and instigate new uprisings, they took it upon themselves to arrest and imprison the influential chief. During a scuffle to avoid imprisonment, Crazy Horse was bayoneted. He died in September of 1877 at age 37.

The cry had gone forth to "avenge" Custer. The Black Hills were taken from the Sioux and other Indian tribes. Any Indian survivor had to be confined to a reservation or be slain. Any leader or chief with influence was hunted down and either killed or imprisoned. Indian language, customs, religion, ceremonies, dances, dress, and burial practices were outlawed as a means of control and punishment.

After the Little Bighorn battle, Sitting Bull was harassed and pursued until he fled with his band into Canada. There they faced starvation and cold. The wily General Terry offered Sitting Bull a pardon if he would surrender to him. Knowing that Crazy Horse had been slain, and other bands were being wiped out or conquered, in 1881, Sitting Bull was compelled to surrender in order to save his remaining people from

571

certain death in the Canadian wilds. He was held prisoner at Fort Randall, then moved frequently to guard his location. At the Standing Rock Reservation, Sitting Bull was allowed some peace for a time. He wrote, spoke, and visited Washington and the "White Chief." His poignant letters and speeches reveal the depth of the Indian suffering.

In 1888 Wovoka began the "Ghost Dance" religion. The whites and military dreaded and respected the power and influence of medicine chiefs and skilled warriors such as Sitting Bull, and they were distressed over this new religion which united and encouraged the spirit of the warriors. Fearing Sitting Bull would escape and stir up new conflicts, he was ordered arrested. His people rebelled against this new humiliation of their chief. On December 15, 1890, a ruckus broke out over the alleged "liberation" of Tatanka Yotanka, and he was declared shot during a confrontation with Indian police.

The death of Sitting Bull convinced many of his followers to flee to the Pine Ridge Reservation near the Black Hills. Miles and Gibbon were ordered to pursue and recapture them. On December 29, 1890, the massacre of Wounded Knee took place, with the slaying of over 300 unarmed Indians of both sexes and all ages. (The second battle at Wounded Knee occurred on February 27, 1973.) Ironically, Custer's Seventh Cavalry was almost annihilated at the Little Bighorn battle; yet it was the Seventh Cavalry who was responsible for the Wounded Knee Massacre fourteen days after the death of Sitting Bull.

Other great chiefs mentioned in this story experienced similar fates. The two major chiefs who signed the Laramie Treaty in 1868 and had agencies and reservations named after them were Red Cloud (Mahpialuta) and Spotted Tail (Sinte Galeska). Red Cloud, whose son was with Crazy Horse at the Little Bighorn, is also known for his poignant speeches and letters to Washington. His remaining spirit was broken after the death of Sitting Bull and the Wounded Knee Massacre. Oglala Chief Red Cloud lived sadly and quietly until his death in 1909. Brule Sioux Chief Spotted Tail, whose sister was the mother of Crazy Horse, was most influential in peace efforts. While living on the Rosebud Reservation, he was shot and killed in 1881. Hunkpapa Sioux Chief Gall (Pizi), adopted brother of Sitting Bull, fled with Sitting Bull into Canada but returned to his old hunting grounds in 1881. Without food and weapons, he was compelled to surrender to Miles. Once one of the fiercest warriors, he became known for his peace efforts which he continued until his death in 1896.

Martha Jane Canary Burke (Calamity Jane) lived and worked in the manner described in this novel. Later she performed in Wild West shows. She died in 1903.

The soldiers included in this story were responsible for the conquest and subjugation of other tribes in addition to the powerful and noble Sioux. Crook and his troops overcame the Apache. With the aid of Miles, the famed Geronimo was captured in

1886. Miles had already defeated the prestigious Nez Perce Chief Joseph in 1877 with the assistance of Gibbon. Sherman had previously ordered the "utter extermination" of the Modocs in 1872, and had suppressed the powerful Kiowa Chief Satanta, whose prison release in 1873 sent Sherman on another rampage. Either by action or order, these soldiers were responsible for the conquest and defeat of most major Western tribes. Oddly, among these white soldiers, Crook and Custer had the most favorable images in the eyes of the Indians.

This author has made every attempt to portray the historical events and characters, Indian and white, as accurately as possible. I extend my appreciation for the assistance and Sioux translations furnished by my friend, Hiram Owen, of the Sisseton-Wahpeton Sioux Tribes.

GET A *FREE* BOOK!

Just answer the following questions and Zebra will send you one of the four books listed on the back—*absolutely free!*

1. Where do you buy paperback books? (*Circle one or more*)
   Supermarket   Convenience Store   Newsstand
   Drugstore   Bookstore   Other

2. How many paperback books do you buy a month? _____ a year? _____

3. What magazines do you buy? _____
   _____

4. Where do you buy magazines? (*Circle one or more*)
   Supermarket   Convenience Store   Newsstand
   Drugstore   Bookstore   Subscription   Other

5. What newspapers do you buy? _____
   _____

6. Where do you buy newspapers? (*Circle one or more*)
   Supermarket   Convenience Store   Newsstand
   Drugstore   Bookstore   Home Delivery   Other

7. Do you buy paperback books in the same place you buy your magazines and newspapers? _____ yes _____ no

8. Where do you buy Zebra books? (*Circle one or more*)
   Supermarket   Convenience Store   Newsstand
   Drugstore   Bookstore   Other

9. If you circled Bookstore in #8, is this because you couldn't find Zebra books at your supermarket, drugstore, newsstand, etc.? _____ yes _____ no

10. Would you spend $6.95 for a large format historical romance? _____ yes _____ no

11. What is the title of your favorite Zebra cover?
    _____

(continues on the reverse side)

GET A *FREE* BOOK!
(*see reverse side*)

12. What is the title of your favorite cover on any paperback?
   _____

13. Who is your favorite Zebra author?
   _____

14. Who is your favorite author?
   _____

15. What radio or TV shows do you listen to or watch?
   _____

16. Do you work outside your home? _____ yes _____ no

Send me the following book—*absolutely free!* (Check only one)

_____ PASSION'S DREAM by Casey Stuart

_____ STORM TIDE by Patricia Rae

_____ PASSION'S PLEASURE by Valerie Giscard

_____ SAVAGE EMBRACE by Alexis Boyard

Mail my book to—

name: _____

address: _____

_____

_____

Tear out and mail questionnaire to Zebra Books, 475 Park Avenue South, New York, New York 10016. Allow 4-6 weeks for delivery. Offer expires July 1, 1985. Offer limited to one per customer.